Classics of Modern Science Fiction

GREENER THAN YOU THINK

10

Books by Ward Moore

Breathe the Air Again (1942)
Greener Than You Think (1947)*
Bring the Jubilee (1953)
Cloud by Day (1956)
Joyleg (with Avram Davidson) (1962 paper; hardcover 1971)
Caduceus Wild (with Robert Bradford) (1978)

Classics of Modern Science Fiction

Classics of Modern Science Fiction

GREENER THAN YOU THINK

YOU THINK

WARD MOORE

Volume 10

Introduction by George Zebrowski
Foreword by Isaac Asimov

Series Editor: George Zebrowski

Crown Publishers, Inc.
New York

For BECKY
1927 – 1937

Introduction copyright © 1985 by Crown Publishers, Inc.
Foreword copyright © 1984 by Isaac Asimov
Copyright 1947 by Ward Moore
Published by Crown Publishers, Inc., One Park Avenue, New York, New York 10016 and simultaneously in Canada by General Publishing Company Limited
Manufactured in the United States of America

Crown is a trademark of Crown Publishers, Inc.

Library of Congress Cataloging in Publication Data
Moore, Ward, 1903–
     Greener than you think.
     (Classics of modern science fiction; v. 10)
     I. Title.   II. Series
PS3563.0668G7   1985   813'.54   85-3767
ISBN 0-517-55866-1
10 9 8 7 6 5 4 3 2 1
First Edition

Retrieving the Lost

by Isaac Asimov

THE HISTORY OF contemporary science fiction begins with the spring of 1926, when the first magazine ever to be devoted entirely to science fiction made its appearance. For a quarter-century thereafter science fiction continued to appear in magazines—and only in magazines.

They were wonderful days for those of us who lived through them, but there was a flaw. Magazines are, by their very nature, ephemeral. They are in the newsstands a month or two and are gone. A very few readers may save their issues, but they are fragile and do not stand much handling.

Beginning in 1950, science fiction in book form began to make its appearance, and some of the books retrieved the magazine short stories and serials in the form of collections, anthologies, and novels. As time went on, however, it became clear that the vast majority of science-fiction books were in paperback form, and these, too, were ephemeral. Their stay on the newsstands is not entirely calendar-bound, and they can withstand a bit more handling than periodicals can—but paperbacks tend to be, like magazines, throwaway items.

That leaves the hardback book, which finds its way into public libraries as well as private homes, and which is durable. Even there, we have deficiencies. The relatively few science-fiction books which appear in hardback usually appear in small printings and few, if any, reprintings. Out-of-print is the usual fate, and often a not very long delayed one, at that.

Some science-fiction books have endured, remaining available in hardcover form for years, even decades, and appearing in repeated paperback reincarnations. We all know which these are because, by enduring, they have come to be read by millions, including you and me.

It is, of course, easy to argue that the test of time and popularity has succeeded in separating the gold from the dross and that we have with us all the science-fiction books that have deserved to endure.

That, however, is too easy a dismissal. It is an interesting and convenient theory, but the world of human affairs is far too complex to fit into theories, especially convenient ones. It sometimes takes time to recognize quality, and the time required is sometimes longer than the visible existence of a particular book. That the quality of a book is not recognizable at once need not be a sign of deficiency, but rather a sign of subtlety. It is not being particularly paradoxical to point out that a book may be, in some cases, too good to be immediately popular. And then, thanks to the mechanics of literary ephemerality, realization of the fact may come too late.

Or must it?

Suppose there are dedicated and thoughtful writers and scholars like George Zebrowski and Martin H. Greenberg, who have been reading science fiction intensively, and with educated taste, for decades. And suppose there is a publisher such as Crown Publishers, Inc., which is interested in providing a second chance for quality science fiction which was undervalued the first time around.

In that case we end up with Crown's *Classics of Modern Science Fiction* in which the lost is retrieved, the unjustly forgotten is remembered, and the undervalued is resurrected. And you are holding a sample in your hand.

Naturally, the revival of these classics will benefit the publisher, the editors, and the writers, but that is almost by the way.

The real beneficiaries will be the readers, among whom the older are likely to taste again delicacies they had all but forgotten, while the younger will encounter delights of whose existence they were unaware.

Read—
And enjoy.

George Zebrowski

WARD MOORE (1903– 1978) is best remembered for his striking novel of alternate American history, *Bring the Jubilee* (1953), and for a number of vividly realized stories, among them "Lot" and "Lot's Daughter." (Inexplicably, there has never been a published collection of his stories.) But his first science fiction story, *Greener Than You Think* (William Sloane, 1947), is a comic novel that may be compared to Kurt Vonnegut's work of the 1950s, as well as to the work of that small band of science fiction humorists, Fredric Brown, William Tenn, and Robert Sheckley. What is even more gratifying is the mature literacy of this novel, which was published at a time when much of genre science fiction could not compare, in terms of quality, with fiction from outside the field.

This was the period when the great John W. Campbell was trying to consolidate his reform of pulp adventure science fiction by asking his writers to concentrate on well-crafted stories with believable people working in well-forecast, technologically possible futures. He had already developed many new writers, among them Isaac Asimov, Robert A. Heinlein, L. Sprague deCamp, and others. But in the late 1940s there were already a number of individual voices not so much given to Campbell's vision of realistic science fiction. They wrote a more flamboyant kind of science fiction, and

Campbell published their work, in contradiction to his views, alongside his best pupils, because they told good stories and he was a better editor than an ideologue. Campbell's two best heretics were A. E. van Vogt and Charles L. Harness. There were others that Campbell published only occasionally, or not at all. They were waiting for the new decade, when the creation of *The Magazine of Fantasy and Science Fiction* and *Galaxy* would give them room to breathe.

One such writer was Ward Moore. In the late 1930s he had written a novel about the labor movement, but it was not published until 1942. This was *Breathe the Air Again*, his first novel, and it was published by Harper & Row Publishers, Inc. *Greener Than You Think* was his second published novel. The British edition appeared in 1949 from Gollancz, but it was not until 1961 that a paperback appeared from Ballantine, revised and abridged. It is the text of the first edition, reportedly preferred by the author, that is presented here.

Greener Than You Think has always had a good reputation. At best it is regarded as a classic, at worst a very good novel with especially fine comic characterizations. I. F. Clarke's *The Pattern of Expectation* (1979) credits Moore with beginning the modern cycle of the ecological disaster story, by preparing the way for such notable books as John Christopher's *No Blade of Grass* (1956), John Wyndham's *Day of the Triffids* (1951), and Thomas M. Disch's *The Genocides* (1965), to name just three that deal with plants. But, as with many good books, it slipped through the cracks. The reasons may be many, among them the fact that publishing is not entirely an enterprise based on the merits of a work. One thing is certain: there were never enough copies outside the hands of collectors to give new readers a chance to discover Ward Moore for themselves.

The reviews of *Greener Than You Think* seem to have been few. H. W. Hall's *Science Fiction Book Review Index* for the years 1923–1973 lists only one review within a year of the novel's publication, one in 1950, and three in the early 1960s. I suspect that the Gollancz edition of 1949 may have received British reviews that may be difficult to track down. The reviewers of the 1960s, P. Schuyler Miller, Alfred Bester, and Britain's John Carnell, were taking notice of the 1961 paperback from Ballantine, and they failed to compare it to the first hardcover edition, making no mention of the relative shortness of the new text: 185 pages as opposed to 358 in the hardcover (the Gollancz edition ran 320 pages). No mention was made as to why the novel was abridged and revised, or whether this version was superior to the first. The reviewers simply passed on their glowing opinions of the original. Carnell seemed to recall that the 1947 edition had made a large impact, but perhaps he was only remembering the British reaction.

From the evidence, the novel has been ignored over the years, but its reputation has continued by word of mouth, by citations in various articles and studies of science fiction, and through the praise of collectors who own all the original hardcovers by now. In 1952, *The Magazine of Fantasy and Science Fiction* (the publication with which Moore has been most closely identified) published a shorter version of *Bring the Jubilee*. Farrar, Straus and Giroux and Ballantine Books then published the full version in simultaneous hardcover and paperback; but even this was apparently not enough to get Moore a paperback reprint of *Greener Than You Think*.

More recent opinions of the novel continue to be laudatory. "Told with broad catastrophic sweep," wrote Sam Moskowitz in his *Seekers of Tomorrow* (1966) as he lamented the novel's neglect. Donald H. Tuck's *The Encyclopedia of Science Fiction and Fantasy* (1978) calls attention to the novel's "fascinating characterization"— always rare praise for a science fictional work. Peter Nicholls's *The Science Fiction Encyclopedia* (1979) describes the work as a "successful comic novel" while citing the better known *Bring the Jubilee* as "the definitive alternate worlds novel." Neil Barron's *Anatomy of Wonder* (1976) inadequately describes the book as a "good satire" and invites us to compare it to novels by Disch, Wyndham, and Christopher. Brian Ash's *Who's Who in Science Fiction* (1976) correctly reminds us that Ward Moore "emerged fully-fledged into the science fiction field with *Greener Than You Think*, a satirical and delightfully zany account of a world overrun by mutated devil grass set off by a wonder fertilizer." Inexplicably, Baird Searles's *et al.* much praised *A Reader's Guide to Science Fiction* (1979) has no entry for Ward Moore at all. W. Warren Wagar's impressive *Terminal Visions* (1982) notes the continuing neglect of Moore's novel while calling attention to the work's central image: human helplessness before nature raging out of control. Brian Ash's *The Visual Encyclopedia of Science Fiction* (1977) lists Moore's novel as one of the notable debuts in book form for 1947. Writing in the same reference work, author Robert Sheckley points out that "the story is told with a satirical lilt which brightens what would otherwise be a harrowing tale."

Nevertheless, despite the continuing esteem in which the body of Ward Moore's work is held, there has been no large critical or publishing support for his work. A major short story collection, *Dominions Beyond*, with an introduction by Avram Davidson and a personal memoir by Raylyn Moore, waits to be published, and there are enough longer stories to make a second volume possible.

But while new readers who do not have access to back runs of magazines wait for Moore's stories to be collected in book form, and for a new edition of *Bring the Jubilee* to be published, I think the author would have approved of this new presentation of his first and most neglected effort in its original form. Its humor, grace, and wit are pleasures to be enjoyed beyond the story's science fictional premise; but in the end we cannot ignore the central drama of nature out of control, which is so much less than human in its blindness, yet which can defeat even intelligence and consciousness—with an army of grass. This tragicomedy is ironically Swiftian and Rabelaisian at the same time, as unsettlingly awesome as it is entertaining.

"... I knew there was but one way; for his nose was as sharp as a pen, and 'a babbled of green fields. 'How now, Sir John!' quoth I; 'what, man! be o' good cheer.' So 'a cried out, 'God, God, God!' three or four times. Now I, to comfort him, bid him 'a should not think of God; I hop'd there was no need to trouble himself with any such thoughts yet. . . ."

Henry V

Neither the vegetation or people in this book are entirely fictitious. But, reader, no person pictured here is you. With one exception. You, Sir, Miss, or Madam—whatever your country or station—are Albert Weener. As I am Albert Weener.

Albert Weener Begins

One

1 I ALWAYS KNEW I should write a book. Something to help tired minds lay aside the cares of the day. But I always say you never can tell what's around the corner till you turn it, and everyone has become so accustomed to fantastic occurrences in the last twenty one years that the inspiring and relaxing novel I used to dream about would be today as unreal as Atlantis. Instead, I find I must write of the things which have happened to me in that time.

It all began with the word itself.

"Grass. Gramina. The family Gramineae. Grasses."

"Oh," I responded doubtfully. The picture in my mind was only of a vague area in parks edged with benches for the idle.

Anyway, I was far too resentful to pay strict attention. I had set out in good faith, not for the first time in my career as a salesman, to answer an ad offering "$50 or more daily to top producers," naturally expecting the searching onceover of an alert salesmanager, back to the light, behind a shinytopped desk. When youve handled as many products as I had an ad like that has the right sound. But the world is full of crackpots and some of the most pernicious are those who hoodwink unsuspecting canvassers into anticipating a sizzling deal where there is actually only a warm hope. No genuinely highclass proposition ever came from a layout without aggressiveness enough to put on some kind of front; working out of an office, for instance, not an outdated, rundown apartment in the wrong part of Hollywood.

"It's only a temporary drawback, Weener, which restricts the Metamorphizer's efficacy to grasses."

The wheeling syllables, coming in a deep voice from the middleaged woman, emphasized the absurdity of the whole business. The snuffy apartment, the unhomelike livingroom—dust and books its only furniture—the unbelievable kitchen, looking like a pictured warning to housewives, were only guffaws before the final buffoonery of discovering the J S Francis who'd inserted that promising ad to be Josephine Spencer Francis. Wrong location, wrong atmosphere, wrong gender.

Now I'm not the sort of man who would restrict women to a place in the nursery. No indeed, I believe they are in some ways just as capable as I am. If Miss Francis had been one of those wellgroomed, efficient ladies who have earned their place in the business world without at the same time sacrificing femininity, I'm sure I would not have suffered such a pang for my lost time and carfare.

But wellgroomed and feminine were alike inapplicable adjectives. Towering above me—she was at least five foot ten while I am of average height—she strode up and down the kitchen which apparently was office and laboratory also, waving her arms, speaking too exuberantly, the antithesis of moderation and restraint. She was an aggregate of cylinders, big and small. Her shapeless legs were columns with large flatheeled shoes for their bases, supporting the inverted pediment of great hips. Her too short, greasespotted skirt was a mighty barrel and on it was placed the tremendous drum of her torso.

"A little more work," she rumbled, "a few interesting problems solved, and the Metamorphizer will change the basic structure of any plant inoculated with it."

Large as she was, her face and head were disproportionately big. Her eyes I can only speak of as enormous. I dare say there are some who would have called them beautiful. In moments of intensity they bored into mine and held them till I felt quite uncomfortable.

"Think of what this discovery means," she urged me. "Think of it, Weener. Plants will be capable of making use of anything within reach. Understand, Weener, anything. Rocks, quartz, decomposed granite—anything."

She took a gold victorian toothpick from the pocket of her mannish jacket and used it energetically. I shuddered. "Unfortunately," she went on, a little indistinctly, "unfortunately, I lack resources for further experiment right now—"

This too, I thought despairingly. A slight cash investment—just enough to get production started—how many wishful times Ive heard it. I was a salesman, not a sucker, and anyway I was for the moment without liquid capital.

"It will change the face of the world, Weener. No more usedup areas, no more frantic scrabbling for the few bits of naturally rich ground, no more struggle to get artificial fertilizers to wornout soil in the face of ignorance and poverty."

She thrust out a hand—surprisingly finely and economically molded, barely missing a piledup heap of dishes crowned by a flowerpot trailing droopy tendrils. Excitedly she paced the floor largely taken up by jars and flats of vegetation, some green and flourishing, others gray and sickly, all constricting her movements as did the stove supporting a glass tank, robbed of the goldfish which should rightfully have gaped against its sides and containing instead some slimy growth topped by a bubbling brown scum. I simply couldnt understand how any woman could so far oppose what must have been her natural instinct as to live and work in such a slatternly place. It wasnt just her kitchen which was disordered and dirty; her person too was slovenly and possibly unclean. The lank gray hair swishing about her ears was dark, perhaps from vigor, but more likely from frugality with soap and water. Her massive, heavychinned face was untouched by makeup and suggested an equal innocence of other attentions.

"Fertilizers! Poo! Expedients, Weener—miserable, make shift expedients!" Her unavoidable eyes bit into mine. "What is a fertilizer? A tidbit, a pap, a lollypop. Indians use fish; Chinese, nightsoil; agricultural chemists concoct tasty tonics of nitrogen and potash—where's your progress? Putting a mechanical whip on a buggy instead of inventing an internal combustion engine. Ive gone directly to the heart of the matter. Like Watt. Like Maxwell. Like Almroth Wright. No use being held back because youve only poor materials to work with—leap ahead with imagination. Change the plant itself, Weener, change the plant itself!"

It was no longer politeness which held me. If I could have freed myself from her eyes I would have escaped thankfully.

"Nourish'm on anything," she shouted, rubbing the round end of the toothpick vigorously into her ear. "Sow a barren waste, a worthless slagheap with lifegiving corn or wheat, inoculate the plants with the Metamorphizer—and you have a crop fatter than Iowa's or the Ukraine's best. The whole world will teem with abundance."

Perhaps—but what was the sales angle? Where did I come in? I didnt know a dandelion from a toadstool and was quite content to keep my distance from nature. Had she inserted the ad merely to lure a listener? Her whole procedure was irregular: not a word about territories and commissions. If I could bring her to the point of mentioning the necessary investment, maybe I could get away gracefully. "You said you were stuck," I prompted, resolved to get the painful interview over with.

"Stuck? Stuck? Oh—money to perfect the Metamorphizer. Luckily it will do it itself."

"I don't catch."

"Look about you—what do you see?"

I glanced around and started to say, a measuring glass on a dirty plate next to half a cold fried egg, but she stopped me with a sweep of her arm which came dangerously close to the flasks and retorts—all holding dirtycolored liquids—which cluttered the sink. "No, no. I mean outside."

I couldnt see outside, because instead of a window I was facing a sickly leaf unaccountably preserved in a jar of alcohol. I said nothing.

"Metaphorically, of course. Wheatfields. Acres and acres of wheat. Bread, wheat, a grass. And cornfields. Iowa, Wisconsin, Illinois—not a state in the Union without corn. Milo, oats, sorghum, rye—all grasses. And the Metamorphizer will work on all of them."

I'm always a man with an open mind. She might—it was just possible—she might have something afterall. But could I work with her? Go out in the sticks and talk to farmers; learn to sit on fence rails and whittle, asking after crops as if they were of interest to me? No, no . . . it was fantastic, out of the question.

A different, more practical setup now . . . At least there would have been no lack of prospects, if you wanted to go miles from civilization to find them; no answers like We never read magazines, thank you. Of course it was hardly believable a woman without interest in keeping herself presentable could invent any such fabulous product, but there was a bare chance of making a few sales just on the idea.

The idea. It suddenly struck me she had the whole thing backwards. Grasses, she said, and went on about wheat and corn and going out to the rubes. Southern California was dotted with lawns, wasnt it? Why rush around to the hinterland when there was a big territory next door? And undoubtedly a better one?

"Revive your old tired lawn," I improvised. "No manures, fuss, cuss, or muss. One shot of the Meta—one shot of Francis' Amazing Discovery and your lawn springs to new life."

"Lawns? Nonsense!" she snorted, rudely, I thought. "Do you think Ive spent years in order to satisfy suburban vanity? Lawns indeed!"

"Lawns indeed, Miss Francis," I retorted with some spirit. "I'm a salesman and I know something about marketing a product. Yours should be sold to householders for their lawns."

"Should it? Well, I say it shouldnt. Listen to me: there are two ways of making a discovery. One is to cut off a cat's hindleg. The discovery is then made that a cat with one leg cut off has three legs. Hah!

"The other way is to find out your need and then search for a method of filling it. My work is with plants. I don't take a daisy and see if I can make it produce a red and black petaled monstrosity. If I did I'd be a fashionable horticulturist, delighted to encourage imbeciles to grow grass in a desert.

"My method is the second one. I want no more backward countries; no more famines in India or China; no more dustbowls; no more wars, depressions, hungry children. For this I produced the Metamorphizer— to make not two blades of grass grow where one sprouted before, but whole fields flourish where only rocks and sandpiles lay.

"No, Weener, it won't do—I can't trade in my vision as a downpayment on a means to encourage a waste of ground, seed and water. You may think I lost such rights when I thought up the name Metamorphizer to appeal on the popular level, but there's a difference."

That was a clincher. Anyone who believed Metamorphizer had salesappeal just wasnt all there. But why should I disillusion her and wound her pride? Down underneath her rough exterior I supposed she could be as sensitive as I; and I hope I am not without chivalry.

I said nothing, but of course her interdiction of the only possibility killed any weakening inclination. And yet . . . yet . . . Afterall, I had to have *something* . . .

"All right, Weener. This pump—" she produced miraculously from the jumble an unwieldy engine dragging a long and tangling tail of hose behind it, the end lost among mementos of unfinished meals "—this pump is full of the Metamorphizer, enough to inoculate a hundred and fifty acres when added in proper proportion to the irrigating water. I have a table worked out to show you about that. The tank holds five gallons; get $50 a gallon—a dollar and a half an acre and keep ten percent for yourself. Be sure to return the pump every night."

I had to say for her that when she got down to business she didnt waste any words. Perhaps this contrasting directness so startled me I was roped in before I could refuse. On the other hand, of course, I would be helping out someone who needed my assistance badly, since she couldnt, with all the obvious factors against her, be having a very easy time. Sometimes it is advisable to temper business judgment with kindness.

Her first offer was ridiculous in its assumption that a salesman's talent, skill and effort were worth only a miserable ten percent, as though I were a literary agent with something a cinch to sell. I began to feel more at home as we ironed out the details and I brought the knowledge acquired with much hard work and painful experience into the bargaining. Fifty percent I wanted and fifty percent I finally got by demanding seventyfive. She became as interested in the contest as she had been before in benefits to humanity and I perceived a keen mind under all her eccentricity.

I can't truthfully say I got to like her, but I reconciled myself and eventually was on my way with the pump—a trifling weight to Miss Francis, judging by the way she handled it, but uncomfortably heavy to me—strapped to my back and ten feet of recalcitrant hose coiled round my shoulder. She turned her imperious eyes on me again and repeated for the fourth or fifth time the instructions for applying, as though I were less intelligent than she. I went out through the barren livingroom and took a backward glance at the scaling stucco walls of the apartment-house, shaking my head. It was a queer place for Albert Weener, the crackerjack salesman who had once led his team in a national contest to put over a threepiece aluminum deal, to be working out of. And for a woman. And for such a woman . . .

---

2 Everything is for the best, is my philosophy and Make your cross your crutch is a good thought to hold; so I reminded myself that it takes fewer muscles to smile than to frown and no one sees the bright side of things if he wears dark glasses. Since it takes all kinds to make a world and Josephine Spencer Francis was one of those kinds, wasnt it only reasonable to suppose there were other kinds who would buy the stuff she'd invented? The only way to sell something is first to sell yourself and I piously went over the virtues of the Metamorphizer in my mind. What if by its very nature there could be no repeat business? I wasnt tying myself to it for life.

All that remained was to find myself a customer. I tried to recall the location of the nearest rural territory. San Fernando valley, probably—a long, tiresome trip. And expensive, unless I wished to demean myself by thumbing rides—a difficult thing to do, burdened as I was by the pump. If she hadnt balked unreasonably about putting the stuff on lawns, I'd have prospects right at hand.

I was suddenly lawnconscious. There was probably not a Los Angeles street I hadnt covered at some time—magazines, vacuums, old gold, nearnylons—and I must have been aware of green spaces before most of the houses, but now for the first time I saw lawns. Neat, sharply confined, smoothshaven lawns. Sagging, slipping, eager-to-keep-up-appearances but fighting-a-losing-game lawns. Ragged, weedy, dissolute lawns. Halfbare, repulsively crippled, hummocky lawns. Bright lawns, insistent on former respectability and trimness; yellow and gray lawns, touched with the craziness of age, quite beyond all interest in looks, content to doze easily in the sun. If Miss Francis' mixture was on the upandup and she hadnt introduced a perfectly unreasonable condition—why, I couldnt miss.

On the other hand, I thought suddenly, I'm the salesman, not she. It was up to me as a practical man to determine where and how I could sell to the best advantage. With sudden resolution I walked over a twinkling greensward and rang the bell.

"Good afternoon, madam. I can see from your garden youre a lady who's interested in keeping it lovely."

"Not my garden and Mrs Smith's not home." The door shut. Not gently.

The next house had no lawn at all, but was fronted with a rank growth of ivy. I felt no one had a right to plant ivy when I was selling something effective only on the family Gramineae. I tramped over the ivy hard and rang the doorbell on the other side.

"Good afternoon, madam. I can see from the appearance of your lawn youre a lady who really cares for her garden. I'm introducing to a restricted group—just one or two in each neighborhood—a new preparation, an astounding discovery by a renowned scientist which will make your grass twice as green and many times as vigorous upon one application, without the aid of anything else, natural or artificial."

"My gardener takes care of all that."

"But, madam—"

"There is a city ordinance against unlicensed solicitors. Have you a license, young man?"

After the fifth refusal I began to think less unkindly of Miss Francis' idea of selling the stuff to farmers and to wonder what was wrong with my technique. After some understandable hesitation—for I don't make a practice of being odd or conspicuous—I sat down on the curb to think. Besides, the pump was getting wearisomely heavy. I couldnt decide exactly what was unsatisfactory in my routine. The stuff had neither been used nor advertised, so there could be no prejudice against it; no one had yet allowed me to get so far as quoting price, so it wasnt too expensive.

The process of elimination brought me to the absurd conclusion that the fault must lie in me. Not in my appearance, I reasoned, for I was a personable young man, a little over thirty at the time, with no obvious defects a few visits to the dentist wouldnt have removed. Of course I do have an unfortunate skin condition, but such a thing's an act of God, as the lawyers say, and people must take me as I am.

No, it wasnt my appearance . . . or was it? That monstrously outsized pump! Who wanted to listen to a salestalk from a man apparently prepared for an immediate gasattack? There is little use in pressing your trousers between two boards under the mattress if you discount such neatness with the accouterment of an invading Martian. I uncoiled the hose from my shoulder and eased the incubus from my back. Leaving them visible from the corner of my eye, I crossed the most miserable lawn yet encountered.

It was composed of what I since learned is Bermuda, a plant most Southern Californians call—with many profane prefixes—devilgrass. It was yellow, the dirty, grayish yellow of moldy straw; and bald, scuffed spots immodestly exposed the cracked, parched earth beneath. Over the walk, interwoven stolons had been felted down into a ragged mat, repellent alike to foot and eye. Perversely, onto what had once been flowerbeds, the runners crept erect, bristling spines showing faintly green on top—the only live color in the miserable expanse. Where the grass had gone to seed there were patches of muddy purple, patches which enhanced rather than relieved the diseased color of the whole and emphasized the dying air of the yard. It was a neglected, unvalued thing; an odious appendage, a mistake never rectified.

"Madam," I began, "your lawn is deplorable." There was no use giving her the line about I-can-see-you-are-a-lady-who-cares-for-lovely-things. Anyway, now the pump was off my back I felt reckless. I threw the whole book of salesmanship away. "It's the most neglected lawn in the neighborhood. It is, madam, I'm sorry to say, no less than a disgrace."

She was a woman beyond the age of childbearing, her dress revealing the outlines of her corset, and she looked at me coldly through rimless glassing biting the bridge of her inadequate nose. "So what?" she asked.

"Madam," I said, "for ten dollars I can make this the finest lawn in the block, the pride of your family and the envy of your neighbors."

"I can do better things with ten dollars than spend it on a bunch of dead grass."

Gratefully I knew I had her then and was glad I hadnt weakly given in to an impulse to carry out the crackpot's original instructions. When they start to argue, my motto is, theyre sold. I took a good breath and wound up for the clincher.

I won't say she was an easy sale, but afterall I'm a psychologist; I found all her weak points and touched them expertly. Even so, she made me cut my price in half, leaving me only twofifty according to my agreement with Miss Francis, but it was an icebreaker.

I got the pump and hose, collecting at the same time an audience of brats who assisted me by shouting, "What ya goin a do, mister?" "What's at thing for, mister?" "You goin a water Mrs Dinkman's frontyard, mister?" "Do your teeth awwis look so funny, mister? My grampa takes his teeth out at night and puts'm in a glass of water. Do you take out your teeth at night, mister?" "You goin a put that stuff on our garden too, mister?" "Hay, Shirley—come on over and see the funnylooking man who's fixing up Dinkman's yard."

They were untiring, shrilling their questions, exclamations and comments, completely driving from my mind the details of the actual application of the Metamorphizer. Anyway, Miss Francis had been concerned with putting it in the irrigation water—which didnt apply in this case. I thought a moment. A gallon was enough for thirty acres;

half a pint should suffice for this—more than suffice. Irrigation water, nonsense—I'd squirt it on and tell the woman to hose it down afterward—that'd be the same as putting it in the water, wouldnt it?

To come to this practical conclusion under the brunt of the children's assault was a remarkable feat. As I dribbled the stuff over the sorry devilgrass they kicked the pump—and my shins—mimicking my actions, tripping me as they skipped under my legs, getting wet with the Metamorphizer—I hoped with mutually deleterious effect—and generally making me more than ever thankful for my bachelor condition.

Twofifty, I thought, angrily squirting a fine mist at a particularly dreary spot—and it isnt even selling. Manual labor. Working with my hands. I might as well be a gardener. College training. Wide experience. Alert and aggressive. In order to dribble stuff smelling sickeningly of carnations on a wasted yard. I coiled up my hose disgustedly and collected a reluctant five dollars.

"It don't look any different," commented Mrs Dinkman dubiously.

"Madam, Professor Francis' remarkable discovery works miracles, but not in the twinkling of an eye. In a week youll see for yourself, provided of course you wet it down properly."

"In a week youll be far gone with my five dollars," diagnosed Mrs Dinkman.

While this might be superficially true, it was an unfair and unkind thing to say, and it wounded me. I reached into my pocket and drew out an old card—one printed before I'd had an irreconcilable difference with the firm employing me at the time.

"I can always be reached at this address, Mrs Dinkman," I said, "should you have any cause for dissatisfaction—which I'm sure is quite impossible. Besides, I shall be daily in this district demonstrating the value of Dr Francis' Lawn Tonic."

That was certainly true; unless I made a better connection. Degrading manual labor or not, I intended to sell as many local people as possible on the strength of having found a weak spot in the wall of salesresistance before the effects of the Metamorphizer became apparent. For, in strict confidence, and despite its being an undesirable negative attitude, I was a little dubious that those effects—or lack of them—would stimulate further sales.

3 My alarmclock, as it did every morning, Sundays included, rang at sixthirty, for I am a man of habit. I turned it off, remembering instantly I had given Miss Francis neither her pump nor her share of the sale. Of course it was more convenient and timesaving to bring them both together and I was sure she didnt expect me to follow instructions to the letter, like an officeboy, any more in these matters than she had in her restriction to agricultural use.

Still, it was remiss of me. The fact is, I had spent her money as well as my own—not on dissipation, I hasten to say, but on dinner and an installment of my roomrent. This was embarrassing, but I looked upon it merely as an advance—quite as if I'd had the customary drawingaccount—to be charged against my next commissions. My acceptance of the advance merely indicated my faith in the future of the Metamorphizer.

I dissolved a yeastcake in a glass of water; it's very healthy and I'd heard it alleviated dermal irritations. Lathering my face, I glanced over the list culled from the dictionary and stuck in the mirror the night before, for I have never been too tired to improve my mind. By this easy method of increasing my vocabulary I had progressed, at the time, down to the letter K.

While drinking my coffee—never more than two cups—it was my custom to read and digest stock and bond quotations, for though I had no investments—the only time I had been able to take a flurry there was an unforeseen recession in the market—I thought a man who didnt keep up with trends and conditions unfitted for a place in the businessworld. Besides, I didnt expect to be straitened indefinitely and I believed in being ready to take proper advantage of opportunity when it came.

As a man may devote the graver part of his mind to a subject and then turn for relaxation to a lighter aspect, so I had for years been interested in a stock called Consolidated Pemmican and Allied concentrates. It wasnt a highpriced issue, nor were its fluctuations startling. For six months of the year, year in and year out, it would be quoted at 1/16 of a cent a share; for the other six months it stood at 1/8. I didnt know what pemmican was and I didnt particularly care, but if a man could invest at 1/16 he could double his money overnight when it rose to 1/8. Then he could reverse the process by selling before it went down and so snowball into fortune. It was a daydream but a harmless one.

Satisfying myself Consolidated Pemmican was bumbling along at its low level, I reluctantly prepared to resume Miss Francis' pump. It seemed less heavy as I wound the hose over my shoulder and I felt this wasnt due to the negligible quantity I'd expended on Mrs Dinkman's grass. I just knew I was going to have a successful day. I had to.

In moments of fancy I often think a salesman is more truly a creative artist than many of those who arrogate the title to themselves. He uses words, on one hand, and the receptivity of prospects on the other, to mold a cohesive and satisfying whole, a work of Art, signed and dated on the dotted line. Like any such work, the creation implies thoughtful and careful preparation. So it was that I got off the bus, polishing a new salestalk to fit the changed situation. "One of your neighbors . . ." "I have just applied . . ." I sneered my way past those houses refusing my services the day before; they couldnt have the Metamorphizer at any price now. Then it hit my eyes.

Mrs Dinkman's lawn, I mean.

The one so neglected, ailing and yellow only yesterday.

It wasnt sad and sickly now. The most enthusiastic homeowner wouldnt have disdained it. There wasnt a single bare spot visible in the whole lush, healthy expanse. And it was green. Green. Not just here and there, but over every inch of soft, undulating surface; a pale applegreen where the blades waved to expose its underparts and a rich, dazzling emerald on top. Even the runners, sinuously encroaching upon the sidewalk, were deeply virescent.

The Metamorphizer worked.

The Metamorphizer not only worked, but it worked with unbelievable rapidity. Overnight. I knew nothing about the speed at which ordinary fertilizers, plant stimulants or hormones took hold, but commonsense told me nothing like this had ever happened so quickly. I had been indulging in a little legitimate puffery in saying the inoculant worked miracles, but if anything that had been an understatement. It just went to show how impossible it is for a real salesman to be too enthusiastic.

Nerves in knees and fingers quivering, I walked over to join the group curiously inspecting the translated lawn. I, I had done this; out of the most miserable I'd made the loveliest—and for a paltry five dollars. I tried to recapture the memory of what it had looked like in order to relish the contrast more, but it was impossible; the vivid present blotted out the decayed past completely.

"Overnight," someone said. "Yessir, just overnight. Wouldnt of believed it if I hadnt noticed just yesterday how much worse an the city dump it looked."

"Bet at stuff's ten inches high."

"Brother, you can say that again. Foot'd be closer."

"Anyhow it's uh fattestlookin grass I seen sence I lef Texas."

"An the greenest. Guess I never did see such a green before."

While they exclaimed about the beauty and vigor of the growth, my mind was racing in high along practical lines. Achievement isnt worth much unless you can harness it, and in today's triumph I saw tomorrow's benefit. No more canvassing with a pump undignifiedly on my back, no more manual labor; no, bold as the thought was, not even any more direct selling for me. This was big, too big to be approached in any cockroach, build-up-slowly-from-the-bottom way. It was a real top deal, in a class with nylon or jukeboxes or bubblegum. You could smell the money in it.

First of all I'd have to tie Josephine Francis down with an ironclad contract. Agents; dealerships; distributors and a general salesmanager, Albert Weener, at the top. Incorporate. Get it all down in black and white and signed by Miss Francis right away. For her own good. An idealistic scientist, a frail woman, protect her from the vultures who'd try to rob her as soon as they saw what the Metamorphizer would do. Such a woman wouldnt have any business sense. I'd see she got a comfortable living out of it and free her from responsibility. Then she could potter around all she liked.

Incorporate. Interest big money. Put it on a nationwide basis. A cut for the general salesmanager on every sale. Besides stock. Take the patent in the company's name. In six months I'd be on my way to being a millionaire. I had certainly been right up on my toes in picking the Metamorphizer as a winner in spite of Miss Francis' kitchen and her lack of aggressiveness. Instinct, the unerring instinct of a wideawake salesman for the right product—and for the right market. I mustnt forget that. Had I been content with her original limitation I d still be bumbling around trying to interest Farmer Hicks in some Metamorphizer for his hay.

"Ja notice how thick it was?"

"Well, that's Bermuda for you. Tell me they actually plant it on purpose in Florida."

"No kiddin?"

"Yessir. Know one thing—even if it looks pretty right now, I wouldnt want that stuff on my place. Have to cut it every day."

"Bet ya. Toughlookin too. I rather take my exercise in bed."

That's an angle, I thought—have to get old lady Francis to modify her formula or something. Else we'll never get rich. Slow down the rate of growth, dilute it—ought to be more profitable too . . . Have to find out how cheaply the inoculant can be produced— no more inefficient hand methods . . . Of course the fastness of growth wouldnt affect the sale to farmers—help it in fact. No doubt she'd had more than I originally thought in that aspect, I conceded generously. We could let them apply it themselves . . . mailorder advertising . . . cut costs that way . . . Think of clover and alfalfa— or werent they grasses? Anyway, imagine hay or wheat as tall as Iowa corn and corn higher than a smalltown cityhall! Fortune—there'd be a dozen fortunes in it.

I began perspiring. The deal was getting bigger and bigger. It wasnt just a simple matter of cutting in on a good thing. All the angles, which were multiplying at a tremendous rate, had to be covered before I saw Miss Francis again; I darent miss any bets. I needed a staff of agricultural experts—anyway someone who could cover the scientific side. Whatever happened to my freshman chemistry? And a mob of lawyers; you'd have to plug every loophole—tight. But here I was without a financial resource— couldnt hire a ditchdigger, much less the highpriced talent I needed—and someone else might get a brainstorm when he saw the lawn and beat me to it. I visioned myself cheated of my million . . .

Yes . . . a really fast worker—some unethical promoter willing to stoop to devious methods—might pass at any moment and grasp the possibilities, have Miss Francis signed up before I'd even got the deal straight in my mind. How could he miss, seeing this lawn? Splendid, magnificent, beautiful. No one would ever call this stuff devilgrass—angelgrass would be more appropriate to the implications of such a heavenly green. Millions in it—simply millions . . .

"Say—arent you the fellow put this stuff on?"

Halfadozen vacant faces gaped at me, the burdening pump, the caudal hose. Curiosity, interest, imbecile amusement argued in their expression with the respect due the worker of the transformation; it was the sort of look connected with salesresistance of the most obstinate kind. They distracted me from thinking things through.

"Miz Dinkman's sure looking for you. Says she's going to sue you."

Here was an unfortunate development, an angle to end all angles. Unfavorable publicity, the abortifacient of new enterprises, would mean you could hardly give the stuff away. My imagination raced through columns of newsprint in which the Metamorphizer was made the butt of reporters' humor. Mrs Dinkman's ire would have to be placated, bought off. Perhaps I'd better discuss developments with Miss Francis right away, after all.

Whatever I decided, it was advisable for me to leave this vicinity. I was in no financial position to soothe Mrs Dinkman and it was dubious, in view of her attitude, whether it would be possible to sell any more in the immediate neighborhood. Probably a new territory was the answer to my problem; a few sales would give me both cash in hand and time to think.

While I hesitated, Mrs Dinkman, belligerency dancing like a sparkling aura about her, came out of her garage with a rusty, rattling lawnmower. I'm no authority on gardentools, but this creaking, rickety machine was clearly no match for the lusty growth. The audience felt so too, and there was a stir of sporting interest as they settled down to watch the contest.

Determination was implicit in the sharply unnatural lines of her corset and the firm set of her glasses as she charged into the gently swaying runners. The wheels turned rebelliously, the mower bit, its rusty blades grated against the knife, something clanked forcibly and the machine stopped. Mrs. Dinkman pushed, her back arched with effort—the mower didnt budge. She pulled it back. It whirred gratefully; the clanking stopped and she tried again. This time it chewed a handful of grass from the edge, found it distasteful and quit once more.

"Anybody know how to make this damn thing work?" Mrs Dinkman asked exasperatedly.

"Needs oil" was helpfully volunteered.

She retired into the garage and returned with a lopsided oilcan. "Oil it," she commanded regally. The helpful one reluctantly pressed his thumb against the wry bottom of the can, aiming the twisted spout at odd parts of the mower. "I dunno," he commented.

"I don't either," said Mrs Dinkman. "You—Greener, Weener—whatever your name is!"

There was no possibility of evasion. "Yes, mam?"

"You made this stuff grow; now you can cut it down."

Uncouth guffaws from the watching idiots.

"Mrs Dinkman, I—"

"Get behind that lawnmower, young man, if you don't want to be involved in a lawsuit."

I wasnt afraid of such a consequence in itself, having at the moment nothing to attach, but I thought of Miss Francis and future sales and that impalpable thing known as "goodwill." "Yes mam," I repeated.

I discarded pump and hose to move reluctantly toward the mower. Under my feet I felt the springiness of the grass; was it pure fancy—or did it truly differ in quality from the lawns I'd trod so indifferently the day before?

I took the handle. If oiling had improved the machine, its previous efficiency must have been slight. It went shakily over the first inch of grass and then, as it had for Mrs Dinkman, it stopped for me.

By now the spectators had increased to a small crowd and their dull humor had taken the form of cheerfully offering much gratuitous advice. "Tie into it, Slim—build up the old muscle." "Back her up and take a good run." "Go home an do some settinup exercises—come back next year." "Got to put the old back behind it, Bud—give her the gas." "Need a decent mower—no use trying to cut stuff like that with an antique." "Yeah—get a good mower—one made since the Civil War." "No one around here got an honestogod lawnmower?"

The last query evidently nettled local pride, for soon a blithe, beamshouldered little man trundled up a shiny, rubbertired machine. "Thisll do the business," he announced confidently as I relinquished the spotlight to him with understandable readiness. "It's a regular jimdandy."

It certainly was. The devilgrass came irreverently above the wheels and flowed with graceful inquisitiveness over the blades, but the brisk little man pushed heartily and the mechanism revolved with a barely audible clicking. It did not balk, complain or hesitate. Cleanly severed ends of grass whirled into the air and floated down on the neat smooth swath left behind. Everyone smiled relievedly at the jimdandy's triumph and my sigh was loudest and most heartfelt. I edged away as unobtrusively as I could.

4 I have no sympathy with weaklings who complain of the cards being stacked, but it did seem as though fate were dealing unkindly with me. Here was a good proposition, coming just at the time I needed it most and it was turning bad rapidly. Walking the short distance to Miss Francis' I was unable to settle my mind, to strike a mental balancesheet. There was money; there had to be money—lots and lots of it—in the Metamorphizer, but it was possible there was trouble—lots and lots of it—also. The thing was, well, dangerous. What was the use of expending ability in selling something which could have kickbacks acting as deterrents to future sales? Of course a man had to take risks . . .

The door, after a properly prudent hesitation, clicked brokenly. Miss Francis looked as though she'd added insomnia to her other abstentions, otherwise she had not changed, even to her skirt and the smudge on her left nostril. "If youve come about the icebox youre a week late. I fixed it myself," she greeted me gruffly.

"Weener," I reminded her, "Albert Weener—remember? I'm selling—that is, I'm going to sell the product you invented to make plants eat anything."

"Oh. Weener—yes." She produced the toothpick and scratched her chin with it. "About the Metamorphizer." She paused and rubbed her elbow. "A mistake, I'm afraid. An error."

Aha, I thought, a new deal. Someone's offered to back her. Steal her brainchild, negate all my efforts to make her independent and cheat me of the reward of my spadework. You wouldnt think of her as a frail credulous woman, easily taken in by the first smooth talker, but a woman is a woman afterall.

"Look, Miss Francis," I argued, "youve got a big thing here, a great thing. The possibilities are practically unlimited. Of course youll have to have a manager to put it across—an executive, a man with business experience—someone who can tap the great reservoir of buying power by the conviction of a new need. Organize a sales campaign; rationalize production. Put the whole thing on a commercial basis. For all this you need a man who has contacted the public on every level—preferably doortodoor and with a varied background."

She strode past the stove, which had gathered new accreta during the night and looked in the cloudy mirror as though searching for a misplaced thought. "No doubt, Weener, no doubt. But before all these romantically streamlined things eventuate there must be a hiatus. In my haste I overlooked a detail yesterday, trivial maybe—perhaps vital. I should never have let you start out so soon."

This was bad; I was struggling now for my job and for the future of the Metamorphizer. "Miss Francis, I don't know what you mean by mistakes or trivial details or how I could have started out too soon, but whatever the trouble is I'm sure it can be smoothed out easily. Sometimes, you know, obstacles which appear tremendous prove to be nothing at all in experienced hands. I myself have had occasion to put things right for a number of different concerns. Really, Miss Francis, you mustnt let opportunity slip through your fingers. Believe me, I know what a big thing your discovery is—Ive seen what it does."

She turned those too sharp eyes on me discomfortingly. "Ah," she said, "so soon?"

"Well," I began, "it certainly acted quickly . . ."

I stopped when I saw she wasnt hearing me. She sat down in the only empty chair and drummed her fingers against big white teeth. "Even under a microscope," she muttered, "no perceptible reaction for fortyeight hours. Laboratory conditions? Or my own idiocy? But I approximated . . ." Her voice trailed off and for a full minute the absolute silence of the kitchen was broken only by the melodramatic dripping of a tap.

She made an effort to pull herself together and addressed me in her old abrupt way. "Corn or wheat?"

"Ay?"

"You said youve seen what it does. I asked you if you had applied it to corn or wheat—or what?"

She was looking at me so fixedly I had a slight difficulty in putting my words in good order. "It was neither, mam. I applied some of the stuff to a lawn—"

"A *lawn*, Weener?"

"Y-yes, mam."

"But I said—"

"General instructions, Miss Francis. I'm sure you didnt mean to tie my hands."

Another long silence.

"No, Weener—I didnt mean to tie your hands."

"Well, as I was saying, I applied some of the stuff to a lawn. Exactly according to your instructions—"

"In the irrigation water?"

"Well, not precisely. But just as good, I assure you."

"Go on."

"A terrible lawn. All shot. Last night. This morning—"

"Stop. What kind of grass? Or don't you know?"

"Of course I know," I answered indignantly. Did she think I was an idiot? "It was devilgrass."

"Ah." She rubbed the back of her hand against her singularly smooth cheek. "Bermuda. *Cynodon dactylon*. Stupid, stupid, stupid. How could I have been so blind? Did I think only the corn would be affected and not the weeds in the furrows? Or that something like this might not happen?"

I didnt feel like wasting any more time listening to her soliloquy. "This morning," I continued, "it was as green—"

"All right, Weener, spare me your poetry. Show it to me."

"Well now, Miss Francis . . ." I wanted, understandably enough, to discuss future arrangements before she saw Dinkman's lawn.

"Immediately, Weener."

When dealing with childish persons you have to cater to their whims. I rid myself of the pump—I'd never dreamed I'd be reluctant to part with the monster—while she made perfunctory and unconvincing motions to fit herself for the street. Of course she neither washed nor madeup, but she peered in the glass argumentatively, pulled her jacket down decisively, threw her shoulders back to raise it askew again and gave the swirl of hair a halfhearted pat.

"I'd like to go over the matter of organizing—"

"Not now."

I was naturally reluctant to be seen on the street with so conspicuous a figure, but I could hardly escape. I tried to match her swinging stride, but as she was at least six inches taller I had to give a sort of skip between steps, which was less than dignified. Searching my mind to find a tactful approach again to the subject of proper distribution of the Metamorphizer, I felt my opportunity slipping away every moment. She, on her part, was silent and so abstracted that I often had to put out a guiding hand to avert collision with other pedestrians or stationary objects.

I doubt if I'd been gone from Mrs Dinkman's threequarters of an hour. I had left a small group excited at the free show consequent upon the too successful beautification of a local eyesore; I returned to a sizable crowd viewing an impressive phenomenon. The homely levity had vanished; no one shouted jovial advice. Opinions and comments passed in whispers accompanied by furtive glances toward the lawn, as though it were sentient and might be offended by rude speculation. As we pushed through the bystanders I was suddenly aware of their cautious avoidance of contact with the grass itself. The nearest onlookers stood a respectful yard back and when unbalanced by the push of those behind went through such antics to avoid treading on it, while at the same time preserving the convention of innocence of any taboo that they frequently pivoted and pirouetted on one foot in an awkward ballet. The very hiding of their inhibition emphasized the new awesomeness of the grass; it was no longer to be lightly approached or frivolously treated.

Now I am not what is generally called a man of religious sensibilities, having long ago discarded belief in the supernatural; and I am not overcome at odd moments by mystical feelings. Furthermore I had been intimate with this particular patch of vegetation for some eighteen hours. I had viewed its decaying state; I had injected life into it; I had seen it in the first flush of resurrection. In spite of all this, I too fell under the spell of the grass and knew something compounded of wonder and apprehension.

The neatly cut swaths of the little man with the jimdandy mower came to a dramatic end in the middle of the yard. Beyond this shorn portion the grass rose in a threatening crest, taller than a man's knees; green, aloof and derisive. But it was not this forbidding sight

which gave me such a queer turn. It was the mown part; for I recalled
how the brisk man's machine had cut close and left behind short,
crisp stems. Now this piece was almost as high as when I'd first seen
it—grown faster in an hour than ordinary grass in a month.

5 I stole a look at Miss Francis to see how she was taking the
sight, but there was no emotion visible on her face. The
toothpick was once more in play and the luminous eyes fixed straight
ahead. Her legs were spread apart and she seemed firmly in position
for hours to come, as though she would wait for the grass to exhaust its
phenomenal growth.

"Why did they quit cutting?" I asked the man standing beside me.

"Mower give out—dulled the blades so they wouldnt cut no
more."

"Going to give up and let it grow?"

"Hell, no. Sent for a gardener with a powermower. Big one. Cut
anything. Ought to be here now."

He was, too, honking the crowd from the driveway. Mrs Dinkman was with him, looking at once indignant, persecuted, uncomfortable and selfrighteous. It was evident they had failed to reach any
agreement.

The gardener slammed the door of the senescent truck with
vehement lack of affection. "I cut lots a devilgrass, lady, but I won't tie
into this overgrown stuff at that price. You got no right to expect it. I
know what's fair and it's not reasonable to count on me cutting this like
it was an ordinary lawn. You know yourself it isnt fair."

"I'll give you ten dollars and that's my last word."

"Listen, lady, when I get through this job I'll have to take my
mower apart and have it resharpened. You think I can afford to do that
for a tendollar job?"

"Ten dollars," repeated Mrs Dinkman firmly.

The gardener appealed to the gallery. "Listen, folks: now I ask
you—is this fair? I'm willing to be reasonable. I understand this lady's
in trouble and I'm willing to help, but I can't do a twentyfivedollar job
for ten bucks, can I?"

It was doubtful if the observers were particularly concerned with
justice; what they desired was action, swift and drastic. A general

resentment at being balked of their amusement was manifest in murmurs of "Go ahead, do it." "What's the matter with you?" "Don't be dumb—do it for nothing—youll get plenty business out of it." They appealed to his nobler and baser natures, but he remained adamant.

Not to be balked by his churlishness, they passed a hat and collected $8.67, which I thought a remarkably generous admission price. When this was added to Mrs Dinkman's ten dollars the gardener, still protesting, reluctantly agreed to perform.

Mrs Dinkman prudently holding the total, he unloaded the powermower with many flourishes, making quite an undertaking of oiling and adjusting the roller, setting the blades; bending down to assure himself of the gasoline in the small tank, finally wheeling the contraption into place with great spirit. The motor started with a disgruntled put! changing into a series of resigned explosions as he guided it over the lawn crosswise to the lines of his predecessor. Miss Francis followed every motion with rapt attention.

"Did you expect this?" I asked.

"Ay? The abnormally stimulated growth, you mean?"

"Yes."

"Yes and no. Work in the laboratory didnt indicate it. My own fault; I didnt realize at once making available so much free nitrogen would have such instant results. But last night—"

"Yes?"

"Not now. Later."

The powermower went nicely, I might almost say smoothly, over the stuff cut before, muttering and chickling happily to itself as it dragged the panting gardener, inescapably harnessed, in its wake. But the mown area was narrow and the machine quickly jerked through it and made the last easy journey along the wall of untouched devilgrass beyond.

The gardener, without hesitation, aimed his machine at the thicket of grass. It growled, slowed, coughed, spat, struggled and thrashed on and finally conked out.

"Ah," said Miss Francis.

"Oh," said the spectators.

"Sonofabitch," said the gardener.

He yanked the grumbling mower back angrily, inspecting its mechanism in the manner of a mother with a wayward son and began again. There was desperate determination in his shoulders as he added his forward thrust to the protesting rhythm. The machine went at the grass like a bulldog attacking a borzoi: it bit, chewed, held on. It cut a new six inches readily, another foot slowly—and then with jolts and misfires and loud imprecations from the gardener, it gave up again.

"You," judged Mrs Dinkman, "don't know how to cut grass."

The gardener wiped his sweaty forehead with the inside of his wrist. "You—you should have a law against you," he answered bitterly and inadequately.

But the crowd evidently agreed with Mrs Dinkman's verdict, for there were mutterings of "It's a farmer's job." "Get somebody with a scythe." "That's right—get a scythe." "Got to have a scythe to cut hay like that." These remarks, uttered loudly enough for him to hear, so discouraged the gardener that after three more futile tries he reloaded his equipment and left amidst jeers and expressions of disfavor without attempting to collect any of the money.

For some reason the failure of the powermower lightened the atmosphere. Everyone, including Mrs Dinkman, seemed convinced that scything was the solution. Tension relaxed and the bystanders began talking in something above a whisper.

6 "This will just about ruin our sales," I said.

Miss Francis suspended the toothpick before her chin and looked at me as though I'd said dirty words in the presence of ladies.

"Well it will," I argued. "You can't expect people to have their lawns inoculated if they find out it's going to make grass act this way."

Her eyes might have been microscopes and I something smeared on a slide. "Weener, youre the sort of man who peddles *Life Begins at Forty* to the inmates of an old peoples' home."

I couldnt see what had upset her. The last idea had sound salesappeal, but it was a low income market . . . Oh well—her queer notions and obscure reactions undoubtedly went with her scientific gift. You have to lead individuals of this type for their own good, otherwise they spend their lives wandering around in a dreamy fog, accomplishing nothing.

"I still believe youve got something," I pointed out. "You yourself said it wasnt perfected, but perhaps you havent realized how far from marketable it actually is yet. Now then," I went on reasonably, "youre just going to have to dilute it or change it or do something to it, so while it will make grass nice and green, it won't let it grow wild like this."

The fixed look could be annoying. It was nearly impossible to turn your eyes away without rudeness once she caught them. "Weener, the Metamorphizer is neither fertilizer nor plantfood. It is a chemical compound producing a controlled mutation in any treated member of the family Gramineae. Dilution might make it not work—the mutation might not take place—but it couldnt make it half work. I could change your nature by forcibly injecting an ounce of lead into your cerebellum. The change would not only be irrevocable, but it wouldnt make the slightest difference if the lead were adulterated with ironpyrites or not."

"But, Miss Francis," I expostulated, "you'll have to do *something.*"

She threw her hands into the air, a theatrical gesture even more than ordinarily unbecoming. "Why?"

"Why? To make your discovery marketable, of course."

"Now? In the face of this?"

"Miss Francis," I said with dignity, "you are a lady and my selfrespect makes me treat you with the courtesy due your sex. You advertised for a salesman. Instead of sneering at my honest efforts to put your merchandise across to the public, I think youd be better advised to worry about such lowbrow things as keeping faith."

"Am I to keep faith in a vacuum? You came to me as a salesman and I must give you something to sell. This is simple morality; but if such a grant entails concomitant evils, surely I am absolved of my original contract."

"I don't know what youre talking about," I told her frankly. "Your stuff made the grass grow too fast, that's all. You should change the formula or find a new one or else . . ."

"Or else youll have been left with nothing to sell. I despair of making the point about changing the formula; your trust in my powers is too reverent. Again, I'm not an arrogant woman and I'll admit to some responsibility. Make the world fit for Alfred Weener to make a living in."

"It's Albert, not Alfred," I corrected her. I'm not touchy, goodness knows, but afterall a name's a piece of property.

"Your pardon, Albert." She looked down at me with such a placatory and genuinely feminine smile I decided I'd been foolish to be offended. She's a nut of course, I thought indulgently, someone whose life is bounded by theories and testtubes, a woman with no conception of practical reality. Instead of being affronted it would be better to show her patiently how essential my help was to her.

"Of all people," she went on, searching my face with those discomfiting eyes, "of all people Ive the least cause for moral snobbery. Anxious to get a few dollars to carry on my work—and what was such anxiety but selfindulgence?—I threw the Metamorphizer to you and the world before I realized that it was not only imperfect, but faulty. Hell is paved with good intentions and the first result of my desire to benefit mankind has been to injure the Dinkmans. Meditation in place of infatuation would have shown me both the immediate and ultimate wrongs. I doubt if youd been gone an hour yesterday when I knew I'd made a blunder in permitting you to go out with danger in both hands."

"I don't know what youre getting at," I said stiffly, for it sounded as though she were regarding me as a child.

"Why, as I was sitting, composing my thoughts toward extending the effectiveness of the Metamorphizer beyond gramina, it suddenly became clear to me I'd erred about not knowing how long the effect of the inoculations would last."

"You mean you found out?" If she brought the thing under control and the effect lasted a specified time there might be repeat business afterall.

"I found out a great deal by using speculation and logic for a change instead of my hands and memory. I sat and thought, and though this is an unorthodox way for a scientist to proceed, I profited by it. I reasoned: if you change the genetic structure of a plant you change it permanently; not for a day or an hour, but for its existence. I'm not speaking of chance mutations, you understand, Weener, coming about over a course of generations, generations which include sports, degenerates, atavars andsoforth; but of controlled changes, brought about through human intervention. Inoculation by the Metamorphizer might be compared to cutting off a man's leg or transplanting part of his brain. Albert—what happens when you cut off a man's leg?"

I was tired of being talked to like a grammarschool class. Still, I humored her. "Why, then he has only one leg," I answered agreeably if idiotically.

"True. More than that, he has a onelegged disposition. His whole ego, his entire spirit is changed. No longer a twolegged creature, reduced, he is another—warped, if you like—being. To come to the immediate point of the grass: if you engender an omnivorous capacity you implant an insatiable appetite."

"I don't catch."

"If you give a man a big belly you make him a hog."

A chevvy coupe, gently breathing steam from its radiator cap, interrupted. From its turtle hung the blade of a scythe and on the nervously hinged door had been hopefully lettered *Arcangelo Barelli, Plowing & Grading*.

While the coupe was trembling for some seconds before quieting down, I sighed a double relief, at Miss Francis' forgetfulness of the money due her and the soothing of my fears for the lawn's eating its way downward to China or India. The remark about gluttonous abdomens was disturbing.

"And of course there will be no further sale of the Metamorphizer," she concluded, her eyes now totally concerned with the farmer who was opening the turtle with the air of a man expecting to be unpleasantly astonished.

Mr Barelli came as to a deathbed, a consoling but hopeless smile widening his narrow face only inconsiderably. At the scythe cradled in his arms someone shouted, "Here's old Father Time himself." Mr Barelli wasnt amused. Brushing his forehead thoughtfully with tender fingers he surveyed with saddened eye the three graduated steps of grass. The last step, unessayed by his predecessors, rose nearly four feet, as alien to the concept of lawn as a field of wheat.

"Think you can cut it?" one of the audience asked.

Mr Barelli smiled cheerlessly and didnt answer. Instead, he uprooted from his hip pocket a slender stone and began phlegmatically to caress the blade of the scythe with it.

"Hay, that stuff's not goin to stop growin while you fool around."

"Got to do things right," explained Mr Barelli gently.

The rhythmic friction of stone against steel prolonged suspense unbearably. All kinds of speculation crowded my mind while the leisurely performance went on. The grass was growing rapidly; faster than vegetation had ever grown before. Could it grow so quickly the farmer's scythe couldnt keep up with it? Suppose it had been wheat or corn? Planted today, it would be ready to harvest next week, fully ripe. The original dream of Miss Francis would pale compared with the reality. There was still—somewhere, somehow—a fortune in the Metamorphizer . . .

Ready at last, Mr Barelli walked delicately across the stubble as if it were a substance too precious to be trampled brutally. Again he measured the rippling, ascending mass with his eye. It was the look of a bridegroom.

"What you waitin for?"

Unheeding, he scraped bootwelt semicircularly on the sward as though to make a stance. Once more he appraised the grass, crooked his knee, rested his hands lightly on the two short, upraised handholds. Satisfied at length with his preparations, he finally drew the scythe back with a sweeping motion of both arms and curved it forward close to the ground. It embraced a sudden island lovingly and a sheaf of grass swooned into a heap. I was reminded of old woodcuts in a history of the French Revolution.

The bystanders sighed in harmony. "Nothing to it . . . should a had him in the first place . . . can't beat the old elbowgrease. No, sir, musclepower'll do it every time . . . guess it's licked now all right, all right . . ." Mr Barelli duplicated his sweep and another sheaf fell. Another. And another . . .

"One of the oldest human rituals," remarked Miss Francis, swaying her body in time with the farmer's. "An act of devotion to Ceres. But all this husbandman reaps is *Cynodon dactylon*. A commentary."

"Progress," I pointed out. "Now they have machines to harvest grain. All uptodate farmers use them; only the backward ones stick to primitive tools and have to make a living by taking on odd jobs."

"Progress," she repeated, looking from the scythewielder to me and back again. "Progress, Weener. A remarkable conception of the nineteenth century . . ."

The less intense spectators began to move off; not, to be sure, without backward glances, but the metronomic swing of Mr Barelli's blade indicated that it was all over with the rank grass now. I too should have been on my way, writing off the Metamorphizer as a total loss and considering methods for making a new and more profitable connection. Not that I was one to leave a sinking ship, nor had I lost faith in the potentialities of Miss Francis' discovery; but she either wasnt smart enough to modify her formula, or else . . . but there really wasnt any "or else". She just wasnt smart enough to make the Metamorphizer marketable and she was cheating me of the handsome return which should be rightfully mine.

She'd made the stuff and deceived me by an unscrupulously worded advertisement, now, no longer interested, she asked airily if further effort were essential. Who wouldnt be indignant? And to cap it all she suddenly ejaculated, "Can't dawdle around here all day" and after snatching up a handful of the scythings, she left, rolling her large body from side to side, galloping her untidy hair up and down over her neck as she took rapid strides. Evidently the attractions of her messy kitchen were more to her taste than the wholesome air of outdoors. Pottering around, producing another mare's nest and eventually, I suppose, getting another victim . . .

7 But I couldnt leave so cavalierly. Every leaf, stem, and blade of the cancerous grass held me in somewhat the same way Miss Francis' intense eyes did. It wasnt an aesthetic or morbid attraction—its basis was strictly practical. If it could have been controlled—if only the growth could be induced on a modified and proper scale—what a product! A fury of frustration rocked my customary calm . . .

The stretch and retraction of the mower's arms, the swift, bright curving as the scythe cut deeper, fascinated me. An unscrupulous man—just as a whimsical thought—might go about in the night inoculating lawns surreptitiously and appear with a crew next day to offer his services in cutting them. Just goes to show how easy it is to make dishonest speculations . . . but of course such things don't pay in the long run . . .

The lush area was being reduced, but perhaps not with the same rapidity as at first when Mr Barelli was at the top of enthusiastic—if the adjective was applicable—vigor. Oftener and oftener and oftener he paused to sharpen his implement and I thought the cropped shocks were becoming smaller and smaller. As the movement of the scythe swept the guillotined grass backward, the trailing stolons entangled themselves with the uncut stand, pulling the sheaves out of place and making the stacks ragged and inadequate looking.

Behind me a cocky voice asked, "What's cooking around here, chum?"

I turned round to a young man, thin as a bamboo pole, elegantly tailored, who yawned to advertise gold inlays. I explained while he looked skeptical, bored and knowing simultaneously. "Who would tha flummox, bah goom?" he inquired.

"Ay?"

He took a pack of playingcards from his pocket and riffled them expertly. "Who you kidding, bud?" he translated.

"No one. Ask anybody here if this wasnt a dead lawn yesterday and if it hasnt grown this high since morning."

He yawned again and proffered me the deck. "Pick any card," he suggested. To avoid rudeness I selected one. He put the pack back and said, "You have the nine of diamonds. Clever, eh?"

I didnt know whether it was or not. He accepted the pasteboard from me and said, peering out from under furry black eyebrows, "If I brought in a story like that, the chief would fire me before you could say James Gordon Bennett."

"Youre a reporter?"

"Acute chap. Newspaperman. Name of Gootes. Jacson Gootes, *Daily Intelligencer,* not *Thrilling Wonder Stories.*"

I thought I saw an answer to my most pressing problem. One has to stoop occasionally to methods which, if they didnt lead to important ends, might almost be termed petty; but afterall there was no reason Mr Jacson Gootes shouldnt buy me a dinner in return for information valuable to him. "Let's get away from here," I suggested.

He fished out a coin, showed it to me, waved his arm in the air and opened an empty palm for my inspection. "Ah sho would like to, cunnel, but Ahve got to covah thisyeah sto'y—even if it's out of this mizzble wo'ld."

"I'm sure I can give you details to bring it down to earth," I told him. "Make it a story your editor will be glad to have."

"'Glad'!" He pressed tobacco into a slender pipe as emaciated as himself. "You dont know W R. If he got a beat on the story of Creation he'd be sore as hell because God wanted a byline."

He evidently enjoyed his own quip for he repeated several times in different accents ". . . God wanted a byline." He puffed a matchflame and surveyed the field of Mr Barelli's effort. "Hardworkin feller, what? Guess I better have a chat with the bounder—probably closest to the dashed thing."

"Mr Gootes," I said impressively, "I am the man who applied the inoculator to this grass. Now shall we get out of here so you can listen to my story?"

"Sonabeesh—thees gona be good. Lead away, amigo—I prepare both ears to leesten."

I drew him toward Hollywood Boulevard and into a restaurant I calculated might not be too expensive for his generosity. Besides, he probably had an expenseaccount. We put a porcelaintopped table between us and he commanded, "Give down." Obediently I went over all the happenings of yesterday, omitting only Miss Francis' name and the revealing wording of the ad.

Gootes surveyed me interestedly. "You certainly started something here, Acne and/or Psoriasis."

Humor like his was beneath offense. "My name's Albert Weener."

"Mine's Mustard." He produced a plastic cup and rapidly extracted from it a series of others in diminishing sizes. "I wouldnt have thought it to look at you. The dirty deed, I mean—not the exzemical hotdog. O K, Mister Weener—who's this scientific magnate? Whyre you holding him out on me?"

"Scientists don't like to be disturbed in their researches," I temporized.

"No more does a man in a whorehouse," he retorted vulgarly. "Story's no good without him."

That was what I thought and I'm afraid my satisfaction appeared on my face.

"Now leely man—no try a hold up da press. Whatsa matter, you already had da beer and da roasta bif sanawich?"

"Maybe you better repeat the order. You know in these cheap

places they don't like to have you sit around and talk without spending money."

"Money! Eh, laddie—I'm nae a millionaire." He balanced a full glass of water thoughtfully upon a knifeblade, looking around for applause. When it was not forthcoming he meekly followed my suggestion.

"Listen, Gootes," I swallowed a mouthful of sandwich and sipped a little beer. "I want to help you get your story."

He waved his hand and pulled a handkerchief out of his ear.

"The point is," I commenced, sopping a piece of bread in the thick gravy, "if I were to betray the confidence involved I couldnt hope to continue my connection and I'd lose my chances to benefit from this remarkable discovery."

"Balls," exclaimed Gootes. "Forget the spiel. I'm not a prospect for your lawn tonic."

I disrgarded the interruption. "I'm not a mercenary man and I believe in enlightening the public to the fullest extent compatible with decency. I'm willing to make a sacrifice for the general good, yet I—"

"—'must live.' I know, I know. How much?"

"It seems to me fifty dollars would be little enough—"

"Fifty potatoes!" He went through an elaborate pantomime of shock, horror, indignation, grotesque dismay and a dozen other assorted emotions. "Little man, youre fruitcake sure. W R wouldnt part with half a C for a tipoff on the Secondcoming. No, brother— you rang the wrong bell. Five I might get you—but no more."

I replied firmly I was not in need of charity—ignoring his pointed look at the remains on my plate—and this was strictly a business proposition, payment for value received. After some bargaining he finally agreed to phone his managingeditor and propose I'd "come clean" for twenty dollars. While he was on this errand I added pie and coffee to the check. It is well to be provident and I'd paid for my meal in more than money.

Jacson Gootes came limply from the phonebooth, his bumptiousness gone. "No soap." He shook his head dejectedly. "Old Man said only pity for the lower mammals prevented him from letting me go to work for Hearst right away. Sorry."

His nerves appeared quite shattered; capable of restoration only by Old Grandad. After tossing down a couple of bourbons he seemed a little recovered, but hardly quite well enough to use an accent or perform a trick.

"I'm sorry also," I said. "Since we can be of no further use to each other—"

"Don't take a powder, chum," he urged plaintively. "What about a last gander at the weed together?"

As we walked back I reflected that at any rate I was saved from submitting Miss Francis to vulgar publicity. Everything is for the best—Ive seen a hundred instances to prove it. Perhaps—who knew—something might yet happen to make it possible for me to profit by the freak growth.

"Needs a transfusion," remarked Gootes as we stood on the sidewalk before it.

Indeed it was anemically green; uneven, hacked and ragged; shorn of its emerald beauty. A high fog filtered the late afternoon light to show Mr Barelli's task accomplished and the curious watchers gone. It was no smoothly clipped carpet, yet it was no longer a freakish, exotic thing. Rather forlorn it looked, and crippled.

"Paleface pay out much wampum to get um cut every day."

"Oh, it probably won't take long till the strength is exhausted."

"Says you. Well, Ive got half a story. Cheerio."

I sighed. If only Miss Francis could control it. A fortune . . .

I walked home, trying to figure out what I was going to do tomorrow.

---

8 I thought I was prepared for anything after the shocks of the day before; I know I was prepared for nothing at all— to find the grass as I'd left it or even reverted to its original decay. Indeed, I was not too sure that my memory was completely accurate; that the thing had happened so fantastically.

But the devilgrass had outdone itself and made my anticipations foolish. It waved a green crest higher than the crowd—a crowd three times the size of yesterday's and increasing rapidly. All the scars inflicted on it, the indignities of scythe and mower, were covered by a new and even more prodigious stand which made all its former growth appear puny. Bold and insolent, it had repaired the hackedout areas and risen to such a height that, except for a narrow strip at the top, all the windows of the Dinkman house were smothered. Of the garage, only the roof, islanded and bewildered, was visible, apparently resting on a solid foundation of devilgrass. It sprawled kittenishly, its deceptive softness faintly suggesting fur; at once playful and destructive. My optimism of the night before was dashed; this voracious growth wasnt going to dwindle away of itself. It would have to be killed, rooted out.

Now the Dinkman lawn wasnt continuous with its neighbors, but, until now, had been set off by chesthigh hedges. The day before these had contained and defined the growth, but overwhelming them in the night, the grass had swept across and invaded the neat, civilized plots behind, blurring sharply cut edges, curiously investigating flowerbeds, barbarously strangling shapely bushes.

But these werent the ravages which upset me; it was reasonable if not entirely comfortable to see shrubbery, plants and blossoms swallowed up. Work of men's hands they may be, but they bear the imprimatur of nature. The cement sidewalk, however, was pure artifice, stamped with the trademark of man. Indignity and defeat were symbolized by its overrunning; it was an arrogant defiance, an outrageous challenge offered to every man happening by. But the grass was not satisfied with this irreverence: it was already making demands on curbing and gutter.

"Junior, youve got a story now. W R fired three copyboys and a proofreader he was so mad at himself. Here." Jacson Gootes made a pass in the air, simulated astonishment at the twentydollar bill which appeared miraculously between his fingers and put it in my hand.

"Thank you," I replied coolly. "Just what is this for?"

"Faith, me boy, such innocence Ive never seen since I left the old sod. Tis but a little token of esteem from himself, to repay you for the trouble of leading me to your scientist, your Frankenstein, your Burbank. Lead on, my boy. And make it snappy, brother," he added, "because Ive got to be back here for the rescue."

"Rescue?"

"Yeah. People in the house." He consulted a scrap of paper. "Pinkman—"

"Dinkman."

"Dinkman. Yeah—thanks—no idea how sensitive people are

when you get their names wrong. Dinkmans phoned the firedepart-
ment. Can't get out. Rescue any minute—got to cover that—impera-
tive—TRAPPED IN HOME BY FREAK LAWN—and nail down
your scientist at the same time."

I was very anxious myself to see what would happen here so I
suggested, since I could take him to the discoverer of the Metamorphizer any time, that we'd better stay and get the Dinkman story
first. With overenthusiastic praise of my acuteness, he agreed and
began practicing his sleightofhand tricks to the great pleasure of some
children, the same ones, I suspect, who had plagued me when I was
spraying the lawn.

His performance was terminated by the rapidly approaching
firesiren. The crowd seemed of several minds about the purpose of the
red truck squealing around the corner to a stop. Some, like Gootes,
had heard the Dinkmans were indeed trapped in the house; others
declared the firemen had come to cut away the grass onceandforall;
still others held the loud opinion that the swift growth had generated a
spontaneous combustion.

But having made their abrupt face-in-the-ground halt, the truck
(or rather the firemen on it) anticlimactically did nothing at all.
Helmeted and accoutered, ready for instant action, they relaxed
contentedly against the engine, oblivious of grass, bystanders, or
presumable emergency. Gootes strolled over to inquire the cause of
their indolence. "Waiting for the chief," he was informed. Thereupon
he borrowed a helmet (possibly on the strength of his presscard) and
proceeded to pull from it such a variety of objects that he received the
final accolade from several of his audience when they told him
admiringly he ought to be on the stage.

The bystanders were not seduced by this entertainment into
approval of the firemen's idleness and inquired sarcastically why they
had left their cots behind or if they thought they were still on WPA?
The men remained impervious until the chief jumped out of his red
roadster and surveyed the scene napoleonically. "Thought somebody
was pulling a rib," he explained to no one in particular. "All right,
boys, there's folks in that house—let's get them out."

Carrying a ladder the men plunged toward the house. Their boots
trod the sprawling runners heavily, spurning and crushing them
carelessly. The grass responded by flowing back like water, sloshing

over ankles and lapping at calves, thoroughly entangling and impeding progress. Panting and struggling the firemen penetrated only a short way into the mass before they were slowed almost to a standstill. From the sidelines it seemed as though they were wrestling with an invisible octopus. Feet were lifted high, but never free of the twining vegetation; the ladder was pulled angrily forward, but the clutch of the grass upon it became firmer with every tug.

At length they were halted, although their efforts still gave an appearance of advance. Thrashing and wrenching they urged themselves and the now burdensome ladder against the invincible wall. The only result was to give the illusion they were burying themselves in the clutching tentacles. Exertions dwindled; the struggle grew less intense; then they retreated, fighting their way out of the enveloping mass in a panic of desperation, abandoning the ladder.

The chief surveyed them with less than approbation. "Cut your way in," he ordered. "You guys think those axes are only to bust up furniture with?"

Obediently, wedges of bright steel flashed against the green wall.

"Impatiently I await the rescue of fair Dinkmans from this enchanted keep," murmured Gootes, vainly trying to balance his pipe on the back of his hand.

It looked as though he would have to contain his impatience for some time. The firemen slashed unenthusiastically at the grass, which gave way only grudgingly and by inches. Halfanhour later they triumphantly dragged out the abandoned ladder. "Stuff's like rubber—bounds back instead of cutting."

"Yeah. And in the meantime those people been telephoning again. Want to know what the delay is. Want to know what they pay taxes for. Threaten to sue the city."

"Let'm sue. Long as theyre in there they can't collect."

"Funny as a flat tire. Get going, goldbrick."

9 Another firetruck rolled up and there was much kidding back and forth between the two crews. This was clearly no situation in which lives or property were at stake; it was rather in line with assisting distraught cats down from tops of telephonepoles or persuading selfimmolated children to unlock the bathroom door and let mommy in; an amusing interval in a tense day. Perhaps those manning the second truck were more naturally ingenious, possibly the original workers sought more diverting labor; at any rate the futile chopping was abandoned. Instead, several long ladders were hooked together and the synthesis lowered from the curb to the edge of Dinkman's roof. It seemed remarkably fragile, but it reached and the watchers murmured approval.

No longer beset by novelty, the men took easily to the swaying, sagging bridge. They passed over the baffled grass, the leader carrying another short ladder which he hung from the roof, stabbing its lower rungs down into the matted verdure below. The crossing was made with such insouciance the wonder was they hadnt done it at first, instead of wasting time on other expedients.

The firemen went down the vertical ladder and forced an entrance into the choked windows. Mrs Dinkman came out first, helped by two of them. She kept pinching her glasses into place with one hand and pulling her skirt modestly close with the other, activities leaving her very little to grasp the ladder with. The firemen seemed quite accustomed to this sort of irrationality, and paying no heed to the rush of words—inaudible to us on the street—bursting from her, they coaxed her expertly up onto the roof. Here she stood, statuesquely outlined against the bright sky, berating her succorers, until Mr Dinkman, rounded, bald, and calm, joined her.

At first Mrs Dinkman refused to try the bridge to the street, but after some urging which was conveyed to us by the gestures of the firemen, she ventured gingerly on the trembling ladders only to draw back quickly. One of the firemen demonstrated the ease and simplicity of the journey, but it was in vain; Mrs Dinkman was carried across gallantly in traditional moviestyle, with Mr Dinkman and the crew following sedately behind.

"A crime," Mrs Dinkman was saying when she came within earshot. "A crime. Malicious mischief. Ought to be locked up for life."

"Don't upset yourself, my dear," urged Mr Dinkman. "It's very distressing, but afterall it might be worse."

"'Worse'! Adam Dinkman, has misfortune completely unhinged your mind? Money thrown in the gutter—imposed on by oily rascals—our house swallowed up by this . . . this unnatural stuff—and the final humiliation of being pulled out of our own home in front of a gawking crowd." She turned around and shouted, "Shoo, shoo—why don't you go home?" And then to Mr Dinkman again, "'Worse' indeed! I'd like to know what could be worse?"

"Well now—" began Mr Dinkman; but I didnt hear the rest, for I was afraid by "rascals" Mrs Dinkman referred, quite unjustly, to me and I thought the time opportune to remind Gootes he hadnt yet completed his assignment.

"Right," he agreed, suddenly assuming the abrupt accents of an improbable Englishman, "oh very right, old chap. Let's toddle along and see what Fu Manchu has to say for himself. First off though I shall have to phone in to Fleet Street—I mean to W R."

"Fine. You can ask him at the same time to authorize you to give me the other thirty."

Gootes lost his British speech instantly. "What other thirty, bum?"

"Why, the balance of the fifty. For an introduction to Mi—to the maker of the Metamorphizer. To compensate me, you know, for my loss of revenue."

"Weener, you have all the earmarks of a castiron moocher. Let me tell you, suh—such methods are unbecoming. They suggest damyankee push and blackmail. Remember Reconstruction and White Supremacy, suh."

If I were hypersensitive to the silly things people say, I should have given up selling long before. I pretended not to hear him. We walked into a drugstore and he dropped a nickel into a payphone, hunching the receiver between ear and shoulder. "Fifty your last word?" he asked out of the corner of his mouth.

I nodded.

"Hello? 'Gencer? Gootes. Hya, beautiful? Syphilis all cleared up? Now . . . now, baby . . . well, if youre going to be formal— gimme W R." He turned to me and leered while he waited.

". . . Chief? Gootes. Got the Dinkman story. You know—Freak Growth Swallows Hollywood Mansion. Yeah. Yeah. I know. But, Chief—this was what I wanted you for—on the followup; I have the fellow who put the stuff on the grass. Yeah. Sure I did. Yeah. And the sonofabitch wants to hold us up for another thirty. Or else he won't sing. Yeah. Yeah. I know. But I can't, Chief. I havent got a lead. I don't know, Chief, not much of a one, I guess. Wait a minute."

He turned to me. "Listen, little man: Mr Le ffaçasé"—he pronounced it l'fassassy and he pronounced it with awe. I too was properly solemn, for I hadnt realized before to whom he referred when he talked so lightly of "W R." I knew—as what newspaper reader didnt—of William Rufus Le ffaçasé, "The Last of the Great Editors," but I hadnt connected him with the *Daily Intelligencer*— "—Mr Le ffaçasé will shoot you another sawbuck and no more. What's the deal?"

Now, the famous editor's reputation was such that you didnt tell him to go to the devil, even through the medium of an agent; it would have been like writing your name on the Lincoln Memorial. It was reluctantly therefore that I shook my head. "I'm sorry, Mr Gootes," I apologized, "I'd certainly like to oblige—"

He cut me off with a waving hand and turned cheerfully back to the telephone. "No soap, Chief. O K. O K. All right—put the rewrite man on." And for the next ten minutes he went over the events at the Dinkmans', carefully spelling out all names including the napoleonic firechief's. I began to suspect Gootes wasnt so inefficient a reporter as he appeared.

The story given in, he hung up and turned to me. "Well, so long, little man—been nice knowing you."

"But—what about meeting the discoverer of the Metamorphizer?"

"Oh, that. Well, W R thinks we don't need him anymore. Not enough in that angle."

I suspected he was bluffing; still it was possible he wasnt. In such a delicate situation there was nothing I could do but bluff in turn. If you are a good salesman, I always say, you must have psychology at your fingertips. "Very well, Mr Gootes; perhaps I shall see you again sometime."

I was immediately confronted by a Frenchman, affable, volatile, affectionate. "Ah cher ami, do not leave me with the abruptness. You desolate mon coeur. Alors—return to me the twenty dollars."

"But, Mr Gootes—"

"None of it, bud." He whisked the cards out and showed them to me, the ace of spades ghoulishly visible, its ominousness tempered only by the word "Bicycle" printed across it. "Don't hold out on your Uncle Jacson or I might have the boys take you for a little trip. A block of concrete tastefully inscribed 'A Weener' ought to make an amusing base for a birdbath, say."

"Listen, Gootes." I was firm. "I'm reasonably certain youve been authorized to advance me the other thirty, but I hope we're both sensible people and I'll be glad to sign a receipt for the full amount if youll let me have twentyfive."

"Albert, youre a fine fellow—a prince." On a page from his notebook he wrote, *Of Jacson Gootes, $50 U. S.* and I signed it. He handed me another twentydollarbill and put his wallet away. "Charge the other five to agent's fees," he suggested. "Lead us to your Steinmetz."

You just can't expect everyone to have the same standards of probity, so philosophically I pocketed my loss and gains together. Life is full of ups and downs and take the bad with the good. Gootes was in high spirits after his piece of chicanery and as we went down the street he practiced, quite unsuccessfully, a series of ventriloquial exercises.

10 The appearance of the apartmenthouse drew the comment from him that it was a good thing for their collective bloodpressures the Chamber of Commerce and the All Year Club didnt know such things existed in the heart of Hollywood. "It's no better than I live in myself," he added.

He whistled at the dismal livingroom and raised his eyebrows at the kitchen. Before I could mutter an introduction, Miss Francis growled without turning around, "If youve come about the icebox—"

"Zounds!" exclaimed Gootes. "A female Linnaeus. Shades of Dorothy Dix!"

"I don't know who you are, young man, but youre extremely impudent to come tramping into my kitchen, adding nothing to the sum of knowledge but a confirmation of my sex which would be plain to any mammal. If youve—"

"Nein, Fräulein Doktor," said Gootes hastily, "about z' kelvinators I know nossing. I represent, Fräulein Doctor, z' *Daily Intelligencer* zeitung—"

Miss Francis pierced his turgid explanation with a sharp spate of words in what I took to be German. Gootes answered with difficult slowness, but he fumbled and halted before long and abandoning the Central European, became again the Southern Gentleman. "I quite understand, mam, how any delicately reared gentlewoman would resent having her privacy intruded upon by rude agents of the yellow press. But consider, mam: we live in a progressive age and having made a great contribution to Science you can hardly escape the fame rightfully yours. You are a public figure now and must stand in the light. Would it not be preferable, mam, to talk as lady to gentleman (I am related to the Taliaferros of Ruffin County on the distaff side) than to be badgered by some hack journalist?"

Miss Francis squatted ungracefully on her heels and looked up from the flowerpot she had been engaged with. "I havent any objection to publicity, hack or otherwise," she said mildly. "I am merely impressed again by the invulnerability of newspapers to thousands of important discoveries and inventions, newsworthy 'contributions to Science' as you call them in your bland ignorance of semantics, in contrast to their acute, almost painful sensitivity to any mischance."

Gootes, unjointing disproportioned length carelessly against the sink to the peril of several jars of specimens, didnt reply. Instead he fluttered his arms and produced a halfdollar, apparently from Miss Francis' hair, which after exhibiting he prudently pocketed.

"Tell me, Dr Francis—"

"Miss. Show me how you did that trick."

"In a minute, Miss Francis. It's a honey, isnt it? Paid fourbits to a funhouse in Utica, New York, for it. Tell me, how did you come to make your great discovery?"

"I was born. I went to school. I read books. I reached maturity. I looked through a microscope."

"Yes?" prodded Gootes.

"That's all."

"Lassie," urged Gootes, underlining the honey of his voice with a tantalizing glimpse of a rapidfire snatching of three colored handkerchiefs out of the air, "tis no sensible course ye follow. Think, gurrl, what the press can do to a recalcitrant lass like yoursel. Ye wouldna like it if tomorrow's paper branded you—and I quote—'an unsexed harpy, a traitor to mankind, a heartless, soulless—'"

"Oh, shut up. What do you want to know?"

"First," said Gootes briskly, "what is this stuff?"

"The Metamorphizer?"

He nodded.

"You want the chemical formula?"

"Wouldnt do me or my readers the least bit of good and you wouldnt give it to me if I asked. Why should you? No, enlighten me in English."

"It is a compound on the order of colchisine, acting through the somaplasm of the plant. It is apparently effective only on the family Gramineae, producing a constitutional metabolic change. I have no means of knowing as yet whether this change is transmissible through seed to offspring—"

"Hay, wait a minute. 'Producing a constitutional metabolic change.' How do you spell metabolic—never mind, the proof-readers'll catch it. What constitutional change?"

"Are you a botanist, young man?" Gootes shook his head. "An agrostologist? Even an agronomist? Then you can't have the slightest idea of what I'm talking about."

"Maybe not," retorted Gootes, "but one of my readers might. Just give me a rough idea."

"Plants absorb certain minerals in suspension. That is, they absorb some and reject others. The Metamorphizer seems to give them the ability to break down even the most stable compound, select what they need, and also fix the inert nitrogen of the air to nourish themselves."

"'Themselves,'" repeated Gootes, writing rapidly. "O K. If I get you—which is doubtful—so far it sounds like a good new fertilizer."

"Really? I tried to make myself clear."

"Now don't get sore, Professor. Just give out on what made the grass go wild."

"I can only hazard a guess. As I told Weener, if you create a capacity, you engender an appetite. I imagine that patch of *Cynodon dactylon* just couldnt stop absorbing once it had been inoculated."

"Aha. Like giving a man a taste for bourbon."

"If it pleases you to put it that way."

"O K. O K. Now let's have an idea how this growth can be stopped. Theoretical, you know."

"As far as I know," said Miss Francis, "it cannot be stopped."

```
         ╭─────────────────────────────────────────╮
        ╭│      Consequences of a Discovery         │╮
         ╰─────────────────────────────────────────╯
              ╲            TWO           ╱
               ╲                        ╱
                ╲_____╱
```

11 BUT IT'S GOT to be stopped," exclaimed Gootes.

Miss Francis turned silently back to her flowerpot as though she'd forgotten us. Gootes coursed the kitchenfloor like a puzzled yet anxious hound. "Damn it, it's got to be stopped." He halfway extracted his pack of cards, then hastily withdrew his hand as though guarding the moment's gravity.

"Otherwise . . . why, otherwise itll swallow the house." He decided on the cards afterall and balanced four of them edgewise on the back of his hand. Miss Francis immediately abandoned the flowerpot to stare childishly at the feat. "In fact, if what you say is true, it will literally swallow up the house. Digest it. Convert it into devilgrass."

"*Cynodon dactylon.* What I say is true. How much elementary physics is involved in that trick?"

"But that's terrible," protested Gootes. He regarded a bowl of algae as if about to make it disappear. Mentally I agreed; one of the greatest potential moneymakers of the age lost and valueless.

"Yes," she agreed, "it is terrible. Terrible as the starvation in a hive when the apiarist takes out the winter honey; terrible as the daily business in an abattoir; terrible as the appetite of grown fish at spawning time."

"Poo. Fate. Kismet. Nature."

"Ah; you are unconcerned with catastrophes which don't affect man."

"Local man," substituted Gootes. "Los Angeles man. *Pithe-*

canthropus moviensis. Stiffs in Constantinople are strictly AP stuff."

"It seems to me," I broke in, "that you are both assuming too much. I don't know of anything that calls for the word catastrophe. I'm sure I'm sorry if the Dinkmans' house is swallowed up as Gootes suggests, but it hasn't been and I'm sure the possibility is exaggerated. The authorities will do something or the grass will stop growing. I don't see any point in looking at the blackest side of things."

Gootes opened his mouth in pretended astonishment. "Wal, I swan. Boy's a philosopher."

"You are not particularly concerned, Weener?"

"I don't know any reason why I should be," I retorted. "I sold your product in good faith and I am not responsible—"

"Oh, blind, blind. Do you imagine one man can suffer and you not suffer? Is your name Simeon Stylites? Do you think for an instant what happens to any man doesnt happen to everyman? Are you not your brother's keeper?" She twisted her hands together. "Not responsible! Why, you are responsible for every brutality, execution, meanness and calamity in the world today!"

I had often heard that the borderline between profundity and insanity was thin and inexact and it was now clear on which side she stood. I looked at Gootes to see how he was taking her hysterical outburst, but he had found a batch of empty testtubes which he was building into a perilously swaying structure.

"Of course, of course," I agreed soothingly, backing away. "Youre quite right."

She walked the floor as if her awkward body were a burden. "Is the instant response to an obvious truth—platitude even—always a diagnosis of lunacy? I state a thought so old no one knows who first expressed it and a hearer feels bound to choose between offense to himself and contempt for the speaker. Believe me, Weener, I was offering no exclusive indictment: I too am guilty—infinitely culpable. Even if I had devoted my life to pure science—perhaps even more certainly then—patterning myself on a medieval monastic, faithful to vows of poverty and singleness of purpose; even if I had not, for an apparently laudable end, betrayed my efforts to a base greed; even if I had never picked for a moment's use such an unworthy—do not be insulted again, Weener, unworthiness is a fact, insofar as there are any facts at all—such an unworthy tool as yourself; even if I had never compounded the Metamorphizer; even if I had been a biologist or an astronomer—even then I should be guilty of ruining the Dinkmans and making them homeless, just as you are guilty and the reporter here is guilty and the garbageman is guilty and the pastor in his pulpit is guilty."

"Guilty," exclaimed Gootes suddenly, "guilty! What kind of a lousy newspaperman am I? Worrying about guilt and solutions in the face of impending calamity instead of serving it redhot to a palpitating public. Guilty—hell, I ought to be fired. Or anyway shot. Where's the phone?"

"I manage a minimum of privacy in spite of inquiring reporters and unemployed canvassers. I have no telephone."

"Hokay. Hole everythings. I return immediate."

I followed him for I had no desire to be left alone with someone who might prove dangerous. But his long legs took him quickly out of sight before I could catch him, even by running, and so I fell into a more sedate pace. All Miss Francis' metaphysical talk was beyond me, but what little I could make of it was pure nonsense. Guilty. Why, I had never done anything illegal in my life, unless taking a glass of beer in dry territory be so accounted. All this talk about guilt suggested some sort of inverted delusions of persecution. How sad it was the eccentricity of genius so often turned its possessors into cranks. I was thankful to be of mere normal intelligence.

12 But I wasted no more thought on her, putting the whole episode of the Metamorphizer behind me, for I now had some liquid capital. It was true it didn't amount to much, but it existed, crinkled in my pocket, and I was sure with my experience and native ability I could turn the *Daily Intelligencer's* forty dollars into a much larger sum.

But a resolve to forget the Metamorphizer didnt enable me to escape Mrs Dinkman's lawn. Walking down Hollywood Boulevard, formulating, rejecting and reshaping plans for my future, I passed a radioshop and from a loudspeaker hung over the door with the evident purpose of inducing suggestible pedestrians to rush in and purchase sets, the latest report of the devilgrass's advance was blared out at me.

". . . Station KPAR, The Voice of Edendale, reaching you from a portable transmitter located in the street in front of what was formerly the residence of Mr and Mrs Dinkman. I guess youve all heard the story of how their lawn was allegedly sprinkled with some chemical which made the grass run wild. I don't know anything about that, but I want to tell you this grass is certainly running wild. It must be fifteen or sixteen feet high—think of that, folks—nearly as high as three men standing on each other's shoulders. It's covered the roof halfway to the peak and it's choking the windows and doorways of the houses on either side. It's all over the side-walk—looks like an enormous green woolly rug—no, that's not quite right—anyway, it's all over the sidewalk and it would be right out here in the street where I'm talking to you from if the fire-department wasnt on the job constantly chopping off the creeping ends as they come over the curb. I want to tell you, folks, it's a frightening sight to see grass—the same kind of grass growing in your backyard or mine—magnified or maybe I mean multiplied a hundred times—or maybe more—and coming at you as if it was an enemy—only the cold steel of the fireman's ax saving you from it.

"While we're waiting for some action, folks—well, not exactly that—the grass is giving us plenty of action all right—I'll try to bring you some impressions of the people in the street. Literally in the street, because the sidewalk is covered with grass. Pardon me, sir—would you like to say a few words to the unseen audience of Station KPAR? Speak right into the microphone, sir. Let's have your name first. Don't be bashful. Haha. Gentleman doesnt care to give his name. Well, that's all right, quite all right. Just what do you think of this phenomenon? How does it impress you? Are you disturbed by the sight of this riot of vegetation? Right into the microphone . . ."

"Uh . . . hello . . . well, I guess I havent . . . uh anything much to say . . . pretty color . . . bad stuff, I guess. Gladsnotgrowing myyard . . ."

"Yes, go right on, sir. Oh . . . the gentleman is through. Very interesting and thank you.

"Theyre bringing up a whole crew of weedburners now—going to try and get this thing under control. The men all have tanks of oil or kerosene on their backs. Wait a minute, folks, I want to find out for sure whether it's oil or kerosene. Mumble. Mumble. Well, folks, I'm sorry, but this gentleman doesnt know exactly what's in the tanks. Anyway it's kerosene or oil and there are long hoses with wide nozzles at the end. Something like vacuumcleaners. Well, that's not quite right. Anyway theyre lighting the nozzles now. Makes a big whoosh. Now I'll bring the microphone closer and maybe you can catch the noise of the flame. Hear it? That's quite a roar. I guess old Mr Grass is cooked now.

"Now these boys are advancing in a straight line from the street up over the curb, holding their fiery torches in front of them. The devilgrass is shriveling up. Yessir, it's shriveling right up—like a gob of tobaccojuice on a hot stove. Theyve burned about two feet of it away already. Nothing left but some smoking stems. Quite a lot of smoking stems—a regular compact mass of them—but all the green stuff has been burned right off. Yes, folks, burned clean off; I wish we had television here so I could show you how that thick pad of stems lies there without a bit of life left in it.

"Now theyre uncovering the sidewalk. I'm following right behind with the microphone—maybe you can hear the roar of the weedburners again. Now I'd like to have you keep in mind the height of this grass. You never saw grass as tall as this unless youve been in the jungle or South America or someplace where grass grows this high. I mean high. Even here at the sidewalk it's well over a man's head, seven or eight feet. And this crew is carving right into it, cutting it like steel with an acetylenetorch. Theyre making big holes in it. You hear that hissing? That noise like a steamhose? Well, that's the grass shriveling. Think of it—grass with so much sap inside it hisses. It's drying right up in a one-two-three! Now the top part is falling down—toppling forward—coming like a breaking wave. Oops! Hay . . . It put out one of the torches by smothering it. Drowned it in grass. Nothing serious—the boy's got it lit again. Progress is slow here, folks—youve got to realize this stuff's about ten feet high. Further in it's anyway sixteen feet. Fighting it's like battling an octopus with a million arms. The stuff writhes around and grows all the time. It's terrific. Imagine tangles of barbedwire, hundreds and hundreds of bales or rolls or however barbedwire comes, covering your frontyard and house—only it isnt barbedwire at all, but green, living grass . . . Just a minute, folks, I'm having a little trouble with my microphone cable. Nothing serious, you understand—tangled a bit in the grass behind me. Those burnt stems. Stand by for just a minute . . ."

"This is KPAR, The Voice of Edendale. Due to mechanical difficulties there will be a brief musical interlude until contact is resumed with our portable transmitter bringing you an onthespot account of the unusual grass . . ."

"Kirk,Quork,krrrmp—AR's portable transmitter. Here I am again, folks, in the street in front of the Dinkman residence—a little out of breath, but none the worse off, ready to resume the blowbyblow story of the fight against the devilgrass. That was a little trouble back there, but it's all right now. Seems the weedburners hadnt quite finished off the grass in the parkwaystrip between the curb and the sidewalk and after I dragged my microphone cable across it, it sort of—well, it sort of came to life again and tangled up the cable. It's all right now though. Everything under control. The boys with the weedburners have come back and are going over the parkwaystrip again, just to make sure.

"I want to tell you—this stuff really can grow. It's amazing, simply amazing. Youve heard of plants growing while you look at them; well, this grows while you don't look at it. It grows while your back is turned. Just to give you an example: while the boys have been busy a second time with the parkwaystrip, the grass has come back and grown again over all they burned up beyond the sidewalk. And now it's starting to come back over the concrete. You can actually see it move. The creepers run out in front and crawl ahead like thousands of little green snakes. Imagine seeing grass traveling forward like an army of worms. An army you can't stop. Because it's alive. Alive and coming at you. It's alive. It's alive. It's al—"

"This is Station KPAR. We will resume our regular programs immediately following the timesignal. Now we bring you a message from the manufacturers of Chewachoc, the Candy Laxative with the Hole . . ."

I continued thoughtfully down the street. The *Daily Intelligencer* was spread on a newsstand, a smudgy black bannerhead fouling its pure bosom. CITY COUNCIL MEETS TO END GRASS MENACE.

I trusted so. Quickly. I was tired of Mrs Dinkman's lawn.

13   Weener sahib, fate has tied us together."

I hoped not. I was weary of Gootes and his phony accents.

"On account of your female Burbank, your scientess (scientistess is a twister. Peder Piber et a peg of piggled pebbers) won't play ball with W R. The chief offered her a fabulous sum—'much beer in little kegs, many dozen hardboiled eggs, and goodies to a fabulous amount'—fabulous for W R, that is—to act as special writer on the grass business. J S Francis, World Renowned Chemist, exclusively in the *Intelligencer.* You know. Suppress her unfortunate sex. ORIGINATOR OF WILD GRASS TELLS ALL.

"Anyway she didnt grasp her chance. Practically told W R to go to hell. Practically told him to go to hell," he repeated, evidently torn between reprehension at the sacrilege and admiration of the daring.

Miss Francis plainly had what might be described as talent that way. I debated whether to inform Gootes of my discovery of her craziness and decided against it on the bare possibility it would be unwise to lower the value of my connection with the Metamorphizer's discoverer. I was soon rewarded for my caution.

"O Weeneru san," continued Gootes, evidently in an oriental vein traveling westward, "not too hard for you to be picking up few yen. You do not hate fifty potatoes from Editor san yesterday?"

"Forty," I corrected.

"Forty, fifty—whats the difference so long as youre healthy?" He produced a card, showed it, tore it in half, waved his hand and exhibited it whole and unharmed. "No kidding, chum; the old man has the bug to make *you* a special correspondent—on my advice yunderstand—always looking out for my pals."

Well, why not? The wheel of Fortune had been a long time turning before stopping at the proper spot. I had never had any doubt I'd someday be in a position to prove my writing ability. Now all those who had sneered at me years before—my English teachers and editors who had been too jealous to recognize my existence by anything more courteous than a printed rejection—would have to acknowledge their injustice. And in the meantime all my accumulated experience had been added to enhance my original talent. I'd sold everything that could be sold doortodoor and a man acquires not only an ease with words but a wide knowledge of human nature this way. Certainly I was better equipped all around than many of these highly advertised magazine or newspaper authors.

"Well . . . I don't know if I could spare the time . . ."

"O K, bigshot. Let me know if the market goes down and I'll come around and put up more margin."

"How much will Mr Le ffaçasé—"

"How the hell do I know? More than youre worth—more than I'm getting, because youre a ninetyday wonder, the guy who put the crap on the grass and sent it nuts. Less than he'd have given Minerva-Medusa. Come and get it straight from the horse's mouth."

My only previous visits to newspaper offices has been to place advertisements, but I was prepared to find the *Daily Intelligencer* a veritable hive of activity. Perhaps some part of the big building which housed the paper did hum, but not the floor devoted to the editorial staff. That simply dozed. Gootes led me from the elevator through an enormous room where men and an occasional woman sat indolently before typewriters, stared druggedly into space or flew paper airplanes out of open windows. The only sign of animation I saw as we walked what might well have been a quartermile was one reporter (I judged him such by the undersized hat on the back of his head) who enthusiastically munched a sandwich while perusing a magazine containing photographs of women with uncovered breasts. Even the nipples showed.

Beyond the cityroom was a battery of private offices. I will certainly not conceal the existence of my extreme nervousness as we neared the proximity of the famous editor. I hung back from the groundglass door inscribed in shabby, peeling letters—in distinction to its neighbors, newly and brightly painted—W.R. Le ffaçasé. Gootes, noting my trepidation, put on the brogue of a burlesque Irishman.

"Is it afraid of Himself you are, me boy? Sure, think no more of it. Faith, and wasnt he born Billy Casey; no better than the rest of us for all his mother was a Clancy and related to the Finnegans? He's written so often about coming from noble Huguenot stock he almost believes it himself, but the Huguenots were dirty Protestants and when his time comes W R'll send for the priest and take the last sacraments like the true son of the Church he is in his heart. So buck up, me boy, and come in and view the biggest faker in journalism."

But Gootes' flippancy reassured me no more than did the bare sunlit office behind the door. I had somehow, perhaps from the movies, expected to see an editor's desk piled with copypaper while he himself used halfadozen telephones at once, simultaneously making incomprehensible gestures at countless underlings. But Mr Le ffaçasé's desk was nude except for an enameled snuffbox and a signed photograph of a president whose administration had been subjected daily to the editor's bitterest jabs. On the walls hung framed originals of the famous political cartoons of the last quarter-century, but neither telephone nor scrap of manuscript was in evidence.

But who could examine that office with detached scrutiny while William Rufus Le ffaçasé occupied it? Somnolent in a leather armchair, he opened tiny, sunken eyes to regard us with less than interest as we entered. Under a shiny alpaca coat he wore an oldfashioned collarless shirt whose neckband was fastened with a diamond stud. Neither collar nor tie competed with the brilliance of this flashing gem resting in a shaven stubblefold of his draped neck. His face was remarkably long, his upperlip stretching inter-minably from a mouth looking to have been freshly smeared with vaseline to a nose not unlike a golfclub in shape. From the snuffbox on his desk, which I'd imagined a pretty ornament or receptacle for small objects, he scooped with a flat thumb a conical mound of graybrown dust and this, with a sweeping upward motion, he pushed into a gaping nostril.

"Chief, this is Albert Weener."

"How do, Mr Weener. Gootes, who the bloody hell is Weener?"

"Why, Chief, he's the guy who put the stuff on the grass."

"Oh." He surveyed me with the attention due a worthy but not particularly valuable specimen. "You bit the dog, ay, Weener?"

Gootes burst into a high, appreciative cackle. Le ffaçasé turned the deathray of his left eye on him. "Youre a syncophant, Gootes," he stated flatly, "a miserable groveling lowlivered cringing fawning mealymouthed chickenhearted toadeating arselicking, slobbering syncophant."

I couldnt see how we were ever to reach the point this way, so I ventured, "I understand in view of the fact that I inoculated Mrs Dinkman's lawn you want me to contribute—"

"Desires grow smaller as intelligence expands," growled Le ffaçasé. "I want nothing except to find a few undisturbed moments in which to read the work of the immortal Hobbes."

"I'm sorry," I said. "I understood you wished me to report the progress of the wildly growing grass."

"Cityeditor's province," he declared uninterestedly.

"No such thing on the *Intelligencer*," Gootes informed me in a loud whisper. Le ffaçasé, who evidently heard him, glared, reached down and retrieved the telephone from its concealment under the desk and snarled into the mouthpiece, "I hate to interrupt your crapgame with the trivial concerns of this organ men called a newspaper till you got on the payroll. I'm sending you a man who knows something about the crazy grass. Divorce yourself from whatever pornography youre gloating over at the moment to see if we can use him."

His immediate obliviousness to our presence was so insulting that if Gootes had not made the first move to leave I should have done so myself. I don't know what vast speculations swept upon him as he hung up the telephone, but I thought he might at least have had the courtesy to nod a dismissal.

"Youre hired, bejesus," proclaimed Gootes, and of course I was, for there was no doubt a brilliantly successful figure like Le ffaçasé—whatever my opinion of his intemperate language or failure in the niceties of deportment, he was a forceful man—had sized me up in a flash and sensed my ability before I'd written a single line for his paper.

14 The wage offered by the *Daily Intelligencer*—even assuming, as they undoubtedly did, that the affair of the grass would be over shortly and my service ended—was high enough to warrant my buying a secondhand car. A previous unpleasantness with a financecompany made the transaction difficult, with as little cash as I had on hand, but a phonecall to the paper established my bonafides and I was soon driving out Sunset Boulevard in a tomatocolored roadster, meditating on the longdelayed upsurge of my fortunes.

The street was closed off by a road barrier quite some distance away and tightly parked cars testified to the attraction of the expanding grass. Scorning these idle sightseers, I pushed and shoved my way forward to what had now become the focus of all my interests.

The Dinkmans had lived in a city block, an urban entity. It was no pretentious group of houses, nor was it a repetitive design out of some subdividing contractor's greedy mind. Moderatesized, mediumpriced, middleclass bungalows; these were the homes of the Dinkmans and their neighbors; a sample from a pattern which varied but was basically the same here and in Oakland, Seattle and St. Louis; in Chicago, Philadelphia, Boston and Cleveland.

But now I looked upon no city scene, no picture built upon the substantial foundation of daddy at the office all day, fixing a leaky faucet of an evening, painting the woodwork during his summer vacation; or mom, after a pleasant afternoon with the girls, unstintedly opening cans for supper and harassedly watching the cleaning woman who came in once a week. An alien presence, a rude fist through the canvas negated the convention that this was a picture of reality. A coneshaped hill rose to a blurred point, marking the burialplace of the Dinkman house. It was a child's drawing of a coneshaped hill, done in green crayon; too symmetrical, too evenly and heavily green to be a spontaneous product of nature; man's unimaginative hand was apparent in its composition.

The sides of the cone flowed past the doors and windows of the adjacent houses, blocking them as it had previously blocked the Dinkmans', but their inhabitants, forewarned, had gone. More than mere desertion was implied in their going; there was an implicit surrender, abandonment to the invader. The base of the cone, accepting capitulation and still aggressive, had reached to the lawns beyond, warning these householders too to be ready for flight; over backfences to dwellings fronting another street, and establishing itself firmly over the concrete pavement before the Dinkmans' door.

I would be suppressing part of the truth if I did not admit that for the smallest moment some perverted pride made me cherish this hill as my work, my creation. But for me it would not have existed. I had done something notable, I had caused a stir; it was the same kind of sensation, I imagine, which makes criminals boast of their crimes.

I quickly dismissed this morbid thought, but it was succeeded by one almost equally unhealthy, for I was ridden by a sudden wild impulse to touch, feel, walk on, roll in the encroaching grass. I tried to control myself, but no willing of mine could prevent me from going up and letting the long runners slip through my half open hands. It was like receiving some sort of electric shock. Though the blades were soft and tender, the stems communicated to my palms a feeling of surging vitality, implacable life and ineluctable strength. I drew back from the green mass as though I had been doing something venturesome.

For, no matter what botanists or naturalists may tell us to the contrary, we habitually think of plantlife as fixed and stolid, insensate and quiescent. But this abnormal growth was no passive lawn, no sleepy patch of vegetation. As I stood there with fascinated attention, the thing moved and kept on moving; not in one place, but in thousands; not in one direction, but toward all points of the compass. It writhed and twisted in nightmarish unease, expanding, extending, increasing; spreading, spreading, spreading. Its movement, by human standards, was slow, but it was so monstrous to see this great mass of verdure move at all that it appeared to be going with express speed, inexorably enveloping everything in its path. A crack in the roadway disappeared under it, a shrub was swallowed up, a patch of wall vanished.

The eye shifted from whole to detail and back again. The overrun crack was duplicated by an untouched one a few inches away—it too went; the fine tentacles on top of the mound reached upward, shimmering like the air on a hot summer's day, and near my feet hundreds of runners crept ever closer, the pale stolons shiny and brittle, supporting the ominously bristling green leaves.

I hope Ive not given the impression there was no human activity all this while, that nothing was being done to combat the living glacier. On the contrary, there was tremendous bustle and industry. The weedburning crew was still fighting a rearguard action, gaining momentary successes here and there, driving back the invading tendrils as they wriggled over concrete sidewalk and roadway, only to be defeated as the main mass, piling higher and ever higher, toppled forward on the temporarily redeemed areas. For on this vastly thicker bulk the smoky fingers of flame had no more effect than did the exertions of the scythemen, hacking futilely away at the tough intricacies, or the rattling reapers entangling themselves to become like waterlogged ships.

But greatest hopes were now being pinned on a new weapon. A dozen black and sootylooking tanktrucks had come up and from them, like the arms of a squid, thick hoses lazily uncoiled. Hundreds of gallons of dark crudeoil were being poured upon the grass. At least ten bystanders eagerly explained to any who would listen the purpose and value of the maneuver. Petroleum, deadly enemy of all rooted things, would unquestionably kill the weed. They might as well call off all the other silly efforts, for in a day or two, as soon as the oil soaked into the ground, the roots would die, the monster collapse and wither away. I wanted with all my heart to believe in this hope, but when I compared the feeble brown trickle to the vast green body I was gravely doubtful.

Shaken and thoughtful, I went back to my car and drove homeward, reflecting on the fortuitousness of human actions. Had I not answered Miss Francis' ad someone else would have been the agent of calamity; had Mrs Dinkman been away from home that day another place than hers, or perhaps no place at all, might have been engulfed.

On the other hand, I might still be searching for a chance to prove my merit to the world. It seemed to me suddenly man was but a helpless creature afterall.

15 It wasnt until I was almost at my own frontdoor I remembered the purpose of my visit, which was not to draw philosophic conclusions, but to order my impressions so the columns of the *Daily Intelligencer* might benefit by the reactions of one so closely connected with the spread of the devilgrass. I began tentatively putting sentences together and by the time I got to my room and sat down with pencil and paper, I was in a ferment of creative activity.

Now I cannot account for this, but the instant I took the pencil in my fingers all thought of the grass left my mind. No effort to summon back those fine rolling sentences was of the least avail. I slapped my forehead and muttered, "Grass, grass, Bermuda, *Cynodon dactylon*" aloud, varying it with such key words as "Dinkman, swallowing up, green hill" and the like, but all I could think of was buying a tire (700 x 16) for the left rear wheel, paying my overdue rent, Gootes' infuriating buffoonery, the possibilities for a man of my caliber in Florida or New York, and with a couple of thousand dollars a nice mailorder business could be established to bring in a comfortable income . . .

I left the chair and walked up and down the cramped room until the lodger below rapped spitefully on his ceiling. I went to the bathroom and washed my hands. I came back and inspected my teeth in the mirror. Then I resumed my seat and wrote, "The Grass—" After a moment I crossed this out and substituted, "Today, the grass—"

I decided the whole approach was unimaginative and unworthy of me. I turned the paper over and began, "Like a dragon springing—" Good, good—this was the way to start; it would show the readers at once they were dealing with a man of imagination. "Like a dragon springing." Springing from what? What did dragons spring from anyway? Eggs, like snakes? Dragons were reptiles werent they? Or werent they? Give up the metaphor? I set my teeth with determination and began again. "Not unlike a fierce and belligerently furious dragon or some other ferocious, blustery and furious chimerical creature, a menacing and comminatory debacle is burning fierily in the heart of our fair and increasingly populous city. As one with an innocent yet cardinal part in the unleashing of this dire menace, I want to describe how the exposure of this threatening menace affected me as I looked upon its menacing and malevolent advance today . . ."

I sat back, not dissatisfied with my beginning, and thought about the neat little bachelor apartment I could rent on what the *Intelligencer* was paying me. Of course in a few days this hullabaloo would be all over—for though I had little faith in the efficacy of the crudeoil I knew really drastic measures would be taken soon and the whole business stopped—but even in so short a time there could be no doubt Mr Le ffaçasé would realize he needed me permanently on his staff and I would be assured of a living in my own proper sphere. Thus fired with the thoughts of accomplishment, I returned to my task, but I cannot say it went easily. I remembered many great writers indulged in stimulants in the throes of composition, but I decided such a course might blunt the keen edge of my mind and afterall there was no better stimulant than plain oldfashioned perseverance. I picked up the pencil again and doggedly went on to the next sentence.

16 What the hell's this?" Demanded the cityeditor, looking at my neatly rolled pile of manuscript.

I disdained to bandy words with an underling too lazy to make an effort to get at what was probably the finest piece of writing ever brought to him, so I unrolled my story, flattening it out so he might read it the more easily.

"By the balls of Benjamin Franklin and the little white fringe on Horace Greeley's chin, this goddamned thing's been wrote by hand! Arent there any typewriters anymore? Did Mister Remington commit suicide unbeknownst to me?"

"I'm sorry," I said stiffly. "I didnt think youd have any difficulty in reading my handwriting." And in fact the whole business was absurd, for if there's anything I pride myself on it's the gracefulness and legibility of my penmanship. Typewriters might well be mandatory for the ephemeral news item, but I had been hired as a special correspondent and someday my manuscript would be a valuable property.

The cityeditor eyed me in a most disagreeable fashion. "I'm an educated man," he stated. "Groton, Harvard and the WPA. No doubt with time and care I could decipher this bid for next year's Pulitzer prize. But I must consider the more handicapped members of the staff: compositors, layoutmen and proofreaders; without my advantages and broadmindedness they might be so startled by this innovation as to have their usefulness permanently crippled. No; I'm afraid, Mr Weener, I must ask you to put this in more orthodox form and type it up."

Just another example of pettish bureaucracy, the officiousness of the jack-in-office. Except for the nuisance, it didnt particularly matter. When Mr Le ffaçasé read my contribution I knew there would be no concern in future whether it was handwritten, type-written, or engraved in Babylonic cuneiform on a freshly baked brick.

Nevertheless I went over to one of the unoccupied desks and began to copy what I had written on the machine. I must say I was favorably impressed by the appearance of my words in this form, for they somehow looked more important and enduring. While still engaged in this task I was slapped so heartily on the back I was knocked forward against the typewriter and Gootes perched himself on a corner of the desk.

"Working the jolly old mill, what? I say, the old bugger wants to know where your stuff is. Fact of the matter, he wants to know with quite a bit of deuced bad language. Not a softspoken chap, you know, W R."

"I'll be through in a minute or two."

He gathered his pipe apparently out of my left ear and his tobacco pouch from the air and very rudely, without asking my permission, picked up the top sheet and started to read it. A thick eyebrow shot up immediately and he allowed his pipe to hang slackly from his mouth.

"Purple," he exclaimed, "magenta, violet, lavender, mauve. Schmaltz, real copperriveted, brassbound, steeljacketed, castiron schmaltz. I havent seen such a genuine sample since my kid sister wrote up Jack the Ripper back in 1889."

The manifest discrepancy in these remarks so confused me my fingers stumbled over the typewriter keys. Evidently he intended some kind of humor or sarcasm, but I could make nothing of it. How could his younger sister . . .?

"Bertie boy," he said, after I had struggled to get another paragraph down, "it breaks my heart to see you toil so. Let's take in as much as youve done to the chief and either he'll be so impressed he'll put a stenographer to transcribing the rest or else—"

"Or else?" I prompted.

"Or else he won't. Come on."

Mr Le ffaçasé had apparently not stirred since last we were in his office. He opened his eyes, thumbed a pinch of snuff and asked Gootes, "Where the bloody hell is that stuff on the grass?"

"Here it is, Chief. No date, no who what when and where, but very litry. Very, very litry."

The editor picked up my copy and I could not help but watch him anxiously for some sign of his reaction. It came forth promptly and explosively.

"What the ingenious and delightfully painful hell is this, Gootes?"

"'As Reported by Our Special Writer, Albert Weener, The Man Who Inoculated the Loony Grass.'"

"Gootes, you are the endproduct of a long line of incestuous idiots, the winner of the boobyprize in any intelligencetest, but you have outdone yourself in bringing me this verminous and maggoty ordure," said Le ffaçasé, throwing my efforts to the floor and kicking at them. The outrage made me boil and if he had not been an older man I might have done him an injury. "As for you, Weener, I doubt if you will ever be elevated to the ranks of idiocy. Get the sanguinary hell out of here and do humanity the favor to step in front of the first tentontruck driving by."

"One minute, Chief," urged Gootes. "Don't be hasty. Seen the latest on the grass? Well, the mayor's asked the governor to call out the National Guard; the *Times*'ll have an interview with Einstein tomorrow and the *Examiner*'s going to run a symposium of what Herbert Hoover, Bernard Shaw and General MacArthur think of the situation. Don't suppose perhaps we could afford to ghost Bertie here?"

Was I never to escape from the malice inspired by the envy my literary talent aroused? I had certainly expected that a man of the famous editor's reputation would be above such pettiness. I was too dismayed and downcast by the meanness of human nature to speak.

Le ffaçasé snuffed again and looked malevolently at the wall. A framed caricature of himself returned the stare. "Very well," he grudgingly conceded at length, "youre on the grass anyway, so you might as well take this on too. Leave you only twentytwo hours a day to sleep in. You, Weener, are still on the payroll—at half the agreedupon figure."

I opened my mouth to protest, but he turned on me with a snarl; baring yellow and twisted teeth, unpleasant to see. "Weener, you look like a criminal type to me; Lombroso couldve used you for a model to advantage. Have you a policerecord or have you so far evaded the law? Let me tell you, the *Intelligencer* is the evildoers' nemesis. Is your conscience clear, your past unsullied as a virgin's bed, your every deed open to search? Do you know what a penitentiary's like? Did you ever hear the clang of a celldoor as the turnkey slammed it behind him and left you to think and stew and weep in a silence accented and made more wretched by a yellow electricbulb and the stink of corrosivesublimate? Back to the cityroom, you dabbling booby, you precious simpleton, addlepated dunce, and be thankful my boundless generosity permits you to draw a weekly paycheck at all and doesnt condemn you to labor forever unrewarded in the subterranean vaults where the old files are kept."

First Miss Francis and now Le ffaçasé. Were all these great intelligences touched? Was the world piloted by unbalanced minds? It seemed incredible, impossible it should be so, but two such similar experiences in so short a time apparently supported this gloomy view. Horrible, I thought as I preceded Gootes out of the maniac's office, unbelievably horrible.

"Son," advised Gootes, "never argue with the chief. He has the makings of a firstclass apoplexy—I hope. You just keep squawking to the bookkeeping department and youll get further than coming up against the Old Man. Now let's go out and look at nature in the raw."

"But my copy," I protested.

"Oh, that," he said airily, "I'll run that off when we come back. Deadlines mean nothing to Jacson Gootes, the compositors'

companion, the proofreaders' pardner, the layoutman's love. Come,
Señor Veener, we take look at el grasso grosso by the moonlight."

17 However, it was not moonlight illuminating the weird
tumulus, but the glare of a battery of searchlights,
suggesting, as Gootes irreverently remarked, the opening of a new
supermarket. During my absence the National Guard had arrived
and focused the great incandescent beams on the mound which
now covered five houses and whose threat had driven the inhabitants from as many more. The powdery blue lights gave the grass an
uncanny yellowish look, as though it had been stricken by a
disease.

The rays, directed low, were constantly being interrupted by
the bodies of the militiamen hurrying back and forth to accomplish
some definite task. "What goes on?" inquired Gootes.

The officer addressed had two gleaming silver bars on his
shoulder. He seemed very young and nervous. "Sorry—no one
allowed this far without special authorization."

"Working press." Gootes produced a reporter's badge from the
captain's bars.

"Oh. Excuse me. Say, that was a sharp little stunt, Mr—"

"Name of Jacson Gootes. *Intelligencer.*"

"Captain Eltwiss. How did you learn stuff like that?"

I looked at him, for the name was somehow vaguely familiar.
But to the best of my knowledge I had never seen that smooth,
boyish face before.

"Talent. Natural talent. What did you say all the shootin was
about?"

"Getting ready to tunnel under," answered the officer affably.
"Blow the thing skyhigh from the middle and get rid of it right now.
Not going to let any grass grow under our feet."

"But I read an article saying neither dynamite, TNT nor
nitroglycerin would be effective against the grass; might even do
more harm than good."

"Writers." Captain Eltwiss dismissed literature without even
resorting to an exclamationpoint. "Writers." To underline his confidence the boneshaking chatter of pneumatic chisels began a

syncopated rattle. Military directness would accomplish in one swift, decisive stroke at the heart of things what civilian fumbling around the edges had failed to do.

I looked with almost sentimental regret at the great conical heap. I had brought it into being; in a few hours it would be gone and whatever fame its brief existence had given me would be gone with it.

With swift method the guardsmen started burrowing. In ordered relays, fresh workers replaced tired, and the pile of excavated dirt grew. Since their activity, except for its urgency and the strangeness of the situation, didnt differ from labors observable any time a street was repaired or a foundation laid, I saw no point in watching, hour after hour. I thought Gootes' persistence less a devotion to duty than the idle curiosity which makes grown men gape at a steamshovel.

My hints being lost on him, I ascertained the hour they expected to be finished and went home. Excitement or no excitement, I saw no reason to abandon all routine. My forethought was proven when I returned refreshed in midmorning as the last shovelfuls of dirt came from the tunnel and the explosive charges were hurried to their place.

There was reason for haste. While the tunneling had been going on, all the grassfighting activity had ceased, for the militia had ordered weedburners, reapers, bulldozers and the rest off the scene. The weed, unhampered for the first time since Mrs Dinkman attacked it with her lawnmover, responded by growing and growing until more and more guardsmen had to be detached to the duty of keeping it back from the excavation—by the very means they had scorned so recently. Even their most frantic efforts could not prevent the grass from sending its most advanced tendrils down into the gaping hole where the wires were being laid to detonate the charge.

There was so much dashing to and fro, so many orders relayed, so many dispatches delivered that I thought I might have been witnessing an outofdate Civilwar play instead of a peacetime action of the California National Guard. Captain Eltwiss—I kept wondering where I'd heard the name—was constantly being interrupted in what was apparently a very friendly conversation with Gootes by

the arrival of officiallooking envelopes which he immediately
stuffed into his pocket with every indication of vexation. "Silly old
fools," he muttered, each time the incident happened.

Quick inspections made, plans checked, an order was rasped to
clear the vicinity. Gootes' agonized protest that he had to report the
occasion for the *Intelligencer's* readers was ignored. "Can't start
making exceptions," explained Captain Eltwiss. Everyone—work-
ingpress, militia, sightseers and all, had to move back a couple of
blocks where intervening trees and houses cut us off from any view
of the green hill.

"This is terrible," exclaimed Gootes frantically. "Tragic. Howll
I live it down? Howm I going to face W R? Godlike wrath. 'What
poolhall were you dozing in, Gootes? Asleep on your bloody feet,
ay, somnambulistic offspring of a threetoed sloth?' Wait all night
for a story and then not get it, like the star legman on the Jackson
Junior Highschool *Jive-Jitterbug*. I'll never be able to hold my head
up again. Say something, say something, Weener—Ive *got* to get
this."

"We'll be able to hear the explosion from here," I remarked to
console him, for his distress was genuine.

"Oh," he groaned. "Hear the explosion. Albert, Albert . . .
you have a fertile mind. Why didnt I get W R to hire a plane? Why
didnt I foresee this and do any of a hundred things? A microphone
and automatic moviecamera . . . Goony Gootes, they called him,
the man who missed all bets . . . A captive balloon, now . . . Hay!
What about a roof?"

"Trees," I objected, with a mental picture of him bursting into
the nearest house and demanding entrance to the roof.

"Bushwa. Zair's no tree in z' way of z' old box over zair—
allons!"

It wasnt till he had urged me inside and up a flight of stairs
that I realized the "box" was Miss Francis' apartmenthouse. It had
been a logical choice, since its height and ugliness distinguished it
even from its unhandsome neighbors. Less than a week had gone
by since I had come here for the first time. As I followed Gootes'
grasshopper leaps upward at a more dignified pace, I reflected how
strangely my circumstances had changed.

The shoddily carpeted halls were musty and still as we

climbed, except for the unheeded squeaking of a radio someone had forgotten to turn off. You could always tell when a radio was being listened to, for when disregarded it sulkily gave off painfully listless noises in frustration and loneliness.

I wasnt at all surprised to find Miss Francis among the spectators crowded on the roof in evidence of having no more important occupation. "I somehow expected you. Have you any new tricks?" she asked Gootes coaxingly.

"Ecod, your worship, wot time ave I for legerdemain? Wif your elp, now, I'd be a fine gentleman-journalist, stead of a noverworked ack."

"Ha," she said genially, busy with the toothpick, "youll find enough respectable laboratory mechanics eager to cooperate. How long will it be before they shoot, do you know?"

Gootes shook his head and I strained my eyes toward the grass. Symmetrical and shimmeringly green, removed as it now was from all connotations of danger by distance and the promise of immediate destruction, it showed serenely beautiful and unaffected by the machinations of its attackers. I could almost have wept as I traced its sloping sides upward to the rounded peak on top. Reversing all previous impressions, it now appeared to be the natural inhabitant and all the houses, roadways, pavements, fences, automobiles, lightpoles and the rest of the evidences of civilization the intruders.

But even as I looked at it so eagerly it moved and wavered and I heard the muffled boom of explosion. The roof trembled and windows rattled with diminishing echoes. The noise was neither a great nor terrifying one and I distinctly remember thinking it quite inadequate to the occasion.

I believe all of us there, when we heard the report, expected to see a vast hole where the grass had been. I'm sure I did. When it was clear this hadnt happened, I continued to stare hard, thinking, since my highschool physics was so hazy, I had somehow reversed the relative speed of sight and sound and we had heard the noise before seeing the destruction.

But the green bulk was still there.

Oh, not unchanged, by any means. The smooth, picturebook slope had become jagged and bruised while the regular, even-lyrounded apex had turned into a sort of phrygian cap with its

pinnacle woundedly askew. The outlines which had been sharp
were now blurred, its evenness had become scraggly. The placid
surface was vexed; the attempt on its being had hurt. But not
mortally, for even with outline altered, it remained; defiant, certain, inexorable.

The air was filled with small green particles whirling and
floating downward. Feathery, yet clumsy, they refused to obey
gravity and seek the earth urgently, but instead shifted and changed
direction, coyly spiraling upward and sideways before yielding to
the inevitable attraction.

"At least there's less of it," observed Gootes. "This much anyway," he added, holding a broken stolon in his fingers.

"*Cynodon dactylon*," said Miss Francis, "like most of the
family Gramineae, is propagated not only by seed, but by cuttings
as well. That is to say, any part of the plant (except the leaves or
flowers) separated from the parent whole, upon receiving water and
nourishment will root itself and become a new parent or entity. The
dispersion of the mass, far from making the whole less, as our
literary friend so ingenuously assumes, increases it to what mathe-
maticians call the nth power because each particle, finding a new
restingplace unhampered by the competition for food it encountered when integrated with the parent mass, now becomes capable
of spreading infinitely itself unless checked by factors which deprive it of sustenance. These facts have been repeated a hundred
times in letters, telegrams and newspaper articles since the project
of attempting to blow up the inoculated batch was known. In spite
of warnings the authorities chose to go ahead. No, make no mistake, this fiasco has not set *Cynodon dactylon* back a millimeter;
rather it has advanced it tremendously."

There was silence while we absorbed this unpleasant bit of
information. Gootes was the first to regain his usual cockiness and
he asked, "You say fiasco, professor. O K—can you tell us just why
it was a fiasco? I know they stuck enough soup under it to blow the
whole works and when it went off it gave out with a good bang."

"Certainly. *Cynodon dactylon* spreads in what may be called
jumps. That is, the stems are short and jointed. Those above-
ground, the true stems, are called stolons, and those below, from
which the roots spread, are rhizomes. Conceive if you will twoinch

lengths of stiff wire—and this plant is vulgarly called wiregrass in some regions just as it is called devilgrass here—bent on either end at rightangles. Now take these bits and weave them horizontally into a thick mass. Then add, vertically, more of the wires, breaking the pattern occasionally and putting in more in odd places, just to be sure there are no logical fracturepoints. Cover this involved web—not forgetting it has three dimensions despite my instructions treating it as a plane—with earth, eight, ten, or twelve inches deep. Then try to blow it up with dynamite or trinitrotoluene and see if you havent—in a much lesser degree—duplicated and accounted for the situation in hand."

Everything now seemed unusually and, perhaps because of the contrast, unreasonably quiet. Downstairs the radio, which had been monotonously soothing a presumptive audience of unsatisfied housewives with languid ballads, raised its pitch several tones as though for the first time it had become interested in what it purveyed.

". . . Yes, unseen friends, God is preparing His vengeance for wickedness and sin, even as you are listening. You have been warned many times of the wrath to come, but I say to you, the wrath is at hand. Even now God is giving you a sign of His displeasure; a cloud no bigger than a man's hand. But, O my unseen friends, that cloud has within it all the storms, cyclones, typhoons, hurricanes and tornadoes necessary to destroy you and yours. Unless you repent of your pride and sloth, Judgment will surely come upon you. The Lord has taken a simple and despisèd weed and caused it to multiply in defiance of all your puny powers and efforts. O my friends, do not fight this grass, but cherish it; do not allow it to be cut down for it is full of significance for you. Call off all your minions and repent, lest if the holy messenger be injured a more terrible one is sent. But now, my friends, I see my time is up; please send your contributions so urgently needed to carry on the Divine Work to Brother Paul care of the station to which you are listening."

"That's one way of looking at it," said Gootes. "Adios amigos."

He went down the stairs at an even more breakneck pace than he had come up. Almost in front of the apartmenthouse door we nearly collided with two officers in angry dispute.

"You mean to tell me, Captain, that not one of the urgent orders to suspend operations came through to you?"

"Colonel, I havent seen a thing against the project except some fool articles in a newspaper."

Suddenly I remembered where I'd seen the name Eltwiss. It was on the financial page, not far away from the elusive quotation on Consolidated Pemmican and Allied Concentrates for which I'd been idly searching. "Eltwiss Explosives Cut Melon." Funny how things come back to you as soon as you put them out of your mind.

Miss Francis, who had followed us down was busy collecting some of the stolons which were still floating lazily downward.

18 An illiterate patchwork of lifeless and uninteresting scribbling appeared under my byline day after day in the *Intelligencer*. Not a word, not a thought of my own was left. I was not restrained from protest by the absurd threats of Le ffaçasé, but prudence dictated not throwing away dirty water before I got clean, and the money from the paper, while negligible of course, yet provided my most pressing needs.

As I was being paid for my name while my talents went to waste, I was free to go anywhere I pleased, but I had little desire to leave the vicinity of the grass. It exerted upon me, more understandably, the same fascination as on the merely curious.

But I was not permitted unmolested access to the phenomenon with which I was so closely concerned. An officious young guardsman warned me away brusquely and I was not allowed to come near until I swallowed my pride and claimed connection with the *Intelligencer*. Even then it was necessary for me to explain myself to several nervous soldiers on pain of being ordered from the spot.

I was struck as I had not been before by the dynamic quality of the grass; never the same for successive instants. Constant movement and struggle as the expanding parts fought for room among themselves, pushing upward and outward, seemed to indicate perceptible sentience permeating the whole body. Preparing, brooding, it was disturbed, searching, alert.

Its external aspect reflected the change. The proportions of height to breadth had altered since the explosion. The peak had disappeared, flattening out into an irregular plateau. Its progress across the ground, however, had been vastly accelerated; it had crossed the streets on all sides of the block and was spreading with great rapidity over the whole district. For the moment no new effort was apparently being made to halt its progress, the activities of the militia being confined to patrolling the area and shooing decent citizens away. I wondered if a new strategy contemplated allowing the thing to exhaust itself. Since it looked more vigorous with each passing hour, I saw myself on the payroll·of the *Intelligencer* for a long time to come.

Captain Eltwiss walked by and I asked him if this were so. "Don't worry," he reassured me. "We're hep now, with the actual, unbeatable mccoy. Park the body and watch what happens to old Mr Grass."

I had every intention of staying and I thought it advisable to remain close to the captain in order, if his boast were wellfounded, to be in on the kill. He was in excellent spirits and although I did not think it tactful to refer to it, it was evident his little difference with the colonel about the unreceived orders had not affected him. We chatted amiably. I mentioned what Miss Francis had said about the weed springing up in new places from each of the shreds dispersed by the explosion, but he merely shrugged and laughed.

"I know these longbearded scientific nuts. They can find calamity around the corner quicker than a drunk can find a bar."

"The discoverer of the Metamorphizer is a woman, so her long beard is doubtful," I told him, just a little irritated by his cocksureness.

He laughed with as much ease at himself as at anything else. "A woman scientist, ay? Funny things womenll do when they can't get a man. But longbearded or flatchested it's all the same. Gruesome, that's what they are, gruesome. Forget it. After we get this cleaned up we'll take care of any others that start, but personally I don't think therell be any. Sounds like a lot of theory to me."

I looked contemptuously at him, for he had that unimaginative approach which disdains Science and so holds Civilization back on its upward path. If the world's future rested with people like this, I thought, we should never have had dynamite or germtheories or airplanes capable of destroying whole cities at a blow.

But Captain Eltwiss was a servant to the Science he looked down on. The answer he had bragged about now appeared and it was a scientific contribution if ever there was one. A division of tanks, twenty or thirty of them with what appeared to be sledrunners invertedly attached to their fronts, rolled into sight. "Wirecutters," he explained with pride. "Same equipment used for barbedwire on the Normandy beachhead. Go through anything like cheese."

The tanks drew up in a semicircle and the drivers came out of their vehicles for lastminute preparations. A final check was made of gas, oil, and the positions of the wirecutters. Maps, showing the location of each house now covered by the grass, were studied and compasspoints checked against them. I admired the thoroughness and efficiency of the arrangements. So did the captain.

"The idea is simple. These tanks are shocktroops. Theyll cut their way into the middle of the stuff. This will give us entranceways and a central operating point, besides hitting the grass where its strength is greatest. From there—" he paused impressively—"from there we'll throw everything in the book at it and a few that arent. All the stuff they used before we came. Only we'll use it efficiently. And everything else. Even hush-hush stuff. Just got the release from Washington. The minute one of these stems shows we'll stamp it out. We'll fight it and fight it until we beat it and we won't leave a bit of it, no, sir, not one bit of it, alive."

He looked at me triumphantly. Behind his triumph was a hint of the vast resources and the slowmoving but unassailable force his uniform represented. It sounded as though he had been correct in his boast and something drastic indeed would "happen to Mr. Grass."

The tanks were ready to go at last and the drivers climbed back into them and disappeared, leaving the steel monsters looking as though theyd swallowed the men. Like bubbles of air in a narrow glass tube they began to jerk backward and forward, until at some signal—I presume given by radio—they jumped ahead, their exhausts bellowing defiance of the grass mauled and torn by their treads.

They went onward with careless scorn, leaving behind a bruised and trampled pathway. The captain followed in the track and I after him, though I must admit it was not without some trepidation I put my feet upon the battered and now lifeless mass packed into a hard roadbed, for I recalled clearly how the grass had wrenched the ladder from the firemen and how it had impishly attacked the broadcaster's equipment.

The tanks moved ahead steadily until the slope of the mound began to rise sharply and the runners of grass, instead of flattening obediently behind, curled and twisted grotesquely as the tracks passed over them, lightly slapping at the impervious steel sides. Small bunches, mutilated and crushed, sprang back into erectness, larger ones flopped limply as their props were pushed aside.

Then, suddenly, the tank we were trailing disappeared. There was no warning; one second it was pursuing its way, an implacable executioner, the next it had plunged into the weed and was lost to sight. The ends of the grass came together spitefully behind it, weaving themselves together, knitting, as we watched, an opaque blanket. It closed over and around so that the smooth track ended abruptly, bitten by a wiry green portcullis.

I was dismayed, but the captain seemed happy. "Now we're getting somewhere," he exclaimed. "The little devils are eating right into the heart of the old sonofabitch."

We stood there gaping stupidly after our lost champion, but the grass mound was enigmatic and offered us no information as to its progress. A survey of the other tracks showed their tanks, too, had burrowed into the heart of the weed like so many hounds after a rabbit.

"Well," said the captain, who by now had apparently accepted me as his confidant, "let's go and see whats coming in over the radio."

I was glad to be reminded the tanks werent lost, even temporarily, and that we would soon learn of their advance. Field headquarters had been set up in a house about two blocks away and there, after exchanging salutes, passwords, and assorted badinage, the captain led. The men in contact with the tanks, shoulders hunched, fingers rapid with pad and pencil, were sitting in a row by a wall on which had been tacked a large and detailed map of the district.

In addition to their earphones, a loudspeaker had also been

thoughtfully set up, apparently to take care of any such curious
visitors as ourselves. The disadvantage, soon manifest, was that no
plan had been dev'sed to unscramble the reports from the various
tanks. As a consequence, whenever two or three came in together,
the reports overlapped, resulting in a jumble of unintelligible
sounds from the loudspeaker.

"Brf brf brm," it was saying as we entered the room. "Rrr rrr
about three hundred meters khorof khorof khorof north by north-
east. Can vou hear me, FHQ? Come in, FHQ."

There vas a further muddle of words, then, "I think my
motor's going to conk out. Shall I backtrack, FHQ? Come in,
FHQ."

"Rugged place to stall," commented captain Eltwiss sympathetically, "but we can pull him out in halfashake soons we get
things under control."

The loudspeaker, after a great deal of gibberish, condescended
to clarity again. ". . . about five hundred meters. Supposed to join
SMT_5 at this point. Can't raise him by radio. What do you have on
SMT_5, FHQ? Come in, FHQ."

I was still speculating as to what had happened to SMT_5 when
the loudspeaker once more became intelligible. ". . . and the
going's getting tougher all the time. I don't believe these goddamned wirecutters are worth a pissinasnowhole. Just fouled up,
that's what they are, just fouled up. Got further if theyd been left
off."

His grumbling was blotted out. For a moment there was complete babel, then ". . . if I can guess, it's somehow got in the motor
and shorted the ignition. Ive got to take a chance and get out to look
at it. This is SMT_3 reporting to FHQ. Now leaving the
transmitter."

". . . stalled so I turned on my lights. Can you hear me,
FHQ? Come in FHQ, O K, O K, don't get sore. So I turned on my
lights. I'm not going to do a Bob Trout, but I want to tell you it's
pretty creepy. I guess this stuff looks pretty and green enough on
top, especially in daylight, but from where I am now it's like an
illustration out of Grimm's *Fairy Tales*—something about the place
where the wicked ogre lived. Not a bit of green. Not a bit of light
except from my own which penetrate about two feet ahead and stop.

Dead. Yellow and reddishbrown stems. Thick. Interlaced. How the hell I ever got this far I'd like to know. But not as much as how I'm going to get out.

"I'm sticking my head out of the turret now. As far as these stemsll let me. Which isnt far. Theyre a solid mass on top of the machine. And beside it. I'm going to take a few tools and make for the engine. Only thing to do. Can't sit here and describe grassroots to you dogrobbers all day long. See if I can't get her running and back out. Then I resign from the state of California. Right then. This is SMT$_7$ leaving the transmitter for essential repairs and signing off."

For hours the reports kept coming in, all in identically the same vein: rapid progress followed by a slowdown, then either engine trouble or a failure to keep rendezvous by another tank, all messages concluding alike: "Now leaving transmitter." It was no use for field headquarters frantically to order them to stay in their tanks no matter what happened. They were young, ablebodied, impatient men and when something went wrong they crawled out to fight their way through a few feet of grass to fix it. Afterall they were in the heart of a great city. Their machines had burrowed straightforwardly into the grass and no threats of courtmartial could make them sit and look silly till help arrived and they were tamely rescued. So one by one they wormed their way out to fix the ignition, adjust the carburetor, or hack free the cogs which moved the tracks. And one by one their radios became silent and were not heard again.

The captain went from cockiness to doubt, from doubt to anxiety, and then to anguished fury. He had been so completely confident of the maneuver's outcome that its failure drove him, not to despair, but to anger. He knew most of the tankdrivers personally and the picture of these friends trapped in their tiny, evernarrowing pockets of green sent him into a frenzy. "SMT$_1$ —that's Lew Brown. Don't get out, Lew—stay where you are, you jackass. Stay where you are Lew," he bellowed into the unresponsive loudspeaker.

"Jake White. Jake White's in four. Said I'd buy him a drink afterwards. Joke. He's a cocacola boy. Why can't you stay inside, Jake? Why can't you stay put?"

Unable to bear it longer, he rushed from field headquarters shouting, "Let's get'm out, boys, let's get'm out," and would personally have led a volunteer party charging on foot into the grass if he had not been forcibly restrained and sympathetically led away, sobbing hysterically, toward hospitalization and calming treatment.

The captain's impulse, though impractical, was shared by all his comrades. For the moment the destruction of the grass became secondary to the rescue of the trapped tankmen. If field headquarters had bustled before, it now turned into a veritable beehive, with officers shouting, exhorting, complaining, and men running backwards and forwards as though there were no specific for the situation except unlimited quantities of their own sweat.

19 It would be futile to relate, even if I could recall them, all the various methods and devices which were suggested and rejected or tried and proved failures in the attempt to rescue the tankdrivers. Press and radio followed every daring essay and carefully planned endeavor until the last vicarious quiver had been wrung from a fascinated public. For twentyfour hours there was no room on the front pages of the newspapers for anything but the latest on the "prisoners of the grass," as they were at first called. Later, when hope for their rescue had diminished and they were forced from the limelight to make way for later developments, they were known simply as "heroes in the fight against the weird enemy."

For the grass had not paused chivalrously during the interval. On the contrary, it seemed to take renewed vigor from the victims it had entombed. House after house, block after block were engulfed. The names of those forced from their homes were no longer treated individually and written up as separate stories, but listed in alphabetical order, like battle casualties. Miss Francis, frantically trying to get all her specimens and equipment moved from her kitchen in time, had been ousted from the peeling stucco and joined those who were finding shelter (with some difficulty) in other parts of the city.

The southernmost runners crept down toward Hollywood

Boulevard where every effort was being marshaled to combat them, and the northernmost wandered around and seemingly lost themselves in the desert of sagebrush and greasewood about Hollywood Bowl. Traffic through Cahuenga Pass, the great artery between Los Angeles and its tributary valley, was threatened with disruption.

But while the parent body was spreading out, its offspring, as Miss Francis foresaw, had come into existence. Dozens of nuclei were reported, some close at hand, others far away as the Sunset Strip and Hollywoodland. These smaller bodies were vigorously attacked as soon as discovered but of course they had in every case made progress too great to be countered, for they were at first naturally indistinguishable from ordinary devilgrass and by the time their true character was determined so rapid was their growth they were already beyond all possibility of control.

The grass was now everyone's primary thought, replacing the moon (among lovers), the incometax (among individuals of importance), the weather (among strangers), and illness (among ladies no longer interested in the moon), as topics of conversation. Old friends meeting casually after many years' lapse greeted each other with "What's the latest on the grass?" Radiocomedians fired gagmen with weeks of service behind them for failure to provide botanical quips, or, conversely, hired raw writers who had inhabited the fringes of Hollywood since Mack Sennett days on the strength of a single agrostological illusion. Newspapers ran long articles on *Cynodon dactylon* and the editors of their garden sections were roused from the somnolence into which thay had sunk upon receiving their appointment and shoved into doubleleaded boldfaced position.

Textbooks on botany began outselling popular novels and a mere work of fiction having the accidental title *Greener Than You Think* was catapulted onto the bestseller list before anyone realized it wasnt an academic discussion of the family Gramineae. Contributors to scientifiction magazines burst bloodvessels happily turning out ten thousand words a day describing their heroes' adventures amid the red grass of Mars or the blue grass of Venus after they had singlehanded—with the help of a deathray and the heroine's pure love—conquered the green grass of Tellus.

Professors, shy and otherwise, were lured from their classrooms to lecture before ladies' clubs hitherto sacred to the accents of transoceanic celebrities and Eleanor Roosevelt. There they competed on alternate forums with literate gardeners and stuttering horticultural amateurs. Stolon, rhizome and culm became words replacing crankshaft and piston in the popular vocabulary; the puerile reports Gootes fabricated under my name as the man responsible for the phenomenon were syndicated in newspapers from coast to coast, and a query as to rates was received from the *Daily Mail.*

Brother Paul's exhortations on the radio increased in both length and intensity as the grass spread. Pastors of other churches and conductors of similar programs denounced him as misled; realestate operators, fearful of all this talk about the properties, complained to the Federal Communications Commission; Sundayschools voted him the Man of the Year and hundreds of motherly ladies stormed the studio with cakes baked by their own hands. Brother Paul's answer to indorser and detractor alike was to buy up more radiotime.

No one doubted the government would at length awaken from its apathy and counter the menace swiftly and efficiently, as always before in crises when the country was threatened. The nation with the highest rate of production per manhour, the greatest efficiency per machine, the greatest wealth per capita, and the greatest vision per mindseye was not going to be defeated by a mere weed, however overgrown. While waiting the inevitable action and equally inevitable solution the public had all the excitement of war without suffering the accompanying privations and bereavements. The grass was a nuisance, but a nuisance with titillating compensations; most people felt like children whose schoolhouse had burned down; they were sorry, they knew there'd be a new one, they were quite ready to help build it—but in the meantime it was fun.

The *Daily Intelligencer* was gorged with letters from its readers on the subject of the grass. Many of them wanted to know what a newspaper of its standing meant by devoting so much space to an ephemeral happening, while many more asked indignantly why more space wasnt given to something affecting their very lives and fortunes. Communist partymembers, using improbable pennames, asked passionately if this was not a direct result of the country's failure to come to a thorough understanding with the Soviet Union? Terrified propertyholders irately demanded that something, SOMETHING be done before realestate became as valueless in Southern California as it already was in Red Russia.

Technocrats demanded the government be immediately turned over to a committee of engineers and competent agronomists who would deal with the situation as it deserved after harnessing the wasted energy of the populace. Nationalists hinted darkly that the whole thing was the result of a plot by the Elders of Zion and that Kaplan's Delicatessen—in conspiracy with A Cohen, Notions—was at the bottom of the grass. Brother Paul wrote—and his letter was printed, for he now advertised his radioprograms in the columns of the *Intelligencer*—that Caesar—presumably the state of California—had been chastened for arrogating to itself things not to be rendered unto Caesar and the tankmen had deservedly perished for their sacrilege. The letter aroused fury—the followers of Brother Paul either didnt read the *Intelligencer* or were satisfied their leader needed no championing, if they did—and other letters poured in calling for various expressions of popular disapproval, from simple boycott up through tarring and feathering to plain and elaborated—with gasoline and castration—lynching. The grass was a hot topic.

With its acute perception of the popular taste Le ffaçasé's paper printed not only most of the communications—the unprintable ones were circulated among the staff till they wore out or disappeared mysteriously in the Gents Room—but maps showing the daily progress of the weed, guesses as to the duration of the plague by local prophets, learned articles by scientists, opinions of statesmen, views of prominent entertainers, in fact anything having any remote connection with the topic of the day. The paper even went further and offered a reward of ten thousand dollars to anyone advancing a suggestion leading to the destruction of the intruder. Its circulation jumped at the expense of less perspicacious rivals and the incoming mail, already many times normal, swelled to staggering proportions.

The contest was taken with deadly seriousness, for the livelihood of many of the paper's readers was suddenly threatened by its subject and from a new quarter. In the same issue as the offered reward there appeared an interview with the accredited head of the

organized motionpicture producers. This retiring gentleman was
rumored to be completely illiterate, an unquestionable slander, for
he had written checks to support every cause dedicated to keeping
wages where they belonged and seeing the wage earners didnt waste
the money so benevolently supplied by their employers.

I got the details of the interview from the interviewer himself.
The magnate—he had no objection to the description—had been
irritable and minced no words. The grass was bad alike for production and boxoffice, taking everyone's mind off the prime business of
making and viewing motionpictures. It was injuring The Industry
and he couldnt conceal the fact that The Industry, speaking
through his mouth and with his vocabulary, was annoyed.

"Unless this disgraceful episode ends within ten days," he had
said sternly, "the Motion Picture Industry will move to Florida."

It was an ultimatum; Southern Californians heard and trembled. The last time this dread interdiction had been invoked—in
the midst of a bitter election fight—it had sent them scurrying to
the polls to do their benefactor's bidding. Now indeed the grass
menace would be taken seriously.

The next day's paper had news of more immediate concern to
me. The governor had appointed a special committee to investigate
the situation and the first two witnesses to be called were Josephine
Spencer Francis and Albert Weener.

20 William Rufus Le ffaçasé was as enthusiastic as his
phlegmatic nature permitted. He called me into his
office and half raised the snuffbox off the desk as though to offer
me an unwelcome pinch. "Youre a made man now, Weener," he
said, thinking better of his generosity and putting the snuffbox
back. "Your name will be in headlines from Alabama to Alberta—
and all due to the *Intelligencer.*"

I would have resented this as a gross misappropriation of
credit—for surely all obligation was on the other side—had I not
been deeply disturbed by the prospect of being haled before this
committee like a criminal before the bar of justice.

"I'd much rather avoid this unpleasant notoriety, Mr. Le
ffaçasé," I protested. "Since the *Intelligencer,* for reasons best

known to itself, chooses not to avail itself of my contributions, but prints my name over words I have not written, there could be no possible objection to my slipping away to Nevada until this investigation ends."

His face became a pretty shade of plum. "Weener, youre a thief, a petty, cadging, sly, larcenous, pilfering, bloody thief. You take the *Daily Intelligencer's* honest dollars without a qualm aye, with a smirk on your imbecile face, proposing with the cool impudence of the born embezzler to return no value for them. Weener, you forget yourself. The *Intelligencer* picked you out of a gutter, a nauseous, dungspattered and thoroughly fitting gutter, and pays you well, mark that, you feebleminded counterfeit of a confidenceman, pays you well, not for your futile, lecherous pawings at the chastity of the English language, but out of the boundless generosity which only a newspaper with a great soul can have. And what do you propose to do in gratitude? To run, to flee, to hide from the expression of authority, to bring disgrace upon the very newspaper whose munificence pumps life into your boneless, soulless, gutless carcass. Not another word, not a sound, not a ghoulish syllable from your ineffective vocabulary. Out of my presence before I lose my temper. Get down to whatever smokefilled and tastelessly decorated room that committee is meeting in and do not leave while it is in session, neither to eat, sleep, nor move those bowels whose possession I gravely doubt. You hear me, Weener?"

For some reason the committee was not attempting to get the story of the grass in chronological order. When I arrived, the six distinguished gentlemen were trying to find out all about the crudeoil poured, apparently without effect, in what now seemed so long ago, but which actually had been less than two weeks before.

Flanked on either side by his colleagues, the little black plug of his hearingaid sticking out like a misplaced unicorn's horn, was the chairman, Senator Jones, his looseskinned old fingers resting lightly on the bright table, the nails square and ridged, the flesh brownspotted. He adjusted a pair of goldrimmed spectacles, quickly found the improvement in his vision unpleasant, and rumbled, "What did it cost the taxpayers?"

On the stand, the chief of police was settled in great discomfort, so far forward on the rounded edge of his chair that his balance was a source of fascinated speculation to the gallery. He squirmed a perilous half inch forward, but before he had time to reply, old Judge Robinson of the State Supreme Court, who scorned any palliation of his deafness such as Senator Jones condescended to, cupped his left ear with his hand and shrieked, "Ay? Ay? What's that? Speak up, can't you? Don't sit there mumbling."

Assemblyman Brown, head of the legislature's antiracketeering committee, intense concentration expressed in the forward push of his vigorous shoulders and the creased lines on his youthful forehead, asked if it were not true that the oil had been held up by a union jurisdictional dispute? There was a spattering of applause from the listeners at this adroit question and one man in the back of the room cried "Sha—" and then sat down quickly.

Attorney General Smith wanted to know just who had ordered the oil in the first place and whether the propertyowners had given their consent to its application. The attorney general's square face, softened and rounded by fat, shone on the wriggling chief like a klieglight; his lips, irresistibly suggesting twin slices of underdone steak, parting into a pleasant smile when his question had concluded. The other two members of the committee seemed about to inquire further when the chief managed to stammer, he was awfully sorry, gentlemen, but he had been out of town and hadnt even heard of the oil till this moment.

He was instantly dismissed from the stand and a new witness, from the mayor's office, was called, with no happier results. He, too, was about to be excused when Dr Johnson, who represented Science on the committee, descended from Himalayan abstraction to demand what effect the oil had had on the grass.

There were excited whisperings and craning of feminine heads as Dr Johnson propounded his question. The interest he excited was, however, largely vicarious. For he was famous, not so much in his own right, as in being the husband of the *Intelligencer's* widely read society columnist whose malapropisms caused more wry enjoyment and fearsome anticipation than an elopement to Nevada.

"And what effect did the oil have on the grass?" he repeated.

The query caused confusion, for it seemed the committee could not proceed until this fact had been ascertained. Various technicians were sent for, and the doctor, tall, solemn and benign, looked over his stiff, turned-down collar and the black string tie drooping around it, as though searching for some profound truth, which would be readily apparent to him alone.

The experts discoursed at some length in esoteric terms—one even bringing a portable blackboard on which he demonstrated, with diagrams, the chemical, geologic and mathematical aspects of the problem—but no pertinent information was forthcoming till some minor clerk in the Department of Water and Power, who had only got to the stand through a confusion of names, said boldly, "No effect whatever."

"Why not?" asked Judge Robinson. "Was the oil adulterated? Speak up, speak up; don't mumble."

Henry Miller, the Southland's bestknown realtor ("Los Angeles First in Population by Nineteen Ninety Nine"), who had connections in the oil industry, as well as in citrus and walnut packing, frowned disapprovingly. The clerk said he didnt know, but he might venture a guess—

Senator Jones informed him majestically that the committee was concerned with facts, not speculations. This created an impasse until Attorney General Smith tactfully suggested the clerk might be permitted to guess, entirely off the record. After the official stenographer had been commanded sternly not to take down a single word of conjecture, the witness was allowed to advance the opinion that the oil hadnt killed the plant because it had never reached the roots.

"Ay?" questioned the learned judge, looking as though neither his lunch nor breakfast nor, for that matter, any nourishment absorbed since the Taft administration, had agreed with him.

"I'm a bit of a gardener myself, gentlemen," the witness assured them confidentially, settling back comfortably. "I putter around my own place Saturdays and Sundays and I know what devilgrass is like. I can well imagine a bunch of it twenty or twentyfive feet high could be coated with many, many gallons of oil without a drop seeping down into the ground."

Mr Miller said magisterially, "Not really good American oil," but no one paid attention, knowing that he was commenting, not as a member of the committee, but in his other capacity as the head of an organization to promote Brotherhood and Democracy by deporting all foreignborn and the descendants of foreignborn to their original countries. Everyone was only too happy to have the oil matter concluded at any cost; and after the stenographer was ordered to resume his labors, the next witness was called.

"Albert Weener!"

I hope I may never again have to submit to the scrutiny of twelve such merciless eyes. I cast my own down at the brown linoleum until every stain and inkspot was impressed ineradicably on my mind. Senator Jones finally broke the tension by asking, "What is your name?"

Judge Robinson enjoined, "Speak up, speak up. Don't mumble."

"Albert Weener," I replied.

There was a faint sigh through the room. Everyone who read the *Daily Intelligencer* had heard of me.

"And what is your occupation, Mr Weener?" asked Henry Miller.

"Salesman, sir," I answered automatically, forgetting my present connection with the newspaper, and he smiled at me sympathetically.

"You belong to a socalled tradesunion?" inquired Assemblyman Brown.

"I will ask the honorable Mr Brown to modify his question by having the word 'socalled' struck from it."

"I will inform the honorable attorney general that my question stands exactly as I phrased it," rejoined Assemblyman Brown sharply. "I'll remind the attorney general I myself am a member in good standing of a legitimate union, namely the International Brotherhood of Embalmers, Morticians, Gravediggers and Helpers, and when I asked the witness if he belonged to a socalled tradesunion I was referring to any one of those groups of Red conspirators who attempt to strangle the economic body by interfering with the normal course of business and mulcting honest citizen of tributary dues before they can pursue their livelihoods."

Judge Robinson cupped his ear again and glared at me. "Speak up man; stop mumbling."

"I don't belong to any union," I answered as soon as there was a chance for my words to be heard. Senator Jones took a notebook from his pocket, consulted it, put it back, scribbled something on the pad in front of him, tore it up, looked at his notebook again and asked, "What is your connection with this . . . um . . . grass?"

"I applied Miss Francis' Metamorphizer to it, sir," I answered.

"Nonsense," said Judge Robinson sharply.

"Explain yourself," demanded Attorney General Smith.

"Tell us just what this stuff is and how you applied it," suggested Henry Miller.

"Don't mumble," ordered Judge Robinson.

"I'm sorry, gentlemen, I don't know exactly what it is. You'll have to ask Miss Francis that. But—"

Senator Jones interrupted me. "You mean to say you applied a chemical to someone's lawn, a piece of valuable property, without knowing its contents?" he asked sternly.

"Well, Senator—" I began.

"Do you habitually act in this irresponsible manner?"

"Senator, I—"

"Don't you understand, sir, that consequences necessarily follow actions? What sort of world would this be if everyone rushed around blindly using things of whose nature they were completely unaware?"

"Don't mumble," warned Judge Robinson.

I began to feel very low indeed and could only say haltingly, "I acted in good faith, gentlemen," when Mr Miller kindly recommended that I be excused since I had evidently given all the information at my command.

"Subject to recall," growled Attorney General Smith.

"Oh, certainly, sir, certainly," agreed Mr Miller, and I was thankfully released from my ordeal.

"Josephine Spencer Francis."

I cannot say Miss Francis had made any concessions in her appearance in deference to the committee, for she looked as though she had come straight from her kitchen, a suspicion strengthened by the strand of grass she carried in her fingers and played with absently throughout. She appeared quite at home as she settled herself in the chair, scanning with the greatest interest the faces of the committeemen as if she were memorizing each feature for future reference.

The honorable body returned her scrutiny with sharply individual emphasis. The attorney general smiled pleasantly at her; Judge Robinson looked more sour than ever and grunted, "Woman; mistake"; Senator Jones bowed toward her with courtesy; Assemblyman Brown gave her a sharp onceover; Mr Miller pursed his lips in amusement; and Dr Johnson gazed at her in horrified fascination.

Senator Jones bowed for a second time and inquired her name. He received the information and chewed it meditatively. Miss Francis took out her gold toothpick, considered the etiquette of using it and regretfully put it away in time to hear the attorney general's question, "Mrs or Miss Francis?"

"Miss," she replied gruffly. "*Virgo intacta.*"

Senator Jones drew back as if attacked by a wasp. Attorney General Smith said, "Hum," very loudly and looked at Assemblyman Brown who looked blank. Dr Johnson's nose raised itself a perceptible inch and Judge Robinson, sensing a sensation among his colleagues, shouted, "Speak up, madam, don't mumble."

Mr. Miller, who hadnt been affected, inquired, "What is your occupation, Miss Francis?"

"Agrostological engineer, specializing in chemical research."

"How's that again?" Judge Robinson managed to put into the simple gesture of cupping his ear a devastating condemnation of Miss Francis, women in general, science and presentday society. She politely repeated herself.

"Astrology—what's that got to do with the grass? Do you cast horoscopes?"

"Agrostology," Dr Johnson murmured to the ceiling.

"Will you explain please in simpler terms, just what you do?" requested Attorney General Smith.

"Local statutes against fortunetelling," burst out Judge Robinson.

"I have spent my life studying reactions of plants to the lighter elements and the effects of certain compounds on their growth, reproduction, and metabolism."

Judge Robinson removed his hand from behind his ear and rubbed his skull irritably. Assemblyman Brown complained, "There's entirely too much talk about reaction." Dr Johnson inspected a paneled wall with no interest whatever and Senator Jones stated pontifically, "You are an agricultural chemist."

Miss Francis smiled at him amiably. "Agriculture is a broad field and I farm one small corner of it."

Attorney General Smith leaned forward with interest. "From what university did you obtain your degrees, Miss Francis?"

She slouched back comfortably, to look more cylindrical than ever. "None," she stated baldly.

"Hay? . . . mumble!"

Senator Jones said, "I'm afraid I did not quite understand your reply, madam."

"I hold no degrees, honors, or diplomas whatever, and I have not wasted one second of my life in any college, university, academy, or other alleged institution of learning. The degrees good enough for Roger Bacon, Erasmus Darwin, Lavoisier, Linnaeus and Lamarck are good enough for me. I am a questioner, gentlemen, a learner, not a collector of alphabetical letters which, strung together in any form your fancy pleases, continue eternally to spell nothing whatever."

Sensation. One of the experts who had been waiting patiently to testify, folded his arms and said in a loud voice, "This is what comes of tolerating women in the professions." Another muttered, "Charlatan . . . ridiculous . . . dangerous thing . . . shameful . . . sex . . ." Two elderly ladies in broadcloth coats with fur collars, later identified as crusaders for antivivisection, cheered feebly and were promptly ejected.

Senator Jones took off his spectacles, polished them exhaustively, tried to put them on upside down, gave up and stated gravely, "This is an extraordinary admission, Miss, um, Francis."

"It is not an admission at all; it is a statement of fact. As for its irregularity, I take the liberty of believing we unlettered ones are in the majority rather than minority."

Judge Robinson warned, "Could be cited for contempt, Miss Harrumph."

Dr Johnson said sharply, "Nonsense, madam, even a—even a tree surgeon has more respect for learning."

Mr Miller leaned slightly over the table. "Do you realize that

in your ignorant dabbling you have ruined hundreds of propertyowners and taxpayers?"

"I thought there was some law against practicing without a
license," speculated Assemblyman Brown.

"There is apparently no law applying intelligence qualifications for members of the legislature," remarked Miss Francis
pleasantly.

Senator Jones lifted his gavel, idle until now, and banged it on
the table, smashing his spectacles thoughtlessly placed in front of
him a moment before. This did nothing to appease his rising
choler. "Silence, madam! We have perhaps been too lenient in
deference to your, um, sex. I'll remind you that this body is vested
with all the dignity of the state of California. Unless you apologize
instantly I shall cite you for contempt."

"I beg the committee's pardon."

The investigators held a whispered conference among themselves, evidently to determine whether this equivocal apology was
to be accepted. Apparently it was, for Dr Johnson now asked loftily
and with an abstracted air, as though he already knew the answer
and considered it beneath notice, "What was this magic formula
you caused to be put on the grass?"

Malicious spirits averred that Dickie Johnson had flunked out
of agricultural school, had an obscure European diploma, and that
his fame as a professor at Creighton University was based on the
gleaming granite and stainless steel building dedicated to research
in agronomy which bore the legend "Johnson Foundation" over the
entrance. No one hearing him pronounce "magic formula" putting
into the word all the contempt of the scientist for the quack, could
ever put credence in the base slander. "What was this 'magic
formula' you caused to be put on the grass?" he repeated.

Miss Francis reeled off a list of elements so swiftly I'm sure no
one but the stenographer caught them all. I know I didn't get more
than half, though I was sitting less than five feet from her. "Magne-
sium," she stated, "iodine, carbon, nitrogen, hydrogen, helium,
potash, sulphur, oxygen . . ."

Dr Johnson seemed to have known its composition since grammarschool days. Senator Jones asked, "And what effect did you
expect this extraordinary conglomeration to have?"

She repeated what she had told me at first and the deductions she had made since. Dr Johnson smiled. "A true Man of Science," he stated, "one who has labored for years to acquire those degrees you affect to despise, would have been trained in selfless devotion to the service of mankind, would never have made whatever gross error your ignorance, heightened by projection into a sphere for which you are probably biologically unfitted—though this is perhaps controversial—has betrayed you into. For had you freely shared your work with colleagues they would have been able to correct your mistakes and this catastrophe brought on by selfish greed—a catastrophe which has already cost millions—would not have occurred."

The entire committee, including Dr Johnson himself, seemed pleased with this indictment. Attorney General Smith looked inquiringly at the witness as though inviting her to answer *that* if she could. Miss Francis evidently took the invitation literally, for she addressed herself directly to Dr Johnson.

"I do not know, Doctor, where these beautiful and eminently sensible ideals you have so eloquently outlined are practiced, where scientists, regardless of biological fitness, share with each other their advances from moment to moment and so add to the security of civilization from day to day. Is it in the great research foundations whose unlimited funds are used to lure promising young men to their staffs, much as athletes used to be given scholarships by universities anxious to improve the physical qualities of American youth? Is it in the experimental laboratories of great industries where technological advances are daily suppressed, locked away in safes, so profits may not be diminished by the expensive retooling necessary to put these advances into effect? Or is it in a field closer to my own, in chemical research—pure science, if you like—where truly secrets are shared on an international scale in order to build up the cartels which choke production by increasing prices and promote those industries which thrive on international illwill?"

Assemblyman Brown rose to his feet and said in measured tones, "This woman is a paid agent of the Communist International. I have heard such rantings from demagogues on streetcorners. I demand the committee listen to no more of this propaganda."

Mr Miller gave a polite wave of his hand toward the assembly-man, indicating at once full agreement with what the legislator said and apology for pursuing his questioning of Miss Francis. He then asked the witness sternly, "What is your real name?"

"I'm afraid I don't quite understand. The only name I have is Josephine Spencer Francis and so far as I know it is thus written on my birth certificate."

"Birth certificate, ay?" Where were you born? Speak up, don't mumble."

"Russia, without a doubt," muttered Assemblyman Brown.

"Youre sure it isnt Franciski or Franciscovitch? Or say, Finkelstein?"

"My name is not Finkelstein, although I do not find myself terrified of that combination of syllables. I was born in Moscow—"

Another sensation. "I thought so!" screamed Judge Robinson triumphantly.

"Aha!" exclaimed Senator Jones profoundly.

"The leopard doesnt change his spots or the Red his (or her) color," asserted Assemblyman Brown.

"A sabatoor," yelled several of the spectators. Only Dr Johnson seemed unimpressed with the revelation; he smiled contentedly.

"—in Moscow, Idaho," concluded Miss Francis, picking her teeth with a flourish.

Judge Robinson screeched, "Ay? Ay? What's all this hubbub?" Assemblyman Brown sneered, "A very unlikely story." Attorney General Smith wanted it proven in blackandwhite while Senator Jones remarked Miss Francis' taste was on a level with her scholarship.

She waved the toothpick toward the chairman and politely waited for either further questions or dismissal. All the while her intense interest in each gesture of the inquisitors and every facet of the investigation had not diminished at all. As she sat there pa-tiently, her eyes darted from one to the other as they consulted and only came to rest on Senator Jones when he spoke directly to her again.

"And what steps can you take to undo, hum, this?"

"So far, none," admitted Miss Francis, "but since this thing has happened I have given all my time to experiment hoping in some manner to reverse the action of the Metamorphizer and evolve a formula whereby the growth it induced will be inhibited. I cannot say I am even on the right road yet, for you must recall I have spent my adult life going, as it were, in one direction and it is now not a matter of merely retracing my steps, but of starting out for an entirely different destination in a field where there are no highwaymaps and few compasspoints. I cannot say I am even optimistic of success, but it is not for want of trying—be assured of that."

Another semisilence while the committee conferred once more. Finally Senator Jones spoke in grave and measured tones: "It is a customary politeness in hearings of this nature to thank the witness for his helpfulness and cooperation. This courtesy I cannot with any sincerity extend to you, madam. It seems to me you have proven yourself the opposite of a good citizen, that you have set yourself up, in your arrogance, against all logical authority and have presumed to look down upon the work and methods of men whose standing and ways of procedure are recognized by all sound people. By your conceit, madam, you have caused the death of young men, the flower of our state's manhood, who gave their lives in a vain attempt to destroy what your ignorance created. If I may be permitted a rather daring and perhaps harsh aside, I think this should strike you doubly, as a woman who has not brought forth offspring to carry on the work of our forefathers and as one who—with doubtful taste—boasts of that sterility. I think the results of your socalled experiments should chasten you and make you heed the words of men properly qualified in a field where you are clearly not so."

Someone in the back of the room applauded the senator's eloquence.

"Senator Jones," said Miss Francis, turning her eyes on him with the attention I knew so well, the look which meant she had found an interest for the moment excluding all others, "you accuse me of what amounts to crime or at least criminal folly and I must answer that your accusations are at once both true and false. I have been foolish, but it was not in despising the constrictions and falsity of the academic world. I *have* flouted authority, but it was not the authority of the movingpicture heroes, whose comic errors

are perpetuated for generations, like those of Pasteur, or so quietly
repudiated their repudiation passes unnoticed, like those of Lister,
in order to protect a vested interest. The authority I have flouted,
in my arrogance as you call it, is that authority all scientists
recognized in the days when science was scientific and called itself,
not boastfully by the name of all knowledge, but more humbly and
decently, natural philosophy. That authority is what theologians
term the Will of God; others, the life force, the immaterial principle, the common unconscious, or whatever you will. When I,
along with all the academic robots whom you admire, denied that
authority, we did not make ourselves, as we thought, men of pure
science, but, on the contrary, by deposing one master we invited in
a horde of others. Since we could not submit to moral force we
submitted in our blind stupidity—we called it the rejection of
metaphysical concepts—to financial force, to political force, to
social force; and finally, since there was no longer any reward in
itself for our speculations, we submitted to the lust for personal
aggrandizement in fortune, in notoriety, in castebound irrespon-
sibility, and even for the hypocritical backslapping of our fellows.

"In the counterrevolution known as the nineteenth century we
even repudiated the name of speculation and it became a term of
disrepute, like metaphysical. We went further than a mere dis-
avowal of the name; we disavowed the whole process and turned
with disgust from the using of our minds to the use of our hands in
a manner which would have revolted the most illiterate of Car-
pathian peasants. We extirpated the salivary glands of dogs in order
to find out if they would slobber without them. We cut off the tails
of mice to discover if the operation affected their greatgrandchildren. We decapitated, emasculated, malnourished, and poi-
soned rodents against whom we had no personal animus for no
other reason than to keep an elaborate apparatus in use.

"Even these pastimes failed to satisfy our undiscriminating
appetite. Someone a little stupider, a little less imaginative—
though such conditions must have been difficult indeed to
achieve—invented what is called the Control Experiment whereby,
if theory tested be correct, half the subjects are condemned without
trial to execution.

"These are my sins: that in despising academic ends I did not despise academic means, that in repudiating the brainlessness of the professorial mind I did not attempt to use my own. Because I was proud of the integrity which made me choose not to do the will of a research foundation or industrial empire, I overlooked the vital fact that I had also chosen not to do God's Will, but what I stupidly thought to be my own. It was not. It was faintheartedness, sloth, placation, doubt, vagueness and romantical misconception. In a word, it was the aimlessness and falsity of the nineteenth century coming back in the window after having been booted out the door; my folly was the failure to recognize it. I have deluded myself, I have taken halfmeasures, I have followed false paths. Condemn me for these crimes. I am guilty."

Attorney General Smith said acidly, "This is neither a psychiatrist's consulting room, a confessional, nor a court of law. I suggest the witness be excused and her last hysterical remarks expunged from the record."

"It is so ordered," ruled Senator Jones. "And now, gentlemen, we shall recess until tomorrow."

21 THE HEARINGS OF the Committee to Investigate Dangerous Vegetation went on for five days and Mr Le ffaçasé was increasingly delighted as the proceedings went down, properly edited and embellished to excite reader interest, in the columns of the *Daily Intelligencer*. He even unbent so far as to call me a fool without any adjectival modification, which was for him the height of geniality.

I don't want to give the impression the committee stole the show, as the saying goes. The show essentially and primarily was still the grass itself. It grew while the honorable body inquired and it grew while the honorable body, tired by its labors, slept. It increased during the speeches of Senator Jones, through the interjections of Judge Robinson, and as Dr Johnson added his wisdom to the deliberations.

While the committee probed, listened and digested, the grass finally pushed its way across Hollywood Boulevard, resisting frantic efforts by the National Guard, the fire and police departments, and a volunteer brigade of local merchants, to stem its course. It defied alike sharpened steel, fire, chemicals and explosives. Even the smallest runner could now be severed only with the greatest difficulty, for in its advance the weed had toughened—some said because of its omnivorous diet, others, its ability to absorb nitrogen from the air—and its rubbery quality caused it to yield to onslaught only to bound back, apparently uninjured, after each blow.

One of the most disquieting aspects of the advance was its variability and unpredictability. To the west, it had hardly gone five blocks from the Dinkman house, while southward it had crossed

Santa Monica Boulevard and was nosing toward Melrose. Its growth had been measured and checked, over and over again, but the figures were never constant. Some days it traveled a foot an hour; on others it leapt nearly a city block between sunrise and nightfall.

It is simple to put down "the grass crossed Hollywood Boulevard"; as simple as saying, "our troops advanced" or "the man was hanged at dawn." But when I write these words less than a generation later, surrounded by rolling hills, gentle brooks, and vast lawns sedate and tame, I can close my eyes and see again the green glacier crawling down the sidestreets and over the low roofs of the shops to pour like a cascade upon the busy artery.

Once more I can feel the crawling of my skin as I looked upon the methodical obliteration of men's work. I can see the tendrils splaying out over the sidewalks, choking the roadways, climbing walls, finding vulnerable chinks in masonry, bunching themselves inside apertures and bursting out, carrying with them fragments of their momentary prison as they pursued their ruthless course.

Now the uproar and clamor of a disturbed public swelled to giant volume. All the disruption and distress going before had been news; this was disaster. "All same Glauman's Chinese, all same Pa'thenon," remarked Gootes, and indeed I have heard far less outcry over the destruction of historic landmarks than was raised when the grass obscured the celebrated footprints.

Recall of the mayor was demanded and councilmen's official limousines were frequently overturned. Meetings denounced the inaction of the authorities; a gigantic parade bearing placards calling for an end to procrastination marched past the cityhall. Democrats blamed Republicans for inefficiency and Republicans retorted that Miss Francis had done her research during a Democratic administration.

Every means previously tried and found wanting was tried again as though it were impossible for human minds to acknowledge defeat by an insensate plant. The axes, the scythes, weedburners and reapers were brought out again, only to prove their inability to cope with the relentless flow of the grass. Robot tanks loaded with explosives disappeared as had those containing the soldiers, and only the stifled sound of their explosion registered the fact that they had fulfilled their design if not their purpose.

It was difficult for the man on the street to understand how the

weapons successful in Normandy and Tarawa could be balked by
vegetation. Like the Investigating Committee's pursuit of the question of the crudeoil's adulteration, they wanted to know if the tanks
were firstline vehicles or some surplus palmed off by the War
Department; if the weedburners were properly accredited gram-
inacides or just a bunch of bums taken from the reliefrolls. The
necessary reverse of this picture was the jubilant hailing of each
new instrument of attack, the brief but hysterical enthusiasm for
each in turn as the ultimate savior.

Because of my unique position I witnessed the trial of them
all. I saw tanks dragging rotary plows and others equipped with
devices like electricfans but with blades of hardened steel sharpened to razor keenness. The only thing this latter gadget did was to
scatter more potential nuclei to the accommodating wind.

I saw the Flammenwerfer, the dreadful flamethrowers which
had scorched the bodies of men like burnt toast in an instant, direct
their concentrated fire upon the advancing runners. I smelled the
sweetly sick smell of steaming sap and saw the runners shrivel and
curl back as they had done on other occasions, until nothing was
presented to the flamethrowers except the tangled mass of interwoven stems denuded of all foliage. Upon this involved wall the fire
had no effect, the stems did not wilt, the hard membranes did not
collapse, the steely network did not retreat. It seemed a drawn
battle in one small sector, yet in that very part where the grass
paused on the ground it rose higher into the air like a poising
tidalwave. Higher and higher, until its crest, unbalanced, toppled
forward to engulf its tormentors.

Then the unruffled advance resumed, again some resource was
interposed against it, again it was checked for an instant and again it
overcame its adversary, careless of obstacles, impartially taking to itself
gouty roominghouses and pimping frenchprovincial ("17 master bed-
rooms") chateaus, hotdogstand and Brown Derby, cornergrocery and
pyramidal foodmart; undeterred by anything in its path.

When you say a clump of weed attacked a city you utter an
absurdity. I think everyone was aware of the fantastic discrepancy
between statement of the event and the event itself. So innocent
and ridiculous the grass looked as it made its first tentative thrust at
the urban nerves; the green blades sloped forward like some prettily
arranged but unimaginative corsage upon the the concrete bosom

of the street. You could not believe those fragile seeming strands would resist the impress of a careless boot, much less the entire arsenal of military and agricultural implements. It must have been this deceptive fragility which broke the spirit of so many people.

From an item in the *Intelligencer* I recalled the existence of one of Mrs Dinkman's neighbors who had rudely refused the opportunity to have his lawn treated with the Metamorphizer. He had left an incoherent suicidenote: "Pigeons in the grass alas. Too many pigeons, too much grass. Pigeons are doves, but Noah expressed a raven. Contradiction lies. Roses are red violets are blue. The grass is green and I am thru. Too too too. Darling kiddies." He then, in full view of the helpless weedfighters, marched on into the grass and was lost to sight.

In the days following, so many selfdestructions succeeded this one that the grass became known in the papers as the Green Horror. Perhaps a peculiar sidelight on human oddity was revealed in most of these suicides choosing to immolate themselves, not in the main body of the grass, but in one of the many smaller nuclei springing up in close proximity.

It was my fortune to witness the confluence of two of these descendant bodies. They had come into being only a few blocks apart; understandably their true character was unrecognized until they were out of control and had enveloped the neighborhoods of their origin. They crept toward each other with a sort of incestuous attraction until mere yards separated them; they paused skittishly, the runners crawled forward speculatively, the green fronds began overlapping like clasping fingers, then with accelerating speed came together much as a pack of cards in the hands of a deft shuffler slides edge under edge to make a compact and indivisible whole. The line of division disappeared, the two became one, and where before there had been left a narrow path for men to tread, now only a serene line of vegetation outlined itself against the unblinking sky.

22 I have said Mr Le ffaçasé had softened his brutality toward me, but his favor did not extend—so pervasive is literary jealousy—to printing my own reports. He continued to subject me to the indignity of being "ghosted," a thoroughly expressive term, which by a combination of bad conjugation and the suggestion of insubstantiality defines the sort of prose produced, by Jacson Gootes. This arrangement, instead of giving me some freedom, shackled me to the reporter, who dashed from celebrity to celebrity, grass to nuclei, office to point of momentary interest, with unflagging energy and infuriating jocosity. I knew his repertory of tricks and accents down to the last yawn.

Most of all I resented his irregular habits. He never arrived at the *Intelligencer* office on time or quit after a proper day's work. He thought nothing of getting me out of bed before I'd had my eight hours' sleep to accompany him on some ridiculous errand. "Bertie, old dormouse, the grass is knocking at the doors of NBC."

"All right," I answered, annoyed. "It started down Vine Street yesterday. It would be more surprising if it obligingly paused before the studios."

"Cynic," he said, pulling the bedclothes away from my face. I consider this the lowest form of horseplay I know of. "How quickly your ideals have been tarnished by contact with the vulgar world of newspaperdom. Front and center, Bertie lad, we must catch the grass making its own soundeffects before they jerk out the microphones."

Protests having no effect I reluctantly went with him, but the scene was merely a repetition of hundreds of previous ones, the grass being no more or less spectacular for NBC than for Watanabe's Nursery and Cut Flower Shop a halfmile away. Its aftereffects, however, were immediate. The governor declared martial law in Los Angeles County and ordered the evacuation of an area five miles wide on the perimeter of the grass.

Furious cries of anguish went up from those affected by the arbitrary order. What authority had any official to dispossess honest people from their homes in times of peace? The right to hold their property unmolested was a prerogative vested in the humblest American and who was the governor to abrogate the Constitution, the Declaration of Independence, and manifold decisions of the Supreme Court? In embittered fury Henry Miller resigned from the Investigating Committee, now defunct anyway, its voluminous and inconclusive report buried in the state archives. Injunctions issued from local courts like ashes from a stirring volcano, but the militia were impervious and hustled the freeholders from their homes with callous disregard for the sacred dues of property.

When the reason behind this evacuation order leaked out a still greater lamentation was evoked, for the National Guard was planning nothing less than a saturation incendiary bombing of the entire area. The bludgeon which reduced the cities of Europe to mere shells must surely destroy this new invader. Even the stoutest defenders of property conceded this must be so—but what was the point of annihilating the enemy if their holdings were to be sacrificed in the process? No, no, let the governor take whatever means he pleased to dispatch the weed so long as the method involved left them homes to enjoy when things were—as they inevitably must be—restored to normal. So frantic were their efforts that the Supreme Court actually forced the governor to postpone his proposed bombing, though it did not discontinue the evacuation.

There were few indeed who understood how the weed would digest the very wood, bricks or stucco and who packed up and moved out ahead of the troops. American flags and shotguns recalled the heroic days of the frontier, and defiance of the governor's edict was the rule instead of the exception. Fierce old ladies dared the militiamen to lay a finger on them or their possessions and apoplectic gentlemen, eyes as glazed as those of the huntingtrophies on their walls, sputtered refusals to stir, no, not for all the brutal force in the world. No one was seriously hurt in this rebellion, the commonest wound being long scratches on the cheeks of the guardsmen, inflicted by feminine nails, as with various degrees of resistance the inhabitants were carried or shooed from their dwellings.

While the wrangling over its destruction went on, the grass continued its progress. Out through Cahuenga Pass it flowed, toward fertile San Fernando Valley. Steadily it climbed to the hilltops, masticating sage, greasewood, oak, sycamore and manzanita with the same ease it bolted houses and pavements. Into Griffith Park it swaggered, mumbling the planetarium, Mount Hollywood and Fern Dell in successive mouthfuls and swarmed down to the concretelined bed of the Los Angeles River. Here ineffectual shallow pools had preserved illusion and given tourists something at which to laugh in the dry season; the weed licked them up like a thirsty cow at a wallow. Up and down and over the river it ran, each day with greater speed.

It broke into the watermains, it tore down the poles bearing electric, telephone and telegraph wires, it forced its way between the threaded joints of gaspipes and turned their lethal vapor loose in the air until all services in the vicinity were hastily discontinued. Short weeks after I'd inoculated Mrs Dinkman's lawn, that part of Los Angeles known as Hollywood had disappeared from the map of civilization and had become one solid mass of green devilgrass.

No one refused to move for this dispossessor as they had for the governor; thousands of homeless fled from it. Their going clogged the highways with automobiles and produced an artificial gasoline shortage reminiscent of wartime. In downtown Los Angeles freightcars stood unloaded on their sidings, their consignees out of business and the warehouses glutted. The strain on local transportation, already enfeebled by a publicservice system designed for a city one twentieth its size and a complete lack of those facilities mandatory in every other large center of population, increased by the necessary rerouting around the affected area, threatened disruption of the entire organism and the further disintegration of the city's already weakened coordination. The values of realestate dropped, houses were sold for a song, officebuildings for an aria, hotels for a chorus.

The San Francisco Chamber of Commerce, secure in the knowledge its city suffered from nothing worse than fires, earthquakes, a miserable climate, and an invincible provincialism, invited displaced businessmen to resettle themselves in an area where improbable happenings were less likely; and the state of Oklahoma organized a border patrol to keep out Californians.

I could not blame the realestate men for attempting to unload their holdings before they suffered the fate of one tall building at Hollywood and Highland. The grass closed about its base like a false foundation and surged on to new conquests, leaving the monolith bare and forlorn in its new surroundings. At first the weed satisfied itself with jocular and teasing ventures up the smooth sides; then, as though rasped by the skyscraper's quiescence, it forced its way into the narrow space between the steel sash, filling the lower floor and bursting out again in a riot of whirling tendrils. Up the sides it climbed like some false ivy; clinging, falling back, building upon its own defeated body until it reached another story—and another and another. At each one the tale was repeated: windows burglariously forced, a floor suffocated, egress effected, and another height of wall scaled. At the end the proud structure was a lonely obelisk furred in a green covering to the very flagpole on its peak, from which waved disappointed yet still aspiring runners.

Upward and outward continuously, empty lot, fillingstation, artistic billboard, all alike to the greedy fingers. Like thumb and index they formed a crescent, a threatening semicircle, reaching forward by indirection. Northward and southeastward, the two aqueducts kept the desert from reclaiming its own; for fifty years the city had scraped up, bought, pilfered or systematically robbed all the water it could get; through the gray, wet lines, siphons, opencuts, pumps, lifts, tunnels, the metropolis sucked life. Now the desert had an ally, the grassy fingers avoided the downtown district, feeling purposefully and dangerously toward the aqueducts.

I spent much of my time, when not actively watching the grass, in the *Intelligencer* office. I had now agreed to write articles for several weekly magazines, and though they edited my copy with a heavy and unappreciative hand, still they never outraged me as Le ffaçasé did by causing another man to usurp my name. Since I was in both senses nominally a member of the staff, I had no qualms about using the journal's typewriters and stationery for the construction of little essays on the grass as seen through the eyes of one who had cause to know it better than anyone else.

"The-uh curse of Garry-baldi be upon the head of that ee-veal man who-uh controls this organeye-zation," rolled out Gootes in pseudoChurchillian tones. "The-uh monster has woven a web; we are-uh summoned, Bertie."

I got up resignedly and followed him to the managingeditor's office. We were not greeted directly. Instead, a question was thrown furiously over our heads. "Where is he? What bristling and baseless egomania sways him to affront the *Daily Intelligencer* with his contumacious and indecent unpunctuality?"

"Who, chief?" asked Gootes.

Le ffaçasé ignored him. "When this great newspaper condescends to shed the light of acceptance, to say nothing of an obese and taxable paycheck, upon the gross corpus of an illiterate moviecameraman, a false Daguerre, a spurious Steichen, a dubious Eisenstein, it has a right to expect a return for the goods showered upon such a deceitful sluggard."

Still ignoring Gootes, he turned to me, and apparently putting the berated one from his mind, went on with comparative mildness: "Weener, an unparalleled experience is to fall to your lot. You have not achieved this opportunity through any excellence of your own, for I must say, after lengthy contact, no vestige of merit in you is perceptible either to the nude eye or through an ultramicroscope. Nevertheless, by pure unhappy chance you are the property of the *Intelligencer*, and as such this illustrious organ intends to confer upon you the signal honor of being a Columbus, a Van Diemen, an Amundsen. You, Weener, in your unworthy person, shall be the first man to set foot upon a virgin land."

This speech being no more comprehensible to me than his excoriation of an unknown individual, I could only stay silent and try to look appreciative.

"Yes, Weener; some refugee from the busy newsroom of the Zwingle (Iowa) *Weekly Patriot*," a disdainful handwave referred this description to Gootes; "some miserable castoff from a fourth-rate quickie studio masquerading as a newscameraman; and a party of sheep—perhaps I could simplify my whole sentence by saying merely a party of bloody sheep—will be landed by parachute on top of the grass this very afternoon."

He smacked his lips. "I can see tomorrow's bannerline now: 'Agent of Destruction Views Handiwork.' Should you chance to survive, your ghostwritten impressions—for which we pay too high a price, far too high a price—will become doubly valuable. Should you come, as I confidently expect, to a logical conclusion, the *Intelligencer* will supply a suitable obituary. Now get the bloody hell out of here and either let me see you never again, or as a triumphant Balboa who has sat, if not upon a peak in Darien, at least upon something more important than your own backside."

23 The inside of the converted armybomber smelled like exactly what it was—a barn. Ten sheep and a solitary goat were tethered to stanchions along the sides. The sheep bleated continuously, the goat looked cynically forbearing, and all gave off an ammoniacal smell which was not absorbed by the bed of hay under their hoofs.

Enthusiasm for this venture was an emotion I found practically impossible to summon up. Even without Le ffaçasé's sanguinary prophecies, I objected to the trip. I had never been in a plane in my life, and this for no other reason than disinclination. I feared every possible consequence of the parachutejump, from instant annihilation through a broken neck in the jerk of its opening, down to being smothered in its folds on the ground. I distinctly did not want to go.

But caution sometimes defeats itself; I was so afraid of going that I hesitated to admit my timidity and so I found myself herded with my two companions, the pilot and crew, in with the sheep and the goat. I was not resigned, but I was quiescent. Gootes and the animals were not.

While we waited he went through his entire stock of tricks including a few new ones which were not completely successful, before the cameraman, panting, arrived ten minutes after our scheduled departure. His name was Rafe Slafe—which I thought an improbable combination of syllables—and he was so chubby in every part you imagined you saw the smile which ought to have gone with such a face and figure. Before his breath had settled down to a normal routine, Gootes had rushed upon him with an enthusiastic, "Ah, Rafello muchacho, give to me the abrazo; como usted, compañero?"

Slafe scorned reply, pushing Gootes aside with one plump hand while with the other he tidied the sparse black hairs of his mustache, which was trimmed down to an eyebrow shading his lip. After inspecting and rejecting several identical bucketseats he found one less to his distaste than the others and stowed his equipment, which was extensive, requiring several puffing trips backandforth, next to it. Then he lowered his backside onto the unyielding surface with the same anxiety with which he might have deposited a fortune in a dubious bank.

His hands darted in and out of pockets which apparently held a small pharmacopoeia. Pulling out a roll of absorbentcotton from which he plucked two wads, he stuck them thoughtfully in his ears. He withdrew a nasalsyringe and used it vigorously, swallowed gulps of a clearly labeled seasickremedy, and then sucked at pills from various boxes whose purpose was not so obvious. To conclude, he unstopped a glass vial and sniffed at it. All the while Gootes hovered over him, solicitously deluging him with friendly queries in one accent or another.

I lost interest in both fellowpassengers, for the plane, after shaking us violently, started forward, and before I was clearly aware of it had left the ground. Looking from the windows I regretted my first airplane ride hadnt been taken under less trying circumstances, for it was an extraordinarily pleasant experience to see the field dwindle into a miniature of itself and the ground beneath become nothing more than a large and highly colored reliefmap.

To our right was the stagnant river, dammed up behind the blockading arm of grass. Leftward, downtown, the thumb of the cityhall pointed rudely upward and far beyond was the listless Pacific. Ahead, the gridiron of streets was shockingly interrupted and severed by the great green mass plumped in its center.

It grew to enormous bigness and everything else disappeared; we were over and looked down upon it, a pasture hummock magnified beyond belief; retaining its essential identity, but made ominous by its unappropriate situation and size. As we hovered above the very pinnacle, the rounded peak which poked up at us, the pilot spoke over the intercommunication system. "We will circle till the load is disposed of. First the animals will be dropped, then the equipment, finally the passengers. Is that clear?"

Everything was clear to me except how we should escape from that green mountain once we had got upon it. This was apparently in the hands of Le ffaçasé, a realization, remembering his grisly conversation, making me no easier in my mind. Nor did I relish the pilot's casual description of myself as part of a "load"—to be disposed of.

Slafe suddenly came to life and after peering through a sort of lorgnette hanging round his neck, mumbling unintelligibly to himself all the while, started his camera which went on clicking magically with no apparent help from him. Efficiently and swiftly the crew fastened upon the helpless and bleating sheep their parachutes and onebyone dropped them through the open bombbay. The goat went last and she did not bleat, but dextrously butted two of her persecutors and micturated upon the third before being cast into space.

I would have forgone the dubious honor of being the first to land upon the grass, but the crew apparently had their orders; I was courteously tapped upon the shoulder—I presume the warders are polite when they enter the condemned cell at dawn—my chute was strapped upon me and the instructions I had already read in their printed form at least sixty times were repeated verbally, so much to my confusion that when I was finally in the air I do not know to this day whether I counted six, sixty, six hundred, or six thousand before jerking the ripcord. Whatever the number, it was evidently not too far wrong, for although I received a marrowexploding shock, the parachute opened and I floated down.

But no sooner were my fears of the parachute's performance relieved than I was for the first time assailed with apprehension at the thought of my destination. The grass, the weed, the destroying body which had devoured so much was immediately below me. I was irrevocably committed to come upon it—not at its edges where other men battled with it heroically—but at its very heart, where there were none to challenge it.

Still tormented and dejected, I landed easily and safely a few feet from the goat and just behind the rearquarters of one of the sheep.

And now I pause in my writing to sit quite still and remember—more than remember, live through again—the sensation of that first physical contact with the heart of the grass. Ecstasy is a pale word to apply to the joy of touching and resting upon that verdure. Soft—yes, it was soft, but the way sand is soft, unyieldingly. Unlike sand, however, it did not suggest a tightlypacked foundation, but rather the firmness of a good mattress resting on a wellmade spring. It was resilient, like carefully tended turf, yet at the same time one thought, not of the solid ground beneath, but of feathers, or even more of buoyant clouds. My parachute having landed me gently on my feet, I sank naturally to my knees, and then, impelled by some other force than gravity, my body fell fully forward in complete relaxation until my face was buried in the thickly growing culms and my arms stretched out to embrace as much of the lush surface as they could encompass.

Far more complex than the mere physical reactions were the psychical ones. When a boy I had, like every other, daydreamed of discovering new continents, of being first to climb a hitherto unscaled peak, to walk before others the shores of strange archipelagoes, to bring back tales of outlandish places and unfrequented

isles. Well, I was doing these things now, long after the disillusion-
ment adolescence brought to these childish dreams. But in addition
it was in a sense *my* island, *my* mountain, *my* land—for I had
caused it to be. A sensation of tremendous vivacity and wellbeing
seized upon me; I could not have lain upon the grass more than
half a second before I leaped to my feet. With a nimbleness quite
foreign to my natural habits I detached the encumbering chute and
jumped and danced upon the sward. The goat regarded me speculatively through rectangular pupils, but did not offer, in true
capricious fashion, to gambol with me. Her criticism did not stay
me, for I felt absolutely free, extraordinarily exhilarated, inor-
dinately stimulated. I believe I even went so far as to shout out loud
and break into song.

The descent of Slafe, still solemnly recording the event, camera before him in the position of present arms, did not sober my
intoxication, though circumspection caused me to act in a more
conventional way. I freed him from his harness, for he was too busy
taking views of the grass, the sky, the animals and me to perform
this service for himself.

I do not know if he was affected the way I was, for his
deceptively genial face showed no emotion as he went on aiming
his camera here and there with sour thoroughness. Then, apparently satisfied for the moment, he applied himself once more to the
nasalsyringe and the pillboxes.

On Gootes, however, the consequence of the landing must have
been much the same as on me. He too capered and sang and his
dialect renderings reached a new low, such as even a burlesqueshow
comedian would have spurned. "Tis the old sod itself," he kept
repeating, "Erin go bragh. Up Dev!" and he laughed inanely.

We must have wasted fully an hour in this fashion before
enough coolness returned to allow anything like calm observation.
When it did, we unpacked the equipment, despite obstacles interposed by Gootes, who, still hilarious, found great delight in making the various instruments disappear and reappear unexpectedly.
It was quite complete and we—or rather Slafe—recorded the thermometer and barometer readings as well as the wind direction and
altitude, these to be later compared with others taken under normal
conditions at the same hour.

Included in the gear were telescope and binoculars; these we put to our eyes only to realize with surprise that we were located in the center of a hollow bowl perhaps a hundred and fifty or two hundred feet across and that an horizon of upsurging vegetation cut off our view of anything except the sky itself. I could have sworn we had landed on a flat plateau, if indeed the contour had not sloped upward to a cap. How, then, did we come to find ourselves in a depression? Did the grass shift like the sea it resembled? Or—incredible thought—had our weight caused us to sink imperceptibly into a soft and treacherous bed?

I felt my happiness oozing away. What is man, I thought, but a pigmy trapped in a bowl, bounded by an unknown beginning and headed for a concealed destination? It was sweet to be, but whether good or evil lay in the unseen, who knew? Uneasiness, which did not quite displace my earlier buoyancy, took hold of me.

The animals, in contrast, gave no signals of disquiet. They cropped at the grass without nervousness, perhaps more from habit than hunger. They did not seem to be obtaining much sustenance; clearly they found it hard to bite off mouthfuls of forage. Rather, they chewed sidewise, like a cat, at the tough rubbery tendrils.

"I tank I want to go home—anyways I tank I want to get out of dis haole," remarked Gootes. Slafe had unpacked another camera and attached various gadgets to it, pursing his lips and running his hands lovingly over the assembled product before thrusting it downward into the stolons where queer shocks of radiance seemed to indicate he was taking flashlight pictures of the subsurface.

But the sheep and the cameraman could not distract my attention from the appearance of a trap which the basin of grass was assuming, while Gootes was so volatile he couldnt even put on a simulated stoicism. In a panic I started to climb frantically, all the elation of my first encounter with the mound completely evaporated. The goat raised her head to note my undignified scrambling, but the sheep kept up their determined nibbling.

The trough, as I said, could not have been more than a couple of hundred feet across and though the loose runners impeded my progress I must have covered twice the distance to the edge of the rim before I realized it was as far from me as when I had started. Gootes, going in a direction oblique to mine, had no better success. His waving arms and struggling body indicated his awareness of his predicament. Only Slafe was undisturbed, perhaps unconscious of our efforts, for he had taken out still another camera and was lying on his back, pointing it over our heads at the boundary of grass and sky.

Hysteria burned my lungs as I continued the dreamlike battle upward. Fear may have confused me, but it seemed as though the enveloping weed was now positively rather than merely negatively hampering me. The runners whipped around my legs in clinging spirals; the surface, always soft, now developed treacherous spots like quicksands and while one foot remained comparatively secure, the other sank deeply, tripping me. Prone, the entangling fronds caught at my arms and neck; the green blades, no longer tender, scratched my face and smothered my useless cries for help. I sobbed childishly, knowing myself doomed to die in this awful morass, drowned in an unnatural sea.

So despairing were my thoughts that I gave up all struggle and lay there weakly crying when I noticed the grass relaxing its hold, I was sinking in no farther; indeed it seemed the lightest effort would set me free. I rose to my knees and finally to my feet, but I was so shaken by my battle I made no attempt to continue forward, but stood gazing around me marveling that I was still, even if only for a few more moments, alive.

"Belly belong you walk about too much, ay? Him fella looklook no got belly." Gootes had given up his endeavor to reach the rim and apparently struggled all the way over to impart, if I understood his *bêchedemer*, this absurd and selfevident piece of information.

"This is hardly a time for levity," I rebuked him coldly.

"Couldnt think of a better. Reality is escaped through one flippancy or another. Rafe has his—" he waved his hand toward the still industrious cameraman "—and I have mine. I bet W R has a telescope or a periscope or a spectroscope somehow trained on us right now and will see to it the rescue party arrives ten minutes after all life is extinct."

To tell the truth I'd forgotten our expedition was but a stunt initiated by the *Daily Intelligencer* to rebound to its greater publicity. Here in this isolate cup it was difficult to conceive of an anterior existence; I thought of myself, as in some strange manner indigenous to and part of the weed. To recall now that we were here purposefully, that others were concerned with our venture, and that we might reasonably hope for succor extricated me from my subjective entanglement with the grass much as the relaxation of my body a short while before freed me from its physical bonds. I looked hopefully at the empty sky: of course we would get help at any moment.

Once more my spirits were raised; there was no point in trying to get out of the depression now, seeing we could as easily be rescued from one portion of the grass as from another. Again the grass was soft and pleasant to touch and Slafe's preoccupation with his pictures no longer seemed either eccentric or heroic, but rather proper and sensible. Like Alice and the Red Queen, since we had given up trying to reach a particular spot we found ourselves able to travel with comparative ease. We inspected Slafe's activities with interest and responded readily to his autocratic gestures indicating positions and poses we should take in order to be incorporated in his record.

But our gaiety was again succeeded by another period of despondency; we repeated all our antics, struggles and despair. Again I fought madly against the enmeshing weed and again I gave myself up to death only to be revived in the moment of my resignation.

The cameraman was still untouched by the successive waves of fear and joyfulness. Invincibly armored by some strange spirit he kept on and on, although by now I could not understand—in those moments when I could think about anything other than the grass— what new material he could find for his film. Skyward and downward, to all points of the compass, holding his cameras at crazy angles, burlesquing all photographers, his zeal was unabated, unaffected even by the force of the grass.

Our alternating moods underwent a subtle change: the spans of defeat grew longer, the moments of hope more fleeting. The sheep too at last were infected by uneasiness, bleating piteously skyward and making no attempt to nibble any longer. The goat, like Slafe, was unmoved; she disdained the emotional sheep.

And now with horror I suddenly realized that a physical change had marched alongside the fluctuations of our temper. The

circumference of the bowl was the same as at first, but imperceptibly yet swiftly the hollow had deepened, sunk farther from the sky,
the walls had become almost perpendicular and to my terror I
found myself looking upward from the bottom of a pit at the
retreating sky.

I suppose everyone at some time has imagined himself irrevocably imprisoned, cast into some lightless dungeon and left to die.
Such visions implied human instrumentality, human whim; the
most implacable jailer might relent. But this, this was an incarcera-
tion no supplication could end, a doom not to be stayed. Silently,
evenly, unmeasuredly the well deepened and the walls became
more sheer.

Like kittens about to be ignominiously drowned we slid into a
huddled bunch at the bottom of the sack, men and animals equally
helpless and distraught. Fortunately it was during one of the now
rare periods of resurgence that we saw the helicopter, for I do not
think we should have had the spiritual strength needful to help
ourselves had it come during our times of dejection. Gootes and I
yelled and waved our arms frenziedly, while Slafe, exhibiting faint
excitement for the first time, contorted himself to aim the camera
at the machine's belly. Evidently the pilot spotted us without difficulty for the ship came to a hovering rest over the mouth of the well
and a jacobsladder unrolled its length to dangle rope sides and
wooden rungs down to us.

"Snatched from the buzzsaw as the express thundered across
the switch and the water came up to our noses," chanted Gootes.
"W R has a vilely melodramatic sense of timing."

The ladder was nearest Slafe, but working more furiously than
ever, he waved it impatiently aside and so I grasped it and started
upward. The terror of the ascent paradoxically was a welcome one,
for it was the common fear which comes to men on the battlefield
or in the creaking hours of the night, the natural dread of ordinary
perils and not the unmanning panic inspired by the awful unknown within the grass.

The helicopter shuddered and dipped, causing the unanchored
ladder to sway and twist until with each convulsive jerk I expected
to be thrown off. I bruised and burned my palms with the tightness

of my grip, my knees twitched and my face and back and chest were wet. But in spite of all this, waves of thankfulness surged over me.

The roaring and rattling above grew louder and I made my way finally into the open glassfronted cockpit, pulling myself in with the last bit of my strength. For a long moment I lay huddled there, exhausted. My eye took in every trifle, every bolthead, rivet, scratch, dent, indicator, seam and panel, playing with them in my mind, making and rejecting patterns. They were artificial, made on a blessed assemblyline—no terrifying product of nature.

I wondered how so small a space could accommodate us all and was devoutly grateful that I, at least, had achieved safety. Reminded of my companions, I looked out and down. The grass walls towered upward almost within reach; beyond the hole they so unexpectedly made in its surface the weed stretched out levelly, peaceful and inviting. I shuddered and peered down the reversed telescope where the ladder once more hung temptingly before Slafe.

Again he waved it aside. Gootes appeared to argue with him for he shook his head obstinately and went on using his camera. At length the reporter seized him forcibly with a strength I had not known he possessed and boosted him up the first rungs of the ladder. Slafe seemed at last resigned to leave, but he pointed anxiously to his other cameras and cans of film. Gootes nodded energetically and waved the photographer upward.

I saw every detail of what happened then, emphasized and heightened as though revealed through a slowmotion picture. I heard Slafe climb on board and knew that in a few seconds now we would be free and away. I saw the bright sun reflect itself dazzlingly upon the blades of the grass, sloping imperceptibly away to merge with the city it squatted upon in the distance.

The sun where we were was dazzling, I say, but in the hole where Gootes was now tying Slafe's paraphernalia to the ladder, the shadow of the walls darkened it into twilight. I squinted, telepathically urging him to hurry; he seemed slow and fumbling. And then . . .

And then the walls collapsed. Not slowly, not with warning, not dramatically or with trumpets. They came together as silently and naturally as two waves close a trough in the ocean, but without disturbance or upheaval. They fell into an embrace, into a coalescence as inevitable as the well they obliterated was fortuitous. They closed like the jaws of a trap somehow above malevolence, leaving only the top of the ladder projecting upward from the smooth and placid surface of the weed.

Whether in some involuntary recoil the pilot pressed a wrong control or whether the action of the grass itself snatched the ladder from the ship I don't know; but that last bit attached to the machine was torn free and fell upon the green. It was the only thing to mark the spot where the bowl which had held us had been, and it lay, a brown and futile tangle of rope and wood, a helpless speck of artifice on an imperturbable mass of vegetation.

24 Mr Le ffaçasé removed the tube of the dictaphone from his lips as I entered. "Weener, although a rigid adherence to fact compels me to claim some acquaintance with general knowledge and a slight cognizance of abnormal psychology, I must admit bafflement at the spectacle of your mottled complexion once more in these rooms sacred to the perpetuation of truth and the dissemination of enlightenment. Everyday you embezzle good money from this paper under pretense of giving value received, and each day your uselessness becomes more conspicuous. Almost anyone would disapprove the divine choice in the matter of taking Gootes and leaving you alive, and while I know the world suffered not the least hurt by his translation to whatever baroque, noisy and entirely public hell is reserved for reporters, at least he attempted to forge some ostensible return for his paycheck."

"Mr Le ffaçasé," I began indignantly, but he cut me off.

"You unalloyed imbecile," he roared, "at least have the prudence if not the intelligence or courtesy to be silent while your betters are speaking. Gootes was a bloody knave, a lazy, slipshod, slack, tasteless, absurd, fawning, thieving, conniving sloven, but even if he had the energy to make the attempt and a mind to put to it, he could not, in ten lifetimes, become the perfect, immaculate and prototypical idiot you were born."

I don't know how long he would have continued in this insult-

ing vein, but he was interrupted by the concealed telephone.
"What in the name of the ten thousand dubious virgins do you
mean by annoying me?" he bellowed into the mouthpiece. "Yes.
Yes. I know all about deadlines; I was a newspaperman when you
were vainly suckling canine dugs. Are you ambitious to replace me?
Go get with child a mandrakeroot, you, you journalist! I will meet
the *Intelligencer*'s deadline as I did before your father got the first
tepidly lustful idea in his nulliparous head and as I shall after you
have followed your useless testes to a worthy desuetude."

He replaced the receiver and picked up the mouthpiece of the
dictaphone again, paying no further attention to me. He enunci-
ated clearly and precisely, speaking in an even monotone, pausing
not at all, as if reading from some prepared script, though his eyes
were fixed upon a vacant spot where wall and ceiling joined.

"In the death today of Jacson Gootes the *Daily Intelligencer*
lost a son. It is an old and good custom on these solemn occasions
to pause and remember the dead.

"Jacson Gootes was a reporter of exceptional probity, of clear
understanding, of indefatigable effort, and of great native ability.
His serious and straightforward approach to an occupation which to
him was a labor of love was balanced by a sunny yet thoughtful
humor, a combination making his company something to be
sought. Beloved of his fellow workers, no one mourns his loss more
sincerely than the editor through whose hands passed all those
brilliant contributions, now finally marked, as all newspaper copy
is, —30—.

"But though the *Intelligencer* has suffered a personal and
deeply felt bereavement, American journalism has given anothe
warrior on the battlefield. Not by compulsion nor arbitrary selec
tion, but of his own free will, he who serves the public through the
press is a soldier. And as a soldier he is ready at the proper time to
go forward and give up his life if need be.

"No member of a sturdy army was more worthy of a gallant end
than Jacson Gootes. He died, not in some burst of audacity such as
may occasionally actuate men to astonishing feats, but doggedly
and calmly in the line of duty. More than a mere hero, he was a
good newspaperman. W.R.L."

There were tears under my eyelids as the editor concluded his eulogy. Under that gruff and even overbearing exterior must beat a warm and tender heart. You can't go by appearance, I always say, and I felt I would never again be hurt by whatever hasty words he chose to hurl at me.

"Wake up, you moonstruck simpleton, and stop beaming at some private vision. The time has passed for you to live on the bounty of the *Intelligencer* like the bloody mendicant you are. You have outlived your usefulness as the man who started all this fuss; it is no longer good publicity; the matter has become too serious.

"No, Weener, from now on, beneath your unearned byline the public will know you only as the first to set foot upon this terra incognita, this verdant isle which flourishes senselessly where only yesterday Hollywood flourished senselessly. So rest no more upon your accidental laurels, but transform yourself into what nature never intended, a useful member of the community. I will make a newspaperman of you, Weener, if I have to beat into your head an entire typefont, from fourpoint up to and including those rare boldfaced letters we keep in the cellar to announce on our final page one the end of the world.

"You will cover the grass as before and you will bring or send or cause in some other manner to be transmitted to me copy without a single adjective or adverb, containing nothing more lethal than verbs, nouns, prepositions and conjunctions, stating facts and only facts, clearly and distinctly in the least possible number of words compatible with the usages of English grammar. You will do this daily and conscientiously, Weener, on pain of instant dismemberment, to say nothing of crucifixion and the death of a thousand cuts."

"The *Weekly Ruminant* and the *Honeycomb* have found little pieces of mine, written without special instructions, suitable for their columns," I mentioned defensively.

He threw himself back in his chair and stared at me with such concentrated fury I thought he would burst the diamond stud loose from his shirtband. "The *Weekly Ruminant*," he informed me, "was founded by a parsimonious whoremaster whose sanctimonious rantings in public were equaled only by his private impieties. It was brought to greatness—if inflated circulation be a synonym—by a veritable journalistic pimp who pandered to the public taste for literary virgins by bribing them to commit their perverse acts in full view. It is now carried on by a spectral corporation, losing circulation at the same rate a haemophilic loses blood.

"As for the *Honeycomb*, it is enough to say that careful research proves its most absorbing reading to be the 'throw away your truss' ads. Is it not natural, Weener, that two such journals of taste and enlightenment should appreciate your efforts? Unfortunately the *Daily Intelligencer* demands accounts written in intelligible English above the level of fourthgrade grammarschool."

I would have been shocked beyond measure at his libelous smirching of honored names and hurt as well by his slighting reference to myself had I not known from the revealing editorial he had dictated what a sympathetic and kindly nature was really his and how he might, beneath this cynical pose, have an admiration great as mine for the characters he had just slandered.

"You will be the new Peter Schlemihl, Weener; from now on you will go forth without a ghost and any revision essential to your puny assault upon the Republic of Letters will be done by me and God help you if I find much to do, for my life is passing and I must have time to read the immortal Hobbes before I die."

In spite of all he'd said I couldn't help but believe Mr Le ffaçasé realized my true worth—or why did he confer on me what was practically a promotion? I was therefore enboldened to suggest the cancellation of the unjust paycut, but this innocent remark called forth such a vituperative stream of epithet I really thought the apoplexy Gootes had predicted was about to strike and I hurried from his presence lest I be blamed for bringing it on.

25 A little reading brought me uptodate on the state of the grass as a necessary background for my new responsibility. It was now shaped like a great, irregular crescent with one tip at Newhall, broadening out to bury the San Fernando Road; stretching over the Santa Monica Mountains from Beverly Glen to the Los Angeles River. Its fattest part was what had once been Hollywood, Beverly Hills and the socalled Wilshire district. The right arm of the semicircle, more slender than the left, curled crookedly eastward along Venice Boulevard, in places only a few blocks wide.

It severed the downtown district from the manufacturing area, crossing the river near the Ninth Street bridge and swallowing the great Searsroebuck store like a capsule. The office of the *Daily Intelligencer*, like the Civic Center, was unthreatened and able to function, but we were without water and gas, though the electric service, subject to annoying interruptions, was still available.

Already arrangements were being completed to move the paper to Pomona, where the mayor and councilmanic offices also intended to continue. For there was no hiding the fact that the city was being surrendered to the weed. Eastward and southward the homeless and the alarmed journeyed carrying the tale of a city besieged and gutted in little more than the time it would have taken a human army to fight the necessary preliminaries and bring up its big guns.

On trains and buses, by bicycles and on foot, the exodus moved. Those who could afford it left their ravished homes swiftly behind by air and to these fortunate ones the way north was not closed, as it was to the earthbound, by the weed's overrunning of the highways. Usedcardealers sold out their stocks at inflated figures and a ceilingprice had to be put on the gasoline supplied to those retreating from the grass.

Though only a fragment of the city had been lost, all industry had come to a practical standstill. Workers did not care to leave homes which might be grassbound by nightfall; employers could not manufacture without backlog of materials, for a dwindling market, and without transportation for their products. Services were so crippled as to be barely existent and with the failure of the watersupply, epidemics, mild at first, broke out and the diseases were carried and spread by the refugees.

Cattlemen, uncertain there would be either stockyards or working butchers, held back their shipments. Truckfarmers found it simpler and more profitable to supply local depots catering at fantastic prices to the needs of the fugitives, than to depend on railroads which were already overstrained and might consign their highly perishable goods to rot on a siding. Los Angeles began to starve. Housewives rushed frantically to clean out the grocer's shelves, but this was living off their own fat and even the most farsighted of hoarders could provide for no more than a few weeks of future.

So even those not directly evicted or frightened by its proximity began moving away from the grass. But they still had possessions and they wanted to take them along, all of them, down to the obsolescent console radio in grandma's room, the busted mantelclock—a weddingpresent from Aunt Minnie—in the garage and the bridgelamp without a shade which had so long rested in the mopcloset. All of this taxed an already overstrained transportation system. Since it was entirely a oneway traffic, charges were naturally doubled and even then shippers were reluctant to risk the return of their equipment to the threatened zone. The greed to take along every last bit of impedimenta dwindled under the impact of necessity; possessions were scrutinized for what would be least missed, then for what could be got along without; for the absolutely essential, and finally for things so dear it was not worth going if they were left behind. This last category proved surprisingly small, compact enough to be squeezed into the family car—"Junior can sit on the box of fishingtackle—it's flat—and hold the birdcage on his lap"—as it made ready to join the procession crawling along the clogged highways.

Time, reporting the progress of the weed, said in part: "Death, as it must to all, came last week to cult-harboring, movie-producing Los Angeles. The metropolis of the southwest (pop. 3,012,910) died gracelessly, undignifiedly, as its blood oozed slowly away. A shell remained: downtown district, suburbs, beaches, sprawling South and East sides, but the spirit, heart, brain, lungs and liver were gone; swallowed up, Jonah-wise by the advance of the terrifying Bermuda grass (TIME Aug. 10). Still at his post was sunk-eyed W. (for William) R. (for Rufus) Le ffaçasé (pronounced L'Fass-uh-say), prolix, wide-read editor of the Los Angeles *Intelligencer.* Till the last press stopped the *Intelligencer* would continue to disseminate the news. Among those remaining was Le ffaçasé's ace-reporter, Jacson C. (for Crayman) Gootes, 28. Gootes' permanent beat: the heart of the menacing grass where he met his death."

Under Religion, *Time* had another note about the weed. "Harassed Angelinos, distracted & terrified by encroaching *Cynodon dactylon* (TIME Aug. 10) now smothering their city (see National Affairs) were further distracted when turning on their radios (those still working) last week. The nasal, portentous boom of the evangelist calling himself Brother Paul (real name: Algernon Knight Mood) announced the 2nd Advent. It was taking place in the heart of the choking grass. What brought death and disaster to the country's 3rd city offered hope and bliss to followers of Brother Paul. 'Sell all you have,' advised the radiopreacher, 'fly to your Savior who is gathering His true disciples at this moment in the very center of the grass. Do not fear, for He will sustain and comfort you in the thicket through which the unsaved cannot pass.' At last report countless followers had been forcibly restrained from self-immolation in the *Cynodon dactylon*, unnumbered others gone joyfully to their beatification. Not yet reported as joining his Savior: Brother Paul."

Under People: "Admitted to the Relief rolls of San Diego County this week were Adam Dinkman & wife, whose front lawn (TIME Aug. 3) was the starting point of the plaguing grass. Said Mrs. Dinkman, 'The government ought to pay . . .' Said Adam Dinkman, '. . . it's a terrible thing . . .'"

I resolved to send the Dinkmans some money as soon as I could possibly afford it. I made a note to this effect in a pocket memorandumbook, feeling the glow of worthy sacrifice, and then went out and got in my car. It was all right to digest facts and figures about the weed from the printed page, but it was necessary to see again its physical presence before writing anything for so critical an editor as W R Le ffaçasé.

I drove through the Second Street tunnel and out Beverly Boulevard. There, several miles from the most advanced runners of the grass, the certainty of its coming lay like a smothering blanket upon the unnaturally silent district. There was no traffic on my side of the street and only a few lastminute straggling jalopies, loaded down with shameless bedding and bundles, coughed their way frantically eastward.

Those few shops still unaccountably open were bare of goods and the idle proprietors walked periodically to the front to scan the western sky to assure themselves the grass was not yet in sight. But most of the stores were closed, their windows broken, their signs already tarnished and decrepit with the age which seems to come so swiftly upon a defunct business. The sidewalks were littered with rubbish, diagonally flattened papers, broken boxes, odd shoes. Garbagecans, instead of standing decorously in alleys or shame-facedly along the curb, sprawled in lascivious abandon over the pavements, their contents strewn widely. Dogs and cats, deserted by fond owners, snarled and fought over choicer tidbits. I had not realized how many people in the city kept pets until the time came to leave them behind.

At Vermont Avenue I came upon what I was sure was a new nucleus, a lawn green and tall set between others withered and yellow, but I did not even bother reporting this to the police for I knew that before long the main body would take it to its bosom. And now, looking westward, I could see the grass itself, a half mile away at Normandie. It rose high in the air, dwarfing the buildings in its path, blotting out the mountains behind, and giving the illusion of rushing straight at me.

I turned the car north, not with the idea of further observation, but because standing still in the face of that towering palisade seemed somehow to invite immediate destruction. I drove slowly and thoughtfully and then at Melrose the grass came in sight again, creeping down from Los Feliz. I turned back toward the Civic Center. It would not be more than a couple of days at most, now, before even downtown was gone.

26 During my drive several walkers loaded with awkward bundles raised imploring thumbs for a ride, but know-ing to what lengths desperation will drive people and not wishing to be robbed of my car, I had pressed my foot down and driven on. But now as I went along Temple near Rampart a beautiful woman, incongruously—for it was in the middle of a hot October—dressed in a fur coat, and with each gloved hand grasping the handle of a suitcase, stepped in front of me and I had to jam on the brakes to avoid running over her.

The car stopped, radiator almost touching her, but she made no attempt to move. A small hat with a tiny fringe of veil concealed her eyes, but her sullen mouth looked furiously at me as rigidly clutching her luggage she barred my path. Fearing some trap, I turned off the ignition and unobtrusively slid the keys into a sidepocket before getting out and going to her.

"Excuse me, miss. Can I help you?"

She threw her head back and her eyes, brown and glistening, appraised me through heavily painted lashes. I stood there stiffly, uncomfortable under her gaze till I suddenly remembered my hat and lifted it with an awkward bow. This seemed to satisfy her, for still without speaking she nodded and thrust the two suitcases at me. Not knowing what else to do, I took them from her and she promptly, after smoothing her gloves, walked toward the passenger's side of the car.

"You want me to take you somewhere, miss?" I inquired quite superfluously.

She bent her head the merest fraction and then rested her fingers on the doorhandle, waiting for me to open it for her. I ran as fast as I could with the bags—they were beautifully matched expensive luggage—to put them in the turtle and then had to make myself still more ridiculous by running back for the forgotten key resting in the sidepocket. When I had finally stowed away the baggage and opened the door for her she got in with the barest of condescending nods for my efforts and sat staring ahead.

I drove very slowly, nipping off little glances of her profile as we moved along. Her cheeks were smooth as a chinadoll's, her nose the chiseled replica of some lovely antique marble, her mouth a living study of rounded lines; never had I been so close to such an alluring woman. We reached the Civic Center and I automatically headed for the *Intelligencer* building. But I could not bear to part company so quickly and so I turned left instead, out Macy Street.

Now we found ourselves caught in the traffic snailing eastward. In low gear I drove a block, then stopped and waited till a clear ten feet ahead permitted another painfully slow forward motion. Still my passenger had no word to say but kept staring ahead though she could see nothing before her except the trunkladen rearend of a tottery ford long past its majority.

"You," I stumbled, "I—that is, I mean wasnt there somewhere in particular you wanted to go?"

She nodded, still without looking at me, and for the first time spoke.

Her voice was deep and had the timbre of some old bronze bell. "Yuma," she said.

"Yuma, Arizona?" I asked stupidly.

Again she nodded faintly. In a panic I reckoned the contents of my wallet. About forty dollars, I thought—no, thirty. Would that take us to Yuma? Barely, perhaps, and I should have to wire the *Intelligencer* for money to return. Besides, in the present condition of the roads the journey would be a matter of days and I knew she would accept nothing but the very best. How could I do it? Should I return to the *Intelligencer* office and try to get an advance on next week's salary? I had heard from more than one disgruntled reporter that it was an impossibility. Good heavens, I thought, I shall lose her.

Whatever happened I must take her as far as I could; I must not let her go before I was absolutely forced to. This resolution made, my first thought was to cut the time, for poking along in this packed mass I was burning gasoline without getting anywhere. Taking advantage of my knowledge of the sideroads, I turned off at the first chance and was able to resume a normal speed as I avoided towns and main highways.

Still she continued silent, until at length, passing orangegroves heavy with coppery fruit, I ventured to speak myself. "My name is Albert Weener. Bert."

The right rear tire kicked up some dust as I nervously edged off the road. Somewhere overhead a plane ripped through the hot silk of the sky.

"Uh . . . what . . . uh . . . won't you tell me yours?"

Still facing ahead, she replied, "It isnt necessary."

After a few more miles I ventured again. "You live—were living in Los Angeles?"

She shook her head impatiently.

Well, I thought, really . . . ! Then: poor thing, she's probably terribly upset. Home and family lost perhaps. Money gone. Destitute. Going East, swallowing pride, make a new start with the help of unsympathetic relatives. She has only me to depend on—I must not fail her. Break the ice, whatever attitude her natural pride dictates, offer your services.

"I'm on the *Daily Intelligencer*," I said. "I'm the man who first walked on top of the grass."

Ten miles later I inquired, "Wouldn't you be more comfortable with that heavy fur coat off? I can put it in the back with your luggage and it won't be crushed."

She shook her head more impatiently.

Suddenly I remembered the car radio installed a few days before. A little cheerful music calms the soul. I turned it on and got a band playing a brandnew hit, "Green as Grass."

"Oh, no. No noise."

Of course. How thoughtless of me. The very word "grass" reminded her of her tragic situation. I kicked myself for my tactlessness.

We skirted Riverside and joined the highway again at Beaumont where we were unavoidably packed into the slowmoving mass. "I'm sorry," I apologized, "but I can take a chance again at Banning and drive up into the mountains to get away from this."

An hour later I suggested stopping for something to eat. She shook her head. "But it's getting late," I said. "Pretty soon we shall have to think about stopping for the night."

She raised her left hand imperatively. "Drive all night."

This would certainly solve part of my financial problem, but I was hungry and unreasonably more irritated by her refusal of food than her unsociability. "I have to eat, even if you don't," I told her rudely. "I'm going to stop at the next place I see." With the same left hand she made a gesture of resignation.

I pulled up before the roadside cafe. "Won't you change your mind and come in? At least for a cup of coffee?"

"No."

I went in angrily and ate. Who was she, to treat me like a hired chauffeur? A mere pickup, I raged, a stray woman found on a street. By God, she would have the courtesy at least to address me, her benefactor, civilly or else I'd abandon her here on the highway and return to Los Angeles. I finished my meal full of determination and strode back purposefully toward the car. She was still sitting rigid, staring through the windshield. I got in.

"You know—" I began.

She did not hear me. I turned on the ignition, pressed the starterbutton, and drove ahead.

Soddeneyed with lack of sleep and outraged at her taciturnity. I breakfasted alone on the soggiest wheatcakes and the muddiest coffee I ever demeaned my stomach with. The absence of my customary morning paper added the final touch to my wretchedness. But one would have thought to look at my companion that she had been refreshed by a lengthy repose, had bathed at leisure, and eaten the most delicate of continental breakfasts. There was not a smudge on her suede gloves nor a speck upon her small hat and the mascara on her eyelashes might have been renewed but a moment before.

The road curved through vast hummocks of sand, which for no good reason reminded me of the grass in its early stages. Reminded, I wanted to know what the latest news was, how far the weed had progressed in the night. Thoughtlessly, without remembering her interdiction, I turned the knob. "Kfkfkk," squeaked the radio.

"Please," she said, in anything but a pleading tone, and turned it off.

Well, I thought, this is certainly going too far. I opened my mouth to voice the angry words but a look at her stopped me. I couldnt help but feel her imperviousness was fragile, that harsh speech might shatter a calm too taut to be anything but hysterical. I drove on without speaking until the hummocks gave way again to smooth desert. "We'll soon be in Yuma," I announced. "Aren't you going to tell me your name?"

"It isnt important," she repeated.

"But it's important to me," I told her boldly. "I want to know who the beautiful lady was whom I drove from Los Angeles to Yuma."

She shook her head irritably and we crossed the bridge into Arizona.

"All right, this is Yuma. Now where?"

"Here."

"Right here in the middle of the road?"

She nodded. I looked helplessly at her, but her gaze was still fixed ahead. Resignedly I got out, took her bags from the turtle and set them beside the road, opened the door. She descended, smoothed her gloves, straightened the edge of her veil, brushed an

immaterial speck from her coat and, after the briefest of acknowl-
edging nods, picked up her grips.

"But . . . can't I carry them for you?"

She did not even answer this with her usual headshake, but
began walking resolutely back over the way we had come. Bewildered, I watched her a moment and then got into the car and
turned it around, trying to keep her in sight in the rearview mirror
as I did so. It was an awkward procedure on a highway heavy with
traffic. By the time I had reversed my direction she was gone.

27 Due either to Le ffaçasé's perverse sense of humor or,
what is more likely, his excessive meanness with money,
my collect telegram asking for funds to return from Yuma received
the following ridiculous reply: KNOW NO SANGUINARY
WEENER INTELLIGENCER NO ELEEMOSYNARY IN-
STITUTION EAT CAKE. The meaning of the last two words
escaped me and it was possible they were added purely to make the
requisite ten. At all events Le ffaçasé's parsimony made a very
inconvenient and unpleasant trip back for me, milestoned by my
few valuable possessions pawned with suspicious and grasping ser-
vicestation owners.

When I left, a map of the downtown district would have
resembled the profile of a bowl. Now it was a bottle with only a
narrow neck still clear. The weed had flung itself upon Pasadena
and was curving back along Huntington Drive, while to the south
the opposing pincer was feeling its way along Soto Street into Boyle
Heights. It was only with the greatest difficulty that I passed
through the police lines into the doomed district.

If I had thought deserted Beverly Boulevard a sad sight only
three days before, what can I say about my impression of the city's
nerve center in its last hour? Abandoned automobiles stood in the
streets at the spot where they had run out of gas or some minor
mechanical failure had halted them. Dead streetcars, like big game
stopped short by the hunter's bullet, stayed where the failure of
electricpower caught them. The tall buildings reeked of desertion
as if their emptying had dulled some superficial gloss and made
them dim and colorless.

But contrast the dying city with the wall of living green, north, west, and south, towering ever higher and preparing to carry out the sentence already passed, and the victim becomes insignificant in the presence of the executioner. I was reminded of the well where Gootes died for here except on one small side the grass rose like the inside of a stovepipe to the sky; but I suffered neither the same despair nor the unaccountable elation I had upon that hill, perhaps because the trough was so much bigger or because the animate thing was not beneath my feet to communicate those feelings directly.

There had evidently been some looting, not so much from greed as from the natural impulse of human nature to steal and act lawlessly as soon as police vigilance is relaxed. Here and there stores were opened nakedly to the street, their contents spilled about. But such scenes were surprisingly rare, the hopelessness of transporting stolen or any other possessions acting as a greater deterrent than morality. One way or another, as the saying has it, crime does not pay.

Few people were visible and these were divided sharply into two categories: those clearly intent upon concluding some business, rushing furiously, papers, briefcases or articles of worth in their hands; and those obviously without purpose, dazed, listless, stumbling against the curbstones as they shambled along, casting furtive glances toward the green glacier in the background.

The newspaper office contained only people of the first type. Le ffaçasé had come out of his sanctuary for the first time within memory of anybody on the staff. Still collarless, snuffbox in hand, he napoleonically directed the removal of those valuables without which the newspaper could not continue. He was cool, efficient, seemed to have eyes everywhere and know everything going on in the entire building. He spent neither greetings nor reproaches on me, indeed was not looking in my direction but somehow sensed my presence through his back, for he said without turning round, "Weener, if you have concluded your unaccountable peregrinations remove the two files marked E1925 and E1926 to Pomona. If you mislay one scrap of paper they contain—the bartering of a thousand Weeners being an inadequate equivalent—your miserable substance will be attached to four tractors headed in divergent directions. Don't come back here, but attempt for once to palliate the offense of your birth and go interview that Francis female. Interview her, not yourself. Bring back a story, complete and terse, or commit the first sensible act of your life with any weapon you choose and charge the instrument to the *Intelligencer.*"

"I havent the slightest idea where Miss Francis is to be found."

He took a pinch of snuff, issued orders to four or five other people and continued calmly, "I am not conducting a school of journalism; if I were I should have a special duncecap imported solely for your use. The lowest copyboy knows better than to utter such an inanity. You will find the Francis and interview her. I'm busy. Get the hell out of here and handle those files carefully if you value that cadaver you probably think of as the repository of your soul."

I am not a drayman and I resented the menial duty of sliding those heavy filecases down four flights of stairs; but at a time like this, I thought philosophically, a man has duties he cannot shirk; besides, Le ffaçasé was old, I could afford to humor him even if it meant demeaning myself.

With one of the cases in back, I sadly regarded the other one occupying most of the front seat. If she had at least given me her name I would have searched and searched until I found her. This train of thought reminded me of Le ffaçasé's command to find Miss Francis and so I concentrated my attention on getting away from the *Intelligencer* office.

It was no light labor; the stalled streetcars and automobiles presented grave hazards to the unwary. The air smelt of death, and nervously I pressed the accelerator to get away quickly from this tomb. I crossed the dry riverbed and made my way slowly to Pomona, delivered the files, and reluctantly began seeking Miss Francis.

28 It was practically impossible to discover any one person among so many scattered and disorganized people, but chance aided my native intelligence and perseverance. Only the day before she had been involved with an indignant group of the homeless who attributed their misfortunes to her and overcoming their natural American chivalry toward the weaker sex had tried to revenge themselves. I was therefore able to locate her, not ten miles from the temporary headquarters of the *Daily Intelligencer.*

Her laboratory was an abandoned chickenhouse which must have reminded her constantly of her lost kitchen. She looked almost jaunty as she greeted me, a cobweb from the roof of the decaying shed caught in her hair. "I have no profitable secrets to market, Weener—youre wasting your time with me."

"I am not here as a salesman, Miss Francis," I said. "The *Daily Intelligencer* would like to tell its readers how you are getting on with your search for some cure for the grass."

"You talk as if *Cynodon dactylon* were a disease. There is no cure for life but death."

Since she was going to be so touchy about the grass—as if it were a personal possession—(why, I thought, it's as much mine as hers)—I substituted a more diplomatic form of words.

"Well, I have made an interesting discovery," she conceded grudgingly and pointed to a row of flowerpots, her eyes lighting as she scanned the single blades of grass perhaps an inch and a half high growing in each. The sight meant nothing to me and she must have gathered as much from my expression.

"*Cynodon dactylon*," she explained, "germinated from seeds borne by the inoculated plant. Obviously the omnivorous capacity has not been transmitted to offspring."

This was probably fascinating to her or a gardener or botanist, but I couldnt see how it concerned me or the *Daily Intelligencer.*

"It could be a vitamin defiency," she muttered incomprehensibly, "or evasion of the laws regarding compulsory education. These plants indicate the affected grass may propagate its abnormal condition only through the extension of the already changed stolons or rhizomes. It means that only the parent, which is presumably not immortal, is aberrant. The offspring is no different from the weed householders have been cursing ever since the Mission Fathers enslaved the Digger Indians."

"Why, then," I exclaimed, suddenly enlightened, "all we have to do is wait until the grass dies."

"Or until it meets some insuperable object," supplemented Miss Francis.

My faith in insuperable objects had been somewhat shaken. "How long do you think it will be before the grass dies?" I asked her.

She regarded me gravely, as though I had been a child asking an absurd question. "Possibly a thousand years."

My enthusiasm was dampened. But after leaving her I remembered how certain types of people always look for the dark side of things. It costs no more to be an optimist than a pessimist; it is sunshine grows flowers, not clouds; and if Miss Francis chose to think the grass might live a thousand years I was equally free to think it might die next week. Thus heartened by this bit of homely philosophy, just as valid as any of the stuff entombed in wordy books, I wrote up my interview, careful to guide myself by all the stifling strictures and adjurations impressed upon me by the tyrannically narrowminded editor. If I may anticipate the order of events, it appeared next day in almost recognizable form under the heading, ABNORMAL GRASS TO DIE SOON, SAYS ORIGINATOR.

29 The small city of Pomona was swollen to boomtown size by the excursion there of so many enterprises forced from Los Angeles. Ordinary citizens without heavy responsibilities when uprooted thought only of putting as much distance as possible between themselves and their persecutor; but the officials, the industrialists, the businessmen, the staffs of great newspapers hovered close by, like small boys near the knothole in the ballpark fence from which theyd been banished by an officious cop.

The *Intelligencer* was lodged over the printshop of a local tributary which had agreed to the ousting with the most hypocritical assurances of joy at the honor done them and payment—in the smallest possible type—by the addition to the great newspaper's masthead of the words, "And Pomona *Post-Telegram*."

Packed into this inadequate space were the entire staff and files of the metropolitan daily. No wonder the confusion obviated all possibility of normal routine. In addition, the disruption of railroad schedules made the delivery of mail a hazard rather than a certainty. Perhaps this was why, weeks after they were due, it was only upon my return from interviewing Miss Francis I received my checks from the *Weekly Ruminant* and the *Honeycomb*.

It may have been the boomtown atmosphere I have already mentioned or because at the same time I got my weekly salary; at any event, moved by an unaccountable impulse I took the two checks to a barbershop where, perhaps incongruously, a wellknown firm of Los Angeles stockbrokers had quartered themselves. I forced the checks upon a troubledlooking individual—too taciturn to be mistaken for the barber—and mumbling, "Buy me all the shares of Consolidated Pemmican and Allied Concentrates this will cover," hurried out before sober thought could cause me to change my mind.

For certainly this was no investment my cool judgment would approve, but the wildest hunch, causing me to embark on what was no less than a speculation. I went back to the desk I shared with ten others, bitterly regretting the things I might have bought with the money and berating myself for my rashness. Only the abnormal pressure of events could have made me yield to so irrational an impulse.

In the meantime things happened fast. Barely had the tardiest *Intelligencer* employees got away when the enveloping jaws of the weed closed tight, catching milions of dollars' worth of property within. The project to bomb the grass out of existence, dormant for some weeks, could no longer be denied.

Even its most ardent advocates, however, now conceded reluctantly that ordinary explosives would be futile—more than futile, an assistance to the growth by scattering the propagating fragments. For the first time people began talking openly of using the outlawed atomicbomb.

The instant response to this suggestion was an overwhelming opposition. The President, Congress, the Army, Navy and public opinion generally agreed that the weapon was too terrible to use in so comparatively trivial a cause.

But the machinery for some type of bombing had been set in motion and had to be used. The fuel was stored, the airfields jammed, all available planes, new, old, obsolescent and obsolete assembled, and for three days and nights the great fleets shuttled backandforth over the jungled area, dropping thousands of tons of incendiary bombs. Following close behind, still more planes dropped cargoes of fuel to feed the colossal bonfire.

Inverted lightning flashes leapt upward, and after them great, rolling white, yellow, red and blue flames. The smoke, the smell of roasting vegetation, the roar and crackle of the conflagration, and the heat engendered were all noticeable as far away as Capistrano and Santa Barbara.

Down from the sky, through the surface of the grass, the incendiaries burned great patches clear to the earth. The weed, which had resisted fire so contemptuously before, suddenly became inflammable and burned like celluloid for days. Miles of twisted stems, cleaned of blade and life, exposed tortured nakedness to aerial reconnoiter. Bald spots the size of villages appeared, black and smoldering; the shape of the mass was altered and altered again, but when, long after, the last spark flickered out and the last ember grew dull, the grass itself, torn and injured, but not defeated or even noticeably beaten back, remained. It had been a brilliant performance—and an ineffective one.

The failure of the incendiary bombing not only produced ruefully triumphant Itoldyousos from disgruntled and doubly outraged propertyowners, but a new crop of bids for the *Intelligencer's* reward to the developer of a saving agent. From suggested emigrations to Mars and giant magnifying glasses set up to wither the grass with the aid of the sun, they ranged to projects for cutting a canal clear around the weed from San Francisco Bay to the Colorado River and letting the Pacific Ocean do the rest. Another solution envisaged shutting off all light from the grass by means of innumerable radiobeams to interrupt the sun's rays in the hope that with an inability to manufacture chlorophyll an atrophy would set in. Several contestants urged inoculating other grasses, such as bamboo, with the Metamorphizer, expecting the two giants of vegetation, like the Kilkenny cats, would end by devouring each other. This proposal received such wide popular support there is reason to believe it got some serious consideration in official quarters, but it was eventually abandoned on the ground that while it gave only a single slim chance of success it certainly doubled the potential growth to contend with. The analogy of a backfire in forest conflagrations was deemed poetic but inapplicable.

More comparatively prosaic courses included walling in the grass with concrete; the Great Wall of China was the only work of man visible from the moon; were Americans to let backward China best them? A concrete wall only a mile high and half a mile thick could be seen by any curious astronomer on the planet Venus—assuming Venerians to be afflicted with terrestrial vices—and would cost no more than a very small war, to say nothing of employing thousands who would otherwise dissipate the taxpayers' money on Relief. A variant of this plan was to smother the weed with tons of dry cement and sand from airplanes; the rainy season, due to begin in a few months, would add the necessary water and the grass would then be encased in a presumably unbreakable tomb.

But the most popular suggestion embodied the use of salt, ordinary table salt. From their own experience in backyard and garden, eager men and women wrote in urging this common mineral be used to end the menace of the grass. "It will Kill ennything," wrote an Imperial Valley farmer. "Its lethal effect on plantlife is instantaneous," agreed a former Beverly Hills resident. "I know there is not anything like Salt to destroy Weeds" was part of a long and rambling letter on blueruled tabletpaper, "In the June of 1926 or 7 I cannot remember exactly it may have been 28 I accidentally dropped Salt on a beautiful Plumbago . . ."

It was proposed to spray the surface, to drive tunnels through the roots to conduct brine, to bombard sectors with sixteeninch guns firing shrapnel loaded with salt, to isolate by means of a wide saline band the whole territory, both occupied and threatened. Salt enthusiasts argued that nothing except a few million tons of an inexpensive mineral would be wasted if an improbable failure occurred, but if successful in stopping the advance the country could wait safely behind its rampart till some weapon to regain the overrun area was found.

But the salt advocates didnt have everything their own way. There arose a bitter antisalt faction taking pleasure at hurling sneers at these optimistic predictions and delight in demolishing the arguments. Miss Francis, they said, who ought to know more about it than anyone else, claimed the grass would break down even the most stable compound and take what it needed. Well, salt was a compound, wasnt it? If the prosalt fanatics had their way they would just be offering food to a hungry plant. The salt supporters asked what proof Miss Francis had ever advanced that the plant

absorbed everything or indeed that her Metamorphizer had anything to do with metabolism and had not merely induced some
kind of botanical giantism? The antisalts, jeering at their enemies
as Salinists and Salinites, promptly threw away Miss Francis' hypo-
thetical support and relied instead on the proposition that if the salt
were to be efficacious—an unlikely contingency—it would have to
reach the roots and if crudeoil, poured on when the plant was
young, had not done so what possible hope could the prosalt cranks
offer for their panacea now the rampant grass was grown to its
present proportions?

The salt argument cut society in half. Learned doctors battled
in the columns of scientific journals. Businessmen dictated sputter-
ing letters to their secretaries. Housewives wrote newspapers or
argued heatedly in the cornergrocery. Radiocommentators cautiously skirted the edge of controversy and more than one enthusi-
ast had to be warned by his sponsor. Fistfights started in taverns
over the question and judicious bartenders served beer without
offering the objectionable seasoning with it.

The *Intelligencer*, at the start, was vehemently antisalt. "Is
there an American Cato," Le ffaçasé asked, "to call for the final
ignominy suffered by Carthage to be applied, not to the land of an
enemy, but to our own?" Shortly after this editorial, entitled "Carthage, California" appeared, the *Intelligencer* swung to the opposite side and Le ffaçasé offered the prosalt argument under the
heading "Lot's Wife."

The Daughters of the American Revolution declared themselves in favor of salt and refused the use of Constitution Hall to an
antisalt meeting. Stung, the Central Executive Committee of the
Communist party circulated a manifesto declaring the use of salt
was an attempt to encircle, not the grass, for that was a mere
subterfuge of imperialism, but the Soviet Union; and called upon
all its peripheral fringe to write their congressmen and demonstrate
against the saline project. From India the aged Mohandas Gandhi
asked in piping tones why such a valuable adjunct was to be wasted
in rich America while impoverished ryots paid a harsh tax on this
necessity of life? And the Council of Peoples' Commissars, careless
of the action of the American Stalinists, offered to sell the United
States all its surplus salt. The herringpicklers of Holland struck in a

body while the American salt refiners bid as one to produce on a costplus basis.

This last was a clincher and the obscurantic antisalts received the deathblow they richly deserved. The Communist party reversed themselves swiftly. All respectable and patriotic people lined up behind salt. With such popular unanimity apparent, the government could do no less than take heed. A band twenty miles wide, stretching from Oceanside to the Salton Sea, from the Salton Sea to the little town of Mojave and from there to Ventura, was marked out on maps to be saltsown by the very same bombercommand which had dropped the spectacular but futile incendiaries. The triumph of the salt people was ungenerous in its enthusiasm; the disgruntled antisalts, now a mere handful of diehards publishing an esoteric press, muttered everyone would be sorry, wait and see.

30 The grass itself waited for nothing. It seemed to take new strength from the indignities inflicted upon it and it increased, if anything, its tempo of growth. It plunged into the ocean in a dozen spots at once. It swarmed over sand which had never known anything but cactus and the Sierra Madres became great humps of green against the skyline. This last conquest shocked those who had thought the mountains immune in their inhospitable heights. *Cynodon dactylon*, uninoculated, had always shunned coldness, though it survived some degrees of frost. The giant growth, however, seemed to be less subject to this inhibition, though it too showed slower progress in the higher and colder regions. The *Intelligencer* planned to move from Pomona to San Bernardino and if necesary to Victorville.

Daily Le ffaçasé became a sterner taskmaster, a more pettishly exacting employer. By the living guts of William Lloyd Garrison, he raged, had no one ever driven the simple elements of punctuation into my bloody head? Had no schoolmaster in moments of heroic enthusiasm attempted to pound a few rules of rhetoric through my incrassate skull? Had I never heard of taste? Was the word "style" outside my macilent vocabulary? What the devil did I mean by standing there with my mouth open, exposing my unfortunate teeth for all the world to see? Was it possible for any allegedly human to be as addlepated as I? And had I been thrust from my mother's womb—I suppress his horrible adjectives—only to torment and afflict his longsuffering editorial patience?

A hundred times I was tempted to sever my connection with this journalistic autocrat. My column was widely read and two publishinghouses had approached me with the idea of putting out a book, any editorial revision and emendations to be taken care of by them without disturbing me at all. I could have allied myself with almost any paper in the country, undoubtedly at better than the meager stipend Le ffaçasé doled out to me.

But I think loyalty is one of the most admirable of virtues and it was not in my nature to desert the *Intelligencer*—certainly not till I could secure a lengthy and ironclad contract, such as for some reason other papers seemed unwilling to offer me. In accord with this innate loyalty of mine—I take no credit for it, I was born that way—I did not balk at the assignments given me though they ranged from the hazardous to the absurd.

One of the more pleasant of these excursions thought up by Mr Le ffaçasé was to fly over the grass and to Catalina, embark on a chartered boat there and survey the parts of the coast now overrun. A fresh point of observation. Accompanying me was the movie-cameraman, Rafe Slafe, as uncommunicative and earnest in his medications as before.

It was a sad sight to see neat rectangular patterns of roads and highways, cultivated fields and orangegroves, checkered towns and sprawling suburbs come to an abrupt stop where they were blotted out by the regimented uniformity of the onrushing grass. For miles we flew above its dazzling green until our eyes ached from the sameness and our minds were dulled from the lack of variety below. On the sea far ahead a frothing whitecap broke the monotony of color, a flyingfish jumped out of the water to glisten for a moment in the sun, loose seaweed floated on the surface, to change in some degree the intense blue. But here below no alien touch lightened the unnatural homogeneity. No solitary tree broke this endless pasture, now healed of the wounds inflicted by the incendiary bombing, no saltlick, wandering stream of struggling bush enlivened this prairie. There was not even an odd conformation, a higher clump here or there, a dead patch to relieve the unimaginative symmetry. I have read of men going mad in solitary confinement from looking at the same unchanging walls; well, here was a solitary cell hundreds of miles in area and its power to destroy the mind was that much magnified.

I got little consolation from the presence of the others, for the pilot was engaged in navigation while Slafe was, as ever, single-mindedly recording mile after mile of the verdant mat beneath, never pausing nor speaking, though how he justified the use of so much film when one foot was identical with what went before and the next, I could not understand.

At last we cleared the awful cancer and flew over the sea. A thousand variations I had never noticed before offered themselves to my suddenly refreshed eyes. Not for one split second was the water the same. Leaping, tossing, spiraling, foaming back upon itself, making its own shadows and mirroring in an infinitely faceted glass the sunlight, it changed so constantly it was impossible to grasp even a fraction of its mutations. But Slafe evidently did not share my blessed relief, for he turned his camera back to catch every last glimpse of the solid green I was so happy to leave behind.

At the airport, on the way to the boat, on the little vessel itself, I expected Slafe to relax, to indulge in a conversational word, to do something to mark him as more than an automaton. But his actions were confined to using the nasalsyringe, to exchanging one camera for another, to quizzing the sun through that absurd lorgnette, and to muttering over cans of film which he sorted and resorted, always to his inevitable discontent.

While we waited to start, a perverse fog rolled between us and the mainland. It made a dramatic curtain over the object of our visit and emphasized the normality and untouchedness of Avalon behind us. As the boat got under way, strain my eyes as I could eastward, not the faintest suggestion of the ominous outline showed. We sped toward it, cutting the purple sea into white foam. Slafe was in the bow, customarily taciturn, the crew were busy. Alone on board I had no immediate occupation and so I took out my copy of the *Intelligencer* and after reading the column which went under my name and noting the incredible bad taste which had diluted when it had not excluded everything I had written, I turned as for consolation to the marketquotations. The Dow-Jones average was down again, as might be expected since the spread of the weed had unsettled the delicate balance of the stockmarket. My eyes automatically ran down the column and over to the corner where stocks were quoted in centers to reassure my faith in Consolidated Pemmican and Allied Concentrates. There it was, immovable through any storm or stress or injudicious investment by Albert Weener, "CP&AC . . . 1/16."

I must have raised my eyes from the newspaper just about the time the fog lifted. Before us, like the smokewreath accompanying the discharge of some giant cannon, the green mass volleyed into the sea. It did not slope gently like a beach or offer a rugged shoulder to be gnawed away as a rocky cliff, but thundered forward into the surging brine, yielding but invincible, a landforce potent as the wave itself. Hundreds of feet into the air it towered, falling abruptly in a sharp wall, its ends and fringes merging with the surf and wallowing in happy freedom. The breakers did not batter it for it offered them no enmity to rage and boil upon, but giving way with each surge, smothered the eternal anger of the ocean with its own placid surety.

The seagulls, the helldivers, pelicans, seapigeons had not been affected. Resting briefly on the weed, they winged out for their food and returned. It mattered no more to them that the manmade piers and wharves, the seacoast towns, gypjoints, rollercoasters, whorehouses, cottages, hotels, streets, gastanks, quarries, potterykilns, oilfields and factories had been swallowed up than if some old wreck in the sand, once offering them foothold, had been taken back by the sea. If I thought the grass awesome from the land, monotonous from the air, it seemed eternal from the water.

But impressive as it was from any angle, there were just so many things I could say about it. My art, unlike Slafe's, not permitting of endless repetition, I was glad to get back to the Pomona office, to pad what little copy I had, retire into the small tent I shared with six other sufferers from the housing shortage, and attempt some sleep.

31 The course mapped for the saltband caused almost as much controversy, anguish and denunciation as the proposal itself. Cities and towns fought to have the saltband laid between them and the approaching grass, understandably ignoring larger calculations and considerations. Cattle ranchers shot at surveying parties and individual farmers or homeowners fought against having their particular piece of property covered with salt. The original plan had contemplated straight lines; eventually the band twisted and turned like a typewriter ribbon plagued by a kitten, avoiding not only natural obstacles, but the domains of those with proper influence.

Recovery plants worked three shifts a day to pile up great mounds of the white crystals, which were hauled to the airfields by trains and trucks. The laden trucks moved over the highways bumper to bumper; the freighttrains' engines nosed the cabooses of those in front. All other goods were shunted on sidings, perishables rotted, valuables were undelivered; all transportation was reserved for the salt.

Not only was the undertaking unprecedented for its magnitude, but the urgency and the breakdowns, bottlenecks, shortages and disruptions caused by the grass itself added to the formidable accomplishment. But the people were aroused and aware of danger, and they put almost the same effort behind the saltsowing as they would have in turning out instruments of war.

The sowing itself was in a way anticlimactic. By the whim of Le ffaçasé I went in one of the planes on the first day of the task. My protests, as always, proving futile, I spent a very boresome time flying backandforth over the same patch of ground. That is, it would have been boresome had it not been for the dangers involved, for in order to sow the salt evenly and thickly it was necessary to fly low, to hedgehop, the pilot called it. If the parachutejump had unnerved me, the flying at terrific speed straight toward a tree, hill or electricpowerline and then curving upward at the last second to miss them by a whisper must have put gray in my hair and taken years from my life.

The rivers, washes and creeks on the inner edge had been roughly dammed to lessen future erosion of the salt and inappropriately gay flags marked the boundaries of the area. Owing to our speed the salt billowed out behind us like powdery fumes, but beyond the evidence of this smoky trail we might merely have been a group of madmen confusedly searching for some object lost upon the ground.

In reporting for the *Intelligencer* it was impossible to dramatize the event; even the rewritemen were baffled, for under the enormous head SALT SOWN they could not find enough copy to carry over from page one.

---

32 The sowing of the salt went on for weeks, and the grass leaped forward as if to meet it. It raced southward through Long Beach, Seal Beach and the deserted dunes to Newport and Balboa; it came east in a fury through Puente and Monrovia, northeastward it moved into Lancaster, Simi and Piru. Only in its course north did the weed show a slower pace; by the time we had been forced to leave Pomona for San Bernardino it had got no farther than Calabasas and Malibu.

The westward migration of the American people was abruptly reversed. Those actually displaced by the grass infected others, through whose homes they passed in their flight, with their own panic. Land values west of the Rockies dropped to practically nothing and the rich farms of the Great Plains were worth no more than they had been a hundred years before. People had seen directly, heard over the radio, or read in newspapers of the countless methods vainly used to stop the grass and there was little confidence in the saltband's succeeding where other devices had failed. True, there were hereandthere individuals or whole families or even entire communities obstinate enough to scorn flight, but in the opinion of most they were like pigheadedly trustful peasants who cling, in the face of all warning, to homes on the slopes of an active volcano.

It was generally thought the government itself, in creating the saltband, was making no more than a gesture. Whatever the validity of this pessimism, the work itself was impressive. Viewed from high in the air only a month after the start it was already visible; after two months it was a thick, glistening river winding over mountain, desert, and what had been green fields, a white crystalline barrier behind which the country waited nervously.

When the salt had been first proposed, batches had been dumped in proximity to the grass, but the quantity had been too small to demonstrate any conclusion and observers had been immediately driven from the scene of the experiments by the grass.

Nevertheless, the very inclusiveness of these trials confirmed the doubts of the waiting country as the narrow gap before the salt was closed and the weed rolled to it near Capistrano. I would like to think of the meeting as dramatic, heightened by inaudible drum-rolls and flashes of invisible lightning. Actually the conflict was pedestrian.

Manipulated once more by my tyrant, I was stationed, like other reporters and radiomen, in a captive balloon. For the utmost in discomfort and lack of dignity let me recommend this ludicrous invention. Cramped, seasickened, inconvenienced—I don't like to mention this, but provisions for answering the calls of nature were, to say the least, inadequate—I swayed and rocked in that inconsiderable basket, chilled, blinded by the dazzle of the salt, knocked about by gusts of irresponsible wind, and generally disgusted by the uselessness of my pursuit. A telescope to the eye and constant radioreports from shuttling planes told of the approaching grass, but under the circumstances weariness rather than excitement or anxiety was the prevailing emotion.

At last the collision came. The long runners, curiously flat from the air, pushed their way ahead. The salt seemed no more to them than bare ground, concrete, vegetation, or any of the hundred obstacles they had traveled. Unstutteringly the vinelike stolons went forward. A foot, two, six, ten. No recoil, no hesitation, no recognition they were traversing a wall erected against them.

Behind these first outposts, the higher growth came on, and still farther off the great bulk itself reared skyward, blotting out the horizon behind, threatening, inexhaustible. It seemed to prod its precursors, to demand hungrily ever more and more room to expand.

But the creeping of the runners over the first few feet of salt dwindled to a stop. This caused experienced observers like myself no elation; we had seen it happen many times before at the encountering of any novel obstacle, and its only effect had been to make the weed change its tactics in order to overcome the obstruction, as it did now. A second rank moved forward on top of the halted first, a third upon the second and so on till a living wall frowned down upon the salt, throwing its shadow across it for hundreds of ominous yards. It towered erect and then, repeating the tactic invariably successful, it toppled forward to create a bridge-head from which to launch new assaults.

The next day new stolons emerged from the mass, but now for the first time excitement seized us up in our bobbing post of observation. Not only were the new runners visibly shorter in length but they crept forward more slowly, haltingly, as though hurt. This impression was generally discredited, people were surfeited with optimism; they felt our reports were wishful thinking. Their pessimism seemed to be confirmed when the weed repeated its action of the day before, falling ahead of itself upon the salt; and few took stock in our excited announcements that the grass had covered only half the previous distance.

Again the probing fingers poked out, again the reserves piled up, again the mass fell. But it fell far short of a normal leap. There could no longer be any doubt about it; the advance had been slowed, almost stopped. The salt was working.

Everywhere along the entire band the story was the same. The grass rushed confidently in, bit off great chunks, then smaller, then smaller, until its movement ceased entirely. That part which embedded itself in the salt lost the dazzling green color so characteristic and turned piebald, from dirty gray through brown and yellow, an appearance so familiar in its normal counterpart on lawns and vacant lots.

The encircled area filled up and choked with the balked weed. Time after time it essayed the deadly band, only to be thwarted. The glistening fortification, hardly battered, stood triumphant, imprisoning the invader within. Commentators in trembling voices broke the joyful news over every receivingset and even the stodgiest newspapers brought out their blackest type to announce GRASS STOPPED!

33 The President of the United States, as befitted a farmer knowing something of grasses on his own account, issued a proclamation of thanksgiving for the end of the peril which had beset the country. The stockmarket recovered from funereal depths and jumped upward. In all the great cities hysterical rapture so heated the blood of the people that all restraints withered. In frantic joy women were raped in the streets, dozens of banks were looted, thousands of plateglasswindows were smashed while millions of celebrants wept tears of 86 proof ecstasy. Torn tickertapes made Broadway impassable and the smallest whistlestops spontaneously revived the old custom of uprooting outhouses and perching them on the church steeple.

I had my own particular reason to rejoice coincident with the stoppage of the grass. It was so unreal, so dreamlike, that for many days I had trouble convincing myself of its actuality. It began with a series of agitated telephone messages from a firm of stockbrokers asking for my immediate presence, which because of my assignments, failed to reach me for some time. So engrossed was I in the events surrounding the victory over the grass I could not conceive why any broker would want to see me and so put off my visit several times, till the urgency of the calls began to pique my curiosity.

The man who greeted me was runcible, with little strands of sickly hair twisted mopwise over his bald head. His striped suit was rumpled, the collar of his shirt was wrinkled, and dots of perspiration stood out on his upperlip and forehead. "Mr Weener?" he asked. "Oh, thank God, thank God."

Completely at a loss, I followed him into his private office. "You recall commissioning us—when we were located in Pomona—to purchase some shares of Consolidated Pemmican and Allied Concentrates for your account?"

To tell the truth, while I had not forgotten the event, I had been sufficiently ashamed of my rashness to have pushed all recollection of the transaction to the back of my mind. But I nodded confirmingly.

"No doubt you would be willing to sell at a handsome profit?"

Aha, I thought, the rise of the market has sent Consolidated Pemmican up for once beyond its usual 1/8. I am probably a rich man and this fellow wants to cheat me of the fruits of my foresight. "You bought the stock outright?"

"Of course, Mr Weener," he affirmed in a hurt tone.

"Good. Then I will take immediate delivery."

He pulled out a handkerchief and wiped his lip and forehead with evident inefficiency for the perspiration either remained or started afresh. "Mr Weener, " he said, "I am authorized to offer you

six times—six times," he echoed impressively, "the amount of your
original investment. This is an amazing return."

If it was worth it to him, it was worth it to me. "I will take
immediate delivery," I repeated firmly.

"And no brokerage fees involved," he added, as one making an
unbelievable concession.

I shook my head.

"Mr Weener," he said, "I have been empowered to make you
an incredible tender for your stock. Not only will the boardofdirec-
tors of Consolidated Pemmican return to you six times the amount
of your investment, but they will assign to you, over and above this
price, 49 percent of the company's votingstock. It is a magnificent
and unparalleled bid and I sincerely advise you to take it."

I pressed my palms into the back of the chair. I, Albert
Weener, was a capitalist. The money involved already seemed
negligible, for it was a mere matter of a few thousand dollars, but to
own what amounted to a controlling interest, even in a defunct or
somnolent corporation, made me an important person. Only a
reflex made me gasp, "I will take immediate delivery."

The broker dropped his hands against his thighs. "Mr Weener,
you are an acute man. Mr Weener, I must confess the truth. You
have bought more shares of Consolidated Pemmican than there are
in existence; you not only own the firm, lock, stock and barrel, but
you owe yourself money." He gave a weak laugh.

"Above and beyond this, Mr Weener, through an unfortunate
series of events due to the confusion of the times—without it, such
an absurd situation would never have occurred—several people: our
own firm, our New York correspondents, and the present heads of
Consolidated Pemmican are liable to prosecution by the Securities
Exchange Commission. We can only throw ourselves on your
mercy."

I waved this aside magnanimously. "Where is my property
located?"

"Well, I believe Consolidated Pemmican has an office in New
York."

"Yes, but the factory, the works; where is the product made?"

"Strictly speaking, I understand active operations ceased back in 1919. However, there is a plant somewhere in New Jersey, I think; I'll look it up for you."

My dream of wealth began fading as the whole situation became clear and suspicions implicit in the peculiar behavior of the stock were confirmed. The corporation had evidently fallen into the hands of unscrupulous promoters who manipulated for the small but steady "take" its fluctuations on the market afforded. Without attempting to operate the factory, my reasoning ran, they had taken advantage of the stock's low price to double whatever they cared to invest twice yearly. It was a neat and wellshaped little racket and discovery, as the broker admitted, would have exposed them to legal action. Only my recklessness with the checks from the *Weekly Ruminant* and the *Honeycomb* had broken the routine.

But . . . they had offered me several thousand dollars, evidently in cold cash. Defunct or not, then, the business was presumably worth at least that. And if they had employed the stock to maintain some sort of income, why, I could certainly learn to do the same. I was an independent man afterall.

Except for the slightly embarrassing detail of being without current funds I was also free of Le ffaçasé and the *Daily Intelligencer.* "Mr Blank," I said, "I need some money for immediate expenses."

"I knew youd see things in a sensible light, Weener. I'll have your check in a minute."

"You misunderstand me. I have no intention of giving up any part of Consolidated Pemmican."

"Ah?"

"No."

He looked at me intently. "Mr Weener, I am not a wealthy man. Above and beyond that, since this grass business started, I assure you any common laborer has made more money than I. Any common laborer," he repeated sadly.

"Oh, I only need about a thousand dollars for immediate outlays. Just write me a check for that much, like a good fellow."

"Mr Weener, how can we be sure you won't call upon us again for more—ah—expensemoney?"

I drew myself up indignantly. "Mr Blank, no one has ever questioned my integrity before. When I say a thousand dollars is all the expensemoney I require, why, it is all the expensemoney I require. To doubt it is to insult me."

"Ah," he said.

"Ah," I agreed.

Reluctantly he wrote the check and handed it to me. Then, more amicably, we settled the details of the stock transfer and he gave me the location of my property. I went back to the *Intelligencer* office with the springy step of a man who acknowledges no master. In my mind I prepared a triumph: I would wait—even if it took days—for the first bullying word from Le ffaçasé and then I would magnificently fling my resignation in his face.

34 When the grass was thought to be invincible, Miss Francis, as the discoverer of the compound which started it on its course, was the recipient of a universal if grudging respect. Those whom the grass had made homeless hated her and would have overcome their natural feeling of protection toward a woman sufficiently to lynch her if they could. Men like Senator Jones instinctively disliked her; others, like Dr Johnson, detested her, but no one thought of her lightly, even when they glibly coupled the word nut with her name.

When it was found the saltband worked Miss Francis immediately became the butt of all the ridicule and contumely which could be heaped upon her head. What could you expect of a woman who meddled with things outside her province? Since she had asserted the grass would absorb everything, its failure to absorb the salt proved beyond all doubt she was an ignoramus, a dangerous charlatan, and a crazy woman, better locked up, who had destroyed Southern California to her own obscure benefit. The victory over the grass became a victory over Miss Francis; of the ordinary gumchewing moviegoing maninthestreet over the pretentious highbrow. She was ignominiously ejected from her chickenhouse-laboratory on the ground that it was more needed for its original use, and she was jeered at in every vehicle of public expression. In spite of my natural chivalry, I cannot say I pitied her in her fall, which she took with an unbecoming humility amounting to arrogance.

35 It was amazing how quickly viewpoints returned to an apparent normality as soon as the grass stopped at the saltband. That it still existed, in undisputed possession of nearly all Southern California after dispersing and scattering millions of people all over the country, disturbing by its very being a large part of the national economy, was only something read in newspapers, an accepted fact to be pushed into the farthest background of awareness, now the immediate threat was gone. The salt patrol, vigilant for erosions or leachings, a select corps, was alert night and day to keep the saline wall intact. The general attitude, if it concerned itself at all with the events of the past half year, looked upon it merely as one of those setbacks periodically afflicting the country like depressions, epidemics, floods, earthquakes, or other manmade or natural misfortunes. The United States had been a great nation when Los Angeles was a pueblo of five thousand people; the movies could set up in business elsewhere, Iowans find another spot for senescence, the country go on much as usual.

One of the first results of the defeat of the grass was the building, almost overnight, it seemed, of a great city on the east bank of the Salton Sea. Displaced realtors from the metropolis found the surrounding mountains ideally suited for subdivision and laid out romantically named suburbs large enough to contain the entire population of California before the site of the city had been completely surveyed. Beyond their claims, the memorial parks, columbariums, homes of eternal rest and elysian lawns offered choice lots—with a special discount on caskets—on the install-mentplan. Magnificent brochures were printed, a skeletal bio-graphical dictionary—$5 for notice, $50 for a portrait—planned, advertisements in leading magazines urged the migration of indus-try: "contented labor and all local taxes remitted for ten years."

These essential preliminaries accomplished, the city itself was laid out, watermains installed, and paving and grading begun. It was no great feat to divert the now aimless Colorado River aqueduct to the site nor to erect thousands of prefabricated houses. The climate was declared to be unequalled, salubrious, equable, pleasant and bracing. Factories were erected, airports laid out, hospitals, prisons, and insane asylums built. The Imperial and Coachella valleys shipped their products in at low cost, and as a gesture to those who might suffer from homesickness it was called New Los Angeles.

Perhaps in relief from the fear and despair so recently dispelled, New Los Angeles began to boom from the moment the mayor first handed the key to a passing distinguished visitor. It grew and spread as the grass had grown and spread, the embryonic skeletons of its unborn skyline rivaled the height of the green mass now triumphant in its namesake, presenting, as newsphotographers were quick to see, an aspect from the west not entirely dissimilar to Manhattan's.

To New Los Angeles, of course, the *Daily Intelligencer* moved as soon as a tent large enough to house its presses could be set up. But I did not move with it. For some reason, perhaps intuitively forewarned of my intention, Le ffaçasé never gave me the opportunity to humiliate him as I planned. On the contrary, I received from him, a few days before the paper's removal, a silly and characteristic note: "Since the freak grass has been stopped it seems indicated other abnormalities be terminated also. Your usefulness to this paper, always debatable, is now clearly at an end. As of this moment your putative services will be no longer required. W.R.L."

Bitter vexation came over me at having lost the opportunity to give this bully a piece of my mind and my impulse was to go immediately to his office and tell him I scorned his petty paycheck, but I reflected a man of his nature would merely find some tricky way of turning the interview to his malicious satisfaction and he would know soon enough it was the paper which was suffering a loss and not I.

I started next morning and drove eastward toward my property, quite satisfied to leave behind forever the scenes of my early struggles. The West had given me only petty irritations. In the East, with its older culture and higher level of intelligence, I looked forward to having my worth appreciated.

36 EVERYTHING I HAD visualized in the broker's office turned out too pessimistically accurate. Consolidated Pemmican and Allied Concentrates was nothing but a mailing address in one of the most forlorn of Manhattan buildings, long before jettisoned by the tide of commerce. The factory, no bigger than a very small house, was a broken-windowed affair whose solid brick construction alone saved it from total demolition at the playful hands of the local children. The roof had long since fallen in and symbolical grass and weeds had pushed their way through cracks in the floor to flourish in a sickly and surreptitious way.

The whole concern, until my stock purchase, had been the chattel and creature of one Button Gwynnet Fles. In appearance he was such a genuine Yankee, lean and sharp, with a slight stoop and prying eyes, that one quite expected a straw to protrude from between his thin lips or have him draw from his pocket a wooden nutmeg and offer it for sale. After getting to know him I learned this apparent shrewdness was a pure defense mechanism, that he was really an artless and ingenuous soul who had been taught by other hands the swindle he practiced for many years and had merely continued it because he knew no way of making an honest living. He was, like myself, unattached, and disarmed whatever lingering suspicions of him I might have by offering to share his quarters with me until I should have found suitable accommodations.

The poor fellow was completely at my mercy and I not only forbore, generously, to press my advantage, but made him vice-president of the newly reorganized concern, permitting him to buy back a portion of the stock he had sold. The boom in the market having sent our shares up to an abnormal 1/2, we flooded our brokers with selling offers, at the same time spreading rumors—by no means exaggerated—of the firm's instability, buying back control when Consolidated Pemmican reached its norm of 1/16. We made no fortunes on this transaction, but I was enabled to look ahead to a year on a more comfortable economic level than ever before.

But it was by no means in my plans merely to continue to milk the corporation. I am, I hope, not without vision, and I saw Consolidated Pemmican under my direction turned into an active and flourishing industry. Its very decrepitude, I reasoned, was my opportunity; starting from scratch and working with nothing, I would build a substantial structure.

One of the new businesses which had sprung up was that of personally conducted tours of the grass. After the experience of Gootes and myself, parachute landings had been ruled out as too hazardous, but someone happily thought of the use of snowshoes and it was on these clumsy means that tourists, at a high cost and at less than snail's pace, tramped wonderingly over the tamed menace.

My thought then, as I explained to Fles, was to reactivate the factory and sell my product to the sightseers. Food, high in calories and small in bulk, was a necessity on their excursions and nourishing pemmican high in protein quickly replaced the cloying and messy candybar. We made no profit, but we suffered no loss and the factory was in actual operation so that no snoopers could ever accuse us of selling stock in an enterprise with a purely imaginary existence.

I liked New York; it accorded well with my temperament and I wondered how I had ever endured those weary years far from the center of the country's financial life, its theaters and its great human drama. Give me the old Times Square and the East Fifties any day and you can keep Death Valley and functional architecture. I was at home at last and I foresaw a future of slow but sure progress toward a position of eminence and respectability. The undignified days of Miss Francis and Le ffaçasé faded from my mind and I was aware of the grass only as a cause for selling our excellent pemmican.

I won't say I didnt read the occasional accounts of the weed appearing in *Time* or the newspapers, or watch films of it in the movies with more than common interest, but it was no longer an engrossing factor in my life. I was now taken up with larger concerns, working furiously to expand my success and for a year after leaving the *Intelligencer* I doubt if I gave it more than a minute's thought a day.

37 The band of salt remained an impregnable bulwark. Where the winter rains leached it, new tons of the mineral replaced those washed away. Constant observation showed no advance; if anything the edge of the grass impinging directly on the salt was sullenly retreating. The central bulk remained, a vast, obstinate mass, but most people thought it would somehow end by consuming itself, if indeed this doom were not anticipated by fresh scatterings of salt striking at its vitals as soon as the rains ceased.

No more than any other reader, then, was I disquieted by the following small item in my morning paper:

FREAK WEED STIRS SPECULATION

San Diego, Mar 7. (AP) An unusual patch of Bermuda grass discovered growing in one of the city parks' flower beds here today caused an excited flurry among observers. Reaching to a height of nearly four feet and defying all efforts of the park gardeners to uproot it, the vivid green interloper reminded fearful spectators of the plague which over ran Los Angeles two years ago. Scientists were reassuring, however, as they pointed out that the giantism of the Los Angeles devil grass was not transmissible by seed and that no stolons or rhizomes of the abnormal plant had any means of traveling to San Diego, protected as it is by the band of salt confining the Los Angeles growth.

I was even more confident, for I had seen with my own eyes the shoots grown by Miss Francis from seeds of the inoculated plant. A genuine freak, this time, I thought, and promptly forgot the item.

Would have forgotten it, I should say, had I not an hour later received a telegram, RETURN INSTANTLY CAN USE YOUR IMPRESSIONS OF NEW GRASS LEFFACASE. I knew from the fact he had only used nine of the ten words paid for he considered the situation serious.

The answer prompted by impulse would, I knew, not be transmitted by the telegraph company and on second thought I saw no reason why I should not take advantage of the editor's need. Business was slack and I was overworked; a succession of petty annoyances had driven me almost to a nervous breakdown and a vacation at the expense of the New Los Angeles *Daily Intelligencer* sounded pleasantly restful after the serious work of grappling with industrial affairs. Of course I did not need their paltry few dollars, but at the moment some of my assets were frozen and a weekly paycheck would be temporarily convenient, saving me the bother of liquidating a portion of my smaller investments.

Besides, if, as was barely possible, this new growth was in some unbelievable way an extension of the old, it would of course ruin our sales of pemmican to the tourists and it behooved me to be on the spot. I therefore answered: CONSIDER DOUBLE FORMER SALARY WIRE TRANSPORTATION. Next day the great transcontinental plane pouterpigeoned along the runway of the magnificent New Los Angeles airport.

I was in no great hurry to see the editor, but took a taxi instead to the headquarters of the American Alpinists Incorporated where there was frank worry over the news and acknowledgment that no further consignments of pemmican would be accepted until the situation became more settled. I left their offices in a thoughtful mood. Pausing only to wire Fles to unload as much stock as he could—for even if this were only a temporary scare it would undoubtedly affect the market—I finally drove to the *Intelligencer.*

Knowing Le ffaçasé I hardly expected to be received with either cordiality or politeness, but I was not quite prepared for the actual salute. A replica of his original office had been devised, even to the shabby letters on the door, and he was seated in his chair beneath the gallery of cartoons. He began calmly enough when I entered, speaking in a low, almost gentle tone, helping himself to snuff between sentences, but gradually working up into a quite artistic crescendo.

"Ah, Weener, as you yourself would undoubtedly put it in your inimitable way, a bad penny always turns up. I could not say *canis revertit suam vomitem*, for it would invert a relationship—the puke has returned to the dog.

"It is a sad thought that the listless exercise which eventuated in your begetting was indulged in by two whose genes and chromosomes united to produce a male rather than a female child. For think, Weener, if you had been born a woman, with what gusto would you have peddled your flaccid flesh upon the city streets and offered your miserable dogsbody to the reluctant use of un-discriminating customers. You are the paradigmatic whore, Weener, and I weep for the physiological accident which condemns you to sell your servility rather than your vulva. Ah, Weener, it restores my faith in human depravity to have you around to attempt your petty confidence tricks on me once more; I rejoice to find I had not overestimated mankind as long as I can see one aspect of it embodied in your 'homely face and bad complexion,' as the great Gilbert so mildly put it. I shall give orders to triplelock the pet-tycash, to count the stampmoney diligently, to watch all checks for inept forgery. Welcome back to the *Intelligencer* and be grateful for nature's mistakes, since they afford you employment as well as existence.

"But enough of the friendly garrulousness of an old man whose powers are failing. Remove your unwholesomelooking person from my sight and convey the decrepit vehicle of your spirit to San Diego. It is but a gesture; I expect no coherent words from your clogged and sputtery pen; but while I am sufficiently like yourself to deceive the public into thinking you have written what they read, I am not yet great enough scoundrel to do so without your visiting the scene of your presumed labors. Go—and do not stop on the way to draw expensemoney from the cashier for she has strict orders not to pay it."

Jealousy, nothing but jealousy, I thought, first of my literary ability and now of my independence of his crazy whims. I turned my back deliberately and walked slowly out, to show my contempt for his rantings.

In my heart, now, there was little doubt the new grass was an extension of the old and it didnt take more than a single look at the overrun park to confirm this. The same creeping runners growing perceptibly from instant to instant, the same brilliant color, the same towering central mass gorged with food. I could have described it line by line and blade by blade in my sleep. I wasted no more time gazing at it, but hurried away after hardly more than a minute's inspection.

I could take no credit for my perceptivity since everyone in San Diego knew as well as I that this was no duplicate freak, but the same, the identical, the fearsome grass. But a quite understandable conspiracy had been tacitly entered into; the knowledge was successfully hushed until property could be disposed of before it became quite worthless. The conspiracy defeated itself, however, with so many frantic sellers competing against each other and the news was out by the time the first of my new columns appeared in the *Intelligencer*.

The first question which occurred to those of us calm enough to escape panic was, how had the weed jumped the saltband? It was answered simultaneously by many learned professors whose desire to break into print and share the front page with the terrible grass overcame their natural academic reticence. There was no doubt that originally the peculiar voracity of the inoculated plant had not been inherited; but it was equally uncontroverted that somehow, during the period it had been halted by the salt, a mutation had happened and now every wind blowing over the weed carried seeds no longer innocent but bearing embryos of the destroyer.

Terror ran before the grass like a herald. The shock felt when Los Angeles went down was multiplied tenfold. Now there was no predictable course men could shape their actions to avoid. No longer was it possible to watch and chart the daily advance of a single body so a partially accurate picture could be formed of what might be expected tomorrow. Instead of one mass there were countless ones; at the whim of a chance wind or bird, seeds might alight in an area apparently safe and overwhelm a community miles away from the living glacier. No place was out of range of the attack; no square foot of land kept any value.

The stockmarket crashed, and I congratulated myself on having sent Fles orders to sell. A day or two later the exchanges were closed and, shortly after, the banks. Business came to a practical standstill. The great industries shut down and all normal transactions of daily life were conducted by means of barter. For the first time in threequarters of a century the farmer was topdog; his eggs and milk, his wheat and corn and potatoes he could exchange for whatever he fancied and on his own terms. Fortunately for starving citydwellers his appetite for manufactured articles and for luxuries was insatiable; their automobiles, furcoats, costume jewelry, washingmachines, files of the *National Geographic*, and their periodfurniture left the city flat for the farm, to come back in the more acceptable form of steaks, butter, fowl, and turnips. The whole elaborate structure of money and credit seemed to disappear overnight like some tenuous dream.

The frenzied actions of the humanbeings had no effect on the grass. The saltband still stood inviolate, as did smaller counterparts hastily laid around the earlier of the seedborne growths, but everywhere else the grass swept ahead like a tidalwave, its speed seemingly increased by the months of repression behind. It swallowed San Diego in a gulp and leaped beyond the United States to take in Baja California in one swift downward lick. It sprang upon the deserts, whose lack of water was no deterrent, now always sending little groups ahead like paratroopers or fifthcolumnists; they established positions till the main body came up and consolidated them. It curled up the high mountains, leaving only the snow on their peaks unmolested and it jumped over struggling rivers with the dexterity of a girl playing hopscotch.

It lunged eastward into Arizona and Nevada, it swarmed north up the San Joaquin Valley through Fresno and spilled over the lip of the High Sierras toward Lake Tahoe. New Los Angeles, its back protected by the Salton Sea, was, like the original one, subjected to a pincer movement which strangled the promising life from it before it was two years old.

Forced to move again, Le ffaçasé characteristically demanded the burden fall upon the employees of the paper, paying them off in scrip on the poor excuse that no money was available. I saw no future in staying with this sinking ship and eager to be back at the center of things—Fles wrote me that the large stock of pemmican which had been accumulating without buyers could now be very profitably disposed of—I severed my connection for the second time with the *Intelligencer* and returned to my proper sphere.

This of course did not mean that I failed to follow each step of the grass; such a course would have been quite impossible since its every move affected the life and fortune of every citizen. By some strange freak it spared the entire coast north of Santa Barbara. Whether it had some disinclination to approach saltwater—it had been notably slow in its original advance westward—or whether it was sheer accident, San Luis Obispo, Monterey and San Francisco remained untouched as the cities to the south and east were buried under grassy avalanches. This odd mercy raised queer hopes in some; perhaps their town or their state would be saved.

The prostration of the country which had begun with the first wave of panic could not be allowed to continue. The government moved in and seized, first the banks and then the railroads. Abandoned realestate was declared forfeit and opened to homesteading. Prices were pegged and farmers forced to pay taxes in produce.

Although these measures restored a similitude of life to the nation, it remained but a feeble imitation of its previous self. Many of the idle factories failed to reopen, others moved with painful caution. Goods, already scarce, disappeared almost completely and at the same time a reckless disregard of formerly sacred symbols seized upon the people. The grass was coming, so what good was the lot on which they were paying installments? The grass was coming, so why gather together the dollars to meet the interest on the mortgage? The grass was coming—what was the use of depositing money in the bank which would probably go bust tomorrow?

The inflation would have been worse had it not been for the pegged prices and other stern measures. The glut on the labor market was tremendous and wages reached the vanishing point in a currency which would buy little. Suddenly, the United States, which had so long boasted of being the richest country in the world, found itself desperately poor.

Government work projects did little to relieve the suffering of the proletariat. Deaths from malnutrition mounted and the feeble strikes in the few operating industries were easily and quickly crushed by starving strikebreakers ashamed of their deed yet desperately eager to feed their hungry families. Riots broke out in New York and Detroit, but the police were fortunately wellfed and the arms wielding the blackjacks which crushed the skulls of the undernourished rioters were stout.

There was a sweeping revival of organized religion and men too broke to afford the neighborhood movie flocked to the churches. Brother Paul, now on a national hookup, repeated his exhortations to all Christians, urging them to join their Savior in the midst of the grass. There was great agitation for restraining him; more reserved pastors pointed out that he was responsible for increasing the national suicide rate, but the Federal Communications Commission took no action against him, possibly because, as some said, it was cheaper to let a percentage of the surplus population find an ecstatic death than to feed it.

On political maps the United States had lost not one foot of territory. Population statistics showed it harbored as many men, women, and children as before. Not one tenth of the national wealth had been destroyed by the grass or a sixth of the country given up to it, yet it had done what seven wars and many vicissitudes had failed to do: it brought the country to the nadir of its existence, to a hopeless despondency unknown at Valley Forge.

At this desperate point the federal government decided it could no longer temporize with the clamor for using atomic power against the grass. All the arguments so weighty at first became insignificant against the insolent facts. It was announced in a Washington pressconference that as soon as arrangements could be made the most fearful of all weapons would be employed.

38 No one doubted the atomicbomb would do the trick, finally and conclusively. The searing, volcanic heat, irresistible penetration, efficient destructiveness and the aftermath of apocalyptic radiation promised the end of the grass.

When I say no one, of course I mean no clearthinking person of vision with his feet on the ground who didnt go deliberately out of his way to look for the dark side of things. Naturally there were crackpots, as there always are, who opposed the use of the bomb for various untenable reasons, and among them I was not surprised to find Miss Francis.

Though her pessimistic and unpopular opinions had been discredited time and again, the newspapers, possibly to enliven their now perpetually gloomy columns with a little humor, gave some space to interviews which, with variations predicated on editorial policy, ran something like this:

Will you tell our readers what you think of using the atom bomb against the grass?

I think it at the very best a waste of time; at the worst, extremely dangerous.

In what way, Miss Francis?

In every way. Did you ever hear of a chain-reaction, young man? Or radioactivity? Can you conceive, among other possibilities—and mind, this is merely a possibility, a quite unscientific guess merely advanced in the vain hope of avoiding one more folly—of the whole mass becoming radioactive, squaring or cubing its speed of growth, or perhaps throwing before it a lethal band miles wide? Mind you, I'm not anticipating any of this, not even saying it is a probability; but these or similar hazards may well attend this illconsidered venture.

You speak wrongly, Miss Francis. None of the rather fantastic things you predict followed Hiroshima, Nagasaki or Bikini.

In the first place, I tried, with apparent unsuccess, to make it clear I'm not predicting. I am merely mentioning possibilities. In the second place, we don't know exactly what were the aftereffects of the previous bombs because of a general inability to correlate cause and effect. I only know that in every case the use of the atomic bomb has been followed at greater or lesser intervals by tidal waves, earthquakes and other 'natural' phenomena. Now do not quote me as saying the Hilo tidal wave was the result of the Nagasaki bomb or the Chicagku earthquake, the Bikini; for I didnt. I only point out that they followed at roughly equal intervals.

Then you are opposed to the bomb?

Common sense is. Not that that will be a deterrent.

What would you substitute for it?

If I had a counteragent to the grass ready I would not be wasting time talking to reporters. I am working on one. When it is found, by me or another, it will be a true counteragent, changing the very structure and habit of *Cynodon dactylon* as the Metamorphizer changed it originally. External weapons, by definition, can at best, at the very best, merely stop the grass—not render it innocuous. Equals fighting equals produce only deadlocks.

And so on. The few reputable scientists who condescended to answer her at all and didnt treat her views with dignified silence quickly demonstrated the absurdity of her objections. Chainreactions and radioactive advanceguard! Sundaysupplement stuff, without the slightest basis of reasoning; not a mathematical symbol or laboratory experiment to back up these fictional nightmares. And not use external weapons, indeed! Was the grass to be hypnotized then? Or made to change its behaviorpatterns through judicious sessions with psychoanalysts stationed along its periphery?

Whether because of Miss Francis' prophesies or not, it would be futile to deny that a certain amount of trepidation accompanied the decision to use the bomb. Residents of Arizona wanted it dropped in California; San Franciscans urged the poetic justice and great utility of applying it to the very spot where the growth originated; all were in favor of the devastation at the farthest possible distance from themselves.

Partly in response to this pressure and partly in consideration of other factors, including the possibility of international repercussions, the Commission to Combat Dangerous Vegetation decided on one of the least awesome bombs in the catalogue. Just a little bomb—hardly more than a toy, a plaything, the very smallest practicable—ought to allay all fears and set everyone's mind at rest. If it were effective, a bigger one could be employed, or numbers of smaller ones.

This much being settled, there was still the question of where to initiate the attack. Edge or heart? Once more there was controversy, but it lacked the enthusiasm remembered by veterans of the salt argument; a certain lassitude in debate was evident as though too much excitement had been dissipated on earlier hopes, leaving none for this one. There was little grumbling or soreness when the decision was finally confirmed to let fall the bomb on what had been Long Beach.

When I read of the elaborate preparations being made to cover the great event, of the special writers, experts, broadcasters, cameramen, I was thankful indeed I was no longer a newspaperman, arbitrarily to be ordered aloft or sent aboard some erratic craft offshore on the bare chance I might catch a comprehensive or distinctive enough glance of the action to repay an editor for my discomfort. Instead, I sat contentedly in my apartment and listened to the radio.

Whether our expectations had been too high or whether all the eyewitnesses became simultaneously inept, I must say the spot broadcast and later newspaper and magazine accounts were uniformly disappointing. It was like the hundredth repetition of an oftentold story. The flash, the chaos, the mushroomcloud, the reverberation were all in precise order; nothing new, nothing startling, and I imagine the rest of the country, as I did, turned away from the radio with a distinct feeling of having been let down.

First observation through telescope and by airplanes keeping a necessarily cautious distance, showed the bomb had destroyed a patch of vegetation about as large as had been expected. Though not spectacular, the bombing had apparently been effective on a comparatively small segment and it was anticipated that as soon as it was safe to come close and confirm this, the action would be repeated on a larger scale. While hundreds more of the baby bombs, as they were now affectionately called, were ordered and preparations made systematically to blast the grass out of existence, the aerial observers kept swooping in closer and closer with cameras trained to catch every aspect of the damage.

There was no doubt an area of approximately four square miles had been utterly cleaned of the weed and a further zone nine times that size had been smashed and riven, the grass there torn and mangled—in all probability deprived of life. Successive reconnoitering showed no changes in the annihilated center, but on the tenth day after the explosion a most startling observation of the peripheral region was made. It had turned a brilliant orange.

Not a brown or yellow, or any of the various shades of decay which Bermuda in its original form took on at times, but a glowing and unearthly, jewellike blaze.

The strange color was strictly confined to the devastated edge of the bombcrater; airmen flying low could see its distinction from the rest of the mass clear and sharp. In the center, nothing; around it, the weird orange; and beyond, the usual and accustomed green.

But on second look, not quite usual, not quite accustomed. The inoculated grass had always been a shade or two more intense than ordinary *Cynodon dactylon*; this, just beyond the orange, was still more brilliant. Not only that, but it behaved unaccountably. It writhed and spumed upward in great clumps, culminating in enormous, overhanging caps inevitably suggesting the mushroomcloud of the bomb.

The grass had always been cautious of the sea; now the dazzling growth plunged into the saltwater with frenzy, leaping and building upon itself. Great masses of vegetation, piers, causeways, isthmuses of grass offered the illusion of growing out of the ocean bottom, linking themselves to the land, extending too late the lost coast far out into the Pacific.

But this was far from the last aftereffect. Though attention had naturally been diverted from the orange band to the eccentric behavior of the contiguous grass, it did not go unobserved and about a week after its first change of color it seemed to be losing its unnatural hue and turning green again.

Not the green of the great mass, nor of the queer periphery, nor of uninspired devilgrass. It was a green unknown in living plant before; a glassy, translucent green, the green of a cathedral window in the moonlight. By contrast, the widening circle about it seemed subdued and orderly. The fantastic shapes, the tortured writhings, the unnatural extensions into the ocean were no longer manifest, instead, for miles around the ravaged spot where the bomb had been dropped, the grass burst into bloom. Purple flowers appeared—not the usual muddy brown, faintly mauve—but a redviolet, brilliant and clear. The period of generation was abnormally shortened; seed was borne almost instantly—but the seed was a sport.

It did not droop and detach itself and sink into the ground.

Instead, tufted and fluffy, like dandelion seed or thistledown, it floated upward in incredible quantities, so that for hundreds of miles the sky was obscured by this cloud bearing the germ of the inoculated grass.

It drifted easily and the winds blew it beyond the confines of the creeping parent. It lit on spots far from the threatening advance and sprouted overnight into great clumps of devilgrass. All the anxiety and panic which had gone before was trivial in the face of this new threat. Now the advance was no longer calculable or predictable; at any moment a spot apparently beyond danger might be threatened and attacked.

Immediately men remembered the exotic growth of flowers which came up to hide some of London's scars after the blitz and the lush plantlife observed in Hiroshima. Why hadnt the allwise scientists remembered and taken them into account before the bomb was dropped? Why had they been blind to this obvious danger? Fortunately the anger and terror were assuaged. Observers soon discovered the mutants were sterile, incapable of reproduction. More than that: though the new clumps spread and flourished and grew rapidly, they lacked the tenacity and stamina of the parent. Eventually they withered and dwindled and were in the end no different from the uninoculated grass.

Now a third change was seen in the color band. The green turned distinctly blue and the sharp line between it and the rest of the weed vanished as the blueness shaded out imperceptibly over miles into the green. The barren spot made by the bomb was covered; the whole mass of vegetation, thousands of square miles of it, was animated by a surging new vigor, so that eastward and southward the rampant tentacles jumped to capture and occupy great new swaths of territory.

Triumphantly Brother Paul castigated the bombardiers and urged repentance for the blasphemy to avert further welldeserved punishment. Grudgingly, one or two papers recalled Miss Francis' warning. Churches opened their doors on special days of humiliation and fasting. But for most of the people there was a general feeling of relief; the ultimate in weapons had been used; the grass would wear itself out in good time; meanwhile, they were thankful the effect of the atomicbomb had been no worse. If anything the spirit of the country, despite the great setback, was better after the dropping of the bomb than before.

I was so fascinated by the entire episode that I stayed by my radio practically all my waking hours, much to the distress of Button Fles. Every report, every scrap of news interested me. So it was that I caught an item in a newscast, probably unheard by most, or smiled aside, if heard. *Red Egg*, organ of the Russian Poultry Farmers, editorialized, "a certain imperialist nation, unscrupulously pilfering the technical advance of Soviet Science, is using atomic power, contrary to international law. This is intolerable to a peace-loving people embracing 1/6 of the earth's surface and the poultrymen of the Collective, *Little Red Father*, have unanimously protested against such capitalist aggression which can only be directed against the Soviet Union."

The following day, *Red Star* agreed; on the next, *Pravda* reviewed the "threatening situation." Two days later *Izvestia* devoted a column to "Blackmail, Peter the Great, Suvarov and Imperialist Slyness." Twentyfour hours after, the Ministerial Council of the Union of Soviet Republics declared a state of war existed— through no action of its own—between the United States and the Soviet Union.

39 At first the people were incredulous. They could not believe the radio reports were anything but a ghastly mistake, an accidental garbling produced by atmospheric conditions. Historians had told them from their schooldays of traditional Russian-American friendship. The Russian Fleet came to the Atlantic coast in 1862 to escape revolutionary infection, but the Americans innocently took it as a gesture of solidarity in the Civil War. The Communist party had repeated with the monotony of a popular hymntune at a revival that the Soviet Union asked only to be let alone, that it had no belligerent designs, that it was, as Lincoln said of the modest farmer, desirous only of the land that "jines mine." At no point were the two nations' territories contiguous.

Agitators were promptly jailed for saying the Soviet Union wasnt—if it ever had been—a socialist country; its imperialism stemming directly from its rejection of the socialist idea. As a great imperialist power bursting with natural resources it must inevitably conflict with the other great imperialist power. In our might we had done what we could to thwart Russian ambition; now they seized the opportunity to disable a rival.

Congressmen and senators shredded the air of their respective chambers with screams of outrage. In every speech, "Stab in the back" found an honorable if monotonous place. Zhadanov, boss of the Soviet Union since the death of the sainted Stalin, answered gruffly, "War is no minuet. We do not wait for the capitalist pigs to bow politely before we rise to defend the heritage of Czar Ivan and our own dear, glorious, inspiring, venerated Stalin. Stab in the back! We will stab the fascist lackeys of Morgan, Rockefeller and Jack and Heinze in whatever portion of the anatomy they present to us."

As usual, the recurring prophets who hold their seances between hostilities and invariably predict a quick, decisive war—in 1861 they gave it six weeks; in 1914 they gave it six weeks; in 1941 they gave it six weeks—were proved wrong. They had been over-weeningly sure this time: rockets, guided missiles or great fleets of planes would sweep across the skies and devastate the belligerents within three hours of the declaration of war—which of course would be dispensed with. Not a building would remain intact in the great cities nor hardly a civilian alive.

But three hours after Elmer Davis—heading an immediately revived Office of War Information—announced the news in his famous monotone, New York and Chicago and Seattle were still standing and so, three days later, were Moscow and Leningrad and Vladivostok.

Astonishment and unbelief were nationwide. The Empire State, the Palmolive Building, the Mark Hopkins—all still intact? Only when commentators, rummaging nervously among old manuscripts, recalled the solemn gentlemen's agreement never to use heavierthanaircraft of any description should the unthinkable war come, did the public give a heartfelt sigh of relief. Of course! Both the Soviet Union and the United States were nations of unstained honor and, rather than recall their pledged word, would have suffered the loss of a dozen wars. Everyone breathed easier, necks relaxed from the strain of scanning the skies; there would be neither bombs, rockets, nor guided missiles in this war.

As soon as the conviction was established that the country was safe from the memory of Hiroshima, panic gave place to relief and for the first time some of the old spirit was manifest. There was no rush to recruitingstations, but selectiveservice, operating smoothly except in the extreme West, took care of mobilization and the war was accepted, if not with enthusiasm, at least as an inescapable fate.

The coming of the grass had not depleted nor unbalanced the country's resources beyond readjustment, but it had upset the sensitive workings of the national economy. This was tolerable by a sick land—and the grass had made the nation sick—in peacetime; but "war is the health of the state" and the President moved quickly.

All large industries were immediately seized, as were the mines and means of transportation. A basic fiftyfivehour workweek was imposed. A new chief of staff and of naval operations was appointed and the young men went off to camp to train either for implementing or repelling invasion. Then came a period of quiet during which both countries attacked each other ferociously over the radio.

40 In the socialistic orgy of nationalizing business, I was fortunate; Consolidated Pemmican and Allied Concentrates was left in the hands of private initiative. Better than that, it had not been tied down and made helpless by the multiplicity of regulations hampering the few types of endeavor remaining nominally free of regimenting bureaucracy. Opportunity, long prepared for and not, I trust, undeserved, was before me.

In the pass to which our country had come it seemed to me I could be of most service supplying our armed forces with fieldrations. Such an unselfish and patriotic desire one would think easy of realization—as I so innocently did—and I immediately began interviewing numberless officers of the Quartermaster's Department to further this worthy aim.

I certainly believe every corporation must have its rules, otherwise executives would be besieged all day by timewasters. The

United States government is surely a corporation, as I always used to say in advocating election of a business administration, and standard procedures and regulations are essential. Still, there ought to be a limit to the number and length of questionnaires to fill out and the number of underlings to interview before a serious businessman can get to see a responsible official.

After making three fruitless trips to Washington and getting exhaustively familiar with countless tantalizing waitingrooms, I became impatient. The man I needed to see was a Brigadier General Thario, but after wasting valuable days and hours I was no nearer reaching him than in the beginning. I had filled out the necessary forms and stated the nature of my business so often I began to be alarmed lest my hand refuse to write anything else and I be condemned for the rest of my life to repeat the idiotic phrases called for in the blank spaces.

I am afraid I must have raised my voice in expressing my exasperation to the young lady who acted as receptionist and barrier. At any rate she looked startled, and I think pressed a button on her desk. A pinkfaced, whitemustached gentleman came hastily through the door behind her. The jacket of his uniform fitted snugly at the waist and his bald head was sunburnt and shiny.

"What's this? What's this? . . . going on here?"

I saw the single star on his shoulderstraps and ventured, "General Thario?"

He hid his white mustache with a forefinger pink as his cheeks. "Yes. Yes. But you must have an appointment to speak to me. That's the rule, you know. Must have an appointment." He appeared extremely nervous and harassed, his eyes darting back to the refuge of his office, but he was evidently held to the spot by whatever distress animated his receptionist.

"General Thario," I persisted firmly, "I quite appreciate your viewpoint, but I have been trying for days to get such an appointment with you on a matter of vital concern and I have been put off every time by what I can only describe as redtape. I am sorry to say so, General Thario, but I must repeat, redtape."

He looked more worried than before and his eyes ranged over the room for some escape. "Know just how you feel," he muttered, "Know just how you feel. Horrible stuff. Swaddled in it here.

Simply swaddled in it. Strangled." He cleared his throat as though to disembarrass it of a garrote. "But, uh, hang it, Mr—"

"Weener. Albert Weener. President of Consolidated Pemmican and Allied Concentrates Incorporated."

"—Well, you know, Mr. Weener . . . man your position . . . appreciate absolute necessity certain amount of routine . . . keep the cranks out, otherwise swarming with them, simply swarming . . . wartime precautions . . . must excuse me now . . . terribly rushed . . . glad to have met—"

Swallowing the rest of the sentence and putting his hand over his mouth lest he should inadvertently regurgitate it, he started for his office. "General Thario," I pleaded, "a moment. Consider our positions reversed. I have long since established my identity, my responsibility. I want nothing for myself; I am here doing a patriotic duty. Surely enough of the routine you mention has been complied with to permit me to speak to you for five or ten minutes. Do for one moment as I say, General, and put yourself in my place. Think of the discouragement you as a citizen would feel to be hampered, perhaps more than is necessary."

He took his hand down from his mouth and looked at me out of blue eyes so pale as to be almost colorless. "But hang it, you know, Mr Weener . . . highly irregular. Sympathize completely, but consider . . . don't like being put in such a position . . . why don't you come back in the morning?"

"General," I urged, flushed with victory, "give me ten minutes now."

He collapsed. "Know just how you feel . . . wanted to be out in the field myself . . . no desk soldier . . . lot of nonsense if you ask me. Come in, come in."

In his office I explained the sort of contract I was anxious to secure and assured him of my ability to fulfill its terms. But I could see his mind was not intent upon the specifications for fieldrations. Looking up occasionally from a dejected study of his knees, he kept inquiring, in elliptical, practically verbless questions, how many men my plant employed, whether I had a satisfactory manager and if a knowledge of chemistry was essential to the manufacture of concentrates; evading or discussing in the vaguest terms the actual business at hand.

However, he seemed very friendly and affable toward me personally once the chill air of the waitingroom had been left behind and as Button Fles had advised me insistently to entertain without regard to expense any officials with whom I came in contact, I thought it politic to invite him to dinner. He demurred at first, but at length accepted, instructing his secretary to phone his wife not to expect him home early. I suggested Mrs Thario join us, but he shook his head, muttering, "No place for women, Mr Weener, no place for women." Whether this referred to Washington or the restaurant where we were going or to his life largely was not clear.

Wartime Washington was in its usual chaotic turmoil and it was impossible to get a taxi, so we had to walk. But the general did not seem at all averse to the exercise. It seemed to me he rather enjoyed returning the salutes with the greatest punctilio and flourish. On our way we came to one of the capital's most famous taverns and I thought I detected a hesitancy in his stride.

Now I am not a drinking man myself. I limit my imbibing to an occasional glass of beer on account of the yeast it contains, which I consider beneficial. I hope, however, I am no prig or puritan and so I asked casually if he would care to stop in for an appetizer.

"Well, now you mention it, Mr Weener . . . hum .   . fact is . . . don't mind if I do."

While I confined myself to my medicinal beverage the general conducted a most remarkable raid on the bar. As I have hinted, he was in demeanor a mild appearing, if not indeed a timid man. In the course of an hour's conversation no word of profanity, such as is affected by many military men, had crossed his lips. The framed photograph of his wife and daughters on his desk and his respectful references to women indicated he was not the type of soldier who lusts for rapine. But seated before that dull mahogany bar, whatever inhibitions, whatever conventional shackles, whatever selfdenials and repressions had been inculcated fell from him swiftly and completely. He barked his orders at the bartender, who seemed to know him very well, as though he were addressing a parade formation of badly disciplined troops.

Not only did General Thario drink enormously, but he broke all the rules I had ever heard laid down about drinking. He began with a small, squat glass, which I believe is called an Oldfashioned glass, containing half cognac and half ryewhisky. He followed this with a tall tumbler— "twelve full ounces . . . none of your eight-ounce thimbles . . . not trifled with"—of champagne into which the bartender, upon his instructions and under his critical eye, poured two jiggers of tropical rum. Then he wiped his lips with a handkerchief pulled from his sleeve and began with a serious air on a combination of benedictine and tequila. The more he imbibed, the longer, more complete and more coherent his sentences became. He dropped his harassed air; his abdomen receded, his chest expanded, bringing to my notice for the first time the rows of ribbons which confirmed his earlier assertion that he was not a desk soldier.

He was sipping curaçao liberally laced with applejack when he suggested we have our dinner sent in rather than leave this comfortable spot. "The fact of the matter is, Mr Weener—I'm going to call you Albert if you don't mind—"

I said I didnt mind with all the heartiness at my command.

"The fact of the matter is, Albert, I have devoted my unfortunate life to two arts: the military and the potatory. As you may have noticed, most of the miserable creatures on the wrong side of a bar adopt one of two reprehensible courses: either they treat drinking as though the aim of blending liquids were to imitate some French chef's fiddlefaddle—a dash of bitters, a squirt of orange, an olive, a cherry, or onion wrenched from its proper place in the saladbowl, a twist of lemonpeel, sprig of mint or lump of sugar and an eyedropperful of whisky; or else they embrace the opposite extreme of vulgarity and gulp whatever rotgut is thrust at them to addle their undiscerning brains and atrophy their undiscriminating palates. Either practice is foreign to my nature and philosophy. I believe the happiest combinations of liquors are simple ones, containing no more than two ingredients, each of which should be noble—that is to say, drinkable in its own right."

He raised his fresh glass, containing brandy and arrack. "No doubt you have observed a catholicity in my taste; I range through the whole gamut from usquebaugh to sake, though during the present conflict for obvious patriotic reasons, I cross vodka from my list, while as a man born south of the Mason-Dixon Line, sir, I leave gin to Nigras."

I must say, though somewhat startled by his manner of imbibing, I was inclined to like General Thario, but I was impatient to discuss the matter of a contract for Consolidated Pemmican. Every time I attempted to bring the subject round to it he waved me grandly aside. "Dinner," he confirmed, when the waiters brought in their trays. "Yes; no drink is complete without a little bit of the right food to garnish it. Eating in moderation I approve of; but mark my words, Albert, the man who takes a meal on an empty stomach is digging his grave with his teeth."

If he would not talk business I could only hope his amiability would carry over till I saw him again in his office tomorrow. I settled down as far as I could, simply to enjoy his company. "You may have been surprised at my referring to my life as unfortunate, Albert, but it is a judicious adjective. Vilely unfortunate. I come of a military family, you know; you will find footnotes mentioning the Tharios in the history of every war this country has had."

He finished what was in his glass. "My misfortunes, like Tristram Shandy's, began before my birth—and in the same way, exactly the same way. My father was a scholar and a gentleman who dreamed his life away over the campaigns of the great captains instead of attempting to become a great captain himself. I do not condemn him for this: the organization of the army is such as to encourage impracticality and inadvertence, but the consequences were unfortunate for me. He named me after his favorite heroes, Stuart Hannibal Ireton Thario, and so aloof was he from the vulgarities of everyday life that it was not until my monogram was ordered painted upon my first piece of luggage that the unfortunate combination of my initials was noted. Hannibal and Ireton promptly suppressed in the interests of decency, nevertheless at West Point my surname was twisted by fellow classmates into Lothario, giving it a connotation quite foreign to my nature. I lived down both vexations only to encounter a third. Though Ireton remained successfully concealed, the Hannibal leaked out and when, during the World War, I had the misfortune to lead a company which was decimated"—his hand strayed to the ribbons on his chest— "behind my back the enlistedmen called me Cannibal Thario."

He began discussing another drink. "Of one thing I'm resolved: my son shall not suffer as I have suffered. I did not send him to West Point so he might win decorations on the field of valor and then be shunted off to sit behind an unsoldierly desk. I broke with tradition when I kept him from a military career, quite on purpose, just as I was thinking of his welfare and not some silly foible of my own when I called him by the simplest name I could find."

"What is your son's name?" I was constrained to ask.

"George," he answered proudly, "George Thario. There is no nickname for George as far as I know."

"And he's not in the army now?" I queried, more in politeness than in interest.

"No, and I don't intend he shall be." The general's pink face grew pinker with his vehemence. "Albert, there are plenty of dunderheads and duffers like me in the country who are good for nothing better than cannonfodder. Let them go and be killed. I'm willing enough—only an idiotic General Staff has booted me into the Quartermaster Corps for which I am no more fitted than to run an academy for lady marines—but I'm not willing for a fine sensitive boy, a talented musician like George to suffer the harsh brutalities of a trainingcamp and battlefield."

"The draft . . ." I began tentatively.

"If George had a civilian position in an essential industry—say one holding a contract with the army for badly needed fieldrations . . ."

"I should like to meet your son," I said. "I have been looking around for some time for a reliable manager . . ."

"George might consider it." General Thario squinted his glass against the light. "I'll have him stop by your hotel tomorrow."

The little radio behind the bar, which had been mumbling to itself for hours, spoke loudly. "We interrupt this program to bring you a newsflash: Eire has declared war on the Soviet Union. I repeat, war has been declared on the Union of Soviet Republics by Eire. Keep tuned to this station for further details. We return you now to our regular program."

There was an absent pattering of applause and General Thario stood up gravely, glass in hand. "Gallant little Eire—or, if I may be permitted once the indulgence of using the good old name we know and love so well—brave old Ireland. When the world was at war, despite every provocation, she stayed peaceful. Now that the

world is disgracefully pacific—and you have all heard foreign ministers unanimously declaring their countries neutral—so fast did
they rush to the microphones that they were still panting when they
went on the air—when the whole world was cautious, Ireland, true
to her traditions, joined the just cause. Gentlemen, I give you our
fighting ally, Eire."

Departing from his usual custom, he drank the toast in one
gulp, but no one else in the room paid any attention. I considered
this lack of enthusiasm for a courageous gesture quite unworthy
and meditated for a moment on the insensitivity into which our
people seemed to have sunk.

As the evening went on, the general grew more and more
affable and, if possible, less and less reticent. He had, he assured
me, been the constant victim, either of men or of circumstances.
At the military academy he had trained for the cavalry only to find
himself assigned to the tank corps. He had reconciled himself,
pursued his duties with zeal, and was shunted off to the infantry,
where, swallowing chagrin, he had led his men bravely into a
crossfire from machineguns. For this he got innumerable decorations and a transfer to the Quartermaster's Department. His marriage to the daughter of an influential politician should have
assured peacetime promotion, but the nuptials coincided with an
election depriving the family's party of power.

Now another war had come and he was a mere brigadier
pigeonholed in an unimportant office with juniors broadly hinting
at his retirement while classmates were leading divisions and even
army corps to glorious victory on the field of battle. At least, they
would have been leading them to glorious victory if there had been
any action at all.

"Invade," insisted General Thario, becoming sufficiently stirred by his fervor to lapse into sober incoherence. "Invade them
before they invade us. Aircraft out . . . gentlemen's agreement . . .
quite understand . . . well . . . landingbarges . . . Bering Sea . . .
strike south . . . shuttle transports . . . drive left wing Transiberian
. . . holding operation by right and center . . . abc . . ."

No doubt it was a pity he was deprived of the opportunity to try
these tactics. I was one of the few who had not become a military
theoretician upon the outbreak of the war, but to my lay mind his

plan sounded feasible. Nevertheless, I was more interested in the possible contract for food concentrates than in any strategy, no matter how brilliant. I'm afraid I showed my boredom, for the general abruptly declared it was time to go home.

41 I was a little dubious that after all the drinking and confidences he would remember to send his son around, and to tell the truth, in the calm morning, I felt I would not be too sorry if he didnt, for he had not given me a very high opinion of that young man. What on earth Consolidated Pemmican could do with a musician and a draftevader as generalmanager—even if the title, as it must be, were purely honorary—I couldnt imagine.

I had been long up, shaved and breakfasted and had attended to my correspondence, before the telephone rang and George Thario announced himself at my disposal.

He was what people call a handsome young man. That is, he was big and burly and slow and his eyelashes were perceptible. His hair was short and he wore no hat, but lounged about the room with his hands, thumbs out, in his jacketpockets, looking at me vaguely through the curling smoke from a bent pipe. I had never seen anyone look less like a musician and I began to wonder if his father had been serious in so describing him.

"I don't like it," he announced abruptly.

"Don't like what, Mr Thario?" I inquired.

"Joe to you," he corrected. "Mister from you to me belies our prospective relationship. Just call me Joe."

"I thought your name was George."

"Baptismal—whim of the Old Man's. But it's a stuffy label—no shortening it, you know, so the fellows all call me Joe. Chummier. Don't like the idea of evading the draft. Shows a lack of moral courage. By rights I ought to be a conchie, but that would just about kill the Old Lady. She's in a firstclass uproar as it is—like to see me in the frontlines right now, bursting with dulce et decorum. I don't believe it would bother the Old Man any if I sat out the duration in a C O camp, but it'd hurt his job like hell and the poor old boy is straining his guts to get into the trenches and twirl a theoretical saber. So I guess I'm slated to be your humble and obedient, Mr Weener."

"I'll be delighted to have you join our firm," I said wryly, for I felt he would be a completely useless appendage. In this I am glad to say I did him an injustice, for though he never denied his essential lack of interest in concentrates and the whole process of moneymaking, he proved nevertheless—at such times as he chose to attend to his duties—a faithful and conscientious employee, his only faults being lack of initiative and a tendency to pamper the workers in the plant.

But I have anticipated; at the moment I looked upon him only as a liability to be balanced in good time by the asset of his father's position. It was therefore with irritation I listened to his insistence on my coming to the Thario home that afternoon to meet his mother and sisters. I had no desire for purely social intercourse, last evening's outing being in the nature of a business investment and it seemed superfluous to be forced to extend courtesies to an entire family because of involvement with one member.

However great my reluctance I felt I couldnt afford to risk giving offense and so at fouroclock promptly I was in Georgetown, using the knocker of a door looking like all the other doors on both sides of the street.

"I'm Winifred Thario and youre the chewinggum man—no, wait a minute, I'll get it—the food concentrate man who's going to make Joe essential to the war effort. Do come in, and excuse my rudeness. I'm the youngest, you know, except for Joe, so everybody excuses me." Her straight, blond hair looked dead. The vivacity which lit her windburned face seemed a false vivacity and when she showed her large white teeth I thought it was with a calculated effort.

She led me into a livingroom peopled like an Earlyvictorian conversationpiece. Behind a low table, in a rockingchair, sat a large, fullbosomed woman with the same dead hair and weather-beaten cheeks, the only difference being that the blondness of her hair was mitigated by gray and in her face were the tiny broken red lines which no doubt in time would come to Winifred.

"This is Mama," said Winifred, accenting the second syllable strongly and contriving at once to be vivacious and reverent.

Mama inclined her head toward me without the faintest smile, welcoming or otherwise, placing her hand as she did so regally upon the teacozy, as upon a royal orb.

"Mrs Thario," I said, "I am delighted to meet you."

Mama found this beneath her condescension.

"And this is Constance, the general's firstborn," introduced Winifred, still retaining her liveliness despite Mama's low temperature. Constance was the perfect connectinglink between Winifred and her mother, not yet gray but soon to be so, without Winifred's animation, but with the same voluntary smile showing the same white teeth. She rose and shook my hand as she might have shaken a naughty puppy, with a vigorous sidewise jerk, disengaging the clasp quickly.

"And this," announced Winifred brightly, "is Pauline."

To say that Pauline Thario was beautiful would be like saying Mount Everest is high. In her, the blond hair sparkled like newly threshed straw, the teeth were just as white and even, but they did not seem too large for her mouth, and her complexion was faultless as a cosmetic ad. She was an unbelievably exquisite painting placed in an appropriate frame.

And yet . . . and yet the painting had a quality of unreality about it, as though it were the delineation of a madonna without child, or of a nun. There was no vigor to her beauty, no touch of the earthiness or of blemish necessary to make the loveliness real and bring it home. She did not offer me her hand, but bowed in a manner only slightly less distant than her mother's.

I sat down on the edge of a petitpoint chair, thoroughly ill-atease. "You must tell us about your pills, Mr Weener," urged Winifred.

"Pills?" I asked, at a loss.

"Yes, the thingamyjigs youre going to have Joe make for you," explained Constance.

Mama made a loud trumpeting noise which so startled me I half rose from my seat. "Damned slacker!" she exclaimed, looking fiercely right over my head.

"Now, Mama—bloodpressure," enjoined Pauline in a colorless voice.

Mama relapsed into immobility and Winifred went on, quite as if there had been no explosion. "Are you married, Mr Weener?"

I said I was not.

"Then here's our chance for Pauline," decided Winifred. "Mr Weener, how would you like to marry Pauline?"

I could do nothing but smile uncomfortably. Was this the sort of conversation habitually carried on in their circle or were they quite mad? Constance mentioned with apparent irrelevance, "Winifred is so giddy," and Pauline smiled at me understandingly.

But Winifred went on, "We've been trying to marry Pauline off for years, you know. She's wonderful to look at, but she hasnt any sexappeal."

Mama snorted, "Damned vulgar thing to have."

"Would you like some tea, Mr Weener?" asked Constance.

"Tea! He looks like a secret cocacola guzzler to me! Are you an American Mr Uh?" Mama demanded fiercely, deigning for the first time to address me.

"I was born in California, Mrs Thario," I assured her.

"Pity. Pity. Damned shame," she muttered.

I was partially relieved from my uneasiness by the appearance of George Thario, who bounded in, waved lightly at his sisters and kissed his mother just below her hairline. "My respectful duty, Mama," he greeted.

"Damned hypocrisy. You did your duty youd be in the army."

"Bloodpressure," warned Constance.

"Have they made you thoroughy miserable, Mr Weener? Don't mind them—there's something wrong with all the Tharios except the Old Man. Blood gone thin from too much intermarriage."

"Just like incest," exclaimed Winifred. "Don't you think incest's fascinating, Mr Weener? Eugene O'Neill and all that sort of thing?"

"Morbid," objected Constance.

"Damned nonsense," grunted Mama.

"Cream or lemon, Mr Weener?" inquired Constance. Mama, noved by a hospitable reflex, filled a grudging cup.

"Cream, please," I requested.

"Turn it sour," muttered Mama, but she poured the cream and handed the cup to Constance who passed it to Pauline who gave it to me with a gracious smile.

"You just mustnt forget to keep Pauline in mind, Mr Weener; she would be a terrific help when you become horribly rich and have to do a lot of stuffy entertaining."

"Really, Winifred," protested Constance.

"Help him to the poorhouse and a damned good riddance."

I spent another uneasy fifteen minutes before I could decently make my departure, wondering whether I hadnt made a mistake in becoming involved with the Tharios at all. But there being no question of the solidity of the general's position, I decided, since it was not afterall incumbent upon me to continue a social connection with them, to bear with it and confine my acquaintance as far as possible to Joe and his father.

42 As soon as the contracts were awarded the struggle began to obtain necessary labor and raw materials. We were straining everything to do a patriotic service to the country in time of war, but we came up against the competition for these essentials by ruthless capitalists who had no thought but to milk the government by selling them supplies at an enormous profit. Even with the wholehearted assistance of General Thario it was an endless and painful task to comply with, break through, or evade the restrictions and regulations thrown up by an uncertain and slowmoving administration, restrictions designed to aid our competitors and hamper us. Yet we got organized at last and by the time three Russian marshals had been purged and the American highcommand had been shaken up several times, we had doubled the capacity of our plant and were negotiating the purchase of a new factory in Florida.

I set aside a block of stock for the general, but its transfer was a delicate matter on account of the indefatigable nosiness of the government and I approached his son for advice. "Alberich!" exclaimed Joe incomprehensibly. "Just wrap it up and mail it to him. Mama, God bless her, takes care of all financial transactions anyway." And doubtless with great force, I thought.

Such directness, I pointed out, might have embarrassing repercussions because of inevitably smallminded interpretation if the facts ever became public. We finally solved the problem by putting the gift in George Thario's name, he making a will leaving it to the general. I informed his father in a guarded letter of what we had done and he replied at great length and somewhat indiscreetly, as the following quotation may show:

". . . In spite of pulling every handy and unhandy wire I am still billeted on this ridiculous desk. The General Staff is the most incompetent set of blunderers ever to wear military uniform since Bull Run. They've never heard of Foch, much less of Falkenhayn and Mackensen, to say nothing of Rommel, Guderian or Montgomery. They rest idly behind their Washington breastworks when the order of the day should be attack, attack, and again attack; keeping the combat entirely verbal, weakening the spirit of our forces and waiting supinely for the enemy to bring the war to us . . ."

Although I was too much occupied with the press of business to follow the daytoday progress of hostilities, there was little doubt the general was justified in his strictures. The war was entirely static. With fear of raids by marauding aircraft allayed, the only remaining uneasiness of the public had been whether the words "heavier than air craft" covered robot or V bombs. But when weeks had passed without these dreadful missiles whistling downward, this anxiety also went and the country settled down to enjoy a wartime prosperity as pleasant, notwithstanding the fiftyhour week, rationing, and the exorbitant incometax, as the peacetime panic had been miserable. In my own case Consolidated Pemmican was quoted at 38 and I was on my way, in spite of all hampering circumstances, to reap the benefits of foresight and industry. Unique among great combats, not a shot had so far been exchanged and everyone, except cranks, began to look upon the academic conflict as an unalloyed benefit.

Gradually the war began leaving the frontpages, military analysts found themselves next to either the chessproblems, Today's Selected Recipe, or the weekly horoscope; people once more began to concern themselves with the grass. It now extended in a vast sweep from a point on the Mexican coast below the town of Mazatlan, northward along the slope of the Rocky Mountains up into Canada's Yukon Province. It was wildest at its point of origin, covering Southern California and Nevada, Arizona and part of New Mexico, and it was narrowest in the north where it dabbled with delicate fingers at the mouth of the Mackenzie River. It had spared practically all of Alaska, nearly all of British Columbia, most of Washington, western Oregon and the seacoast of northern California.

Why it surged up to the Rockies and not over them when it had conquered individually higher mountains was not understood, but people were quick once more to take hope and remember the plant's normal distaste for cold or think there was perhaps something in the rarefied atmosphere to paralyze the seeds or inhibit the stolons, so preventing further progress. Even through the comparatively low passes it came at such a slow pace methods tried fruitlessly in Los Angeles were successful in keeping it back. Everyone was quite ready to wipe off the Far West if the grass were going to spare the rest of the country.

General Thario's indiscreet letters kept coming. If anything, they increased in frequency, indiscretion, and length as his continued frustration in securing a field command was added to his helpless wrath at the generalstaff's ineptitude. ". . . They have got hold of that odd female scientist, Francis," he wrote, "and have made her turn over her formula for making grass go crazy. It's to be used as a war weapon, but how or where I don't know. Just the sort of silly rot a lot of armchair theorists would dream up . . ."

Later he wrote indignantly: ". . . They are sending a group of picked men to Russia to inoculate the grasses on the steppes with this Francis stuff. Sheer waste of trained men; bungling incompetence. Why not send a specially selected group of hypnotists to persuade the Russians to sue for peace? It would be better to have given them Mills bombs and let them blow up the Kremlin. Time and effort and good men thrown away . . ."

Still later he wrote with unconcealed satisfaction: ". . . Well, that silly business of inoculating the steppes came to exactly nothing. Our fellows got through of course and did their job, but nothing happened to the grass. Either Francis gave them the wrong formula (possibly mislaid the right one in her handbag) or else what worked in California wouldn't do elsewhere. She is busy trying to explain herself to a military commission right now. For my part they can either shoot her or put her in charge of the WAC. It's of no moment. You can't fight a determined enemy with sprayguns and formulas. Attack with infantry by way of Siberia . . ."

43 While everyone, except possibly General Thario and others in similar position, was enjoying the new comradeinarms atmosphere the abortive war had brought on, a sudden series of submarine attacks on the Pacific Fleet provided a disagreeable jolt and ended the bloodless stage of the conflict. Tried and proved methods of detection and defense became useless; the warships were nothing more than targets for the enemy's torpedoes.

In quick succession the battleships *Montana, Louisiana, Ohio,* and *New Hampshire* were sunk, as were the carriers *Gettysburg, Antietam, Guadalcanal,* and *Chapultepec* as well as the cruisers *Manitowoc, Baton Rouge, Jackson, Yonkers, Long Beach, Evanston* and *Portsmouth,* to say nothing of the countless destroyers and other craft. Never had the navy been so crippled and the people, presaging correctly a forthcoming invasion, suffered a new series of terrors which was only relieved by the news of the Russian landings on the California coast at Cambria, San Simeon and Big Sur.

". . . What did I tell you? What did I tell them, the duffers and dunderheads? We could have been halfway across Asia by now; instead we waited and hemmed and hawed till the enemy, from the sheer weight of our inertia, was forced to attack. The whole crew should be courtmartialed and made to study the campaigns of Generals Shafter and Wheeler as punishment." General Thario's always precise handwriting wavered and trembled with the violence of his disgust.

An impalpable war, pregnant with annihilating scientific devices and other unseen bogies was one thing; actual invasion of the sacred soil over which Old Glory flew, and by presumptuous foreigners who couldnt even speak English, was quite another. At once the will of the nation stiffened and for the first time something approaching enthusiasm was manifest. Cartoonists, moved by a common impulse, unanimously drew pictures of Uncle Sam rolling up his sleeves and preparing to give the pesky interlopers a good trouncing before hurling them back into the Pacific.

Unfortunately the presence of the grass prevented quick eviction of the unwelcome visitors. Only a small portion of the armed forces was based on the Pacific coast, because of the logistical problems presented by inadequacies of supply and transportation.

Of these only a fraction could be sent to the threatened places for fear dispersions of the main body would prove disastrous if the landings were feints. Thus the enemy came ashore practically unopposed at his original landingpoints and secured small additional beachheads at Gorda, Lucia, Morro Bay and Carmel.

East of the grass there were whole armies who had completed basic training, fit and supple. The obvious answer to the invasion was to load them on transports and ship them to the theater of operations. Unfortunately the agreement not to use heavierthanaircraft was an insuperable bar to this action.

That the pact had never been designed to prevent nations from defending their soil against an invader was certain; thousands of voices urged that we keep the spirit of the treaty and disregard the letter. No one could expect us to sit idly by and let our homeland be invaded because of overfinicky interpretation of a diplomatic document.

But in spite of this clear logic, the American people were swept by a wave of timidity. "If we use airplanes," they argued, "so will the Russians; airplanes mean bombs; bombs mean atombombs. Better to let the Russians hold what advantage their invasion has given them than to have our cities destroyed, our population wiped out, our descendants—if any—born with six heads or a dozen arms as a result of radioactivity."

According to General Thario, for a while it was touchandgo whether the President would yield to the men of vision or the others. But in the end apprehension and calculation ordained that every effort must be made to reinforce the defense of the West Coast—except the effective one.

Of course every dirigible was commandeered and work speeded up on those under construction; troopships, heedless of their vulnerability, rushed for the Panama Canal; while negotiations were opened with Mexico, looking toward transporting divisions over its territory to a point south of the weed.

While confusion and defeatism took as heavy a toll of the country's spirit as an actual defeat on the battlefield, the Russians slowly pushed their way inland and consolidated their positions. The American units offered valiant resistance, but little by little they were driven northward until a fairly fixed front was established south of San Francisco from the ocean to the bay and a more fluid one from the bay to the edge of the grass. Army men, like the public, were suspicious of the enemy's apparent contentment with this line, for they reasoned it presaged further landings to the north.

General Thario's jubilation contrasted with the common gloom. "At last the blunderers have given me active duty. I have a brigade in the Third Army—finest of all. Can't write exactly where I'm stationed, but it is not far from a well-known city noted for its altitude, located in a mining state. Brigade is remarkably fit, considering, and the men are rearing to go. Keep your ear open for some news—it won't be long . . ."

44 The news was of the heroic counterlandings. The entire fleet, disdainful of possible submarine action, stood off from the rear of the Russian positions, bombarding them for forty-eight hours preliminary to landing marines who fought their way inland to recapture nearly half the invaded territory. Simultaneously the army below San Francisco pushed the Russians back and made contact at some points with the marines. The enemy was reduced to a mere foothold.

But the whole operation proved no more than a rearguard action. As General Thario wrote, "We are fighting on the wrong continent." Joe was even broader and more emphatic. "It's a putup job," he complained, "to keep costplus plants like this operating. If they called off their silly war (Beethoven down in the cellar during the siege of Vienna expresses the right attitude) and went home, the country would fall back into depression, we'd have some kind of revolution and everybody'd be better off."

I had suspected him of being some kind of parlor radical and although he would doubtless outgrow his youthful notions, it made me uneasy to have a crank in my employ. But beyond urging him to keep his ideas strictly to himself and not leave any more memopads scribbled over with clef signs on his desk, I could do nothing, for upon his retention depended his father's goodwill—the general's assignment to a fieldcommand hadnt altered the status of our contracts—and we had too many unscrupulous competitors to rely solely upon merit for the continuance of our sales.

George Thario's attitude was symptomatic of the demoralization of the country, apparent even during our momentary success. There was no will to victory, and the generalstaff, if one could believe General Thario, was too unimaginative and inflexible to meet the peculiar conditions of a war circumscribed and shaped by the alien glacier dividing the country and diverting normal operations into novel channels.

So the new landings at Astoria and Longview, though anticipated and indeed precisely indicated by the flimsiness of the Russian resistance to the counteroffensive, caught the highcommand by surprise. "Never was a military operation more certain," wrote General Thario, "and never was less done to meet the certainty. Albert, if a businessman conducted himself like the military college he would be bankrupt in six months." Wherever the fault lay, the American gains were wiped out and the invaders swept ahead to occupy all of the country west of the grass.

Boastfully, they sent us newsreels of their entries into Portland and Seattle. They established headquarters in San Francisco and paraded forty abreast down Market Street—renamed Krassny Prospekt. The Russians also renamed Montgomery Street and Van Ness after Mooney and Billings respectively, but for some reason abandoned these designations almost immediately.

But for all their celebrations and 101 gun salutes, this was as far as they could go; the monstrous growth which had clogged our defense now sealed the invaders off and held them in an evershrinking sector. Now came another period of quiescence in the war, but a period radically different in temper from the first. There were many, perhaps constituting a majority, who like George Thario wanted a peace, almost any kind of peace, to be made. Others attempted to ignore the presence of a war entirely and to conduct their lives as though it did not exist. Still others seemed to regard it as some kind of game, a contest carried on in a bloodless vacuum, and from these to the newspapers and the Wardepartment came the hundreds of plans, nearly all of them entirely fantastic, for conquering an enemy now unassailably entrenched.

But while pessimism and lassitude governed the United States the intruders were taking energetic measures to increase their successes. "I have been present at the questioning of two spies," reported General Thario, "and I want to tell you the enemy is not going to miss a single opportunity, unlike ourselves. What they have in mind I cannot guess; they can't fly over the grass any more than we can as long as they want to conciliate world opinion and I doubt if they can tunnel under it, but that they intend to do *something* is beyond question."

Often the obvious course is the surprising one; since the Russians couldnt go over or under the grass they decided to march on top of it. They had heard of our prewar snowshoe excursions on its surface and so they equipped a vast army with this clumsy footgear and set it in motion with supplytrains on wide skis pulled by the men themselves. Russian ingenuity, boasted the Kremlin, would succeed in conquering the grass where the decadent imperialists had failed.

"It is unbelievable—you might even call it absurd, but at least they are doing something, not sitting twiddling their thumbs. My men would give six months' pay to be as active as the enemy. To be sure they are grotesque and inefficient—so was the Army of Italy. Imagine sending an army—or armies if our reports are correct—on a six hundred mile march without an airforce, without artillery, without any mechanized equipment whatsoever. Unless, like the Army of Italy, they have a Bonaparte concealed behind their lunacy they have no chance at all of success, but by the military genius of Joseph Eggleston Johnston, if I were a younger man and not an American I would like to be with them just for the fun they are having."

By its very nature the expedition was composed exclusively of infantry divisions carrying the latest type of automatic rifle. The field commissaries, the ambulances, the baggagetrains, had to be cut to the barest minimum and General Thario wrote that evidently because of the impossibility of taking along artillery the enemy had also abandoned their light and heavy machineguns. Against this determined threat, behind the wall of the Rockies, the American army waited with field artillery, railway guns, bazookas and flamethrowers. For the first time there was belief in a Russian defeat if not in eventual American victory.

But the waiting Americans were not to be given the opportunity for handtohand combat. Since planes could not report the progress of the snowshoers over the grass, dirigibles and free balloons drifting with the wind gave minutetominute reports. Though many of the airships were shot down and many more of the balloons blown helplessly out of the area, enough returned to give a picture of the rapid disintegration of the invading force.

Nothing like it had happened to an army since 1812. The snowshoes, adequate enough for short excursions over the edge of the grass, became suicidal instruments on a march of weeks. Starting eastward from their bases in northern California, Oregon and Washington, in military formation, singing triumphantly in minor keys, the Slavic steamroller had presented an imposing sight. Americans in the occupied area, seeing column after column of closely packed soldiers tramping endlessly up and over the grass, said it reminded them of old prints of Pickett's charge at Gettysburg.

The first day's march went well enough, though it covered no more than a few miles. At night they camped upon great squares of tarpaulin and in the morning resumed their webfooted way. But the night had not proved restful, for over the edges of every tarpaulin the eager grass had thrust impatient runners and when the time came to decamp more than half the canvases had been left in possession of the weed. The second day's progress was slower than the first and it was clear to the observers the men were tiring unduly. More than one threw away his rifle to make the marching easier, some freed themselves of their snowshoes and so after a few yards sank, inextricably tangled into the grass; others lay down exhausted, to rise no more. The men in the balloons could see by the way the feet were raised that the inquisitive stolons were more and more entangling themselves in the webbing.

Still the Soviet command poured fresh troops onto the grass. Profiting perhaps by the American example, they transported new supplies to the army by dirigibles, replacing the lost tarpaulins and rifles, daringly sending whole divisions of snowshoers by parachute almost to the eastern edge. This last experiment proved too reckless, for enough of these adventurers were located to permit their annihilation by longrange artillery.

"Their endurance is incredible, magnificent," eulogized Gen-

eral Thario enthusiastically. "They are contending not only with
the prospect of meeting fresh, unworn troops on our side, but
against a tireless enemy who cannot be awed or hurt and even more
against their own feelings of fear and despair which must come
upon them constantly as they get farther into this green desert,
farther from natural surroundings, deeper into the silence and
mystery of the abnormal barrier they have undertaken to cross.
They are supermen and only supernatural means will defeat them."

But there was plenty of evidence that the general credited the
foe with a stronger spirit than they possessed. Their spirit was
undoubtedly high, but it could not stand up against the relentless
harassment of the grass. The weary, sodden advance went on,
slower and slower; the toll higher and higher. There were signs of
dissatisfaction, mutiny and madness. Some units turned about to
be shot down by those behind, some wandered off helplessly until
lost forever. The dwindling of the great army accelerated, airborne
replacements dependent on such erratic transport failed to fill
the gaps.

The marchers no longer fired at the airships overhead; they
moved their feet slowly, hopelessly, stood stockstill for hours or
faltered aimlessly. Occasional improvised white flags could be
seen, held apathetically up toward the balloonists. Long after their
brave start the crazed and starving survivors began trickling into the
American lines where they surrendered. They were dull and listless
except for one strange manifestation: they shied away fearfully from
every living plant or growth, but did they see a bare patch of soil, a
boulder or stretch of sand, they clutched, kissed, mumbled and
wept over it in a very frenzy.

45 But the catastrophic loss of their great armies was not
all the enemy had to endure. As the grass had stood our
ally and swallowed the attackers, helping us in a negative fashion as
it were, it now turned and became a positive force in our relief.
Unnoticed for months, it had crept northwestward, filching precious mile after mile of the hostile foothold. Now it spurted ahead
as it had sometimes done before, at a furious pace, to take over the
coast as far north as the Russian River, which now doubled the

irony of its name, and added thousands of square miles to its area at the enemy's expense. It surged directly westward too, making what was left of the invader's foothold precarious in the extreme.

The stockmarket boomed and the country went wild with joy at the news of the Soviet defeats. At the darkest moment we had been delivered by forces outside ourselves, but still indubitably American. Hymns of praise were sung to the grass as the savior of the nation and in a burst of gratitude it was declared a National Park, forever inviolate. Rationing restrictions were eased and many industries were sensibly returned to private ownership. Good old Uncle Sam was unbeatable afterall.

But if the Americans were jubilant, the Russians were cast into deepest gloom. Accustomed to tremendous wartime losses of man-power, they had at first taken the news stoically, interpreting it as just another defeat to be later redeemed by pouring fresh troops and then more fresh troops after those which had gone down. But when they realized they had lost not divisions but whole armies, that they had suffered a greater blow than any in their history, that their reserve power was little greater than the armies remaining to the Americans, and finally that the grass, the foe which had dealt all these grievous blows, was rapidly wiping out what remained of their bridgehead, they began to murmur against the war itself.

"Under our dear little Uncle Stalin," they said, "this would never have taken place. Our sons and brothers would not have been sent to die so far away from Holy Mother Russia. Down with the enemies of Stalin. Down with the warmongering bureaucracy."

The Kremlin hastened to assure the population it was carrying out the wishes of the sainted Stalin. It convinced them of the purity of its motives by machinegunning all demonstrators and executing after public trials all Trotskyite-fascist-American saboteurs and traitors. For some reason these arguments failed to win over the people and on November 7 a new slogan was heard, "Long live Stalin and Trotsky," which proved so popular that in a short time the entire bureaucracy was liquidated, the Soviet Union declared an unequivocal workers' state, the army replaced by Redguards, the selling of Soviet bonds decreed a contravention of socialist econ-omy, wages of all were equalized, and the word stakhanovism erased from all Russian dictionaries.

No formal peace was ever made. Neither side had any further appetite for war and though newspapers like the *Daily Intelligencer* continued for months to clamor for the resumption of hostilities, even to using aircraft now that there was less danger of reprisal, both countries seemed content to return quietly to the status quo. The only results of the war, aside from the tremendous losses, was that in America the grass had been unmolested for a year, and the Soviet Union had a new constitution. One of the peculiar provisions of this constitution was that political offenders—and the definition was now severely limited, leaving out ninetynine percent of those formerly jeoparded—should henceforth expiate their crimes by spending the term of their sentence gazing at the colossal and elaborate tomb of Stalin which occupied the center of Red Square.

46 General Stuart Thario, rudely treated by an ungrateful republic, had the choice of a permanent colonelcy or retirement. I have always thought it was his human vanity, making him cling to the title of general, which caused him to retire. At any rate there was no difficulty in finding a place for him in our organization, and if his son's salary and position were reduced in consequence, it was all in the family, as the saying goes.

One of the happy results of our unique system of free enterprise was the rewarding of men in exact proportion to their merits and abilities. The war, bringing disruption and bankruptcy to so many shiftless and shortsighted people, made of Consolidated Pemmican one of the country's great concerns. The organization welcoming General Thario was far different from the one which had hired his son. I now had fourteen factories, stretching like a string of lustrous pearls from Quebec down to Montevideo, and I was negotiating to open new branches in Europe and the Far East. I had been elected to the directorship of several important corporations and my material possessions were enough to constitute a nuisance—for I have always remained a simple, literary sort of fellow at heart—requiring secretaries and stewards to look after them.

It is a depressing sidelight on human nature that the achievement of eminence brings with it the malice and spite of petty minds and no one of prominence can avoid becoming the target of stupid and unscrupulous attack. It would be pointless now to go into those carping and unjust accusations directed at me by irresponsible newspaper columnists. Another man might have ignored these mean assaults, but I am naturally sensitive, and while it was beneath my dignity to reply personally I thought it perhaps one of the best investments I could make to add a newspaper to my other properties.

Now I am certainly not the sort of capitalist portrayed by cartoonists in the early part of the century who would subvert the freedom of the press by handpicking an editor and telling him what to say. I think the proof of this as well as of my broadmindedness is to be found in the fact that the paper I chose to buy was the *Daily Intelligencer* and the editor I retained was William Rufus Le ffaçasé. The *Intelligencer* had lost both circulation and money since it had, so to speak, no home base. But moved perhaps by sentiment, I was not deterred from buying it for this reason, and anyway it was purchasable at a more reasonable figure on this account.

Small circulation or no, it—or rather Le ffaçasé himself—still possessed that intangible thing called prestige and I was satisfied with my bargain. Le ffaçasé showed no reluctance—as why indeed should he?—to continue as managingeditor and acted toward me as though there had never been any previous association, but I did not object to this harmless eccentricity as a smallerminded person might have.

As publisher I named General Thario. I never knew exactly what purpose a publisher serves, but it seemed necessary for every newspaper to have one. Whatever the duties of the office, it left the general plenty of time to attend to the concerns of Consolidated Pemmican. I fed the paper judiciously with money and it was not long before it regained most of the circulation it had lost.

---

47 There was no doubt the grass, our ally to such good purpose in the war, had definitely slowed down; now it was looked upon as a fixture, a part of the American heritage, a natural phenomenon which had outlived its sensational period and come to be taken for granted. Botanists pointed out that *Cynodon* *dactylon*, despite its ability to sheathe itself against a chill, had never flourished in cold areas and there was no reason to suppose the inoculated grass, even with its abnormal metabolism, could withstand climates foreign to its habit. It was true it had touched, in one place, the arctic tundra, but it was confidently expected this excursion would soon cease. The high peaks of the Rockies with the heavy winter snowdrifts lying between them promised no permanent hospitality, and what seeds blew through the passes and lighted on the Great Plains were generally isolated by saltbands, and since they were confined to comparatively small clumps they were easily wiped out by salt or fire. To all appearance the grass was satiated and content to remain crouching over what it had won.

Only a minority argued that in its new form it might be infinitely adaptable. Before, when stopped, it had produced seeds capable of bearing the parent strain. So now, they argued, it would in time acclimate itself to more rigorous temperatures. Among these pessimists, Miss Francis, emerging from welldeserved obscurity, hysterically ranged herself. She prophesied new sudden and sweeping advances and demanded money and effort equal to that expended in the late war be turned to combating the grass. As if taxes were not already outrageously high.

Those in authority, with a little judicious advice from persons of standing, quite properly disregarded her querulous importunities. The whole matter of dealing with the weed was by now in the hands of a permanent body, the Federal Disruptions Commission. This group had spent the first six months of its existence exactly defining and asserting its jurisdiction, which seemed to spread just as the vegetation calling it into being did; and the second six months wrangling with the Federal Trade Commission over certain "Cease and Desist" orders issued to firms using allusions to the grass on the labels of their products, thereby implying they were as vigorous, or of as wide application, as the representation. The Disruptions Commission had no objection in principle to this castigation; they merely thought it should have come from their regulatory hands.

But with the end of the war a new spirit animated the honorable members of the commission and as a token of revived energy they issued a stern directive that no two groups engaged in antigraminous research were to pool their knowledge; for competition, the commission argued in the sixtyseven page order, spurred enthusiasm and the rivalry between workers would the sooner produce a solution. Having settled this basically important issue they turned their attention to investigating the slower progress of the grass to determine whether it was permanent or temporary and whether its present sluggishness could be turned to good account. As a sort of side project—perhaps to show the wideness of their scope—they undertook as well to study the reasons for the failure of the wartime inoculation of the steppes as contrasted with the original too successful California one. They planned a compilation of their findings, tentatively scheduled to cover a hundred and fortyseven foliovolumes which would remain the basic work for all approaching the problem of attacking the grass; and as an important public figure who had some firsthand knowledge of the subject they requested me to visit, at my own expense, the newest outposts of the weed and favor them with my observations. I was not averse to the suggestion, for the authority of the commission would admit me to areas closed to ordinary citizens and I was toying with the idea it might be possible in some way to use the devilgrass as an ingredient in our food products.

48 George Thario having shown in many ways he was growing stale on the job and in need of a vacation, I decided to take him with me. Besides, if the thought of using the weed as a source of cheap rawmaterial came to anything, the engagement of his interest at an early stage would increase his usefulness. Before setting out for the field I read reports of investigators on the spot and was disquieted to note a unanimous mention of new stirrings on the edges of the green glacier. I decided to lose no time and we set out at once in my personal plane for a mountain lodge kindly offered by a business acquaintance. Here, for the next few weeks, keeping in touch with my manifold affairs only by telephone, Joe and I devoted ourselves to observing the grass.

Or rather I did. George Thario's idea of gathering data differed radically from mine—I feel safe to say, as well as from that of almost any other intelligent man. In a way he reminded me of the

cameraman Slafe in his brooding obliviousness to everything except the grass; but Slafe had been doing a job for which he was
being paid, whereas Joe was only yielding to his own mood. For
hours he lay flat on his belly, staring through binoculars; at other
times he wandered about the edge, looking at, feeling, and smelling
it and once I saw him bend down and nibble at it like a sheep.

"You know, A W," he observed enthusiastically—he always
called me "A W" with just enough of a curious intonation to make
it doubtful whether the use of the initials was respectful or satirical— "you know, A W, I understand those fellows who went and
chucked themselves into the grass. It's sublime; it has never happened in nature before. Ive read newspaper and magazine accounts
and either the writers have no eyes or else they lie for the hell of it.
They talk about the 'dirty brown' of the flowers, but A W, Ive seen
the flowers myself and theyre a vivid glorious purple. Have you
noticed the iridescent sparkle when the wind ripples the blades? All
the colors of the spectrum against the background of that marvelous
green."

"There's nothing marvelous about it," I told him a little irritably. "It used to be really green, a bright, even color, but up here
where it's high and cold it doesnt look much different from ordinary
devilgrass—dirty and ugly." I thought his enthusiasm distinctly out
of place in the circumstances.

He did not seem to hear me, but went on dreamily, "And the
sounds it makes! My God, A W, a composer'd give half the years of
his life to reproduce those sounds. High and piercing; soft and
muted; creating tonepoems and études there in its lonely grandeur."

I have spoken before of the noise produced by the weed, a
thunderous crackling and snapping attributable to its extraordinary
rate of growth. During its dormancy the sound had ceased and, in
the mountains at least, was replaced by different notes and combinations of notes as the wind blew through its culms and scraped
the tough stems against each other. Occasionally these ululations
produced reflections extremely pleasing, more often it hurt the ears
with a shrieking discordance; but even at its best it fell far short, to
my mind—and I suppose I may say I'm as sensitive to beauty as
anybody—of meriting Joe's extravagant rhapsodies.

But he was entranced beyond the soberness of commonsense.

He filled notebooks, those thick pulppapered volumes which children are supposed to use in school but never do, with his reactions. In idle moments when he was away, I glanced through them, but for the most part they were incoherent. Meterless poems, lists of adjectives, strained interpretations of the actions of the grass, and many musical notations which seemed to get no farther than a repetitive and faltering start.

I reproduce a few pages of the less chaotic material for what it is worth: "The iceage drove the Cromagnon from the caves which prophesied Cnossus and Pithom and the Temple of Athena in the Acropolis. This grass, twentiethcentury ice, drives magnates from their twentyroom villas to their twentyroom duplexes. The loss was yesterday's. Walt Whitman.

"For it is the animals. Cows and pigs, horses, goats, sheep and rabbits abandoned by the husbandman, startled, puzzled; the clock with the broken mainspring running backward. The small game: deer, antlered, striped, and spotted; wildsheep, *ovis poli*, Teddy Rooseveltshot and Audubonprinted, mountaingoats leaping in terror to hazardous safety on babel's top, upward to the pinpoint where no angels dance. But not alone.

"Meat and meateater, food and feeder, predator and prey; foxes, lynx, coyotes, wolves, wildcats, mountainlion (the passengerpigeon's gone, the dung they pecked from herds thick as man born and man yet to be born lies no more on the plains, *night and day we traveled, but the birds overhead gave cover from the sun and the buffalo before us stretched from the river to the hills*), driven by the ice not ice, but living green, up and up. Pause here upon this little shelf to nibble bark, to mate and bear; to snarl and claw and rend and suck hot blood from moving jugularvein; and then move again upward with docile hoof or else retreat with lashing tail and snarling fangs. Biter and bitten transfused with fear, the timberline behind, the snow alone welcoming, ironically the glacier meets another glacier and only glacier gives refuge to glacier's hunted.

"Here little islands on the peaks. Vegetation's sea is death creeping upward to end at the beginning. The carnivores, whippedtailed, seek the top, ambition's pinnacle, surveying nothing. Tomorrow is for man, the lower mind is reasonable and ponders food and dung and lust, so obstinate the padclaw prowls higher till nothing's left but pedestal and would then wing, but being not yet man can only turn again.

"The ruminants, resigned, nibble at the edges of their death, converting death to life, chewing, swallowing, digesting, regurgitating and digesting again inescapable fate. Reluctant sustenance. Emptybellied, the pointed teeth descend again to take their food at secondhand, to go back sated, brown blood upon the snow and bits of hide and hair, gnawedat bones, while fellows, forgetting fear, remaining stoic, eat, stamp and stamp without impatience and eat again of that which has condemned them.

"Learned doctor, your addingmachine gives you the answer: so many carnivores, so many herbivores, the parallel dashes introduce extinction. Confusedly the savor of Abel's sacrifice was sweet to His nostrils, not Cain's fruits. So is the mind confounded. Turning and devouring each other over prostrate antlers the snarlers die, their furry hides bloat and then collapse on rigid bones to make a place for curious sniffings and quick retreat in trampled snow. There is no victory without harshness, no hope in triumph. The placid ruminants live—the conquerors have conquered nothing.

"The grass comes to the edge of the snow; they eat and fill their meager bellies, they chew the cud and mate and calve and live in wretched unawareness of the heat of glory and death. So is justice done and mercy and yet not justice and yet not mercy. Who was victor yesterday is not victor today, but neither is he victim. Who was victim yesterday is not victor, but neither is he victim . . ."

49 In all this confused rambling I thought there might be a curious and interesting little observation about animal migration—if one could trust the accuracy of an imagination more romantic than factual—and I reduced it to some kind of coherence and added it not only to my report for the Federal Disruptions Commission, but for the dispatches I found time to send in to the *Intelligencer*. I hardly suppose it is necessary to mention that by now my literary talents could no longer be denied or ignored and that these items were not edited nor garbled but appeared exactly as I had written them, boxed and doubleleaded on page one. Though the matter was really trivial and in confessing it I don't mind admitting all of us are subject to petty vanities I was gratified to notice too that Le ffaçasé had the discernment to realize how much the public appreciated my handling the news about the grass, for he advertised my contributions lavishly.

In my news stories I could tell no less than the full truth, which was that the grass, after remaining patriotically dormant throughout the war except for the spurt northward to destroy the remnants of the invading host, had once more set out upon the march. The loss of color I had pointed out to Joe was less apparent each day of our stay as the old vividness revived with its renewed energy and the sweet music which entranced him gave place to the familiar crackling, growing louder with each foot it advanced down the slope, culminating every so often in thunderous explosions.

For down the thousand mile incline of the Mississippibasin it was pouring with accelerating tempo, engulfing or driving everything before it. It was the old story of the creeping stolons, the steppedup tangled mass and the great, towering bulk behind; the falling forward and then the continued headway. Once more the eastbound trains and highways clogged with refugees.

My affairs not permitting a longer stay, I returned to New York, but I could not pry Joe from his preoccupation. "A W," he argued, "I'd be no more use to Consolidated Pemmican right now than groundglass in a ham sandwich. My backside might be in a swivelchair, but my soul would be right up here. It's Whitman translated visibly and tangibly, A W, 'Come lovely and soothing death, undulate round and round.' Besides, youve got the Old Man now, he's worth more to you than I ever will be; he loves business. It's just like the army—without a doddering old generalstaff to pull him back every time he gets enthusiastic."

If anyone else in my organization had talked like this I would have fired him immediately, but I was sure down underneath his aesthetic poses and artistic pretensions there was a foundation of good commonsense inherited from the general. Give the boy his head, I thought; let him stay here and rhapsodize till he gets sick of it; he'll come back the better executive for having got it out of his system. Also, as he himself pointed out, I had his father to rely on and he was a man to whip up production if ever there was one.

50 The chief purpose of my visit to the grass was, at least momentarily, a failure. There was little point sampling and analyzing the weed for its possible use as an ingredient in a food concentrate if it were impossible to set up a permanent place to gather and process it. I won't say I considered my time wasted, but its employment had not been profitable.

But even immersed in the everexpanding affairs of Consolidated Pemmican and Allied Industries, as we now called the parent company, I could not get away from the grass. Each hour's eastward thrust was reported in detail by an hysterical radio and every day the newspapers printed maps showing the newly overrun territory. Once more the grass was the most prominent thought in men's minds, not only over the land of its being, but throughout the world. Scientists of every nationality studied it at firsthand and only strict laws and rigid searches by customs inspectors prevented the importation of specimens for dissection in their own laboratories.

The formula of Miss Francis, now at length revealed in its entirety, was discussed by everyone. There was hardly a man, woman or child who did not dream of finding some means to destroy or halt the grass and thereby make of himself an unparalleled benefactor. A new crop of suggestions was harvested by the *Intelligencer*; in addition to the old they included such expedients as reinoculating the grass with the Metamorphizer in the hope either of its cannibalistically feeding upon itself or becoming so infected with giantism as to blow up and burst—the failure of the experiment on the Russian steppes was ignored or forgotten by these contributors; building barriers of dryice; and the use of infrared lamps.

One of the proposals which tickled the popular imagination was a plan for vast areas to be roofed and glassenclosed, giant greenhouses to offer refuge for mankind in the very teeth of the grass. Artesian wells could be sunk, it was argued, power harnessed to the tides of the sea and piped underground, the populace fed by means of concentrates or hydroponic farming. Everyone—except those in authority, the ones who would have to approve the expenditure of the vast sums necessary—thought there was something in the idea, but nothing was done about it.

Many, believing physical means could be of little avail, suggested metaphysical ones, and these were always punctiliously printed by the *Intelligencer*. They ranged from disregarding the existence of the weed and carrying on ordinary life as though it presented no threat, through Holding the Correct Thought, praying daily for its miraculous disappearance, preferably at a simultaneous moment, to reorganizing the spiritual concepts of the human totality.

51 But even without the newspapers George Thario would have kept me informed. "Piteous if not too comprehensive for small emotions," he wrote in a letter only a little more intelligible than the stuff in his notebooks. "Yesterday I stopped by a small farm or ranch as local grandiloquence everseeking purple justification has it here. Submarginal land the tabulating minds of governmentofficials (spectacles precise on nosebridge, daily ration of exlax safe in briefcase) would have labeled it, sitting in expectant unease on hilltops and the uncomfortable slopes between. Dryfarming; the place illegally acquired from cattlerange (more proper and more profitable) by nester grandsire; surviving drought and duststorm, locust, weevil, and straying herds; feeding rachitic kids, dull women and helpless men for halfcentury.

"The Farm Resettlement Administration would have moved them to fatter ground a hundred times, but blindly obstinate they held to what was theirs and yet not theirs. In the frontseat the man and wife and what remained of quick moments of dropjawed ecstasy, in back unwieldly chickencoop, slats patched with bits of applebox and wire, weathered gray; astonished cocks crowing out of time and hens heads down. Hitched behind, the family cow, stiffribbed and emptyuddered. The grass, deaf lover, had seized the shack, its fingers curled the solid door, body pressed forward for joyful rape. The nesters don't look back but pant ahead; the bumping of the car accommodates the cow.

"Ive had to leave the lodge of course and spend my nights in a thin house with a roof shaped like two playingcards, with the misleading sign, in punishment crippled, half fallen from its support, 'Tourists Accommodated' (if accommodation be empty spaces

with mottoes and porcelain pisspots then punishment was un-
righteous). I shall move on soon, perhaps for the worse since there
is green now, beneath the blue.

"If I can ever come away I shall, but I'd not miss this gladiator
show, this retiarii swing.

"Give my best to the Old Boy—tell him I'd write direct, but
family feeling makes it hard. Joe."

I showed the letter to the general, expecting him perhaps to be
annoyed by Joe's instability, but he merely said, "Boy shouldnt be
wasting his talents . . . put it in sound . . . orchestrate it."

Just as Joe's enthusiasm covered only one aspect of the grass so
his retreat from lodge to wayside hostel, to city hotel, embraced
only a minute sector of the great advance. Neither moral nor brute
force slowed the weed. It clutched the upper reaches of the Rio
Grande and ran down its course to the Gulf of Mexico like quick-
silver in a broken thermometer. It went through Colorado,
Oklahoma and Kansas; it nibbled at the forks of the Platte; it left
behind the Great Salt Lake like a chip diamond lost in an enormous setting.

There is no benefit to be derived from looking at the darker
side of things and indeed it is a universal observation that there is
no misfortune without its compensation. The loss of the great
cattlegrazing areas of the West increased the demand for our concentrated foods by the hundredfold. We paid no duty on the
products shipped in from our South American factories for they
competed only with ourselves and we did the country the humanitarian service of preventing a famine by rushing carload after
carload westward, rising above all thoughts of petty gain by making
no increase whatever in our prices despite the expanding demand.

52 About this time it became indisputable that Button
Gwinnet Fles was no longer of value to Consolidated
Pemmican. His Yankee shrewdness and caution which enabled him
to run the corporation when it was merely a name and a quotation
on the stockmarket had the limits of its virtues. He was extraordinarily provincial in outlook and quite unable to see the concern

on a world scale. In view of our vast expansion such narrowness had become an unbearable hindrance.

I had permitted him to hold a limited number of shares and to act nominally as secretary in order to comply with the regulations of the Security and Exchange Commission, but now it was expedient to add to our officers directors of other companies whose fields were complementary to ours. Besides, in General Thario I had a much abler assistant and so, perhaps reluctantly because of my oversensitivity, I displaced Fles and making the general president of the corporation I accepted the post of chairman of the board.

I must say he took a perfectly natural business move with unbecoming illgrace. "It was mine, Mr Weener, you know it was mine and I did not protest when you stole it; I worked loyally and unselfishly for you. It isnt the money, Mr Weener, really it isnt—it's the idea of being thrown out of my own business. At least let me stay on the Board of Directors; youll never have any trouble from me, I promise you that."

It distressed me to reject his abject plea, but my hands were tied by my devotion to the welfare of the company. Besides, he annoyed me by his palpably untrue reference to what had been a legitimate transaction, never giving a thought to my generosity in not exposing his chicanery, nor the fact that the dummy he manipulated bore no resemblance whatever to the firm I had brought by my own effort to its present size.

Leaving matters in the able hands of General Thario, after warning Joe he had better soon return to his father's assistance, I went abroad to arrange for wider European representation. There I found a curious eagerness to be of help to me and almost fawning servility antipathetic to my democratic American notions. Oddly enough, the Europeans looked upon the United States as a doomed country, thinking I, like some members of our wealthier classes, had come to escape disruption and dislocation at home. Only in England did I find the belief prevalent that the Americans would somehow muddle through because afterall theyre the same sort of chaps we are, you know.

After a highly successful trip I returned home the same day the Grass reached the headwaters of the Mississippi.

53 William Rufus Le ffaçasé astonished me, as well as every newspaperman in the country by resigning as editor of the *Daily Intelligencer*, a post he had held before many of its reporters were born. When I phoned him to come to my office and explain himself he refused, in tones and manner I had not heard from any man since the days when I had wasted my talents as a subordinate. Having none of the pettiness of pride which makes some men fearful of their position, since he would not come to my office, I went to his. There he shocked me for the third time: a high, glossy collar, a flowing and figured cravat concealed the famous diamond stud, while instead of the snuffbox his hands hovered over a package of cheap cigarettes.

"Weener," he rasped, jettisoning all those courtesies to which I had become accustomed, "I never thought I'd be glad to see your vapid face again, unless on a marble slab in some city morgue, but now youre here, moneybags slapping the insides of your thighs in place of the scrotum for which you could have no possible use, I am delighted to tell you in person to take my paper—my paper, sir, note that well, for all your dirty pawings could not make it anything but mine—and supposit it. I hope it frets you, Weener, for the sake of your sniveling but immortal soul, I sincerely hope it rasps you like a misplaced hairshirt. You will get some miserable lickspittle to take my place, some mangy bookkeeping pimp with a permanentwaved wife and three snottynosed brats, but the spirit and guts of the *Intelligencer* depart with W R Le ffaçasé."

I disregarded both his illmanners and his bombast. "What's the matter, Bill?" I asked kindly, "Is it more money? You can write your own ticket, you know. Within reason, of course."

His fingers looked for the snuffbox, but found only the cigarettes which he inspected puzzledly. "Weener, no man could do you justice. You are the bloody prototype of all the arselickers, panders, arsonists, kidnapers, cutthroats, pickpockets, abortionists, pilferers, cheats, forgers, sneakthieves, sharpers and blackmailers since Jacob swindled his brother. Do not fawn upon me little man, I am too old to want women or money. The sands are running out and I shall never now read the immortable Hobbes, but I'll not die in your bloody harness. In me you do not see the man who picked up the torch of Franklin and Greeley and Dana where Henry

Watterson dropped it. Loose of your gangrenous chains, you behold the freelance correspondent of the North American Newspaper Alliance, the man who will devote his declining years to reporting in the terse and vivid prose for which he is justly famous the progress of the grass which strangles the country as you have tried to strangle me."

Again I put personal feelings aside. "If your mind is really made up, we'll want your stuff for the *Intelligencer*, Bill."

"Sir, you may want. I hope the condition persists."

There being no profit in arguing with a madman, I made arrangements to replace him immediately. I reproduce here, not for selfjustification, which would be superflous, but merely for what amusement it may afford, one of his accounts which appeared in the columns of so many third and fourth rate newspapers. I won't say it shows the decay of a once possibly great mind, but it certainly reveals that the *Intelligencer* suffered no irreparable loss.

"Today at Dubuque, Iowa, the Mississippi was crossed. Not by redmen in canoes, nor white on logs or clumsy rafts, nor yet by multiwheeled locomotives gliding over steel bridges nor airplanes so high the wide stream was a thread below. Nature and devastation, hand in hand, for the moment one and the same, crossed it today as Quantrell or Kirby Smith or Nathan Bedford Forrest crossed it, sabers glittering, so many forgotten years ago. But if the men in gray and butternut raided a store or burned a tavern they thought it a mighty victory and went home rejoicing; the green invader is an occupier and colonizer, come to remain for all time, leaving no town, no road, no farm where it has passed.

"A few weeks ago Dubuque was still here, quiet, old and pleasant, the butt of affectionate jokes, the Grass still miles away, the population still hopeful of salvation. And then, because of the panic, the frantic scurry to save things once valuable and now only valued, no one noticed when a betraying wind blew seeds beyond the town, over the river, to find receptive soil on the Wisconsin side. The seeds germinated, the clump flourished. It cut the highway and reached down the banks into the Mississippi, waiting. And while it waited it built up greater bulk for itself, behind and beside. Each day it pushed a little farther toward midstream, drowning its own foremost runners so those behind might have solidity to advance upon.

"Meanwhile from the west the continent imposed upon a continent came closer. The other day Dubuque went, its weathered bricks and immature stucco alike obliterated. The Grass ran out like a bather on a cold morning, hastening to the water before timidity halts him. Although I was watching I could not tell you at what exact instant the gap was closed, at what moment the runners from one clump intertwined with those of the other. But such a moment did occur, and shedding water like a surfacing whale the united bodies rose from the riverbed to form a verdant bridge.

"You could not walk across it, at least no man I know would want to try, but it gives the illusion of permanency no work of man, stone or steel or concrete, has ever given and it is a dismaying thing to see man's trade taken over by nature in this fashion.

"The bridge is a dam also. All the debris from the upper reaches collects against it and soon there will be floods to add to the other distress the Grass has brought. More than half the country is gone now: the territories pillaged from Mexico, argued from Britain, bought from France, have all been lost. Only the original states and Florida remain. Shall we be more successful in defending our basic land than all the acquisitions of a century and a half?"

But why add any more? Dry, senile, without feeling, my only wonder was that his stuff was printed, even in the obscure media where it appeared.

54   With twothirds of the country absorbed and a hundred fifty million people squeezed into what was left, economic conditions became worse than ever. No European ghetto was as crowded as our cities and no overpopulated countryside farmed so intensively to so little purpose. An almost complete cessation of employment except in the remnant of the export trade, valueless money—English shillings and poundnotes illegally circulated being the prized medium of exchange—starvation only irritated rather than relieved by the doles of food seized from the farmers and grudgingly handed out to the urban dwellers.

Each election saw another party in power, the sole demand of the voters being for an administration capable of stopping the Grass. Since none was successful, the dissatisfaction and anger grew together with the panic and dislocation. Messiahs and fuehrers sprang up thickly. Riots in all cities were daily occurrences, rating no more than obscure paragraphs, while in many areas gangs of hoodlums actually maintained themselves in power for weeks at a time, ruling their possessions like feudal baronies and exacting tribute from all travelers through their domain.

Immigration had long ago been stopped, but now the government, in order to preserve what space was left for genuine Americans, canceled the naturalization of all foreignborn and ordered them immediately deported. All Jews who had been in the country less than three generations were shipped to Palestine and the others deprived of political rights in order to encourage them to leave also. The Negroes, who except for a period less than a decade in length had never had any political or civil rights, planned a mass migration to Africa, a project enthusiastically spurred by such elder statesmen as the learned Maybank and the judicious Rankin. This movement proved abortive when statisticians showed there were not enough liquid assets among the colored population to pay a profit on their transportation.

An attempt to oust all Catholics failed also, for the rather odd reason that many of the minor Protestant sects joined in a body to oppose it. The Latterday Saints—now busy building New Deseret in Central Australia—and the Church of Christ, Scientist, as well as the Episcopalians, Doweyites, Shakers, Christadelphians, and the congregation of the Chapel of the Former and Latter Rains presented a united front for tolerance and equity.

An astonishing byproduct of the national despair and turmoil was the feverish activity in all fields of creative endeavor. Novels streamed from the presses, volumes of poetry became substantial items on publishers' lists and those which failed to find a publisher were mimeographed and peddled to a receptive public, while painters working with Renascence enthusiasm turned out great canvases as fast as their brushes could spread the oils. We had suddenly become a nation madly devoted to the arts. When Orpheus Crisodd's Devilgrass Symphony was first played in Carnegie Hall an audience three times as great as that admitted had to be accommodated outside with loudspeakers and when the awesome crescendo of horns, drums, and broken crockery rubbed over slate surfaces announced the climax of the sixth movement, the crowds wept. Even for Mozart the hall was full, or practically full.

In the lively arts the impact of the Grass was more overt. On the comicpage, Superman daily pushed it back and there was great regret his activities were limited to a fourcolor process, while Terry Lee and Flash Gordon, everinspirited by the sharp outlines of mammaryglands, also saved the country. Even Lil Abner and Snuffy Smith battled the vegetation while no one but Jiggs remained absolutely impervious. The *Greengrass Blues* was heard on every radio and came from every adolescent's phonograph until it was succeeded by *Itty Bitty Seed Made Awfoo Nasty Weed*.

Perhaps the most notable feature of this period was a preoccupation with permanency. Jerrybuilding, architectural mode since the first falsefront was erected over the first smalltown store, practically disappeared. The skyscrapers were no longer steel skeletons with thin facings of stone hung upon them like a slattern's apron, while the practice of daubing mud on chickenwire hastily laid over paper was discontinued. Everyone wanted to build for all time, even though the Grass might seize upon their effort next week. In New York the Cathedral of St John the Divine was finally completed and a new one dedicated to St George begun. The demand for enduring woods replaced the market for green pine and men planned homes to accommodate their greatgrandchildren and not to attract prospective buyers before the plaster cracked.

Naturally, forwardlooking men like Stuart Thario and myself, though we had every respect for culture, were not swamped by this sudden urge to encourage the effervescent side of life. Our feet were still upon the ground and though we knew symphonies and novels and cathedrals had their place, it was important not to lose sight of fundamentals; while we approved in principle the desire for permanency, we took reality into account. We had every faith in the future of the country, being certain a way would be found before long to stop the encroachments of the weed; nevertheless, as a proper precaution—a safeguarding counterbalance to our own enthusiastic patriotism—we invested our surplus funds in Consols and European bonds, while hastening our plans for new factories on other continents.

I'm sure George Thario must have been a great cross to his father although the general never spoke of him save in the most affectionate terms. Living like a tramp—he sent a snapshot once showing him with a long starveling beard, dressed in careless overalls, his arm over the shoulder of a slovenly looking girl—he stayed always on the edge of the advancing weed, moving eastward only when forced. He wrote from Galena:

"Eagle forgotten. The rejected accepted, for yesterday's eagle is today's, the hero is man and man his own hero. I was with him when he died and when he died again and a hundred miles to the south is another eagle forgotten and all the prairies, green once more, will be as they were before men insulted them. O eagle forgotten, O stained prairie, O gallows, thirsty mob, knife, torch, revolver. Contumely, parochialism, the shortvision forever gone; and the long vision too, the eagle forgotten is the national bird, the great merging with the greater, so gained too late a vision and saw the hope that was despair.

"I named the catalogue of states and the great syllables rolled from my tongue to echo silence. My sister, my bride. Gone and gone; the Conestoga wagons have no more faint ruts to follow, the Little Big Horn is a combination of letters, the marking sunflowers exist no more. We destroyed, we preempted; we are destroyed and we have been thrust out. Illinois admitted to the Union on suchandsuch a date, the Little Giant rubbed stubby fingers through pompous hair heavy with beargrease, the Honorable Abe in Springfield's most expensive broadcloth, necktie in the latest mode but pulled aside to free an eager adamsapple; the drunken tanner, punctual with the small man's virtues, betrayed and dying painfully with so much blood upon his hands; and the eagle himself, forgotten and now again forgotten.

"I move once more. Step by step I give it up, the land we took and the land we made. Each foot I resign leaves the rest more precious. O precious land, O dear and fruitful soil. Its clods are me, I eat them, give them back; the bond is indissoluble. Even the land gone is still mine, my bones rest in it, I have eaten of its fruits and laid my mark on it . . ."

All of which was a longwinded way of saying the Grass was overrunning Illinois. In contrast I cannot forbear to quote Le ffaçasé, though his faults, at the opposite end of the scale, were just as glaring: "It is in Kentucky now, birthstate of Abraham Lincoln, sixteenth president of the United States, a country which once stretched south of the Forty-ninth Parallel from the Atlantic to the Pacific. I have been traveling extensively in what is left of Lincoln's nation. 'Dukes,' remarked Chesterton, 'don't emigrate.' This country was settled by the poor and thriftless and now few more than the poor and thriftless remain in it.

"Let me try to present an overall picture: What is left of the country has become a nineteenth century Ireland, with all economic power in the hands of absentees. It is not that everyone below the level of a millionaire is too stupid to foresee possibility of complete destruction; or the middle and lower classes virtuously imbued with such fanatical patriotism they are prepared for mass suicide rather than leave. Because dukes *are* emigrating and sending the price of shippingspace into brackets which make the export of any commodity but diamonds or their own hides a dubious investment, even the pawning of all the family assets would not buy steerage passage for a year old baby. Besides there are not enough bottoms in the world to transport a hundred and fifty million people. If the Grass is not stopped, except for a negligible few, it will cover Americans when it covers America.

"No wonder a strange and conflicting spirit animates our people. Apathy? Yes, there is apathy; you can see it on the faces in a line of relief clients wondering how long an industrially stagnant country can continue their dole—even though now it consists of nothing but unpalatable chemicals—socalled 'Concentrates.' Despair? Certainly. The riots and lootings, especially the intensified ones recently in Cleveland and Pittsburgh, are symptoms of it. The overcrowded churches, the terrific increase in drugging and drinking, the sex orgies which have been taking place practically in the open in Baltimore and Philadelphia and Boston are stigmata of desperation.

"Hope? I suppose there is hope. Congress sits in uninterrupted session and senators lend their voices night and day to the destruction of the Grass. The Federal Disruptions Commission has published the eleventh volume of its report and is currently holding hearings to determine how closely the extinct buffalograss is related to *Cynodon dactylon.* Every research laboratory in the country, except those whose staffs and equipment have been moved with their proprietary industries, is expending its energies in seeking a salvation.

"Perhaps only in the Deep South, as yet protected by the width of the lower Mississippi, is there something approaching a genuine hope, although ironically that may be the product of ignorance. Here the overlords have gone and the poor whites, unsupported by an explicit kinship, have withdrawn into complete listlessness. Some black men have fled, but to most the Grass is a mere bogey, incapable of frightening those who have survived so much. Now, for the first time since 1877 the polls are open to all and there are again Negro governors and black legislatures. And they are legislating as if forever. Farm tenancy has been abolished, the great plantations have been expropriated and made cooperative, the Homestead Act of 1862 has been applied in the South and every citizen is entitled to claim a quartersection. There is a great deal of laughter at this childish lawmaking, but it goes on, changing the face of the region, the lawmakers themselves not at all averse to the joke."

Everything Le ffaçasé wrote was not only dull, but biased and unjust as well. It was true capital was leaving the country rapidly, but what other course had it? To stay and attempt to carry on industry in the midst of the demoralization was obviously impractical. The plants remained and when a way was found to conquer the Grass we would be glad to reopen them, for this would be a practical course, just as the flight of capital and no captain, no matter how valiant, has ever feared to use it."

"Pop," George Thario had retorted goodhumoredly, "you dragged in the metaphor, not I. Youve heard of the Alamo and Vicksburg and Corregidor? Well, this is them—all rolled into one."

56 The first snows of this ominous winter halted progress of the Grass. It went sluggish and then dormant first in the far north, where only the quick growingseason, once producing cabbages big as hogsheads, had allowed it to spread at a rate at all comparable to its progress farther south. But by now there could be no doubt left that *Cynodon dactylon,* once so sensitive to cold that it had covered itself, even in the indistinguishable Southern California winter, with a protective sheath, had become inured to frost and chill, hibernating throughout the severest cold and coming back vigorously in the spring.

It now extended from Alaska to Hudson Bay, covering all Manitoba and parts of Ontario. It had taken to itself Minnesota, the northern peninsula of Michigan, Wisconsin, a great chunk of Illinois, and stood baffled on the western bank of the Mississippi from Cairo to its mouth. The northwestern, underpopulated half of Mexico was overrun, the Grass moving but sluggishly into the estados bordering the Gulf Coast.

I cannot say this delusive safety was enjoyed, for there was unbelievable hardship. In spite of the great bulk of the country's coalfields lying east of the Grass and the vast quantities of oil and natural gas from Texas, there was a fuel famine, due largely to the breakdown of the transportation system. People warmed themselves after a fashion by burning furniture and rubbish in improvised stoves. Of course this put an additional strain on firedepartments, themselves suffering from the same lack of new equipment, tires, and gasoline, afflicting the general public and great conflagrations swept through Akron, Buffalo and Hartford. Garbage collection systems broke down and no attempt was made to clear the streets of snow. Broken watermains, gaspipes and sewers were followed by typhus and typhoid and smallpox, flux, cholera and bubonic plague. The hundreds of thousands of deaths relieved only in small degree the overcrowding; for the epidemics displaced those refugees sheltered in the schoolhouses, long since closed, when these were made auxiliary to the inadequate hospitals.

The strangely inappropriate flowering of culture, so profuse the year before, no longer bloomed. A few invincible enthusiasts, mufflered and raincoated, still bore the icy chill of the concert hall, a quorum of painters besieged the artist supply stores for the precious remaining tubes of burntumber and scarletlake, while it was presumed that in traditionally unheated garrets orthodox poets nourished their muse on pencil erasers. But all enthusiasm was individual property, the reaction of single persons with excess adrenalin. No common interests united doctor and stockbroker, steelworker and truckdriver, laborer and laundryman, except common fear of the Grass, briefly dormant but ever in the background of all minds. The stream of novels, plays, and poems dried up; publishers, amazed that what had been profitable the year before was no longer so, were finally convinced and stopped printing anything remotely literate; even the newspapers limped along crippledly, their presses breaking down hourly, their circulation and coverage alike dubious.

The streets were no more safe at night than in sixteenth century London. Even in the greatest cities the lighting was erratic and in the smaller ones it had been abandoned entirely. Holdups by individuals had been practically given up, perhaps because of the uncertainty of any footpad getting away with his loot before being hijacked by another, but small compact gangs made life and property unsafe at night. Tempers were extraordinarily short; a surprised housebreaker was likely to add battery, mayhem and arson to his crimes, and altercations which commonly would have terminated in nothing more violent than lurid epithets now frequently ended in murder.

Since too many of the homeless took advantage of the law to commit petty offenses and so secure some kind of shelter for themselves, all law enforcement below the level of capital crimes went by default. Prisoners were tried quickly, often in batches, rarely acquitted; and sentences of death were executed before nightfall so as to conserve both prison space and rations.

In rural life the descent was neither so fast nor so far. There was no gasoline to run cars or tractors, but carefully husbanded storagebatteries still provided enough electricity to catch the news on the radio or allow the washingmachine to do the week's laundry. To a great extent the farmer gave up his dependence on manufactured goods, except when he could barter his surplus eggs or milk for them, and instead went back to the practices of his forefather, becoming for all intents and purposes practically selfsufficient. Soap from woodashes and leftover kitchen grease might scratch his skin and a jacket of rabbit or wolverine hide make him self-conscious, but he went neither cold nor hungry nor dirty while his urban counterpart, for the most part, did.

One contingency the countrydweller prepared grimly against:

roaming hordes of the hungry from the towns, driven to plunder by
starvation which they were too shiftless to alleviate by purchasing
concentrates, for sale everywhere. Shotguns were loaded, corncribs
made tight, stock zealously guarded. But except rarely the danger
had been overestimated. The undernourished proletariat lacked the
initiative to go out where the food came from. Generations had
conditioned them to an instinctive belief that bread came from the
bakery, meat from the butcher, butter from the grocer. Driven by
desperation they broke into scantily supplied food depots, but sel-
dom ventured beyond the familiar pavements. Famine took its
victims in the streets; the farmers continued to eat.

I arrived in New York on the clipper from London in midJanu-
ary of this dreadful winter. I had boarded the plane at Croydon,
only subconsciously aware of the drive from London through the
traditionally neat hedgerows, of the completely placid and lawabid-
ing England around me, the pleasant officials, the helpful yet not
servile porters. Long Island shocked me by contrast. It had come to
its present condition by slow degrees, but to the returning traveler
the collapse was so woefully abrupt it seemed to have happened
overnight.

Tension and hysteria made everyone volatile. The customs
officials, careless of the position of those whom they dealt with,
either inspected every cubic inch of luggage with boorish suspicion
and resultant damage or else waved the proffered handbags airily
aside with false geniality. The highways, repeating a pattern I had
cause to know so well, were nearly impassable with brokendown
cars and other litter. The streets of Queens, cluttered with wreckage
and refuse, were bounded by houses in a state of apathetic disrepair
whose filthy windows refused to look upon the scene before them.
The great bridges over the East River were not being properly
maintained as an occasional snapped cable, hanging over the water
like a drunken snake, showed; it was dangerous to cross them, but
there was no other way. The ferryboats had long since broken
down.

At the door of my hotel, where I had long been accustomed to
just the right degree of courteous attention, a screaming mob of
men and boys wrapped in careless rags to keep out the cold, their
unwashed skins showing where the coverings had slipped, begged

abjectly for the privilege of carrying my bags. The carpet in the lobby was wrinkled and soiled and in the great chandeliers half the bulbs were blackened. Though the building was served by its own powerstation, the elevators no longer ran, and the hot water was rationed, as in a fifthrate French pension. The coverlet on the bed was far from fresh, the window was dusty and there was but one towel in the bathroom. I was glad I had not brought my man along for him to sneer silently at an American luxury hotel.

I picked up the telephone, but it was dead. I think nothing gave me the feeling that civilization as we knew it had ended so much as the blank silence coming from the dull black earpiece. This, even more than the automobile, had been the symbol of American life and activity, the essential means of communication which had promoted every business deal, every social function, every romance; it had been the first palliation of the sickbed and the last admission of the mourner. Without telephones we were not even in the horse and buggy days—we had returned to the oxcart. I replaced the receiver slowly in its cradle and looked at it a long minute before going back downstairs.

---

57 I had come home on a quixotic and more or less unbusinesslike mission. It had long been the belief of Consolidated Pemmican's chemists that the Grass might possibly furnish raw material for food concentrates and we had come to modify our opinion about the necessity for a processing plant in close proximity. However, at secondhand, no practicable formula had been evolved. Strict laws against the transportation of any specimens and even stricter ones barring them from every foreign country made experiment in our main research laboratories infeasible; but we still maintained a skeleton staff in our Jacksonville plant and I had come to arrange the collection of a large enough sample for them to get to work in earnest. It was a tricky business and I had no one beside myself whom I could trust to undertake it except General Thario, and he was fully occupied.

In addition to being illegal it also promised little profit, for while dislocation of the normal foodsupply made the United States our main market for concentrates, American currency had fallen so low—the franc stood at $5, the pound sterling at $250—it was hardly worthwhile to import our products. Of course, as a good citizen, I didnt send American money abroad, content to purchase Rembrandts, Botticellis, Titians or El Grecos; or when I couldnt find masterpieces holding a stable price on the world market, to change my dollars into some of the gold from Fort Knox, now only a useless bulk of heavy metal.

My first thought was Miss Francis. Though she had more or less dropped from public sight, my staff had ascertained she was living in a small South Carolina town. My telegrams remaining unanswered, there was nothing for me to do but undertake a trip there.

Despite strict instructions my planes had not been kept in proper condition and I had great difficulty getting mechanics to service them. There were plenty of skilled men unemployed and though they were not eager to earn dollars they were willing to work for other rewards. But the pervading atmosphere of tension and anxiety made concentration difficult; they bungled out of impatience, committed stupidities they would normally be incapable of; they quit without cause, flew into rages at the machines, the tools, their fellows, fate, at or without the slightest provocation.

My pilot was surly and hilarious by turn and I suspected him of drinking, which didnt add to my confidence in our safety. We flew low over railroadtracks stretching an empty length to the horizon, over smokeless factorychimneys, airports whose runways were broken and whose landinglights were dark. The land was green and rich, the industrial life imposed upon it till yesterday had vanished, leaving behind it the bleaching skeleton of its being.

The field upon which we came down seemed in slightly better repair than others we had sighted. The only other ship was an antique biplane which deserved housing in a museum. As I looked around the deserted landingstrip a tall Negro emerged leisurely from one of the buildings and walked toward us.

"Where are the airport officials?" I asked rather sharply, for I didnt relish being greeted by a janitor.

"I am the chief dispatcher. In fact, I am the entire personnel at the moment."

My pilot, standing behind me, broke in. "Boy, where're the white folks around here?"

The chief dispatcher looked at him steadily a long moment before answering. "I imagine you will find people of various shades all over town, including those allegedly white. Was there anyone in particular you were interested in or are you solely concerned with pigmentation?"

"Why, you goddam—"

I thought it advisable to prevent a possible altercation. I recalled Le ffaçasé's articles on the Black South which I had considered vastly overdrawn. Evidently they were not, for the chocolate-colored man spoke with all the ease and assurance of unquestioned authority. "I want to get to a Miss Francis at—" I consulted my notes and gave him the address. "Can you get me a taxi or car?"

He smiled gravely. "We are without such luxuries at present, I regret to say. But there will be a bus along in about twenty minutes."

It had been a long time since I suffered the wasted time and inconvenience of public transportation. However, there was no help for it and I resigned myself philosophically. I walked with the chief dispatcher into the airport waitingroom, dull with the listless air, not of unoccupancy, but disuse.

"Not much air travel," I remarked idly.

"Yours is the first plane in a month."

"I wonder you bother to keep the airport open at all."

"We do what we can to preserve the forms of civilization. The substance, unfortunately, cannot be affected by transportation, production, distribution, education or any other such niceties."

I smiled inwardly. What children these black people were, afterall. I was relieved from further ramblings by the arrival of the bus which was as laughable as the chief dispatcher's philosophizing. The dented and rusty vehicle had been disencumbered of its motor and was hitched to four mules who seemed less than enthusiastic over their lot. I got in and seated myself gingerly on one of the dilapidated seats, noting that the warning signs "For White" and "For Colored" had been smeared over with just enough paint to make the intent of obliteration clear without actually doing so.

58 How Miss Francis continued to make every place she lived in, apartment, chickenhouse or cottage, look exactly alike was remarkable. Nothing is more absurd than the notion that socalled intellectual workers are always alert—as Miss Francis demonstrated by her greeting to me.

"Well, Weener, what is it this time? Selling on commission or an interview?"

It was inconceivable any literate person in the United States could be ignorant of my position. "It is neither," I returned with some dignity. "I am here to do you a favor. To help you in your work." And I explained my proposition.

She squatted back on her heels and gave me that old, familiar, searching look. "So you have made a good thing out of the Metamorphizer afterall," she said irrelevantly and untruthfully. "Weener, you are a consistent character—a beautifully consistent character."

"Please come to the point, Miss Francis. I am a busy man and I have come down here simply to see you. Will you accept?"

"No."

"No?"

"I doubt if I could combine my research with your attempt to process the inoculated *Cynodon dactylon*. However, that would not prevent me from taking you up and using you in order to further a good cause. But I am not yet ready—I shall not be ready for some time, to go directly to the Grass. That must come later. No, Weener."

I was exasperated at the softness of my impulse which had made me seek out this madwoman to do her a favor. I could not regret my charitable nature, but I mentally resolved to be more discriminating in future. Besides, the thought of Miss Francis for the work had been sheer sentimentality, the sort of false reasoning which would make of every mother an obstetrician or every hen an oologist.

As I sauntered through the drowsy streets, killing time till the driver of the ridiculous "bus" should decide to guide his mules back to the airport, I was struck by the lack of tension, of apprehension and anxiety, so apparent in New York. Evidently the Black South suffered little from the brooding fear and terror; I put it down to their childish thoughtlessness.

Walking thus reflectively, head down, I looked up suddenly—straight into the face of the Strange Lady I had driven from Los Angeles to Yuma.

I'm sure I opened my mouth, but no words came out. She was hurrying rapidly along, paying no attention either to me or to her surroundings, aloof and exquisite. I think I put out my hand, or made some other reflexive gesture to stop her, but either she failed to notice or misunderstood. When I finally recovered myself and set out after her, she had vanished.

I waited for the bus, wondering if I had been victim of an hallucination . . .

59 In spite of Miss Francis' blindness to her own interest I still had a prospective superintendent for the gathering and shipping of the grass: George Thario. Unless his obsession had sent him down into Mississippi or Louisiana, I expected to find him in Indianapolis.

The short journey west was tedious and uncomfortable, repeating the pattern of the one southward. At the end of it there was no garrulous chief dispatcher, for the airport was completely deserted, and I was thankful for an ample stock of gas for the return flight.

I had no difficulty locating Joe in an immense, highceilinged furnishedroom in one of the ugliest gray weatherboarded houses, of which the city, never celebrated for its architecture, could boast. The first thing to impress me was the room's warmth. For the first time since landing I did not shiver. A woodfire burned in an open grate and a kerosene heater smelled obstinately in an opposite corner. A grandpiano stood in front of the long narrow windows and on it slouched several thick piles of curlyedged paper.

He greeted me with something resembling affection. "The tycoon himself! Workers of the world—resume your chains. A W, it's a pleasure to see you. And looking so smooth and ordinary and unharassed too, at the moment everyone else is tearing himself with panic or anguish. How do you do it?"

"I look on the bright side of things, Joe," I answered. "Worry never helped anybody accomplish anything—and it takes fewer muscles to smile than to frown."

"You hear that, Florence?"

I had not noticed her when I came in, the original of the snapshot, sitting placidly in a corner darning socks. I must say the photograph had done her less than justice, for though she was undoubtedly commonlooking and sloppy, with heavy breasts and coarse red cheeks and unconcealedly dyed hair, there was yet about her an air of great vitality, kindness, and good nature. Parenthetically she acknowledged my presence with a pleasant smile.

"You hear that? Remind me the next time I am troubled by a transposition or a solopassage that it takes less muscles to smile than to frown. For I have got to work at last, A W; the loafing and inviting of my soul is past, my soul has responded to my invitation. You remember Crisodd's Devilgrass Symphony? A horrible misconception if ever there was one, a personal insult to anyone who ever saw the Grass; a dull, unintentional joke; bad Schoenberg—if that isnt a tautology—combined with faint memories of the most vulgar Wagner—if that isnt another tautology—threaded together on *Mighty Like a Rose* and *Alexander's Ragtime Band*. But what am I saying, A W, to you who are so free from the virus of culture? What the hell interest have you in Crisodd's symphony or my symphony or anybody's symphony, except the polyphony of profits?"

"I hope no one thinks I'm a narrowminded man, Joe," I reproved him. "I venture to say I have as much interest in Art as the next person. Ive done a bit of writing myself, you know, and literature—"

"Oh sure. I didnt mean to hurt your feelings."

"You did not. But while I believe Music is a fine thing in its place, I came to discuss a different subject."

"If you mean taking Joe back to Europe with you, youre out of luck, Mr Weener," put in Florence placidly. "He's almost finished the first movement and we'll never leave the Grass till it's all done."

"You mistake me, Mrs Thario. I have a proposition for your husband, but far from taking him away from the Grass, it will bring him closer to it."

"Impossible," exclaimed Joe. "I am the Grass and the Grass is me; in mystical union we have become a single entity. I speak with its voice and in the great cadences which come from its heart you can hear Thario's first, transfigured and magnified a hundred thousand times."

I was sorry to note his speech, always so simple and unaffected in contrast to his letters, was infected with an unbecoming pomposity. Looking at him closely I saw he had lost weight. His flesh had shrunk closer to his big frame and the lines of his skull stood out sharply in his cheek and jaw. There was the faintest touch of gray in his hair and his fingers played nervously with the ragged and illadvised beard on his chin. He hardly looked the man who had evaded serious work in order to encourage a silly obsession, comfortably supported all the while by a sizable remittance from his father.

I outlined to them my plans for gathering samples of the weed. Florence tucked her stillthreaded needle between her teeth and inspected the current pair of socks critically. Joe walked over to the piano and struck several discordant notes.

"I understand there are several parties making expeditions onto the Grass," I said.

"Lots," confirmed Joe. "There's a group sent out by Brother Paul on some very mysterious missions. It's called the Sanctification of the Forerunner. God knows how many thousands he's made his suckers cough up, for theyre equipped with all the latest gadgets for polar exploration, skis and dogsleds, moompitcher cameras, radios and unheardof quantities of your very best pemmican. They started as soon as the snow was thick enough to bear their weight and if we have an untimely thaw theyll go to join the Russians.

"Then there's the government bunch, the Disruptions Commission having finally and reluctantly produced an idea, but exactly what it is they havent confided to an eager citizenry. Smaller groups too: scientists and nearscientists, enthusiasts who have got the notion somehow that animals or migratory game are roaming the snow on top of the grass—exactly how they got there is not explained—planning to photograph, hunt or trap; and just plain folk making the trip for the hell of it. We might have gone ourselves if it hadnt been for the symphony."

"Your symphony is concerned with the Grass?" I asked politely.

"It's concerned with combinations of sound." He looked at me sharply and banged out harsher discords. "With life, if you want to talk like a programnote."

"If you go on this expedition it will give you an opportunity to gather new material," I pointed out.

"If I look out the window or consult my navel or 'meditate

while at stool' or cut my finger I will get new material with much less hardship. The last thing a composer or writer or painter needs is material; it is from excess of material he is the besotted creature he is. He may lack leisure or energy or ability or an active colon, but no masterpiece ever was or conceivably could be thwarted from lack of material."

"Yet you have tied yourself to the Grass."

"Not to prostitute it to whatever talents I have, but because it is the most magnificent thing on earth."

"Then of course youll go," I said.

"Why don't you go yourself, A W? Do you good to live out in the open."

"I can't afford the time, Joe; I have too many things that need my personal attention."

He struck a series of great thumping notes. "And so have I, A W, so have I. I'm afraid youll have to get somebody else."

I could neither understand nor shake his obstinacy and when I left them I had almost determined to abandon the whole project, for I could not think whom else trustworthy I could get. His idea of my own participation was fantastic; I had long since come to the point where it was necessary to delegate all such duties to subordinates.

60 Perhaps it was Joe's sly remark about it doing me good to be out in the open, or the difficulty of getting a conveyance, but I decided to walk to my hotel. Taxis of course disappeared with gasoline, but ingenious men, unwilling to be pauperized by accepting the dole, had devised rickshaws and bicycle carriages which were the only means of local transportation. The night was clear and cold, the stars gleaming in distant purity, but all around, the offensive smell of the disheveled city played on my disgusted nostrils.

"In the name of Jesus Christ, Amen. Brother, are you saved?"

When the figure had come out from the shadow of a building to accost me my first thought had been of a holdup, but the odd salutation made this seem unlikely. "What do you want?" I asked.

"Brother, are you a Christian man?"

I resented the impertinence and started to walk on; he followed close beside me. "Harden not your heart, miserable sinner, but let Jesus dissolve your pride as he washes away your other sins. Be not high and mighty for the high shall be low and the mighty powerless; in a short time you will be food for grass. The Grass is food for the Ox, the divine Ox with seven horns which shall come upon the world with a great trumpeting and bellowing soon after the Forerunner."

I knew of the great multiplication of insanity and hoped I could reach the hotel before he grew violent. "What is your name?" I temporized.

"Call me Brother Paul, for I was once Saul the worldly; now I am your brother in Christ."

"Brother Paul! The radio preacher?"

"We are all members one of another and He who watches the sparrow fall makes no distinction between one manmade label and another. All of us who have found Christ Jesus with the help of Brother Paul are called Brother Paul. Come to the Loving Arms, O miserable sinner, and be Brother Paul also."

I thought it might be very confusing. "I have always been interested in religion."

"O puny man. Interested in life and interested in death, interested in being and interested in begetting, interested in religion and interested in dung. Turn from those interests which the devil pays upon your soul's mortgage; your Savior resides in the heart of the Grass—withhold not your precious soul from Him. At this very moment the Forerunner is being sanctified and after her there will come the Ox to eat the Grass and then the end of the world. Give Brother Paul your worthless earthly possessions, give your soul to Jesus and hasten that glorious day. Hallelujah!"

The fervid jumble ended in a near scream. What a waste of oratorical and perhaps organizational energy, I mused as I strode along rapidly, still intent on escaping the fanatic. Under different circumstances, I thought, a man like this might turn out to be a capable clerk or minor executive. Suddenly I had a hunch.

"Mr—?"

"Brother Paul. I have no earthly name."

"I wish youd come with me for a few minutes; I have a proposition which might interest you."

In the darkness I could see him peering at me suspiciously. "Is this some worldly seduction from the Christian path?"

"I think you will find what I have to offer a material aid to your church."

"I have no church," he said. "We are Christians and recognize no manmade institution."

"Well, then, to your movement or whatever you call it." In spite of his reluctance, which was now as great as mine had been originally, I persuaded him to accompany me. He sat uneasily forward while I told him who I was and sketched the plan for collecting some of the Grass.

"What is this to me? I have long ago put aside all material thoughts and now care only for the life of the spirit."

This must be true, I thought, noting his shabby clothes, sweat-greasy muffler at once hiding and revealing lack of necktie, and cracked shoes, one sock brown, the other black. "It is this to you: if you don't want the salary and bonus attached to organizing and superintending the expedition—and I am prepared to be generous—you can turn it over to Brother Paul. I imagine it will be acceptable."

He shook his head, muttering, "Satan, Satan." The lower part of his face was wide and divided horizontally, like an inverted jellymold. It tapered up into bracketing ears, supporting gingery eaves. I pressed home my arguments.

"I will put your proposition to Brother Paul," he conceded at length.

"I thought distinctions between one man and another were worldly and trivial," I prodded him. "Arent you Brother Paul?"

"Satan, Satan," he repeated.

I'm sure it could have been nothing but one of those flashes of intuition for which successful executives are noted which caused me to pick this man in spite of his absurd ranting and illfavored appearance. Not intuition really, but an ability to evaluate and classify personalities instantly. I always had this faculty; it helped me in my early experiences as a salesman and blossomed out when I entered my proper field.

Anthony Preblesham—for that was his worldly name—did not disappoint my judgment for he proved one of the most aggressive men I ever hired. The Brother Paul hocuspocus, which he quickly dropped, had merely caught and canalized an abounding energy that would otherwise have flowed aimlessly in a stagnant world. In Consolidated Pemmican he found his true faith; his zeal for our products proved as great if not greater than his former hysteria for the salvation of mankind. It was no fault of his that the expedition he led proved fruitless.

The men Tony Preblesham took with him were all Brother Pauls who—since they disdained them—had not been told of material rewards but given the impression they were furthering their fanatical creed. They built a camp upon the Grass, or rather upon the snow which overlay the Grass, near what had once been Springfield, Illinois. Digging down through the snow to the weed, they discovered it to have lost most of its rubbery qualities of resistance in dormancy, and cut with comparative ease more than four tons which were transported with the greatest difficulty to the Florida plant. Here, to anticipate, their work came to nothing, for no practicable method was found for reducing the grass to a form in which its nutritive elements could be economically extracted.

61 The secrecy surrounding the government expedition could not be maintained and it was soon learned that what was planned was nothing less than an attempt to burn great areas of the weed while in its dormant state. All previous attempts to fire the Grass had been made when the sap was running and it was thought that in its dryer condition some measure of success might be obtained. The public instantly translated possibility into probability and probability into virtual certainty, their enthusiastic optimism making the winter more bearable.

The party proceeded not more than a couple of miles beyond the eastern edge, dragging with them a flexible pipeline through which was pumped fueloil, now priceless in the freezing cities. Methodically they sprayed a square mile and set it afire, feeding the flames with the oil. The burning area sank neatly through the snow, exposing the grass beneath; dry, yellow and brittle. The stiff, interwoven stolons caught; oil was applied unstintedly; the crackling and roaring and snapping could be heard by those well beyond the perimeter of the Grass and the terrific heat forced the temporary abandonment of the work.

The spotbroadcasters in emotional voices gave the news to those whose radios still functioned. Reporters flashed their editors, BURNING SUCCESSFUL. WILL STOP GRASS IF MULTIPLIED. All over the country volunteer crews were instantly formed to repeat the experiment.

When the flames died down the men crept closer to inspect the results. The heat had melted the snow for many yards outside the orbit of fire, revealing a border of dull and sodden grass. Beyond this border a blackened crater had eaten its way straight down to the reclaimed earth below. Shouting and rejoicing greeted this evidence of triumph. What if the Grass could advance at will in summer? It could be subdued in winter and thus kept in check till the ingenuity which devised this one victory could win another.

Working furiously, the oil was again sprayed, this time over a still larger piece and again the flames lit the sky. The President issued a Proclamation of Thanksgiving; the American dollar rose to $175 to the pound, and several prominent expatriates began to think seriously of returning home.

The second fire burned through the night and aided by a slight change in the weather thawed the snow over a great area. Eagerly the expedition, now swollen into a small army, returned to continue their triumphant labors. The bright sun shone upon the dirtied snow, upon naked muddy earth in the center of the crater, upon the network of burnt and blackened stems and upon the wide band of grayishgreen grass the retreating snow had laid open to its rays. Grayishgreen, but changing in color at every moment as the work of spraying began again.

Changing color, becoming more verdant, thrusting blades into the air, moving its long runners upward and sideways and downward toward the destroyed part. Revived by the heat, relieved of the snow, the Grass, fighting for its life with the same intensity which animated its attackers, burst into a fury of growth. It covered the evidences of destruction in less time than the burning had taken. It tore the pipeline from its tormentors' hands and drove them away with threats of swift immolation. Defiantly it rose to a pinnacle, hiding its mutilation, and flaunted its vivid tendrils to bear witness to its invulnerability till a killing frost followed by another snowfall covered it again.

Since the delusive hope had been so high, the disappointment threw the public into a despair greater than ever before. The nervous tension of anxiety was replaced by a listlessness of resignation and the suicide rate, high before, now doubled. For the first time a general admission was to be heard that no solution would be found and in another season the end would come for the United States. Facing the prospect squarely, an exodus of the little people, as distinguished from the earlier flight of men of wealth and foresight, from the country began.

This was the first countermeasure attempted since the Grass crossed the Mississippi, and in reaction to its collapse, the return of Brother Paul's expedition passed almost unnoticed. Only *Time*, now published in Paris, bothered to report it for general circulation: "Last week from some undisclosed spot in mid U.S. returned Mother, 'The Forerunner' Joan (real name: unknown), and party. Dispatched Grassward by Brother Paul, doom-predicting, advent-prophesying graminophile evangelist, the purpose of Mother Joan's expedition had been her 'Sanctification,' above the exact spot where the Savior was waiting in the midst of the Grass to receive His faithful disciples. Said Brother Paul to reporters after embracing The Forerunner enthusiastically, 'The expedition has been successful.' Said Mother Joan, off the record, 'My feet hurt.'"

62 The coming of spring was awaited with grim foreboding, but the Grass was not bound by any manmade almanac and unable to contain itself till the melting of the snow, again leaped the barrier of the Mississippi, this time near Natchez, and ran through the South like water from a sloshed dishpan. The prized reforms of the black legislatures were wiped out more quickly even than their greatgrandfathers' had been in 1877. The wornout cotton and tobacco lands offered hospitable soil while cypress swamps and winterswollen creeks pumped vitality into the questing runners. Southward and eastward it spread, waiting only the opening of the first pussywillow and the showing of the first crocus to jump northward and meet the western advance there.

The dwindling remnants of cohesion and selfcontrol existing before now disappeared completely. The capital was moved to Portland, Maine. Local law and order vanished. The great gangs took over the cities and extracted what tribute they could from the impoverished inhabitants. Utilities ceased functioning entirely, what little goods remained were obtainable only by barter, and epidemic after epidemic decreased the population to fit the shrinking boundaries.

Brother Paul, deprived of the radio, now multiplied himself infinitely in the person of his disciples, preaching unremittingly against resistance, even by thought, to the oncoming Grass. Mother Joan's infrequent public appearances attracted enormous crowds as she proclaimed, "O be joyful; give your souls to Jesus and your bodies to the Grass. I am The Forerunner and after me will come the Ox. Rejoice, brothers and sisters, for this is the end of all your suffering and misery."

On foot or rarely with the aid of a horse or mule, the panicstricken population marched northward and eastward. Canadian officials, anxious to apply immigration controls with the greatest possible latitude, were thrust aside as though their existence were an irrelevance. Along the lower reaches of the St Lawrence the refugees came like locusts to devour the substance of the *habitants*. Into empty Ungava and almost equally empty Labrador the hardier ones pushed, armed like their forebears with only ax and shotgun. Northward and eastward, beyond the Arctic Circle and onto the polar ice they trickled, seeking some place which promised security from the Grass. Passenger rates to Europe or South America, formerly at a premium, now shot to unparalleled heights.

I wound up my own affairs, disappointed at the failure to find a use for the Grass, but still keeping it in view as a future objective, and arranged for the removal of the Florida factory to Brazzaville. Heeding the cabled importunities of Stuart Thario I risked my life to travel once more into the interior to see Joe and persuade him to come back with me. I found them in a small Pennsylvania town in the Alleghenies, once a company owned miningvillage. The Grass, advancing rapidly, was just beyond the nearest mountainridge, replacing the jagged Appalachian horizon with a softer and more ominous one.

They appeared serene and content, Joe's haggard look of the winter erased. "I'm in the middle of the third movement, A W," he told me, like a man who had no time to waste on preliminaries or indirections. "Here." He thrust an enormous manila envelope at me. "Here are the first two movements. There are no copies and I cannot trust the mails or any other messenger to get them out. If possible I'll send the Old Man the third movement as soon as it's finished—and the fourth, if I have time. But take the first two anyway; at least I'll know they're preserved."

"Joe, Florence!" I exclaimed. "This is ridiculous. Insane. Come back with me."

Silence.

"You can compose just as well in Europe, if it is so important to you. In France, say, or England, away from this danger and discomfort. There is no doubt the country is finished; come to safety while you can."

Florence was busy with a stack of musicpaper and offered no comment. Joe put his hand for a second on my shoulder and then turned away, talking with his eyes fixed out the window in the direction of the Grass.

"General Herkimer had both legs shot off at the battle of Oriskany. He made his men put his back to a treestump and with a flintlock rifle fired at the enemy until he bled to death. Commodore Lawrence, mortally wounded, had only one order. Schoolbooks hold the words of John Paul, selfnamed Jones, and of Hiram Ulysses Grant. Even yesterday, the old tradition was alive: 'Enemy landing: issue in doubt.' If I finish my symphony—"

"When you finish your symphony—" I encouraged.

"If you finish your symphony—" said Florence quietly.

"If I finish my symphony, it must be in Maine, New Hampshire, Vermont." His speech took on a hushed, abstracted tone. "Massachusetts, Rhode Island or Connecticut. New York, New Jersey, Pennsylvania—" his voice rose higher— "Maryland, Virginia or West Virginia—" his shoulders shook and he seemed to be crying— "North Carolina, South Carolina, Georgia, Florida . . ."

I left them, convinced the madness of the country had found still another victim. That night I thankfully boarded the European

Clipper for the last time. The next day I sank back into civilization as into a comfortable bed.

---

63   The United States, July 4 (N.A.N.A.)— 'A decent respect for the opinion of mankind' dictates the content of this summary. Less than two centuries past, a small group of smugglers, merchants and planters united in an insurrection which in its course gathered to itself such an accreta of riffraff—debtors, convicts, adventurers, careerists, foreigners, theoreticians, idealists, revolutionaries, soldiers of fortune and restless men, that at the height of their numbers they composed with their sympathizers, perhaps a third of the people in the country. After seven years of inept war in which they had all the breaks, including that of a halfhearted enemy, they established 'upon this continent a new nation.' Some of the phrases thrown off in the heat of propaganda were taken seriously and despite shocked opposition written into basic law.

"The cryptogram is readable backward or forward, straightaway or upside down. Unparalleled resources, the fortuitous historical moment, the tide of immigration drawing on the best of the world, the implicit good in conception necessarily resultant in the explicit best of being; high purpose, inventive genius, exploratory urge, competitive spirit, fraternal enthusiasm, what does the ascription matter if the end product was clear for all to see?

"Is it not fitting that a nation calling itself lightly 'God's Country,' meaning a land abundantly favored by nature, should find its dispatch through an act of the benefactor become understandably irritable? This is not to pose the editorial question of justice, but to remember in passing the girdled forests, abused prairies, gullied lands, the stupidly harnessed plains, wasted coal, gas, petroleum; the millions of tons of rich mud denied hungry soil by Mississippi levees and forced profitlessly into the salt sea.

"A small part, a heartbreakingly small part of the United States remains at this moment. In a matter of weeks even this little must be overrun, stilled and covered green as all graves are. Scattered through the world there will be Americans, participants in a bitter diaspora. For them—and for their children to be instructed zealously in the formalities of an antique civilization—there can be no Fourth of July, no Thanksgiving; only one holiday will remain, and that continue through all the year. Its name, of course, is Memorial Day. W. R. L."

64 This was the last dispatch from the once great editor. It was assumed generally that he had perished with so many others. It was only some time later I heard a curious story, for whose authenticity I cannot vouch.

True to the flippant prediction of Jacson Gootes, Le ffaçasé returned to the Church into which he had been born. He went further and became a lay brother, taking upon himself the obligation of silence. Though an old man, he stayed close to the advancing Grass, giving what assistance and comfort he could to the refugees. The anecdotes of his sudden appearance in typhusridden camps, mute and gaunt, hastening with water for the feverish, quieting the terrified with a light touch, praying silently beside the dying, sound improbable to me, but I mention them for what they are worth.

65 When winter came again, the Canadian government petitioned the Parliament at Westminster for crowncolony status and the assent of the Queen's Privy Council was given to the ending of the premier Dominion. All that was left of the largest landmass within the British Commonwealth was eastern and northern Quebec, the Maritime Provinces and part of the Northwest Territories.

The United States and more than half of Mexico had been wiped from the map. From the Pacific to the Atlantic, from Nome to Veracruz stretched a new Sargasso Sea of *Cynodon dactylon*. A hundred and eighty million men, women, and children had been thrust from their homes by a despised weed.

I cannot say life on the other continents—and I could call any of them, except possibly Africa, my home—was undisturbed by the disappearance of the United States. American competition gone, the tempo of businesslife seemed to run slower and slower. Production dwindled, prices rose; luxury articles were made in abundance, but manufacturers hesitated to adopt American methods of massproduction for necessities.

Russia, after her new revolution, was a quiet backwater economically, although politically she caused turmoil by giving a home to the Fourth International. Germany became the leading iron and steel country, but it was not an aggressive leadership, rather it was a lackadaisical acceptance of a fortuitous role; while Britain, often on deathbed but never a corpse, without question took the lead in international affairs.

Consolidated Pemmican and Allied Industries was now, if not the largest, certainly one of the largest companies in the world. We purchased sheep in Australia, beef and wheat and corn in South America, rice and millet and eggs in Asia, fruit and sugar and milo in Africa, and what the farmers of Europe could spare, to process and ship back in palatable, concentrated form to a world which now constituted our market. Besides all this we had of course our auxiliary concerns, many of which dominated their respective fields. Ministers of finance consulted me before proposing new budgets and there was not a statesman—outside the Socialist Union—who didnt listen respectfully to my suggestions.

Tony Preblesham had proved an invaluable find. Never the type to whom authority in the largest matters could be delegated, nevertheless he was extremely handy as troubleshooter, exploiter of new territory or negotiator with competitors or troublesome laborleaders. The pioneers who had fled to the north had little to offer in payment for the vast quantities of food concentrates they required, but the land was rich in furs, timber, and other resources. With permission of the Danish authorities I sent Preblesham to Julianthaab. There he established our headquarters for Greenland, Iceland, and all that was left of North America. From Julianthaab immediately radiated a network of posts where our products were traded for whatever the refugees could bring in.

But the Americans who had gone into the icy wastes were not seeking subsistence. They were striving mightily to reach some place of sanctuary where they could no longer be menaced by the Grass. Beyond the Arctic Circle? Here they might learn to imitate the Innuit, living on fish and seals and an occasional obligingly beached whale. But could they be sure, on territory contiguous or very nearly contiguous to that supporting the weed, that they could count on immunity? They did not believe so. They filled up Newfoundland in the hope that the narrow Gulf of St Lawrence and the narrower Straits of Belle Isle might offer protective barriers. They crossed on sleds to Baffin Island and in homemade boats to Greenland. Before the Grass had wiped out their families, and their less hardy compatriots left behind in Nova Scotia and Prince Edward Island, these pioneers abandoned the continent of their origin; the only effect of their passage having been to exterminate the last of the Innuit by the propagation of the manifiold diseases they had brought with them.

In the south the tempo was slower, the striving for escape less hysterical and more philosophic. When the Mexican peon heard the Grass was in the next village he packed his few belongings and moved farther away. From Tampico to Chiapas the nation journeyed easily south, not regretting too loudly the lands left behind, not crowding or jostling rudely on the highways, not failing to pause for siestas when the sun was hot, but traveling steadily in a quiet resignation that seemed beyond resignation—the extension of a gracious will.

66 But the rest of the world, even in the lethargy which had come upon it in viewing the loss of most of North America, could not afford to leave the Grass to its own devices, content to receive the refugees it drove out or watch them die. A World Congress to Combat the Grass was hastily called in London. It was a distinguished body of representatives from all the nations and resembled at its best the now functionless Federal Disruptions Committee.

At the opening sitting a delegation with credentials from the President of the United States attempted to join in the proceedings. One of the French members rose to inquire of the chairman, Where was the United States? He, the delegate, had read of such a country, had heard it spoken of—and none too favorably—but did it exist, *de facto?*

The delegate from Haiti asked for the floor and wished to

assure his distinguished colleague from the motherland of culture—especially did he wish to assure this learned gentleman, bound as they were by the same beautiful and meticulous language—that his country had good reason to know the United States actually existed—or had done so at one time. His glorious land bore scars inflicted by the barbarians. His own grandfather, a great patriot, had been hunted down by the United States Marines as a bandit. He implored a congress with humanitarian designs to refuse admission to the delegates of the socalled United States.

One of the German delegates, after wiping the perspiration from the three folds on the back of his neck, said he spoke with great diffidence for fear of being misunderstood. The formerly existent country had twice defeated, or apparently defeated, his own in a war and his distinguished colleagues might misinterpret the spirit which moved him. Nevertheless, he could not refrain from remarking that it appeared to him that a Just Providence had wiped out the United States and therefore it would be illogical if not blasphemous for this august body to admit a delegation from a nonexistent country.

The American delegation attempted to point out feebly that Hawaii still remained and Puerto Rico and Guam. The members from the various sections of the British Commonwealth, arguing the precedents of the governmentsinexile, urged the acceptance of their credentials. The representative of Switzerland called for a vote and the credentials were rejected.

This controversy being settled, the body, in high good humor, selected a governing committee to take whatever measures it deemed necessary to protect the rest of the world from the menace. After lengthy debate and much conflicting testimony from experts a bold plan was endorsed. It was decided to complete the digging of the Nicaragua Canal and blow up that part of Central America lying between it and the Isthmus of Panama. It was a colossal feat of engineering which would cost billions of pounds and untold manpower, but the nations of the world, not without some grumbling, finally agreed to the expenditure.

While technicians from all over the world directed laborgangs and steamshovels, ammunitionships loaded with tons of explosives sailed from every port for Panama and Colon. Though at first reluctant with their contributions, the countries had reconsidered and poured forth their shares without stint. All obsolete war-materials were shipped to the scene of action. Prisons were emptied to supply the needed manpower and when this measure fell short all without visible means of support were added to the roll.

Shortsightedly Costa Rica protested vigorously the proposed destruction of its entire territory and there were even momentary uprisings of patriots who proposed to defend their nation with the last drop of blood, but commonsense and international amity prevailed, especially when Costa Ricans were promised a territory twice as big as their native country in the hinterland between Colombia and Venezuela, a valueless tract both nations had been trying in vain to settle for decades.

Night and day the detonations of highexplosives killed fish on both the Atlantic and Pacific sides of Central America and brought stunned birds plummeting down from the skies to their death. The coastal plains fell into the sea, great mountains were reduced to powder and little by little the gap between North and South America widened.

But the progress of the work was infinitesimal compared with the advance of the Grass. It swept over the ancient Aztec empire down to the Isthmus of Tehuantepec. The ruins of Mayan civilization, excavated once, were buried anew. The demolition engineers measured their daily progress in feet, the Grass in miles. When the waters of the Atlantic and Pacific met in Lake Nicaragua, the Grass was in Yucatan. When the first green runners invaded Guatemala, a bare twenty miles of northern Panama had been demolished and hardly a start had been made in the destruction of Costa Rica.

Fleets of airplanes bombed the connecting strip in the area left by engineers to the last, but as their flights went on the Grass crept into British Honduras. The workers sent another twenty miles of Panama into nothingness and the Grass completed the conquest of Guatemala. They blew up another ten miles and the Grass took over El Salvador. Dynamite widened the Nicaragua Canal to a ridiculously thin barrier as the Grass overran Honduras.

They stood now almost facetoface, the width of one pitiful little Banana Republic between them. On one hand the Grass, funneled and constricted to a strip of land absurdly inadequate to support its gargantuan might, on the other the combined resources of man, desperately determined to destroy the bridge before the invader. In tropic heat the work was kept up at superhuman pace. Gangs of native laborers fainting under their loads were blown skyhigh by impatient technicians unwilling to waste the time necessary to revive them. In selfdefense the South American states doubled their contributions. At the edge of the weed all the offensive weapons of the world were massed to stay it as long as possible, for even a day's—even an hour's delay might be invaluable.

But the Grass overbore the heavy artillery, the flamethrowers, the bombs, the radium, and all the devices in its path. The inventions of war whose constant improvement was the pride of the human race offered no more obstacle to the Grass than a few anthills might to a herd of stampeding elephants. It swept down to the edge of the ditch and paused at the fiftymile stretch of saltwater between it and the shapeless island still offering the temptation of a foothold in front of the now vastly enlarged Panama Canal.

If those engaged in the task, from coordinator-in-chief down to the sweating waterboys, had worked like madmen before, they worked like triple madmen now, for the wind might blow a single seed onto what had been Costa Rica and undo all they had so far accomplished. The explosions were continuous, rocking the diminishing territory with ceaseless earthquakes. After an hour on the job men reeled away, deafened, blinded and shocked.

On the South American side, as had been planned, great supercyclone fans were set up to blow back any errant seed. Fed by vast hydroelectric plants in the Colombian highlands, the noise of their revolving blades drowned out the sounds of the explosions for all those nearby. The oceans became interested participants and enormously high tides possibly caused by the difference in level between the Atlantic and Pacific, clawed away great hunks of land. The great island became a small island, the small island an islet. At last nothing but ruffling blue water lay between the Grass and South America. Over this stretch of sea the great fans blew their steady breath, protecting the continent behind from the fate of its northern twin.

The passage between was forbidden to all ships for fear they might inadvertently act as carriers of the seed. The lost continent was not only isolated, it was sealed off. From the sharp apex of the inverted triangle to its broad base in the arctic ice the Grass flourished in one undisputed prairie, the sole legatee of all the hopes, trials, afflictions, dreams and victories of the men and women who had lived there since the first alien foot was set upon its soil.

The South Pacific Sailing Discovery

FIVE

67   I CANNOT SAY the world greeted the end of the North American continent with either rejoicing or regret. Relief, yes. When the news of the last demolition was given and it was clear the Grass was unable to bridge the gap, the imaginative could almost hear mankind emit a vast sigh. The world was saved, they could go about their business now, having written off a sixth of themselves.

I was reminded of Miss Francis' remark that if you cut off a man's leg you bestow upon him a crippled mentality. For approximately two centuries the United States had been a leg of the global body, a limb so constantly inflicted with growingpains it caused the other parts to writhe in sympathy. Now the member was cut off and everyone thought that with the troublesome appendage gone life would be pleasanter and simpler. Debtor nations expanded their chests when they remembered Uncle Shylock was no more. Industrial countries looked eagerly to enlarge their markets in those places where Americans formerly sold goods. Small states whose inhabitants were occasionally addicted to carrying off tourists and holding them for ransom now felt they could dispense with those foreign undersecretaries whose sole business it had been to write diplomatic notes of apology.

But it was a crippled world and the lost leg still twitched spectrally. I don't think I speak now as a native of the United States, for with my international interests I believe I have become completely a cosmopolitan, but for everyone, Englishman, Italian, Afrikander or citizen of Liberia. The disappearance of America created a revolution in their lives, a change perhaps not immediately apparent, but eventually to be recognized by all.

It was the trivial things we Americans had taken for granted as part of our daily lives and taught the rest of the world to appreciate which were most quickly missed. The substitution of English, Turkish, Egyptian or Russian cigarettes for good old Camels or Luckies; the impossibility of buying a bottle of cocacola at any price; the disappearance of the solacing wad of chewinggum; the pulsing downbeat of a hot band—these were the first things whose loss was noticed.

For a long time I had been too busy to attend movingpictures, except rarely, but a man—especially a man with much on his mind—needs relaxation and I would not choose the foreign movies with their morbid emphasis on problems and crime and sex in preference to the cleancut American product which always satisfied the nobler feelings by showing the reward of the honest, the downfall of evildoers and the purity of love and motherhood. Art is all very well, but need it be sordid?

As I told George Thario, I am no philistine; I think the Parthenon and the Taj Mahal are lovely buildings, but I would not care to have an office in either of them—give me Radio City. I don't mind the highbrow programs the British Broadcasting Corporation put on; I myself am quite capable of understanding and enjoying them, but I imagine there are thousands of housewives who would prefer a good serial to bring romance into their lives. I don't object to a commercial world in which competitors go through the formality of pretending to be scrupulously fair in talking about each others' products, but I must admit I missed the good old American slapdash advertising which yelled, Buy my deodorant or youll stink; wash your mouth with my antiseptic or youll lose your job; brush your teeth with my dentifrice or no one will kiss you; powder your face with my leadarsenate or youll keep your maidenhead. I would give a lot of money to hear a singing commercial once more or watch the neon lights north of Times Square urge me to buy something for which I have no possible use. Living within your income is fine, but the world lacks the goods youd have bought on the installmentplan; getting what you need is sound policy, but how many lives were lightened by the young men working their way through college, or the fullerbrushman?

I think there was a subconscious realization of this which

came gradually to the top. In the beginning the almost universal opinion was that the loss of the aching limb was for the better. I have heard socalled cultured foreigners discuss the matter in my presence, doubtless unaware I was an American. No more tourists, they gloated, to stand with their backs to the Temple of Heaven in Pekin and explain the superior construction of the Masonic Hall at Cedar Rapids; no more visitors to the champagne caves at Rheims to inquire where they could get a shot of real bourbon; no more music lovers at Salzburg or Glyndebourne to regret audibly the lack of a peppy swingtune; no more gourmets in Vienna demanding thick steaks, rare and smothered in onions.

But this period of smug selfcongratulation was soon succeeded by a strange nostalgia which took the form of romanticizing the lost land. American books were reprinted in vast quantities in the Englishspeaking nations and translated anew in other countries. American movies were revived and imitated. Fashionable speech was powdered with what were conceived to be Yankee expressions and a southern drawl was assiduously cultivated.

Bestselling historical novels were laid in the United States and popular operas were written about Daniel Boone, Davy Crockett, and Kit Carson. Men told their growing sons to work hard, for now there was left no land of opportunity to which they could emigrate, no country where they could become rich overnight with little effort. Instead of fairytales children demanded stories of fortyniners and the Wedding of the Rails; and on the streets of Bombay and Cairo urchins, probably quite unaware of the memorial gesture, could be heard whistling *Casey Jones*.

But handinhand with this newfound romantic love went a completely practical attitude toward those Americans still existing in the flesh. The earliest expatriates, being generally men of substance, were well received. The thousands who had crossed by small boats from Canada to Greenland and from Greenland to Iceland to Europe were by definition in a different category and found the quota system their fathers and grandfathers had devised used to deny their own entrance.

They were as bewildered and hurt as children that any nation could be at once so shortsighted and so heartless as to bar homeless wanderers. We bring you knowledge and skills and our own need, they said in effect, we will be an asset to your country if you admit us. The Americans could not understand; they themselves had been fair to all and only kept out undesirable immigrants.

Gradually the world geared itself to a slower tempo. The gogetter followed the brontosaurus to extinction, and we Americans with the foresight to carry on our businesses from new bases profited by the unAmerican backwardness of our competitors. At this time I daresay I was among the hundred most important figures of the world. In the marketing and packaging of our original products I had been forced to acquire papermills and large interests in aluminum and steel; from there the progression to tinmines and rollingmills, to coalfields and railroads, to shippinglines and machineshops was not far. Consolidated Pemmican, once the center of my business existence, was now but a minor point on its periphery. I expanded horizontally and vertically, delighted to show my competitors that Americans, even when deprived of America, were not robbed of the traditional American enterprise.

68 It was at this time, many months after we had given up all hope of hearing from Joe again, that General Thario received a longdelayed package from his son. It contained the third movement of the symphony and a covering letter:

"Dear Father—Stuart Thario—General—I shall not finish this letter tonight; it will be sent with as much of the First Symphony as makes a worthy essence when it goes. The whole is greater than the sum of its parts, but there is a place (perhaps not in life, but somewhere) for the imperfect, for the incomplete. The great and small alike achieve fulfillment, satisfaction—must this be a ruthless denial of all between?

"I have always despised musicologists, makers of programnotes, little men who tell you the opening chords of Opus 67 describe Fate Knocking at the Door or the call of the yellowhammer. A child draws a picture and writes on it, 'This is a donkey,' and when grown proves it to be a selfportrait by translating the Jupiter Symphony into words. Having said this, let me stultify myself—but for private ears alone—as a bit of personal history, not an explanation to be appended to the score.

"I started out to express in terms of strings and winds the emotions roused in me by the sight and thoughts of the Grass, much as LvB took a mistaken idealization of his youth as a startingpoint for Opus 55; but just as no man is an island, so no theme stands alone. There is a cord binding the lesser to the greater; a mystic union between all things. The Grass is not an entity, but an aspect. I thought I was writing about my country, conceived of myself in a reversed snobbishness, a haughty humility, a proud abasement, as a sort of superior Smetana. (Did you know that as a boy I dreamed of the day when I should receive my commission as second lieutenant?)

Boston, Massachusetts

"I interrupted this letter to sketch some of the middle section of the fourth movement and I have wasted a precious week following a false trail. And of course the thought persists that it may not have been a false trail at all, but the right one; the business of saying something is a perpetual wrestle with doubts.

"We leave here tomorrow for an unknown destination—Portsmouth probably and then somewhere in Maine, hoping to wrench from fate the time to finish the score. It seems more than a little pompous to continue my explanation. The Grass, the United States, humanity, God—whatever we write about we write about the same things.

"Still there is a limit to individual perception and it seems to me my concern—at least my musical concern—is enclosed by Canada and Mexico, the Pacific and Atlantic. So, rightly or wrongly, even if the miracle occur and I do finish in time, I cannot leave. A short distance, such a short distance from where I scribble these words, Vanzetti died. No more childish thought than atonement was ever conceived. It is a base and baseless gratification. Evil is not recalled. So I do not sentence myself for the murder of Vanzetti or for my manifold crimes; who am I to pass judgment, even on me? But all of us, accusers and accused, condemners and condemned, will remain—forever indistinguishable. If the requiem for our faults and our virtues, if the celebration of our past and the prayer for our resurrection can be orchestrated, then the fourth movement will be finished. If not—

Aroostook, Maine

"By the best calculations we have about three more days. I do not think the symphony can be finished, but the thought no longer disturbs me. It would be a good thing to complete it, just as it would be a good thing to sit on fleecy clouds and enjoy eternal, nevermelting, nevercloying icecreamcones, celestially flavored.

"The man who is to carry this letter waits impatiently. I must finish quickly before his conviction of my insanity outweighs the promises I have made of reward from you and causes him to run from me. My love to Mama, the siblings and yourself and kindly regards to the great magnate.

Joe"

69 About the same time I also received a letter which somehow got through the protective screening of my secretaries:

"Albert Weener,
Savoy Hotel,
Thames Embankment, WC1.
"Sir:
You may recall making an offer I considered premature. It is now no longer so. I am at home afternoons from 1 until 6 at 14, Little Bow Street, EC3 (3rd floor, rear).

Josephine Spencer Francis"

In spite of her rudeness at our last meeting, my good nature caused me to send a cab for her. She wore the identical gray suit of years before and her face was still unlined and dubiously clean.

"How do you do, Miss Francis? I'm glad to find you among the lucky ones. Nowadays if we don't hear from old friends we automatically assume their loss."

She looked at me as one scans an acquaintance whose name has been embarrassingly forgotten. "There is no profit for you in this politeness, Weener," she said abruptly. "I am here to beg a favor."

"Anything I can do for you, Miss Francis, will be a pleasure," I assured her.

She began using a toothpick, but it was not the oldfashioned gold one—just an ordinary wooden splinter. "Hum. You remember asking me to superintend gathering specimens of *Cynodon dactylon?*"

"Circumstances have greatly altered since then," I answered.

"They have a habit of doing so. I merely mentioned your offer because you coupled it with a chance to advance my own research as an inducement. I am on the way to develop the counteragent, but to advance further I need to make tests upon the living grass itself. The World Control Congress has refused me permission to use specimens. I have no private means of evading their fiat."

"An excellent thing. The decrees of the congress are issued for the protection of all."

"Hypocrisy as well as unctuousness."

"What do you expect me to do?"

"You have a hundred hireling chemists, all of them with a string of degrees, at your service. I want to borrow two of them and be landed on some American mountain, above the snowline, where I can continue to work."

"Besides being illegal—to mention such a thing is apparently hypocritical—such a hazardous and absurd venture is hardly in the nature of a business proposition, Miss Francis."

"Philanthropic, then."

"I have given fifty thousand pounds to set up nurseryschools right here in London—"

"So the mothers of the little brats will be free to work in your factories."

"I have donated ten thousand pounds to Indian famine relief—"

"So that you might cut the wages of your Hindu workers."

"I have subscribed five thousand pounds for sanitation in Szechwan—"

"Thereby lessening absenteeism from sickness among your coolies."

"I will not stoop to answer your insinuations," I said. "I merely mentioned my gifts to show that my charities are on a worldwide scale and there is little room in them for the relief of individuals."

"Do you think I come to you for a personal sinecure? I don't ask if you have no concern outside selfish interest, for the answer is immediate and obvious; but isnt it to that same selfish interest to protect what remains of the world? If the other continents go as North America has gone, will you alone be divinely translated to some extraterrestrial sphere? And if so, will you take your wealth and power with you?"

"I am supporting three laboratories devoted exclusively to antigraminous research and anyway the rest of the world is amply protected by the oceans."

She removed the toothpick in order to laugh unpleasantly. "Once a salesman always a salesman, Weener. Lie to yourself, deny facts, brazen it out. The world was safe behind the saltband too, in the days when Josephine Francis was a quack and charlatan."

"Admitting your great attainments, Miss Francis, the fact remains that you are a woman and the adventure you propose is hardly one for a lady to undertake."

"Weener, you are ineffable. I'm not a lady—I'm a chemist."

The conversation deadlocked as I waited for her to go. Oddly enough, in spite of her sex and the illegality of her proposal, I was inclined to help her, if she had approached me in a reasonable manner and not with the uncouth bearing of a superior toward an inferior. If she *could* find a counteragent, I thought . . . if she could find a weapon, then the possibility of utilizing the Grass as a raw material for food concentrates, a design still tantalizingly just beyond the reach of our researchworkers, might be realized. Labor costs would be cut to a minimum . . .

I could not let the woman be her own worst enemy; I was big enough to overlook her unfortunate attitudes and see through the cranky exterior to the worthy idealist and true woman beneath. I was interrupted in my thoughts by Miss Francis speaking again.

"North American landtitles have no value right now, but a man with money who knew ahead of time the Grass could be destroyed . . ."

How clumsy, I thought, trying to appeal to a cupidity I don't possess; as if I would cheat people by buying up their very homes for sordid speculation. "Miss Francis," I said, "purely out of generosity and in remembrance of old times I am inclined to consider helping you. I suppose you have the details of the equipment you will need, the qualifications of your assistants, and a rough idea of what mountain you might prefer as a location?"

"Of course," and she began rattling off a catalogue of items, stabbing the air with her toothpick as a sort of running punctuation.

I stopped her with a raised hand. "Please. Reduce your list to writing and leave it with my secretary. I will see what can be done."

As soon as she had gone I picked up the phone and cabled Tony Preblesham to report to me immediately. The decision to send him with Miss Francis had been instantaneous, but had I thought about it for hours no happier design could have been conceived. Outside of General Thario there was not another man in my organization I could trust so implicitly. The expedition required double, no, triple secrecy and Preblesham could not only guard against any ulterior and selfish aims Miss Francis might enter-tain—to say nothing of the erratic or purely feminine impulses which could possibly operate to the disadvantage of all concerned—but take the opportunity to give the continent a general survey, both to keep in view the utilization of the weed, whether or not it could be conquered; and whatever possibilities a lay observer might see as to the Grass perishing of itself.

70 Mr Albert Weener,
Queen Elizabeth Hotel,
Perth, Western Australia, A.C.

"Dear Sir:—

According to yr. instructions our party left Paramaribo on the 9th inst. for Medellin, giving out that we were going to see possible tin deposits near there. At Medellin I checked with our men & was told that work gangs with the stuff needed to make landing fields together with caches of gas & oil enough for 3 times the flying required had been dropped both at Mt. Whitney & on Banks Island. A.W., I tell you the boys down there are on their toes. Of course I did not tell them this, but gave them a real old fashioned Pep Talk, & told them if they really made good they might be moved up to Rio or Copenhagen or maybe even London.

"Everything being O.K. in Medellin, we left on the 12th inst., heading at first South to fool any nosey cops & then straight West so as to be out of range of the patrol boats. It was quite late before we could head North and the navigator was flying by instruments so it was not until dawn that we saw land. You can sneer all you like at Bro. Paul (& of course he has not had the benefits of an Education like you, A.W.) but I want to tell you that when I looked out of the port & saw nothing but green grass where houses & trees & mtns. ought to have been, I remembered that I was a backslider & sinful man. However, this is beside the point.

"The lady professor, Miss Francis I mean, & Mr. White & Mr. Black were both so excited they could hardly eat, but kept making funny remarks in some foreign language which I do not understand. However I do not think there was any thing wrong or disloyal to you in their conversation.

"You would have thought that flying over so much green would have got tiresome after some time, but you would have been wrong. I am sorry I cannot describe it to you, but I can only say again that it made me think of my Account with my Maker.

"While I think of it, altho it does not belong here, in

Paramaribo I had to fire our local man as he had got into trouble with the Police there & was giving Cons. Pem. a bad name. He said it was on the Firm's account, but I told him you did not approve of breaking the Law at all.

"We had no trouble sighting the party at Mt. Whitney & I want to tell you, A.W., it was a great relief to get rid of the Scientists altho they are no doubt all right in their way. Some of the work gang kicked at being left behind altho that was in our agreement. They said they were sick of the snow & the sight of the Grass beyond. I said we only had room in the transport for the Banks Is. gang & anyway they would have company now. I promised them we would pick them up on our next trip.

"Miss Francis & the 2 others acted like crazy. They kept shaking each other's hands & saying We are here, we are here, altho any body but a Nut would have thought saying it was a waste of time as even a small child could have seen that they were. And any way, why any body should want to be there is some thing beyond me.

"We took off from Whitney on the 14th inst., flying back S. West. There were no land marks, but the navigator told me when we were over the Site of L.A. I have to report that the Grass looked no different in this Area, where it is the oldest. Then we flew North E., looking for the Gt. Salt Lake according to yr. instructions. I am sorry to say that we could not find it altho we flew back & forth for some time, searching while the instruments were checked. The Lake has disappeared in the Grass.

"We headed North E. by E., finding no land marks except a few peaks above the snow on the Rocky Mtns. I am very glad to say that the Gt. Lakes are still there, altho much smaller & L. Erie & L. Ontario so shrunk I might have missed them if the pilot had not pointed them out. The St. Lawrence River is of course gone.

"We followed the line of the big Canadian Lakes N., but except for Depressions (which may be Swamps) in the latitudes of the Gt. Bear Gt. Slave Lakes, there is nothing but Grass. We stayed over night at Banks Is. & it was very cold &

miserable, but we were happy to remember that there was no Grass underneath the Snow below us. Next morning (the 16th) after fueling up we took off (with the ground crew) for the Homeward trip.

"Stopping at Whitney, everything was O.K. except that I did not see the lady professor (Miss Francis, I mean) as Mr. White and Mr. Black said she was too busy.

"I will be in London to meet you on the 1st as arranged & give you any further news you want. Until then, I remain,
Yrs. Truly,
A. Preblesham, Vice-Pres. in Chge of Field
Operations, Cons. Pem."

I cannot say Preblesham's report was particularly enlightening, but it at least squelched any notion the Grass might be dying of itself. I did not expect any great results from the scientists' expedition, but I felt it worth a gamble. In the meantime I dismissed the lost continent from my mind and turned to more immediate concerns.

71 The disappearance of American foundries and the withdrawal of the Russian products from export after their second revolution had forced a boom in European steel. English, French, and German manufacturers of automobiles, rails, and locomotives, anticipating tremendously enlarged outlets for their output—even if those new markets still fell short of the demand formerly drawing upon the American factories—had earmarked the entire world supply for a long time to come.

Since I owned large blocks of stock, not only in the industries, but in the rollingmills as well, this boom was profitable to me. I had long since passed the point where it was necesary, no matter how great my expenses or philanthropies, for me to exert myself further; but as I have always felt anyone who gains wealth without effort is no better than a parasite, I was contracting for new plants in Bohemia, Poland, Northern Italy and France. I did not neglect buying heavily into the Briey Basin and into the Swedish

oremines to ensure the future supply of these mills. In spite of the
able assistance of Stuart Thario and the excellent spadework of
Preblesham, I was so busy at this time—for in addition to everything else the sale of concentrates diagrammed an everascending
spiral—that food and sleep seemed to be only irritating curtail-
ments of the workingday.

It was the fashion when I was a youth for novelists to sneer at
businessmen and proclaim that the conduct of industry was a
simple affair, such as any halfwit could attend to with but a portion
of his mind. I wish these cynics could have come to know the
delicate workings and balances of my intricate empire. We in
responsible positions, and myself most of all, were on a constant
alert, ready for instant decision or personal attention to a mass of
new detail at any moment.

72 On one of the occasions when I had to fly to
Copenhagen it was Winifred and not General Thario
who met me at the airport. "General T is so upset," she explained
in her vivacious way, "that I had to come instead. But perhaps I
should have sent Pauline?"

I assured her I was pleased to see her and hastened to express
concern for her father.

"Oh, it's not him at all, really," she said. "It's Mama. She's all
bothered about Joe."

I lowered my voice respectfully and said I was sure Mrs
Thario was overcome with grief and perhaps I had better not
intrude at such a time.

"Poo!" dissented Winifred. "Mama doesnt know what grief
is. She's simply delighted at Joe's doing a Custer, but she's awfully
bothered about his music."

"In what way?" I asked. "Do you mean getting it performed?"

"Getting it performed, nothing. Getting it suppresed. That a
long line of generals and admirals should wind up in a composer is
to her a disgrace which will need a great deal of living down. It
preys on her mind. Poor old Stuart is home now reading her choice
passages from the *Winning of the West* by Theodore Roosevelt to
soothe her nerves."

I had been more than a little apprehensive of meeting Mama again, but Winifred's report seemed to reassure me that she would be confined, if not to bed, at least to her own apartments. I was sadly disillusioned to find her ensconced in a comfortable armchair beside a brightly burning fire, the general with a book held open by his thumb. He greeted me with his usual affection. "Albert, I'm sorry I wasnt able to get to the airport."

I shook his hand and turned to his wife. "I regret to hear you are indisposed, Mrs Thario."

"Spare me your damned crocodile tears. Where is my son?"

"In his last letter he suggested he would remain in our country as long as it existed; however it is possible—even probable he escaped. Let us hope so, Mrs Thario."

"That's the sort of damned hogwash you feed to green troops, not to veterans. My son is dead. In action. My grandfather went the same way at Chancellorsville. Do you think me some whimpering broompusher to weep at the loss of a son on the battlefield?"

Stuart Thario put his hand on her arm. "Easy . . . blood-pressure . . . no excitement."

"Not in regimentals," said Mama, and relapsed into silence.

We had a very uneasy dinner, during which we were unable to discuss business owing to the presence of the ladies. Afterward the general and I withdrew with our coffee—he did not drink at home, so I missed the clarity which always accompanied his indulgence—and were deep in figures and calculations when Winifred summoned us hastily.

"General, Mr Weener, come quickly! Mama . . ."

We hurried into the living room, I for one anticipating Mama if not in the throes of a stroke at least in a faint. But she was standing upright before the open fire, an unsheathed cavalry saber in her hand. It was clearly a family relic, for from its guard dangled the golden tassel of the United States Army and on its naked blade were little spots of rust, but it looked dangerous enough as she warned us off with a sweep of it. In her other hand I recognized the bulky manuscript of George Thario's First Symphony which she was burning, page by page.

"Some damned impostor," she said. "Some damned impostor."

"Harriet," protested the general, "Harriet, please . . . the boy's work . . . only copy . . ."

She fed another leaf to the fire. ". . . impostor . . ."

"Harriet—" he advanced toward her, but she waved him away with the sharp blade—"can't burn George's work this way . . . gave his life . . ."

I had not thought highly of Joe's talents as a musician, believing them byandlarge to be but reflections of his unfortunate affectations. I think I can say I appreciate good music and Ive often taken a great deal of pleasure from hearing a hotelband play Rubinstein's Melody in F, or like classical numbers, during mealtimes. But even if Joe's symphony was but a series of harsh and disjointed sounds, I thought its destruction a dreadful thing for Mama to do and the more shocking, aside from any question of artistic taste, because of its reversal of all we associate with the attitude of true motherhood.

"Mrs Thario," I protested, "as your son's friend I beg you to consider—"

"Impudence," declared Mama, pointing the sword at me so that I involuntarily backed up although already at a respectful distance.

"Damned impudence," she repeated, feeding another page to the fire. "Came into my house, bold as brass and said, 'Cream if you please.' Ha! I'll cream him, I will!" And she made a violent gesture with the saber as though skewering me upon its length.

I whispered to Constance, who was standing closest, that her mother had undoubtedly lost her reason and should be forcibly restrained. Unhappily the old lady's keen ears caught my suggestion.

"Oho. 'Deranged,' am I? I spend my life making more money than I can spend, do I? I push my way against all decency into the company of my betters, boring them and myself for no earthly reason, do I? I live on crackers and milk because Ive spent my nervous energy piling up the means to buy an endless supply of steaks and chops my doctor forbids me to eat? I starve my employees half to death in order to give the money I steal from them to some charity which hands a small part of it back, ay? I hire lobbyists or bribe officials to pass laws and then employ others to break them? I foster nationalist organizations with one hand and build up international cartels with the other, do I? I'm crazy, am I?"

Excited by her own rhetoric she put several pages at once into the flames. Constance pleaded, "Mama, this is all we have left of Joe. Please, Mama."

"Sundays the church banner is raised above the Flag. I never heard a post chaplain say immortality was contained on pieces of paper."

"Comfort, then, Mama," suggested Winifred.

"Creative work," muttered the general.

"Is it some trivial thing to endure the pangs of childbed that the creations of men are so exalted? I have offered my life on a battlefield no less and no more than my grandfather fought on at Chancellorsville. Little minds do not judge, but I judge. I bore a son; he was my extension as this weapon is my extension."

She thrust the sword forward to emphasize her utterance. "I will not hestitate to judge my son. If he did not die in proper uniform at least I shall not have him go down as a maker of piano notes instead of buglecalls." She threw the balance of the score into the fire and stirred it into a blaze with the steel's point.

The ringing of the telephonebell put a period to the scene. Constance, who spoke several languages, answered it. She carried on an incomprehensible conversation for a minute and then motioned to me with her head. "It's for you, Mr Weener. Rio. I'll wait till they get the connection through." She turned to the mouthpiece again and encouraged the operator with a soothing flow of words.

I was vastly relieved at the interruption. It was undoubtedly Preblesham calling me on some routine matter, but it served to distract attention from the still muttering old lady and give her a chance to subside.

Preblesham's voice came in a bodiless waver over the miles. "A W? Can you hear me? I can give you a tip. Just about three hours ahead of the radio and newspapers. Can you understand me? Our big competitor has bought the adjoining property. Do you get me, A W?"

I nodded at the receiver as though he could see me, my thoughts racing furiously ahead. I had understood him all right:

the Grass had somehow jumped the saltwater gap and was loose upon another continent.

73 I had about three hours in which to dispose of all my South American holdings before their value vanished. Telephone facilities in the Thario house, though adequate for the transaction of the general's daily business, were completely unequal to the emergency. Even if they had not been, Mama's occasional sallies from her fireplace fort, saber waving threateningly, frequently endangered half our communications and we suffered all the while from the idiosyncrasies of the continental operators who seem unable ever to make a clear connection, varying this annoyance by a habit of either dropping dead or visiting the nearest café at those crucial moments when they did not interrupt a tense interchange by polite inquiries as to whether msieu had been connected.

I must say that in this crisis Stuart Thario displayed all his soldierly qualities to the full. Sweeping aside his domestic concerns as he would at the order of mobilization, he became swift, decisive, vigorous. The first call he put through was to the Kristian IV Hotel, engaging every available empty room so that we might preempt as much of the switchboard as possible. Pressing Constance and Winifred into service as secretaries until his own officestaff could be summoned and leaving Pauline to deal with Mama, he had us established in the hotel less than threequarters of an hour from the time Preblesham phoned.

Even as the earliest calls were being put through a barely perceptible signal passed from the general to Winifred and presently large parts of the Kristian IV bar were being arranged on a long table at the general's elbow. I had little time for observation since I had to exert all my powers of salesmanship on unseen financiers to persuade them by indirection that I was facing a financial crisis and they had a chance to snap up my South American holdings at fractions of their values; but out of the corner of my eye I admired the way Stuart Thario continuously sipped from his constantly refilled glass without hesitating in his duplicating endeavors.

I expected the news to break and end our efforts at any moment, but the quickness with which I had seized upon Preblesham's information confirmed the proverb about the early bird; the threehour reprieve stretched to five and by the time Havas flashed the news I had liquefied almost all of my now worthless assets—and to potential financial rivals. Needless to say I had not trusted solely to the honor of the men with whom I had conversed, but had the sale confirmed in each case by an agent on the spot who accepted a check, draft, or cash from the buyer. Only on paper did I suffer the slightest loss; in actuality my position became three times as strong as before.

74 The world took the extension of the Grass to South America with a philosophic calm which can only be described as amazing. Even the Latins themselves seemed more concerned with how the Grass had jumped the gap than with the impending fate of their continent. The generally accepted theory was that it had somehow mysteriously come by way of the West Indies, although as yet the Grass had not appeared on any of those islands, and even Cuba, within sight of the submerged Florida Keys, was apparently safe behind her protective supercyclone fans. But the fact the Grass had appeared first at Medellin in Colombia rather than in the tiny bit of Panama remaining seemed to show it had come directly from the daggerpointed mass poised above the continent.

La Prensa of Buenos Aires said in a long editorial entitled "Does Humanity Betray Itself?": "When the Colossus of the North was evilly enchanted, many Americans (except possibly our friends across the River Plate) breathed more easily. Now it would seem their rejoicing was premature and the doom of the Yankee is also to be the doom of our older civilization. How did this verdant disease spread from one continent to another? That is the question which tortures every human heart from the Antarctic to the Caribbean.

"It is believed the cordon around North America has not been generally respected. Scientists with the noblest motives, and adventurers urged on by the basest, are alike believed to have visited the forbidden continent. It may well be that on one of these trips the seeds of the gigantic *Cynodon dactylon* were brought back. It is well known that the agents of a certain Yankee capitalist have been accustomed to taking off on mysterious journeys near the very spot now afflicted by the emerald plague."

It was a dastardly hint and the sort of thing I had long come to look upon as inseparable from my position. Of all peoples the Latinamericans have long been known as the most notoriously ungrateful for the work we did in developing their countries. Why, in some backward parts, the natives had been content to live by hunting and fishing till we furnished them with employment and paid them enough so they could buy salt fish and canned meats. Fortunately *La Prensa's* innuendo, so obviously inspired by envy, was not taken up, and attention soon turned from the insoluble problem of the bridging of the gap to the southward progress of the weed itself.

From the very first, everyone took for granted the victory of the Grass. No concerted efforts were made either to confine or to destroy it. The World Congress to Combat the Grass, far from being inactive, worked heroically, but it got little cooperation from the peoples most closely affected. When at one time it seemed as though the congress had got hold of a possible weapon, the Venezuelans refused them the necessary sites and Brazil would not allow passage of foreign soldiers over its soil. Nationalism suddenly became rampant. "We will die as Ecuadorians, descendants of the Incas," exclaimed the leading newspaper of Quito. *El Gaucho* of Lima pointed out caustically that most of Ecuador's area really belonged to Peru and the Peruvians were the true descendants of the Incas anyway. "We shall all die as unashamed Peruvians!" thundered *El Gaucho.*

In vain the Church pointed out the difference between Christian resignation and sinful suicide. The reply of most South Americans, when they bothered to reply at all, was either that the coming of the Grass expressed God's will toward them or else to scorn the Church entirely. Imitations of Brother Paul's movement flourished, with additions and refinements suited to the Latin temperament.

So the efforts of the World Congress were almost entirely limited to searching each ship, plane, and individual leaving the doomed continent to be sure none of the fatal seeds were transported. Even this precaution was resented as an infringement on national sovereignty, but the resentment was limited to bellicose pronouncements in the newspapers; the republics looked on sullenly while their honor was systematically violated by phlegmatic inspectors.

75 The grass grew to unheardof heights in the tropical valley of the Amazon. It washed the slopes of the Andes as it had the Cordilleras and the Rockies, leaving only the highest peaks free of its presence. It raced across the llanos, the savannas and the pampas and covered the high plateaus in a slow relentless growth.

The people ran from the Grass, not in a straight line from north to south, but by indirection, seeking first the seacoasts and then escape from the afflicted land. Those North Americans who had eluded the Grass once did not satisfy themselves with halfmeasures when their sanctuary was lost, but bought passage on any bottom capable, however dubiously, of keeping out the sea and embarked for the farthest regions.

76 In point of time, I am now about halfway through my narrative. It is hard to believe that only eleven years have passed since the Grass conquered South America; indeed, it is extraordinarily difficult for me to reconstruct these middle years at all. Not because they were hard or unpleasant—on the contrary, they carried me from one success to another—but because they have, in memory, the dreamlike quality of unreality, elusive, vague and tantalizing.

Like a dream, too, was the actual progress of the Grass. We were all, I think, impressed by the sense of repetition, of a scene enacted over and over again. It was this quality which gives my story, now that I look back upon it, a certain distortion, for no one, hearing it for the first time, and not as any reader of these words must be, thoroughly familiar with the events could believe in the efforts made to combat the Grass. These efforts existed; we did not yield without struggles; we fought for South America as we had fought for North America. But it was a nightmare fight; our endeavors seem retrospectively those of the paralyzed . . .

The Grass gripped the continent's great northern bulge, squeezed it into submission and worked its way southward to the slender tip, driving the inhabitants before it, duplicating previous acts by sending an influx from sparsely to thickly settled areas, creating despair, terror, disruption and confusion; pestilence, hysteria and famine.

The drama was not played through in one act, but many; to a world waiting the conclusion it dragged on through interminable months and years, offering no change, no sudden twists of fortune, no elusive hopes. At least, mercifully, the tragedy ended; the green curtain came down and covered the continent to the Strait of Magellan. The Grass looked wistfully across at Tierra del Fuego, the land of ice and fire, but even its voracity balked, momentarily at any rate, at the inhospitable island and left it to whatever refugees chose its shores as a slower but still certain death.

South America finally gone, the rest of the globe breathed easier. It would be a slander on humanity to say there was actual rejoicing when the World Congress sealed off this continent too, but whatever sorrow was felt for its loss was balanced by the feeling that at long last the peril of the Grass was finally ended. No longer would speculative Germans, thoughtful Chinese or wakeful Englishmen wonder if the supercyclone fans were indeed an effective barrier; no longer would Cubans, Colombians or Venezuelans look northward apprehensively. Oceanic barriers now confined the peril and though the world was shrunken and hurt it was yet alive. More, it was free from fear for the first time since the mutated seeds had blown over the saltband.

I must not give the impression that a wiping off of the Grass from the account books of humanity was universal and complete. The World Congress periodically considered proposals for countermeasures. On the top of Mount Whitney Miss Francis still labored. New assistants were flown to her as the old ones wandered down the great rockslide from the old stone weatherhouse off into the Grass during fits of despondency, went mad from the realization that, except for problematical survivors on the polar caps, they were alone in an abandoned hemisphere, or died of simple homesickness. In the research-laboratories of Consolidated Pemmican formulas for utilizing the Grass were still tinkered with, and the death of almost every publicspirited man of fortune revealed a will containing bequests to aid those seeking means of controlling the weed.

77 It is not, afterall, a detached history of the past twentyone years I am writing. Contemporaries are only too well aware of the facts and posterity and will find them dehydrated in textbooks. I started out to tell of my own personal part in the coming of the Grass, not to take an Olympian and aloof view of the passion of man.

The very mention of a personal part brings to mind a subject which might be painful were I of a petty nature. There were people who, willfully blind to the facts, held me responsible, in the face of all reason, for the Grass itself. Although it is difficult to believe, there have been many occasions when I have been denounced by demagogues and my blood called for by vicious mobs.

But enough of morbid retrospection. I think I can say at this time there was, with the exception of certain Indian nabobs, hardly a wealthy man left in the world who did not owe in some way the retention of his riches to me. I controlled more than half the steel industry; I owned outright the majority stocks of the world oil cartel; coal, iron, copper, tin and other mines either belonged directly to me or to tributary companies in which I held large interests.

Along with the demagoguery of attributing the Grass to Albert Weener there was the agitation for socialism and the expropriation of all private property, the attempt to deprive men of the fruit of their endeavor and reduce everyone to a regimented, miserable level. It is hardly necessary to say that I spared no effort to combat the insidious agents of the Fourth International. Fortunately for the preservation of the free enterprise system, I had tools ready to hand.

The overrunning of the United States wiped out the gangs which operated so freely there, but remnants made their escape, taking with them to the older continents their philosophy of life and property. Gathering native recruits, they began following the familiar patterns and would in time no doubt have divided the world into countless minute baronies.

However, I was able to subsidize and reason with enough of their leaders to persuade them that their livelihood and very existence rested on a basis of private property and that their great danger came not from each other, but from the advocates of socialism. They saw the point, and though they did not cease from warring on each other, or mulcting the general public, they were ruthless in exterminating the socialists and they left the goods and adjuncts of Consolidated Pemmican and Allied Industries scrupulously unmolested.

Strange as it sounds, it was not my part in protecting the world from the philosophy of equality, nor my ramified properties, which gave me my unique position. Unbelievably, because the change had occurred so gradually, industry, though still a vital factor, no longer played the dominant role in the world, but had given the position back to an earlier occupant. Food was once more paramount in global economy. Loss of the Americas had cut the supply in half without reducing the population correspondingly. The Socialist Union remained selfsufficient and uninterested, while Australia, New Zealand and the cultivated portions of Africa strove to feed the millions of Europeans and Asiatics whose lands could not grow enough for their own use. The slightest falling off of the harvest produced famine.

At this point Consolidated Pemmican practically took over the entire business of agriculture. Utilizing byproducts, and crops otherwise not worth gathering, waste materials, and growths inedible without processing, with plants strung out all over the four continents and with tremendously reduced shipping costs because of the small compass in which so much food could be contained, we were able to let our customers earn their daily concentrates by gathering the raw materials which went into them. I was not only the wealthiest, most powerful man in the world, but its savior and providence as well.

With the new feeling of security bathing the world, tension dissolved into somnolence and the tempo of daily life slackened until it scarcely seemed to move at all. The waves of anxiety, suspicion and distrust of an earlier decade calmed into peaceful ripples, hardly noticeable in a pondlike existence.

No longer beset by thoughts or fears of wars, nations relaxed their pride, armies were reduced to little more than palaceguards, brassbands and parade units; while navies were kept up—if periodic painting and retaining in commission a few obsolete cruisers and destroyers be so termed—only to patrol the Atlantic and Pacific shores of the lost hemisphere.

The struggle for existence almost disappeared; the wagescales set by Consolidated Pemmican were enough to sustain life, and in a world of limited horizons men became content with that. The bickering characteristic of industrial dispute vanished; along with it went the outmoded weapon of the tradesunion. It was a halcyon world and if, as cranks complained, illiteracy increased rapidly, it could only be because with everyman's livelihood assured his natural indolence took the upper hand and he not only lost refinements superficially acquired, but was uninterested in teaching them to his children.

78 I don't know how I can express the golden, sunlit quality of this period. It was not an heroic age, no great deeds were performed, no conflicts resolved, no fundamentshaking ideas broached. Quiet, peace, content—these were the keywords of the era. Preoccupation with politics and panaceas gave place to healthier interests: sports and pageants and giant fairs. Men became satisfied with their lot and if they to a great extent discarded speculation and disquieting philosophies they found a useful substitute in quiet meditation.

Until now I had never had the time to live in a manner befitting my station; but with my affairs running so smoothly that even Stuart Thario and Tony Preblesham found idle time, I began to turn my attention to the easier side of life. Of course I never considered making my permanent home anywhere but in England; for all its parochialism and oddities it was the nearest I could come to approximating my own country.

I bought a gentleman's park in Hampshire and had the outmoded house torn down. It had been built in Elizabethan times and was cold, drafty and uncomfortable, with not one modern convenience. For a time I considered preserving it intact as a sort of museumpiece and building another home for myself on the grounds, but when I was assured by experts that Tudor architecture was not considered to be of surpassing merit and I could find in addition no other advantageous site, I ordered its removal.

I called in the best architects for consultation, but my own artistic and practical sense, as they themselves were quick to acknowledge, furnished the basis for the beautiful mansion I put up. Moved by nostalgic memories of my lost Southland I built a great and ample bungalow of some sixty rooms—stucco, topped with asbestos tile. Since the Spanish motif natural to this form would have been out of place in England and therefore in bad taste, I had timbers set in the stucco, although of course they performed no function but that of decoration, the supports being framework which was not visible.

It was delightful and satisfying to come into the spacious and cozy livingroom, filled with overstuffed easychairs and comfortable couches, warmed by the most efficient of centralheating systems or to use one of the perfectly appointed bathrooms whose every fixture was the best money could buy and recall the dank stone floors and walls leading up to a mammoth and—from a thermal point of view—perfectly useless fireplace flanked by the coatsofarms of deadandgone gentry who were content to shuffle out on inclement mornings to answer nature's calls in chilly outhouses.

So large and commodious an establishment required an enormous staff of servants, which in turn called for a housekeeper and a steward to supervise their activities, for as I have observed many times, the farther down one goes on the wagescale the more it is necessary to hire a highsalaried executive to see that the wage is earned.

I cannot say in general that I ever learned to distinguish between one retainer and another, except of course my personal manservant and Burlet, the headbutler whom I hired right from under the nose of the Marquis of Arpers—his lordship being unable to match my offer. But in spite of the confusion caused by such a multiplicity of menials, I one day noticed an undergardener whose face was tantalizingly familiar. He touched his cap respectfully as I approached, but I had the curious feeling that it was a taught gesture and not one which came naturally to him.

"Have you been here long, my good man?" I asked, still trying to place him.

"No, sir," he answered, "about two weeks."

"Funny. I'm almost certain Ive noticed you before."

He shook his head and made a tentative gesture with the hoe or rake or whatever the tool was in his hand, as though he would now, with my permission, resume his labors.

"What is your name?" I inquired, not believing it would jog my memory, but out of a natural politeness toward inferiors who always feel flattered by such attention.

"Dinkman," he muttered. "Adam Dinkman."

. . . That incredibly dilapidated frontlawn, overrun with sickly devilgrass and spotted with bald patches. Mrs Dinkman's mean bargaining with a tired man who was doing no more than trying to make a living and her later domineering harshness toward someone who was in no way responsible for the misfortune which overcame her. I wondered if she were still alive or had lost her life in the Grass while an indigent on public charity. It is indeed a small world, I thought, and how far we have both come since I humbled myself in order to put food in my stomach and keep a roof over my head.

"Thank you, Dinkman," I said, turning away.

A warm feeling for a fellow American caused me to call in my steward and bid him give Dinkman £100, a small fortune to an undergardener, and let him go. Though he might not realize it immediately, I was doing him a tremendous favor, for an American with £100 in England was bound to do better for himself in some small business than he could hope to do as a mere servant.

Looking back upon this too brief time of tranquillity and satisfaction I cannot help but sigh for its passing. Preceded and followed by periods of turbulence and stress, it stands out in my life as an incredible moment, a soothing dream. Perhaps a faint defect, so small as to be almost unnoticed, was a feeling of solitariness— an inevitable concomitant of my position—but this was so slight that I could not even define it as loneliness and like many another defect it merely heightened the charm of the whole.

I had wealth, power, the respect of the world. The unavoidable detachment from the mob was mitigated by simple pleasures. My estate was a constant delight; the quaint survivals of feudalism among the tenantry amused me; and though I could not bring myself to pretend an interest in the absurd affectation of foxhunting, was well received by the county people, whose insularity and aloofness I found greatly exaggerated, perhaps by outsiders not as cosmopolitan as myself.

Excursions to London and other cities where my presence was demanded or could be helpful afforded me a frequent change of scene and visits by important people as well as more intimate ones by Preblesham and the Tharios prevented The Ivies—for so my place was called—from ever becoming dull to me.

The general fell in love with a certain ale which was brewed on the premises and declared, in spite of his lifelong rule to the contrary, that it could be mixed with Irish whisky to make a drink so agreeable that no sane man would want a better. The girls, particularly Winifred, were enchanted with my private woods, the gardens and the deerpark; but Mama, throughout their visits, remained almost entirely silent and aloof except for the rare remarks which seemed to burst from her as though by an inescapable inward compulsion. These were always insulting and always directed at me, but I overlooked them, knowing her to be deranged.

79 Perhaps one of the things I most enjoyed about The Ivies was wandering through its acres, breathing through my pores, as it were, the sense of possession. I was walking through the cowslips and violets punctuating the meadow bordering one of the many little streams, when I came upon a fellow roughly dressed, the pockets of his shootingjacket bulging and a fishingline in his hand. For a moment I thought him one of the gamekeepers and nodded, but his quick look and furtive gestures instantly revealed him as a poacher.

"Youre trespassing, you know," I said with some severity.

"I know, guvner," he admitted readily, "but I wasnt doing no harm; just looking at this bit of water here and listening to the birds."

"With a fishingline in your hands?"

"Well, now, guvner, that's by way of being a precaution. You see, when I go out on a little expedition like this, to inspect the beauties of nature—which I admit I have no right to do, they being on someone else's land—I always say to myself, 'Suppose you run into some gent looking at a lovely fat trout in a brook and he hasnt got no fishline with him? What could be more philanthropic than I produce my bit of string and help him out?' Aint that a proper Christian attitude, guvner?"

"Possibly; but what, may I ask, makes your pockets bulge so suspiciously? Is that another philanthropy?"

"Accident, guvner, sheer accident. Walking along like this with my head down I always seem to come upon two or three dead hares or now and then a partridge or grouse. Natural mortality, you understand. Well, what could be more humane than to stuff them in my pockets and take them home for proper burial?"

"You know in spite of all the Labour governments and strange doings in Parliament, there are still pretty strict laws against poaching."

"Poaching, govner? I wouldnt poach. I respect what's yours, just as I respect what's my own. Trespassing maybe. I likes to look at a little bit of sky or hear a meadowlark or smell a flower or two, but poaching—! Really, guvner, you hadnt ought to take away a man's character."

I thought it a shame so sturdy and amusing a fellow should have to eke out his living so precariously. "I'll tell you what I'll do," I said. "I'll give you a note right now to my head gamekeeper and have him put you on as an assistant. Thirty shillings a week I think it pays."

"Well, now, thank you, guvner, but really, I don't want it. Thirty bob a week! What should I do with it? Nothing but go down to the Holly Tree and get drunk every night. I'm much better off as I am—total abstinence, in a manner of speaking. No, no, guvner, I appreciate your big heart, but I'm happy with my little bit of fish and a rabbit in the pot—why should I set up to be an honest workingman and get dissatisfied with my life?"

His refusal of my wellintentioned offer did not irk me. In a large and tolerant view you could almost say we were both parasites upon The Ivies and it would not hurt me if he stole a little of my game to keep himself alive. I gave him a note to protect him

against any of the keepers who might come upon him as I had, and
we parted with mutual liking; I remembering for my part that I was
an American and all men, poacher and landlord alike, were created
equal, no matter how far each had come from his beginnings.

80 Shortly after, Miss Francis ended her long sojourn at
Mount Whitney and returned to England. The ordeal
of living surrounded by the Grass, which had destroyed her assistants, seemed to have made no other change in her than the
fading of her hair, which was now completely white, and a loss of
weight, giving her a deceptive appearance of fragility at variance
with the forthrightness of her manner.

I put down her immunity to agorophobia as just another evidence that she was already mad. Her refusal to accept the limits of
her sex and her complete indifference to our respective stations
were mere confirmations. With her usual disregard of realities she
assumed I would go on financing her indefinitely in spite of the
hundreds of thousands of pounds I had paid out without visible
result.

"I've really got it now, Weener," she assured me in a tone
hardly befitting a suppliant for funds. "In spite of the incompetents
you kept sending, in spite of mistakes and blind alleys, the work on
Whitney is done—and successfully. The rest is routine laboratory
work—a matter of quantities and methods of application."

"I don't know that I can spare you any more money, Miss
Francis."

She laughed. "What the devil's the matter with you, Weener?
Are your millions melting away? Or do you think any of the spies
you set on me capable of carrying on—or are you just trying to
crack the whip?"

"I set no spies and I have no whip. I merely feel it may not be
profitable to waste any more money on fruitless experiments."

She snorted. "Time has streamlined and inflated your platitudes. When I am too old to work and ready for euthanasia I shall
have you come and talk me to death. To hear you one would almost
think you had no interest in finding a method to counter the
Grass."

Her egomania and impertinence were really insufferable; her notion of her own importance was ludicrous.

"Interested or not, I have no reason to believe you alone are capable of scientific discovery. Anyway, the world seems pretty well off as it is."

She tugged at her hair as if it were false and would come off if she jerked hard enough. "Of course it's well enough off from your pointofview. It offers you more food than you could eat if you had a million bellies, more clothes than you could wear out in a million years, more houses than you could live in if the million contradictions which go to make up any single human were suddenly made corporeal. Of course youre satisfied; why shouldnt you be? If the Grass were to be pushed back and the world once more enlarged, if hope and dissatisfaction were again to replace despair and content, you might not find yourself such a big toad in a small puddle—and you wouldnt like that, would you?"

I had intended all along to give her a small pension to keep her from want and allow her to putter around, but her irrational accusations and insults only showed her to be the kind from whom no gratitude could be expected.

"I'm afraid we can be of no further use to each other."

"Look here, Weener, you can't do this. The life of civilization depends on countering the Grass. Don't tell me the world can go on only half alive. Look around you and notice the recession every day. Outside of your own subservient laboratories what scientific work is being done? Since Palomar and Mount Wilson and Flagstaff went what has happened in astronomy? If you pick up the shrunken pages of your *Times* or *Tatler*, do you wonder at the reason for their shrinkage or do you realize there are fewer literates in the world than there were ten years ago?

"The Americas were upstart continents, werent they? I am not speaking sarcastically, my point is not a chauvinistic one, not even hemispherically prideful. And the Old World the womb of culture? But how much culture has that womb borne since the Americas disappeared? Without a doubt there are exactly the same number of composers and painters, writers, and sculptors alive on the four continents today as there were when there were six, but in this drowsy halfworld how many books of importance are being produced?"

"There are plenty of books already in existence; besides, those things go by cycles."

"God give me patience; this is the man who has humanity prostrate."

"Humanity seems quite content in the position you ascribe to it."

"Of course, of course—that's the tragedy. It's content the same way a man who has just had his legs cut off is content; suffering from shock and loss of blood he enters a merciful coma from which he may never emerge. The legs do not write the books or think the thoughts, whether these activities wait for the cyclical moment or not, but the brain, dependent on the circulation of the blood and the wellbeing of the rest of the body for proper functioning. And who are you, little man, to stand in the way of assisting the patient?"

"I shall not argue with you any further, Miss Francis. If mankind is really as subject to your efforts as your conceit leads you to believe then I am sure you will find some way to continue them."

"I'm sure I will," she said, and we left it at that.

To say her accusations had been gravely unjust would be to defend myself where no defense is called for. I merely remark in passing that I gave orders to set aside a still greater fund toward finding a reagent against the Grass, and to put those who had lately assisted Miss Francis in charge. I did this, not because I swallowed her strained analogy about a sufferer with his legs cut off, but for purely practical reasons. The world was very well as it was, but an effective weapon against the Grass might at last make possible the neverdiscarded vision of utilizing it beneficially.

81 Meanwhile life went on with a smoothness strange and gratifying to those of us born into a period of strife and restlessness. No more wars, strikes, riots, agitation for higher wages or social experiments by wildeyed fanatics. Those whose limitations laid out a career of toil performed their function with as much efficiency as one could expect and we others who had risen and separated ourselves from the herd carried our responsibilities and accepted the rewards which went with them. The ships of the World Congress continued patrolling the coasts of the deserted continents and restrictions were so far relaxed as to permit plane-flights over the area to take motionpictures and confirm the Grass had lost none of its vigor. Beyond this, the generality of mankind forgot the weed and the regions it covered, living geographically as though Columbus had never set forth from Palos.

It was at this time a new philosophic idea was advanced—giving the lie to Miss Francis' dictum that no new thoughts were being thought—which was, briefly, that the Grass was essentially a good thing in itself; that the world had not merely made the best of a bad situation, but had been brought to a beneficent condition through the loss of the Western Hemisphere. Mankind had desperately needed a brake upon its heedless course; some instrumentality to limit it and bring it to realization of its proper province. The Grass had acted as such an agent and now, rightly chastised, man could go about his fit business.

This concept gained almost immediate popular support, so far as it filtered down to the masses at all; prominent schoolmen endorsed it wholeheartedly; statesmen gave it qualified approval— "in principle"—and the Pope issued an encyclical calling for a return of Christian resignation and submission. Hardly was the ink dry upon the expressions of thanksgiving for the punishment which had brought about a new and better frameofmind than the philosophy was suddenly and dramatically tested by events.

The island of Juan Fernandez, Robinson Crusoe's island, a peak pushed out of the waters of the Pacific 400 miles west of Chile, densely populated with refugees and a base for patrolboats, was overrun by the Grass. It was an impossible happening. Every inhabitant had had personal experience of the Grass and was fearfully alert against its appearance. The patrols covered the sea between it and the mainland constantly; the distance was too far for windborne seeds. The tenuous hypothesis that gulls had acted as carriers was accepted simply for want of a better.

But the World Congress wasted no time looking backward. Although between Juan Fernandez and the next land westward the distance was three times greater than between it and South America, the Congress seized upon the only island to which it could possibly spread, Sala-y-Gomez, and made of it a veritable fortress against the Grass. Not only did ships guard its waters by day and keep it brilliantly lit with their searchlights at night, but swift pursuitplanes bristling with machineguns brought down every bird in flight within a thousand miles.

The island itself was sown with salt a halfmile thick after being mined with enough explosives to blow it into the sea. The world, or that portion of it which had not fully accepted all the implications of the doctrine of submission, watched eagerly. But the ships patrolled an empty sea, the searchlights reflected only the glittering saline crystals, the migrant birds never reached their destination. The outpost held, impregnable. Again everyone breathed easier.

Five hundred miles beyond this focalpoint, its convict settlement long abandoned, was Easter Island, Rapa Nui, home of the great monoliths whose origin had ever been a puzzle. Erect or supine, these colossal statues were strewn all over the island. Anthropologists and archaeologists still came to give them cursory inspection and it was on such a visit an unmistakable clump of Grass was found.

Immediately the ships were rushed from Sala-y-Gomez, planes carrying tons of salt took off from Australia and the whole machinery of the World Congress was swiftly put in operation. But it was too late; Easter Island was swamped, uninhabited Ducie went next, and Pitcairn, home of the descendants of the *Bounty* mutineers followed before even the slightest precautions could be taken. The Grass was jumping gaps of thousands of miles in a breathless steeplechase.

On Pitcairn there was nothing to do but rescue the inhabitants. Vessels stood by to carry them and their livestock off. The pale-brown men and women left for the most part docilely, but the last Adams and the last McCoy refused to go. "Once before, our people were forced to leave Pitcairn and found nothing but unhappiness. We will stay on the island to which our fathers brought their wives."

There was no stopping the Grass now, even if the means had been to hand. The Gambiers, the Tuamotus and the Marquesas were swallowed up. Tahiti, dwellingplace of beautiful if syphilitic women, disappeared under a green blanket, as did the Cook Islands, Samoa and the Fijis. The Grass jumped southward to a foothold in New Zealand and northward into Micronesia. Panic infected the Australians and a mass migration to the central part of the country was begun, but with little hope the surrounding deserts would offer any effective barrier.

82 My first thought when I heard the Grass for the second time had broken its bounds, was that I had perhaps been a little hasty with Miss Francis. It was not at all likely she would succeed where so many better trained and better equipped scientists had so far failed, but I felt a vicarious sympathy with her, as being out of the picture when all her colleagues were striving with might and main to save the world; especially after the years she had spent on Mount Whitney. It would be an act of simple generosity on my part, I thought, to give her the wherewithal to entertain the illusion of importance. When all was said and done, she was a woman, and I could afford a chivalrous gesture even in the face of her overweening arrogance.

I am sorry to say she responded with complete illgrace. "I knew youd eventually have to come crawling to me to save your hide."

"You mistake the situation entirely, Miss Francis," I informed her with dignity. "I am conferring, not asking favors. I have every confidence in my research staff—"

"My God! Those guineapig murderers; those discoveryforgers; those whitesmocked acolytes in the temple of Yes. You value your life or your purse at exactly what theyre worth if you expect those drugstoreclerks to preserve them for you."

"I doubt if either is in the slightest danger," I assured her confidently. "Hysterics have lost perspective. Long before the Grass becomes an immediate concern my drugstoreclerks, with less exalted opinions of their talents than you, will have found the means to destroy it."

"A soothing fairytale. Weener, the truth is not in you. You know the reason you come to me is that youre frightened, scared, terrified. Well, strangely enough, I'm not going to reject your munificence. I'll accept it, because to do God's work is more important than any personal pride of mine or any knowledge that one of the best things *Cynodon dactylon* could do—if I do not take too much upon myself in judging a fellowcreature—would be to bury Albert Weener."

I remained unmoved by her tirade. "When you returned from Whitney you told me there remained only details to be worked out. About how long do you think it will be before you have a workable compound?"

She burst into a laugh and took out her toothpick to point it at me. "Go and put your penny in another slot if you want an answer to an idiot question like that. How long? A day, a month, a year, ten years."

"In ten years—" I began.

"Exactly," she said and put away the toothpick.

---

83 I phoned Stuart Thario to fly over right away for a conference. "General," I began, "we'll have to start looking ahead and making plans."

He hid his mustache with the side of his forefinger. "Don't quite understand, Albert—have details here of activities . . . next three years . . ."

I pressed the buzzer for my secretary. "Bring General Thario some refreshment," I ordered.

The command was not only familiar on the occasion of his visits, but evidently anticipated, for she appeared in a moment with a trayful of bottles.

"Bad habit of yours, Albert, teetotalism . . . makes the brain cloudy . . · insidious." He took a long drink. "Very little real bourbon left . . . European imitation vile . . . learning to like Holland gin." He drank again.

"To get back to the business of making plans, General," I urged gently.

"Not one of those people getting worried about the Grass?"

"Not worried. Just trying to look ahead. I can't afford to be caught napping."

"Well, well," he said, "can't pull another South American this time."

"No, no—and besides, I'm not concerned with money."

"Now, Albert, don't tell me youve finally got enough."

"This is not the time to be avaricious," I reproved him. "If the Grass continues to spread—and there seems to be little doubt it will—"

"All of New Zealand's North Island was finished this morning," he interrupted.

"I heard it myself; anyway, that's the point. As the Grass advances there will be new hordes of refugees—"

He was certainly in an impatient mood this morning, for he interrupted me again. "New markets for concentrates," he suggested.

I looked at him pityingly. Was the old man's mind slipping? I wondered if it would be necessary to replace him. "General," I said gently, "with rare exceptions these people will have nothing but worthless currency."

"Goods. Labor."

"Have you seen the previous batches of refugees foresighted enough to get out any goods of value before starting off? And as for labor, all our workers are now so heavily subsidized by the dole that to cut wages another cent—"

"Ha'penny," corrected General Thario.

"Centime if you like. —would be merely to increase our taxes."

"Well, well," he said. "I see I have been hasty. What did you have in mind, Albert?"

"Retrenchment. Cut production; abandon the factories in the immediate path of the Grass. Fix on reasonably safe spots to store depots of the finished concentrates, others for raw materials. Or perhaps they might be combined."

"What about the factories?"

"Smaller," I said. "Practically portable."

"Hum." He frowned. "You do intend to do business on a small scale."

"Minute," I confirmed.

"What about the mines? The steelmills, the oilfields, the airplane and automobile factories? The shipyards?"

"Shut them down," I ordered. "Ruthlessly. Except maybe a few in England."

"The countries where theyre located will grab them."

"There isnt a government in existence who would dare touch anything belonging to Consolidated Pemmican. If any should come into existence our individualistic friends would take care of the situation."

"Pay gangsters to overturn governments?"

"They would hardly be legitimate governments. Anyway, a man has a right to protect his property."

"Albert," he complained querulously, "youre condemning civilization to death."

"General," I said, "youre talking like a wildeyed crackpot. A businessman's concern is with business; he leaves abstractions to visionaries. Our plants will be closed down, because until the Grass is stopped they can make us no profit. Let some idealistic industrialist take care of civilization."

"Albert, you know very well no business of any size can operate today without your active support. Think again, Albert; listen to me as a friend; we have been associated a long time and to some extent you have taken Joe's place in my mind. Consider the larger aspects. Suppose you don't make a profit? Suppose you even take a loss. You can afford to do it for common humanity."

"I certainly think I do my share for common humanity, General Thario, and it cuts me to the heart that you of all people should imply such a sentimental and unjust reproach against me. You know as well as I do I have given more than half my fortune to charitable works."

"Albert, Albert, need there be this hypocrisy between you and me?"

"I don't know what you mean. I only know I called you to evolve specific plans and you have embarked instead on windy platitudes and personal insult."

He sat for a long time quietly, his drink untouched before him. I did not disturb his meditation, but indulged in one on my own account, thinking of all I had done for him and his family. But only a foolish man expects gratitude, or for that matter any reward at all for his kindnesses.

At last he broke his silence, speaking slowly, almost painfully. "I have not had what could be called a successful life, even though today I am a wealthy man." He resumed his drink again and I wondered what this remark had to do with the subject in hand.

Perhaps nothing, I thought; he is just rambling along while he reconciles himself to the situation. I was glad he was going to be sensible afterall. Not that it mattered; I could get many able lieutenants, but for oldtime's sake I was pleased at the abandonment of his recalcitrance. He relaxed further into the chair while I waited to resume the practical discussion.

"When you first came to me in Washington, Albert, seeking warcontracts for your microscopic business, I suppose there was even then a mark upon your forehead, but I was too heavy with the guilt of my own affairs to see it. We all have our price, Albert, sometimes it is another star on the shoulderstraps or a peerage or wealth or the apparent safety of a son . . .

"I have come a long way with you since then, Albert, through shady deals and brilliant coups and dark passages which would not bear too much investigation. I'm afraid I cannot go any further with you. You will have to get someone else to kill civilization."

"As you choose, General Thario," I agreed stiffly.

"Wait, I'm not finished. I have always tried, however inadequately, to do my duty. Articles of War . . . holding commission in the Armies of the United States . . ." Emotion seemed to be sobering him rapidly. "Duty to you . . . Consolidated Pemmican . . . resign commission. Must mention spot . . . try Sahara . . ."

He stood up.

"Thank you, General Thario," I said. "I shall certainly consider the Sahara as location for depots."

"You won't change your mind about this whole thing, Albert?"

I shook my head. How could I fly in the face of commonsense to gratify the silly whim of an old man whose intelligence was clearly not what it had once been?

"I was afraid not," he muttered, "afraid not. I don't blame you, Albert. Men are as God created them . . . or environment, as the socialist fellers say . . . you didnt put the mark on your forehead . . . Not successful . . . Joe (I called him George but he was Joe all the time) wanted to go to West Point afterall. . . . First Symphony in the fire . . . I burned Joe's First Symphony . . . Do you understand me, Albert? Though I refuse, I am still guilty . . . Cannibal Thario, they said . . . Chronos would be better . . . classical allusion escapes the enlistedman . . ."

He walked out, still mumbling inarticulately and I sat there saddened that a man once alert and vigorous as the general should have come at last to senility and an enfeebled mind.

84 The defection of General Thario threw a great burden of work upon my shoulders. Preblesham was able enough in his own sphere, but his vision was not sufficiently broad to operate at the highest levels. The process of closing down our plants was more complicated than had been anticipated and Thario's military mind would have been more useful than Preblesham's theological one. The employees, conceiving through some fantastic logic that their jobs were as much their property as the mills or mines or factorybuildings were mine, rioted and had to be pacified—the first time such a tactic was resorted to in years. In some places these misguided men actually took possession of the places where they worked and tried to operate them, but of course they were balked by their own inefficiency. Human nature being what it is, they tried to blame their helplessness on my control of their sources of raw material and their consequent inability to obtain vital supplies; as well as the cutting off of light and power from the seized plants, but this was mere buckpassing, always noticeable when some radical scheme fails.

But the setting up of depots in the Sahara, as General Thario had suggested, and by extension, in Arabia, was a different matter. Here Preblesham's genius shone. He flew our whole Australian store of raw materials out without a loss. He recruited gangs of Chinese coolies with an efficiency which would have put an oldtime blackbirder to shame. He argued, cajoled, bullied, sweated for twentyfour hours a day and when in six months he had completed his task, we had seven depots, two in Arabia and five in Africa, complete with four factories, with enough concentrates on hand to feed the world for a year—if the world had the means to pay, which it didnt—and to operate for five.

During those six months the Grass ravenously snatched morsel after morsel. New Zealand's South Island, New Caledonia, the Solomons and the Marianas were gobbled at the same moment. It gorged on New Guinea and searched out the minor islands of the East Indies as a cat searches for baby fieldmice in a nest her paw has discovered. It took a bite of the Queensland coast just below the Great Barrier Reef. The next day it was reported near Townsville and soon after on the Cape York peninsula, the Australian finger pointing upward to islands where lived little black men with woolly hair.

The people of Melbourne and Sydney and Brisbane took the coming of the Grass with calm anger. Preparations for removal had been made months before and this migration was distinguished from previous ones by its order and completeness. But although they moved calmly in accordance with clear plans their anger was directed against all those in authority who had failed to take measures to protect their beloved land.

Queensland, New South Wales, Victoria and Tasmania went. The Grass swept southward like a sickle, cutting through South Australia and biting deep with its point into Western. Although we were amply provided with raw material, considering the curtailment of our activities, Preblesham, on the spot, could not resist buying up great herds of sheep for a penny on the pound and having them driven northward in the hope of finding somehow a means to ship them. I am sorry to say—though I'm afraid I could have predicted it—this venture was a total loss.

85 Burlet, unfolding the *Times* on my breakfastplate, coughed respectfully. "If I could speak to you at your convenience, sir?"

"What is it, Burlet? Lord Arpers finally come through with a higher offer?"

"Not at all, sir. I consider the question of service closed as long as you find yourself satisfied, sir."

"Quite satisfied, Burlet."

"I 'ad in mind the discussion of quite another matter, sir. Not relating to domestic issues."

"Very well, Burlet. Come into the library after breakfast.'

"Very good, sir."

With a world of problems on my mind I thought it would be wryly amusing to resolve whatever difficulties troubled my butler. Promptly after I had settled myself at my desk and before I rang for my secretary, Burlet appeared in the doorway, his striped vest smoothed down over his rounded abdomen, every thin hair in place over the dome of his balding head.

"Come in, Burlet. Sit down. Whats on your mind?"

"Thank you, sir." To my surprise he accepted my invitation and seated himself opposite me. "I ave been speculating, sir."

"Really, Burlet? Silly thing to do. Lost all your wages, I suppose, and would like an advance?"

"You misappre—end me sir. Not speculating on Change. Speculating on the Grass."

"Oh. And did you arrive at any conclusion, Burlet?"

"I believe I ave, sir. As I understand it, scientists and statesmen are exerting their energies to fight the Grass."

"That's right." I was beginning to be bored. Had the butler fallen prey to one of the graminophile sects like Brother Paul's and gone through all this rigmarole merely to give me notice previous to immolating himself?

"And so far they ave achieved no success?"

"Obviously, Burlet."

"Well then, sir, would it not be a sensible precaution to find some means of refuge until and if they find a way to kill the Grass?"

"There is no 'if,' Burlet. The means will be found, and shortly—of that I am sure. As for temporary refuge until that time, no doubt it would be excellent, if practicable. What do you pro- pose—emigration to Mars or floating islands in the oceans?" Both of these expedients had long ago been put forth by contestants in the *Intelligencer.*

"Journeys to other planets would not solve things, sir. Assum- ing the construction of a vessel—an assumption so far unwar- ranted, if I may say so, sir—it would accommodate but a fraction of the affected populations. As for floating islands, they would be no more immune to airborne seeds than stationary ones."

"So it was discovered long ago, Burlet."

"Quite so, sir. Then, if I may say so, protection must be afforded on the spot."

"And how do you propose to do that?"

"Well, sir, by the building of vertical cities."

"Vertical cities?"

"Yes, sir. I believe sites should be selected near bodies of fresh water and tremendous excavations made. The walls and floor of the excavations should be lined with concrete, through which the water is piped. The cities could be on many levels, the topmost perhaps several miles in the air—glass enclosed—and with pipes reaching still igher to bring air in, and completely tight against the Grass. They should be selfcontained, generating their own power and providing their food by ydroponic farming. Such cities could hold millions of people now doomed until a way is found to kill the Grass."

There was a faintly familiar ring to the scheme.

"You seem to have worked it out thoroughly, Burlet."

"Polishing the plate, sir."

"Polishing the plate?"

"It leaves the mind free for cerebration. I ave a full set of blueprints and specifications, if youd like to inspect them, sir."

It was fantastic, I thought, and probably quite impractical, but I promised to submit his plans to those with more technical knowledge than I possessed. I sent his carefully written papers to an undersecretary of the World Congress and forgot the matter. Idleness certainly led to queer occupations. Vertical cities—and who in the world had the money to erect these nightmare structures? Only Albert Weener—that was probably why Burlet took advantage of his position to approach me with the scheme. Completely absurd. . . .

86 Probably the complaints of the Australians gave final impetus to the Congress to Combat the Grass. They met in extraordinary session in Budapest and declared themselves the executive body of a world government, which did not of course include the Socialist Union. All qualified scientists were immediately ordered to leave whatever employment they had and place themselves at the disposition of the World Government. Affluence for life, guaranteed against any fluctuations of currency, was promised to anyone who could offer, not necessarily an answer, but an idea which should lead to the solution of the problem in hand. While they were issuing their first edicts the Grass finished off the

East Indies, covered threequarters of Australia and attacked the southern Philippines.

Millions of Indonesians traveling the comparatively short distances in anything floatable crowded the already overpopulated areas of Asia. As I had predicted to General Thario, these refugees carried nothing with which to purchase the concentrates to keep them alive, and conditions of famine in India and China, essentially due to the backwardness of these countries, offered no subsistence to the natives—much less to an influx from outside.

The Grass sped northward and westward through the Malay States and Siam, up into China and Burma. In the beginning the Orientals did not flee, but stood their ground, village by village and family by family, opposing the advance with scythes, stones, and pitiful bonfires of their household belongings, with hoes, flails, and finally with their bare hands. But the naked hand, no matter how often multiplied, was as unable to halt the green flow as the most uptodate weapons of modern science. And the Chinese and the Hindus dying at their posts were no more an obstacle than mountain or desert or stretches of empty sea had been.

It was now deemed expedient, in order to keep public hysteria from rising to new selfdestructive heights, to tone down and modify the news. This proved quite difficult at first, for the people in their shortsightedness clamored for the accounts of impending doom which they devoured with a dreadful fascination. But eventually, when the wildest rumors produced by the dearth of accurate reports were disproved, many of the people in Western Europe and Africa actually believed the Grass had somehow failed to make headway on the Asiatic continent and would have remained in their pleasant ignorance had it not been for the premature flight of masses of Asiatics.

For the phenomenon contemporary with the close of the Roman Empire was repeated. A great, struggling, churning, sprawling, desperate efflux from east to west began; once more the Golden Horde was on the march. They did not come, as had their ancestors, on wildly charging horses, threatening with lances and deadly scimitars, but on foot, wretched and begging. Even had I been as maudlin as Stuart Thario desired I could not have fed these people, for there were no longer railroads with rollingstock adequate to carry the freight, no fleets of trucks in good repair, nor was the fuel available had they existed. The world receded rapidly from the machineage, and as it did so famine and pestilence increased in evermounting spirals.

The mob of refugees might be likened to a beast with weak, almost atrophied legs, but with a great mouth and greater stomach. It moved with painful slowness, crawling over the face of southern Asia, finding little sustenance as it came, leaving none whatever after it left. The beast, only dimly aware of the Grass it was fleeing from, could formulate no thoughts of the refuge it sought. Without plan, hope, or malice, it was concerned only with hunger. Day and night its empty gut cried for food.

The starving men and women—the children died quickly—ate first all that was available in the stores and homes, then scrabbled in the fields for a forgotten grain of rice or wheat; they ate the bark and fungus from the trees and gleaned the pastures of their weeds and dung. As they ate they moved on, their faminedistended stomachs craving more to eat, driving the ones who were but one step further from starvation ever before them.

Long ago they had chewed on the leather of their footgear and devoured all cats, dogs and rodents. They ate the stiffened and putrid carcasses of draft animals which had been pushed to the last extremity; they turned upon the corpses of the newly dead and fed on them, and at length did not wait for death from hunger to make a new cadaver, but mercifully slew the weak and ate the still warm bodies.

The Asiatic influx was a social accordion. The pulledout end, the high notes, as it were, the Indian princes, Chinese warlords, arrived quickly and settled into a welcoming obscurity. They came by plane, with gold and jewels and government bonds and shares of Consolidated Pemmican. The middle creases of the accordion came later, more slowly, but as quickly as money could speed their way. Men of wealth when they began their journey, they arrived little more than penniless and were looked upon with suspicion, tolerated only so long as they did not become a public charge.

The low notes, the thick and heavy pleats, took not days nor weeks nor months, but years to make the trek. They kept but a step ahead of the Grass, traveling at the same pace. They came not alone, but with accretions, pushing ahead of them millions of their same dispossessed, hungry, penniless kind. These were not greeted with suspicion, but with hatred; machineguns were turned upon the advancing mobs, the few airplanes in service were commandeered to bomb them, and only lack of fuel and explosives allowed them to sweep into Europe and overwhelm most of it as the barbarians had overwhelmed Rome.

But I anticipate. While the bulk of the Orientals was still beyond the Himalayas and the Gobi, Europe indulged in a wild saturnalia to celebrate its own doom. All pretense of sexual morality vanished. Men and women coupled openly upon the streets. The small illprinted newspapers carried advertisements promising the gratification of strange lusts. A new cult of Priapus sprang up and virgins were ceremoniously deflowered at his shrine. Those beyond the age of concupiscence attended celebrations of the Black Mass, although I was told by one communicant that participation lacked the necessary zest, since none possessed a faith to which blasphemy could give a shocking thrill.

Murder was indulged in purely for the pleasure. Men and women, hearing of the cannibalism raging among the refugees, adopted and refined it for their own amusement. Small promiscuous groups, at the end of orgies, chose the man and woman tiring soonest; the two victims were thereupon killed and devoured by their late paramours.

As there was a cult to Priapus, so there was an equally strong cult to Diana. The monasteries and convents overflowed. But in the tension of the moment many were not satisfied with mere vows of celibacy. In secret and impressive ceremonies women scarified their tenderest parts with redhot irons, thus proving themselves forever beyond the lusts of the flesh; men solemnly castrated themselves and threw the symbols of their manhood into a consuming fire.

I wouldnt want to give the impression bestial madness of one kind or another overtook everyone. There were plenty of normal people like myself who were able to maintain their selfcontrol and canalize those energies promoting crimes and beastly exhibitions in the unrestrained into looking forward to the day when the Grass would be gone and sanity return.

Nor would I like anyone to think law and order had completely abdicated its function. As offenses multiplied, laws grew more severe, misdemeanors became felonies, felonies capital offenses. When death by hanging became the prescribed sentence for any type of theft it was necessary to make the punishment for murder more drastic. Drawing and quartering were reinstituted; this not proving an efficient deterrent, many jurists advocated a return to the Roman practice of spreadeagling a man to death; but the churches vigorously objected to this suggestion as blasphemous, believing the ordinary sight of crucified murderers would debase the central symbol of Christianity. A less common Roman usage was adopted in its stead, that of being torn by hungry dogs, and to this the Christians did not object.

But the utmost severity of local and national officials, even when backed by the might of World Government, could not cope with the waves of migrants from the East nor the heedlessness of law they brought with them. As the Grass pushed the Indians and Chinese westward, they in turn sent the Mongols, the Afghans and the Persians ahead of them. These naturally warlike peoples were displaced, not by force of arms, but by sheer weight of numbers; and so, doubly overcome by being dispossessed of their homes—and by pacifists at that—they vented their pique upon those to the west.

As the starving and destitute trickled into Europe and North Africa, giving a hint of the flood to follow, I congratulated myself on the foresight which led to our retrenchment, for I know these ravening hordes would have devoured the property of Consolidated Pemmican with as little respect as they did the scant store of Ah Que, Ram Singh or Mohammed Ali. My chief concern was now to keep my industrial and organizational machinery intact against the day when a stable market could again be established. To this end I kept our vast staff of researchworkers—exempt from the draft of the World Government which had been quite reasonable in the matter—constantly busy, for every day's delay in the arresting of the Grass meant a dead loss of profits.

87 Josephine Francis alone, and as always, proved completely uncooperative. Undoubtedly much of her stubbornness was due to her sex; the residue, to her unorthodox approach to the mysteries of science. When I prodded her for results she snarled she was not a slotmachine. When I pointed out tactfully that only my money made possible the continuation of her efforts, she told me rudely to seek the Wailing Wall in Jerusalem before it was covered by the Grass. Again and again I urged her to give me some idea how long it would be before she could produce a chemical even for experimental use against the Grass and each time she turned me aside with insult or rude jest.

I had set her up in—or rather, to be more accurate, she had insisted upon—a completely equipped and isolated laboratory in Surrey. As it was convenient to my Hampshire place I dropped in almost daily upon her; but I cannot say my visits perceptibly quickened her lethargy.

"Worried, Weener?" she asked me, absently putting down a coffeepot on a stack of microscope slides. "*Cynodon dactylon*'ll eat gold and banknotes, drillpresses and openhearths as readily as quartz and mica, dead bodies and abandoned household goods."

I couldnt resist the opening. "Anything in fact," I pointed out, "except salt."

"A Daniel!" she exclaimed. "A Daniel come to judgment. Oh, Weener, thou shouldst have been born a chemist. And what is the other mistake? Give me leave to throw away my retorts and test-tubes and bunsen burners by revealing the other element besides sodium *Cynodon dactylon* refuses. For every mistake there is another mistake which supplements it. Sodium was the blindspot in the Metamorphizer; when I find the balancing blindspot I shall know not only the second element which the Grass cannot absorb but one which will be poison to it."

"I'm not a chemist, Miss Francis," I said, "but it seems to me Ive heard there are a limited number of elements."

"There are. And three states for each element. And an infinite number of conditions governing their application. What's the matter—aren't your trained seals performing?"

"All the research laboratories of Consolidated Pemmican are going night and day."

"Then what the devil are you hounding me for? Let them find the counteragent."

"Two heads are better than one."

"Nonsense. Two blockheads are worse than one insofar as they tend to regard each other as a source of wisdom. I shall conquer the

Grass, I alone, I, Josephine Spencer Francis—and as soon as possible. Now you have all the data in its most specific form. And I shall accomplish this because I must and not because I love Albert Weener or care a litmuspaper whether or not his offal is swallowed up. I have done what I have done (God forgive me) and I shall undo it, but the matter is between me and a Larger Accountant than the clerk who signs your monthly checks."

"What do you think about temporary protective measures in the meanwhile?"

"What the devil do you mean, Weener? 'Temporary protective measures'? What euphuistic gibberish is this?"

I outlined briefly my butler's plan of vertical cities. Miss Francis startled me with a laugh resembling the burst of machinegun fire. "Someone's been pulling your leg, poor terrified Maecenas. Or else youre befuddled with too many *Thrilling Wonder Scientifictions*. Pipes into the stratosphere! Watersupply piped in through concrete walls! Doesnt your mad inventor know the seeds would find these apertures in an instant?"

"Oh, those are possibly minor flaws which could be remedied."

"Well, go and remedy them and leave me to my work. Or pin your faith on substantialities instead of flights of fancy."

I went up to London, my mind full of a thousand problems. I had caught the economical British habit of using the trains, conserving the petrol and tyres on my car. The first thing I saw on the Marylebone platform was the crude picture in green chalk of a stolon of *Cynodon dactylon*. What idiot, I thought as I irritably rubbed at it with the sole of my shoe, what feebleminded creature has been let loose to do a thing like this? The brittle chalk, smeared beneath my foot, but the representation remained, almost recognizable. On my way to the Savoy I saw it again, defacing a hoarding, and as I paid off my driver I thought I caught another glimpse of the nonsensical drawing on the side of a lorry going by.

Perhaps my sensitivity perceived these signs before they were common property, but in a few days they were spread all over Europe, through what insane impulse I do not know. For whatever reason, symbols of the Grass blossomed on the Arc de Triomphe, on the Brandenburger Tor, on the pavement of the Ringstrasse and on the bridges spanning the Danube between Buda and Pesth.

88 I find myself, in retrospect, involuntarily telescoping the time of events. Looking backward, years become days, and months minutes. At the time I saw the first reproductions of the Grass in London the thing itself was continents away, busy absorbing the fringes of Asia. But its heralds and victims went before it, changing the life of man as it had itself changed the face of the world.

The breakdown of civilization beyond the Channel was almost complete. Only Consolidated Pemmican and the World Government still maintained communication facilities; and with the blocking of the normal ways of commerce the World Government found it difficult to spread either news or decrees to the general public. The most fantastic and contradictory ideas about the Grass were held by the masses.

When the Grass was in the Deccan and still well below the Yangtze, the Athenians were thrown into panic by the rumor it had appeared in Salonika. At the same time there was wild rejoicing in the streets of Marseilles based on the belief large stretches of North America had become miraculously free. The cult of the Grass idolaters flourished despite the strictest interdictions and great massmeetings were frequently held during which the worshipers turned their faces toward the southeast and prayed fervently for speedy immolation. It was quite useless for the World Government to attempt to spread the actual facts; the earlier censorship together with a public temper that preferred to believe the extremes of good or bad rather than the truth of gradual yet relentless approach, made people heedless of broadcasts rarely received even by state operated publicaddress systems or of handbills which even the still literate could not bother to decipher.

The idealization of the Socialist Union—once the Soviet Union—which had risen and fallen through the years, was quickened among those not enamored of the Grass. There must be some intrinsic virtue in this land which had not only been immune to inoculation by the Metamorphizer, but kept the encroaching weed from invading its borders in spite of its long continued proximity across Bering Strait and the Aleutians. The Grass had jumped gaps thousands of ocean miles and yet it had not bridged that narrow strip of water. It would have been a shock to these people had they known, as I knew and as the World Government had vainly tried to tell them, what Moscow had recently and reluctantly admitted: the Grass had long since crossed into Siberia and was now working its will from Kamchatka to the Lena River.

The people of Japan, caught between the jaws of a closing vise, responded in a manner peculiar to themselves. The Christians, now forming a majority, declared the Grass a punishment for the sins of the world and hoped, by their steadfastness in the face of certain death, to earn a national martyr's crown and thus perhaps redeem those still benighted. The Shintoists, on the other hand, agreed the Grass was a punishment—but for a different crime. Had the doctrine of the Eight Corners of the World never been abandoned the Japanese would never have permitted the Grass to overwhelm the Yamato race. The new emperor's reign name, Saiji, they argued, ought not to mean rule by the people as it was usually interpreted, but rule of the people and they called for an immediate Saiji Restoration, under which the subjects of the Mikado would welcome death on the battlefield in a manner compatible with bushido, thus redeeming previous aberrations for which they were now being chastised. Both parties agreed that under no circumstances would any Japanese demean himself by leaving Nippon and the world was therefore spared an additional influx from these islands.

But the Japanese were the only ones who refused to join the westward stampede plunging the world daily deeper into barbarism. We in England had cause to congratulate ourselves on our unique position. The Channel might have been a thousand miles wide instead of twenty. The turmoil of the Continent and of Africa was but dimly reflected. There was still a skeletal vestige of trade, the dole kept the lazy from starvation, railways still functioned on greatly reduced schedules, and the wireless continued to operate from, "Good morning, everybody, this is London," to the last strains of *God Save the Queen*. Although I was constantly rasped by inactivity and by the slowness of the researchworkers to find a weapon against the Grass, I was happy to be able to wait out this terrible period in so ameliorative a spot.

True, our depots in the Arabian and Sahara deserts were unthreatened by either the Grass or the horde, but I should have found it uncomfortable indeed to have lived in either place. In Hampshire or London I felt myself the center of what was left of the world, ready to jump into action the moment the great discovery was finally made and the Grass began to recede.

Preblesham, my right hand, flew weekly to Africa and Asia Minor, weeding out those workers who threatened to become useless to us because of their reaction to the isolated and monotonous conditions at the depots; keeping the heavily armed guards about our closed continental properties alert and seeing our curtailed activities in Great Britain were judiciously profitable. This period of quiescence suited his talents perfectly, for it required of him little imagination, but great industry and force.

I had noticed for some time a slight air of preoccupation and constraint in his demeanor during his reports to me, but I put it down to his engrossment with our affairs and resolved to make him take an extended vacation as soon as he could be spared, never dreaming of disloyalty from him.

I was shocked, then, and deeply wounded when at the close of one of our conferences he announced, "Mr Weener, I'm leaving you."

I begged him to tell me what was wrong, what had caused him to come to this decision. I knew, I said, that he was overworked and offered him the badly needed vacation. He shook his head.

"It aint that. Overwork! I don't believe there is such a thing. At least Ive never suffered from it. No, Mr Weener, my trouble is something no amount of vacations can help, because I can't get away from a Voice."

"Voice, Tony?" Hallucinations were certainly a symptom of overwork. I began mentally recalling names of prominent psychiatrists.

"A Voice within," he repeated firmly. "I am a sinful man, a miserable backslider. Maybe Brother Paul was not treading a true path; I doubt if he was or I would not have been led aside from following him so easily; but when I was doing his work I was at least trying to do the will of God and not the will of another man no better—spiritually, you understand, Mr Weener, spiritually—than myself.

"But now His Voice has sought me out again and I must once

more take up the cross. I feel a call to go on a mission to the poor heathens and urge on them submission to their Father's rod."

"Among those savages across the Channel! They will tear you limb from limb."

"Christ will make me whole again."

"Tony, you are not yourself. Youre upset."

"I am not myself, Mr Weener, I have become as a little child again and do my Father's bidding. I am upset, yes, turned up-sidedown and insideout by a Force not content to leave men in wrong attitudes or sinful states. But upset, I stand upright and go about my Father's business. God bless you, Mr Weener."

Miss Francis and Preblesham, at opposite ends of the intellectual scale, both maundering on about doing the Will of God and General Thario talking about marks on foreheads—what sort of feebleminded, retrogressive world was I living in? All the outworn superstitions of religion taking hold of people and intruding themselves into otherwise normal conversation. A wave of madness, akin to the plague of the Grass, must be sweeping over the earth, was my conclusion.

If General Thario's desertion had thrown an extra weight on my shoulders, Preblesham's burdened me with all the petty details of routine. It was now I who had to inspect our depots periodically and make constant trips into the dangerous regions across the Channel to see that the shutdown plants were being properly cared for. I resented bitterly the trick of fate preventing me from finding for any length of time subordinates to whom I could delegate authority.

Nor even on whom I could rely. What were Miss Francis and her wellpaid staff doing all this time? Why had they produced nothing in return for the fat living they got from me? The Grass was halfway across Asia, lapping the High Pamirs from the south and from the north, digesting Korea, Manchuria, Mongolia, thrusting runners into Turkestan—and still no progress made against it. It would be a matter of mere months now until our Arabian depots would be in the danger zone. I could only conclude these socalled scientists were little better than fakers, completely incompetent when confronted by emergency.

They were ready enough to announce useless and inapplicable

discoveries and conclusions; byproducts of their research, they called them, with an obviously selfconscious attempt to speak the language of industry. The insects living in and below the Grass were growing ever larger and more numerous. Expeditions had found worms the size of snakes and bugs big as birds, happy in their environment. The oceans, they announced, were drying up, due to the retention of moisture in the soil by the Grass, and added complacently that in a million years or so, assuming the Grass in the meantime covered the earth, there would be no bodies of water left. Climates were equalizing themselves, the polar icecaps were melting and spots previously too cold for *Cynodon dactylon* were now covered. I felt it to be a clear case of embezzlement that they had used my money, paid for a specific purpose, to make these useless, if possibly interesting, deductions.

For while they dawdled and read learned papers to each other, the Grass touched the Persian Gulf and the Caspian, paused before Lake Balkash and reached the Yenisei at the Arctic Circle. Far to the south it jumped from India to the Maldives, from the Maldives to the Seychelles and from the Seychelles on to the great island of Madagascar. I hammered the theme of "Time, time" at Miss Francis, but her only response was a helpless sneer at my impatience.

At intervals Burlet inquired of me what progress was being made with his plan for cities of refuge. I could only answer him truthfully that as far as I knew the World Government had it under consideration.

"But—if you will excuse my saying so, sir—in the meantime those people are dying."

"Quite so, Burlet, but there is nothing you or I can do about it."

For the first time since he entered my service I caught him looking almost impertinently at me. I faced him back and he dropped his eyes. "Very good, sir. Thank you."

He had made an understatement when he talked about "those people" dying. Europe was a madhouse. In selfdefense all strangers were instantly put to death and in retaliation the invading throngs spared no native. Peasants feared to stay their ground in terror of the oncoming Orientals and equally dared not move westward where certain killing awaited them at the hands of those who yesterday had been their neighbors. In an effort to cling to life they formed small bands and fought impartially both the static and dynamic forces. Farming was practically abandoned and the swollen population lived entirely on wild growth or upon human flesh.

In Africa the situation was little better. Internecine wars and slavery made their reappearance; the South African whites mercilessly slaughtered the blacks against a possible uprising and the Kaffirs, fleeing northward, repeated the European pattern of overcrowding, famine and pestilence.

89 The day our Arabian depots were abandoned before the oncoming Grass I felt my heart would nearly break with anguish. All that labor, all that forethought, all those precious goods gone. And all because Miss Francis and those like her were too lazy or incompetent to do the work for which they were paid. I flew to the spot, trying vainly to salvage something, but lack of planes and fuel made it impossible. During this trip I caught my first sight of the Grass for years.

I suppose no human eye sees anything abstractly, but only in relation to other things known and observed. With more than half the world in its grip, the towering wave of green bore no more resemblance to its California prototype than a brontosaurus to the harmless lizard scuttling over the sunny floor of an outhouse. Between the dirtysugar sands of the desert and the oleograph sky it was a third band of brilliant color, monstrously outofplace. A tidalwave would have seemed less alien and awful.

The distance was great enough so that no individual part stood out distinctly; instead, it presented itself as a flat belt of green, menacing and obdurate. As my plane rose I looked back at it stretching northward, southward and eastward to the horizon, a new invader in a land weary of many invaders; and I thought of the dead civilizations it covered: Bactria, Parthia, Babylon; the Empire of Lame Timur, Cathay, Cambodia, and the dominions of the Great Mogul.

The refuge of mankind narrowed continually, an island diminished daily by a lapping surf. Africa was thrice beset, in the south from Madagascar; in the center from the steppingstones in the Indian Ocean, and across the Red Sea where the Grass sucked renewed life from the steaming jungles and grew with unbelievable rapidity, in the highlands of Rhodesia and Abyssinia it crept slowly over the plateaus toward the slopes of Kilimanjaro and the Drakensberg. Unless something were done quickly our Sahara depots would go the way of the Arabian ones and we would be left with only our limited British facilities until the day when Africa and Asia would be reconquered.

The violence and murder which had gone before were tame compared with the new fury that shook the feartortured people of Europe, helpless in the nightmareridden days, dreaming through twitching nights of an escape geographically nonexistent. Dismembered corpses in the streets, arenas packed with dead bodies, fallow fields newly fertilized with human blood added their stench to that of an unwashed, disease riddled continent. A rumor was circulated that there were still Jews alive and those who but yesterday had sought each other in mortal combat now happily united to hunt down a common prey. And sure enough, in miserable caverns and cellars hitherto overlooked, shunning daylight, a few men in skullcaps and prayingshawls were found, dragged out into the disinterested sunlight with their families and exterminated. It was at this time the Grass crossed the Urals and leaped the Atlantic into Iceland.

In England, George Bernard Shaw, whose reported death some years before had been mourned by those who had never read a word of his, rose apparently from the grave to deliver himself of a last message:

> "If any who wept over my senile and useless carcass had taken the trouble to read *Back to Methuselah*, they could have reassured themselves regarding my premature demise. If ever there was to be a Longliver, that Longliver would have to be me. This was determined by the Life Force in the middle of the XIX Century. That Life Force could not afford to rob a squinting world of a man of perfect vision.

"Like Haslam (I forget his first name—see my complete works if you're interested) I gave myself out as dead in order to avoid the gawking of a curious and idle multitude. I was recuperating from the labors of my first century in order to throw myself into the more arduous ones of the second.

"But as I have pointed out so many times, the race was between maturity and the petulant self-destruction of protracted adolescence. Mankind had either to take thought or to perish, and it has chosen (perhaps sensibly after all) to perish. I am too old now to protest against selfindulgence.

Is it too late? Is it still possible to survive? The ship is now indeed upon the rocks and the skipper in his bunk below drinking bottled ditchwater. But perhaps a Captain Shotover, drunk on the milk of human kindness rather than rum, will emerge upon the quarterdeck and, blowing his whistle, call all hands on deck before the last rending crash. In that unlikely event, one of those emerging from the forecastle will be

G. Bernard Shaw."

90 In spite of the anarchic and unspeakable conditions on the Continent, I could not refrain from making one last tour of inspection. The thought of flooded mines, pillaged factories and gutted mills was more than I could bear. The stocks of oil in England were running short, but I commanded enough to fill my great transportplane. We flew low over roads crawling with humanity as a sick animal crawls with vermin. Some cities were empty, obscenely bereft of population; others choked with wanderers.

The Ruhr was a valley filled with the dead, with men tearing each other's throats in a frenzy of hunger, with the unburied and the soon to be buried sleeping sidebyside through restless nights. Not a building was still whole; what had not been torn down in

pointless rage had been razed by reasonless arson. Not one brick of
the great openhearths had been left in place, not one girder of the
great sheds remained erect.

The Saar was in little better case and the mines of Alsace were
useless for the next quartercentury. The industrial district around
Paris had been leveled to the ground by the mobs and Belgium
looked as it had after the worst devastation of war. I had expected to
find a shambles, but my utmost anticipations were exceeded. I
could bring myself to look upon no more and my pilot informing
me that our gas was low, I ordered him to return.

We were in sight of the Channel, not far from Calais, when
both starboard engines developed trouble simultaneously and my
pilot headed for a landingfield below. "What are you about, you
fool?" I shouted at him.

"Gasline fouled. I think I can fix it in a few minutes, Mr
Weener."

"Not down among those savages. We wouldnt have a chance."

"We wouldnt have a chance over the Channel, sir. I'd rather
risk my neck among fellow humans than in the water."

"Maybe you would, but I wouldnt. Straighten out the plane
and go on."

"Sorry, Mr Weener; I'm going to have to land here."

And in spite of my protests he did so. I was instantly proved
right, for before we came to a stop we were surrounded by an
assortment of filthy and emaciated men and women bearing
scythes and pitchforks, shouting, yelling and gesticulating, making
in fact, such an uproar that no comprehension was possible. However, there was no misunderstanding their brusque motions order-
ing us away from the plane or the threatening noises which
reinforced the command. No sooner had we reluctantly complied
than they proceeded methodically to puncture the tires and smash
the propellers.

My horror at this marooning among the degenerates was not
lessened by their ugly and illdisposed looks and I feared they would
not be content with smashing the plane, but would take out their
animus against those who had not sunk into their own bestial state
by destroying us as well. Since I do not speak much French, I could
only say to the man nearest me, a sinister fellow in a blue smock

with a brown stockingcap on his head, "C'est un disgrace, ça; je demandez le pourquoi."

He looked at me for a baffled moment before calling, "Jean, Jean!"

Jean was even more illfavored, having a scar across his mouth which gave him an artificial hairlip. However, he spoke English of a kind. "Your airship has been confiscated, citizen."

"What the devil do you mean? That plane is my personal property."

"There is no personal property in the Republic One and Indivisible," replied Jean. "Be thankful your life is spared, Citizen Englishman, and go without further argumentations."

I suppose it was reasonable to take this advice, but I could not resist informing him, "I am not an Englishman, but an American. We also had a Republic one and indivisible."

He shook his head. "On your ways, citizen. The Republic does not make distinctions between one bourgeois and another."

I looked around for the pilot, but he had vanished. Alone, furious at the act of robbery and not a little apprehensive, I began walking toward the coast; but I was not steeled against isolation among the barbarians of the Continent, nor dressed for such an excursion. Between anxiety lest I run into a less pompous and more bloodthirsty group of representatives of the Republic One and Indivisible—when it had come into being, how far its authority extended or how long it lasted I never learned—and the burning and blistering of my feet in their thinsoled shoes, I doubt if I was more than a few miles from the airfield and therefore many from the coast when darkness fell. I kept on, tired, anxious, hungry, in no better plight than thousands of other wretches who at the same moment were heading the same way under identical conditions.

The only advantage of traveling by night was the removal of my fear of the intentions of men, but nature made up for this by putting her own obstacles in my way. The hedgerows which had been allowed to grow wild, the unrepaired roadways, sunken and marked by deep holes and ruts and a hundred other pitfalls made my progress agonizingly slow.

As the moon rose I had a sudden feeling of being near water, and coming out from a thicket I was confirmed in this by seeing the light break into ripples on an uneven surface. But tragically, it was not the Channel I had come upon, merely a river, too wide to cross, which though it undoubtedly led to my goal, would increase the length of my journey by many miles. I'm afraid I gave way to a quite unmanly weakness as I threw myself upon the hard ground and thought of my miserable fate.

I may have lain there for ten minutes, or twenty. The moon went behind a cloud, the air grew chilly. I was nerving myself to get up and resume my journey—though to what purpose I could not conceive for I would be little better off on a Norman beach than inland—when a timid hand was put on my shoulder and someone said questioningly, "Angleterre?"

I sprang up. "England. Oh, yes, England. Can you help me get there?"

The moon stayed covered and I could not see his face in the dark. "England," he said. "Yes, I'll take you."

I followed him to a little backwater, where was beached a rowboat. Even by feel, in the blackness, it seemed to me a very small and frail craft to chance the voyage across the choppy sea, but I had no choice. I seated myself in the stern while he took the oars, cast off and rowed us down the river toward the estuary.

I decided he must be one of that company of smugglers who were ferrying refugees into Britain despite the strictest watch. No doubt he thinks to make a pretty penny for tonight's work, I thought, but no coastguard would turn back Albert Weener. I would pay him well for his help, but he could not blackmail me for fabulous ransom.

Still the moon did not come out. My eyes, accustoming themselves to the dark, vaguely discerned the shape opposite me and I saw he was a short man, but beyond this I could not distinguish his features. The river broadened, the air became salty, the wind rose and soon the little boat was bobbing up and down in a manner to give discomfort to my stomach. The water, building terraces and battlements, reflected enough light to impress me with the diminutiveness of the boat, set in the vastness on which it floated.

Behind us the French coast was a looming mass, then a thick blob, finally a thin blur hardly perceptible to strained eyes. I was thoroughly seasick, retching and vomiting over the narrow freeboard. Steadily and rhythmically the man rowed with tireless arms, apparently unaffected by the boat's leaping and dropping in response to the impulse of the waves and in my intervals of relief from nausea I reflected that he must have gained plenty of practice, that he was an old hand in making this trip. It was a peculiar way to gain wealth, I thought, caught in another spasm of sickness, enriching oneself on the misery of others.

I vomited and dozed, dozed and vomited. The night was endless, the wind was bitter. What riches, I wondered, could compensate a man for such hardships? By the time the wanderers got to the Channel they could not very well have much left and unless my smuggler were gifted with secondsight he could not know, judging by the way he had accosted me, whether he was carrying a man who could pay £10, £100 or £500 for the accommodation. Well, I philosophized, it takes all kinds to make a world, and who am I to say this illicit trafficker isnt doing as much good in his way as I in mine?

I don't know when my nausea finally left me, unless it was after nothing whatever remained in my stomach. I sat limp and cold, conscious only of the erratic bobbing of the little vessel and the ceaseless rhythm of the oars. At last, unbelievably, the sky turned from black to gray. I could not believe it anything but an optical illusion in the endless night and I strained to dissipate whatever biliousness was affecting my vision. But it was dawn, sure enough, and soon it revealed the pettish, wallowing Channel and the fragile outline of our boat, even tinier than I had conceived. I shuddered with more than cold—had I known what a cockleshell it was I might have paused before trusting my life so readily to it.

Line by line the increasing light drew the countenance of my guide. At first he was nothing but a shape, well muffled, with some kind of flat cap upon his head. A little more light revealed a glittering eye, more, a great, hooked nose with wide nostrils. He was a man of uncertain age, bordering upon the elderly, with a black skullcap under which curled outward two silvergray horns of hair. The lower part of his face was covered with a grizzled beard.

He must have been studying me as intently, for he now broke the silence which had prevailed all night. "You are not a poor man," he announced accusingly. "How is it you have waited so long?"

"I'm afraid youve made a mistake in me, my friend," I told him

jovially, "we shan't be making an illegal entry. I am resident in
England and can come home at any time."

He was silent; from disappointment, I concluded. "Never
mind, I'll pay you as much as a refugee—within reason."

"You are a follower of reason, sir?"

I tried hard to make out more of his still obscured face for there
was a note of irony in his voice. "I believe we'd all be better off if
everyone were to accept things philosophically. Responsible people
will find a way to end our troubles eventually and in the meantime
madness and violence—" I waved my hand to the French coast
behind— "don't help at all."

"Ah," he said without pausing in his rowing, "men alone, then,
will solve Man's problem."

"Who else?"

"Who Else, indeed?"

The smuggler's answer or confirmation or whatever the equivocal echo was irritated me. "You think our problems can be solved
from the outside?"

He managed to shrug his shoulders without breaking the
rhythm of his arms. "Perhaps my English is unequal to understanding what you mean by outside. All the forces I know are represented
within."

I was baffled and switched the subject to more immediate
themes. "Are we about halfway, do you think?"

The light now exposed him fully. His hands were small and I
doubted if the arms extended from them were muscular, but he
radiated an air of great vitality. His face was lined, his eyes fierce
under outthrust eyebrows, his lips—where the crisp waves of his
beard permitted them to show—stern, but his whole demeanor was
not unkindly.

"It is easy to measure how far we have come, but who can say
how far we have to go?"

This metaphysical doubletalk annoyed me. "I don't know what
is happening to people," I said. "Either they act like those over
there," I gestured toward the Republic One and Indivisible, "or else
they become mystics."

"You find questions without immediate answers mystical, sir?"

"I like my questions to be susceptible to an answer of some
kind."

"You are a man of thought."

It amused me to speak intimately to this stranger. "I have lived inside myself a great many years. Naturally my mind has not been idle all the while."

"You have not married?"

"I never had the time."

"Ah." He rowed quietly for some moments. "'Never had the time,'" he repeated thoughtfully.

"You think marriage is important?"

"A man without children disowns his parents."

"Sounds like a proverb."

"It is not. Just an observation. I suppose since you have not had the time to marry you have devoted your life to good works."

"I have given employment to many, and help to the pauperized."

"It is commanded to be charitable."

"I have given millions of dollars—hundreds of thousands of pounds to philanthropies."

"Anonymously, of course. You must be a godly man, sir."

"I am an agnostic. I do not know if there is such a thing."

He shook his head. "Beneath us there are fish who do not know it is the sea in which they swim; above us there are birds unaware of the reaches of the sky. The fish have no conception of sky; the birds know nothing of the deep. They are agnostics also."

"Well, it doesnt seem to do them any harm. Fishes continue to spawn and birds to nest without the benefits of esoteric knowledge."

"Exactly. Fish remain fish in happy ignorance; doubt does not cause a bird to falter in its flight."

The sun was pushed into the air from the waters as a ball is pushed by the thumb and forefinger. The chalkcliffs were outlined ahead of me and I calculated we had little more than an hour to go. "You have chosen a strange way of earning a living, my friend," I ventured at last.

"Upon some is laid the yoke of the Law, others depend upon the sun for light," he said. "Perhaps, like yourself, I have committed some great sin and am expiating it in this manner."

"I don't know what you mean. I am conscious of no sin—if I understand the meaning of the theological term."

"'We have trespassed,'" he murmured dreamily, "'we have

been faithless, we have robbed, we have spoken basely, we have committed iniquity, we have wrought unrighteousness——'"

"Since the rational world discarded the superstitions of religion halfacentury ago," I said, "we have learned that good and evil are relative terms; without meaning, actually."

For the first time he suspended his oars and the boat wallowed crazily. "Excuse me," he resumed his exertions. "Good is evil sometimes and evil is good upon occasion?"

"It depends on circumstances and the point of view. What is beneficial at one time and place may be detrimental under other circumstances."

"Ah. Green is green today, but it was yellow yesterday and will be blue tomorrow."

"Even such an exaggeration could be defended; however, that was not my meaning."

"'We have wrought unrighteousness, we have been presumptuous, we have done violence, we have forged lies, we have counseled evil, we have lied, we have scoffed, we have revolted, we have blasphemed, we have been rebellious, we have acted perversely, we have transgressed, we have persecuted——'"

"Perhaps you have," I interrupted with some asperity, "but I don't belong in that category. Far from persecuting, I have always believed in tolerance. Live and let live, I always say. People can't help the color of their skins or the race they were born into."

"And if they could they would naturally choose to be white northEuropean gentiles."

"Why should anyone voluntarily embrace a status of inconvenience?"

"Why, indeed? 'We have persecuted, we have been stiffnecked, we have done wickedly, we have corrupted ourselves, we have committed abominations, we have gone astray and we have led astray. . .'"

We both fell silent after this catalogue, quite inapplicable to the situation, and it was with heartfelt thanks I distinguished each fault and seam in the Dover Cliffs as well as the breaking line of surf below.

I presumed because of what I'd said about legal entry he was not avoiding the coastguard, but with a practiced oar he suddenly veered and drove us onto a minute sandy beach at the foot of the cliffs, obviously unfrequented and probably unknown to officialdom. A narrow yet clearly defined path led upward; this was evidently his customary haven. Were I an emotional man I would have kissed the little strip of shingle, as it was I contented myself with a deep sigh of thanksgiving.

My guide stood on the sand, smoothing the long, shapeless garment he wore against his spare body. He had taken a small book from his pocket and was mumbling some unintelligible words aloud. I was struck again by the nervous vigor of the man which had given him the strength to row all night against a harsh sea—and presumably would generate the energy necessary for the return trip.

I pulled out my wallet and extracted two £100 banknotes. No one could say Albert Weener didnt reward service handsomely. "Here you are, my friend," I said, "and thank you."

"I accept your thanks." He bowed slightly, putting his hands behind him and moving toward his boat.

Perversely, since he seemed bent on rejecting my reward, I became anxious to press it upon him. "Don't be foolish," I argued. "This is a perilous game, this running in of refugees. You can't do it for pleasure."

"It is a work of charity."

I don't know how this shabby fellow conceived charity, but I had never understood that virtue to conflict with the law.

"You mean you ferry all these strays for nothing?"

"My payment is predetermined and exact."

"You are foolish. Anyone using your boat for illegal entry would be glad to give everything he possessed for the trip."

"There are many penniless ones."

"Need that be your concern—to the extent of risking your life and devoting all your time?"

"I can speak for no one but myself. It need be my concern."

"One man can't do much. Oh, don't think I don't sympathize with your attitude. I too pity these poor people deeply; I have given thousands of pounds to relieve them."

"Their plight touches your heart?"

"Indeed it does. Never in all history have so many been so wretched through no fault of their own."

"Ah," he agreed thoughtfully. "For you it is something strange and pathetic."

"Tragic would be a better word."

"But for us it is an old story."

He pushed his boat into the water. "An old story," he repeated.

"Wait, wait—the money!"

He jumped in and began rowing. I waved the banknotes ridiculously in the air. His body bent backward and forward, urging the boat away from me with each pull. "Your money!" I yelled.

He moved steadily toward the French shore. I watched him recede into the Channel mists and thought, another madman. I turned away at last and began to ascend the path up the cliff.

91 When I finally got back to Hampshire, worn out by my ordeal and feeling as though I'd aged ten years, there was a message from Miss Francis on my desk. Even her bumptious rudeness could not conceal the jubilation with which she'd penned it.

"To assuage your natural fear for the continued safety of Albert Weener's invaluable person, I hasten to inform you that I believe I have a workable compound. It may be a mere matter of weeks now before we shall begin to roll back *Cynodon dactylon.*"

Mr Weener Sees It Through

SIX

92 WHETHER IT WAS from the exposure I endured on that dreadful trip or from disease germs which must have been plentiful among the continental savages and the man who rowed me back to England, I don't know, but that night I was seized with a violent chill, an aching head and a dry, enervating fever. I sent for the doctor and went to bed and it was a week before I was myself enough to be cognizant of what was going on around me.

During my illness I was delirious and I'm sure I afforded my nurses plentiful occasion to snicker at the ravings of someone of no inconsiderable importance as he lay helpless and sick. "Paper and pencil, you kep callin for, Mr Weener—an you that elpless you couldnt old up your own and. You said you ad to write a book—the Istory of the Grass. To purge yourself, you said. Lor, Mr Weener, doctors don't prescribe purges no more—that went out before the first war."

I never had a great deal of patience with theories of psychology—they seem to smack too much of the confessional and the catechism. But as I understand it, it is claimed that there exists what is called an unconscious—a reservoir of all sorts of thoughts lurking behind the conscious mind. The desires of this unconscious are powerful and tend to be expressed any time the conscious mind is offguard. Whether this metaphysical construction be valid or not, it seemed to me that some such thing had taken place while I was sick and my unconscious, or whatever it was, had outlined a very sensible project. There was no reason why I shouldnt write such a history as soon as I could take the time from my affairs. Certainly I had the talent for it and I believed it would give me some satisfaction.

My pleasant speculations and plans for this literary venture were interrupted, as was my convalescence, by the loss of the Sahara depots. When I got the news, my principal concern wasnt for the incalculable damage to Consolidated Pemmican. My initial reaction was amazement at the ability of the devilgrass to make its way so rapidly across a sterile and waterless waste. In the years since its first appearance it had truly adapted itself to any climate, altitude, or condition confronting it. A few months before, the catastrophe would have plunged me into profound depression; now, with the resilience of recovery added to Miss Francis' assurance, it became merely another setback soon to be redeemed.

From Senegal, near the middle of the great African bulge, to Tunis at the continent's northern edge, up through Sardinia and Corsica, the latest front of the Grass was arrayed. It occupied most of Italy and climbed the Alps to bite the eastern tip from Switzerland. It took Bavaria, and the rest of Germany beyond the Weser. Only the Netherlands, Belgium, France, Spain and Portugal—a geographical purist might have added Luxembourg, Andorra and Monaco—remained untouched upon the Continent. Into this insignificant territory and the British Isles were packed all that was left of the world's two billion people: a blinded, starving mob, driven mad by terror. How many there were there, squirming, struggling, dying in a desperate unwillingness to give up existence, no matter how intolerable, no one could calculate; any more than a census could be taken of the numbers buried beneath the Grass now holding untroubled sway over ninetenths of the globe.

Watchers were set upon the English coast in a manner reminiscent of 1940. I don't know exactly what value the giving of the alarm would have been; nevertheless, night and day eyes were strained through binoculars and telescopes for signs of the unique green on the horizon or the first seed slipping through to find a home on insular soil.

Miss Francis' optimistic news had been communicated to the authorities, but not given out over the BBC. This was an obvious precaution against a wave of concerted invasion by the fear obsessed horde beyond the Channel. While they might respect our barriers if the hope for survival was dim, a chance pickup of the news that the Grass was doomed would be sure to send its destined victims frenziedly seeking a refuge until the consummation oc- cured. If such a thing happened our tiny islands would be suffo- cated by refugees, our stores would not last a week, and we should all go down to destruction together.

But in the mysterious way of rumor, the news spread to hearten the islanders. They had always been determined to fight the Grass—if necessary as the Chinese had fought it till over- whelmed—indeed, what other course had they? But now their need was only to hold it at bay until the new discovery could be imple- mented. And there was good chance of its being put to use before the Grass had got far beyond the Rhine.

93 Now we were on the last lap, my interest in the progress of the scientific tests was such that I insisted upon being present at every field experiment. For some reason Miss Francis didnt care for this and tried to dissuade me, both by her disagreeable manner (her eccentricity—craziness would undoubt- edly be a more accurate term—increased daily) and by her as- surances I couldnt possibly find anything to hold my attention there. But of course I overruled her and didnt miss a single one of these fascinating if sometimes disappointing trials.

I vividly recall the first one. She had reiterated there would be nothing worth watching—even at best no spectacular results were expected—but I made myself one of the party just the same. The theater was a particularly dismal part of Dartmoor and for some reason, probably known only to herself, she had chosen dawn for the time. We arrived, cold and uncomfortable, in two saloon cars, the second one holding several long cylinders similar to the oxygen or acetylene tanks commonly used in American industry.

There was a great deal of mysterious consultation between Miss Francis and her assistants, punctuated by ritualistic samplings of the vegetation and soil. When these ceremonies were complete four stakes and a wooden mallet were produced and the corners of a square, about 200 by 200, were pegged. The cylinders were un- loaded, set in place at equal intervals along one side of the square, turncocks and nozzles with elongated sprayjets attached, and the valves opened.

A fine mist issued forth, settling gently over the stakedout area. Miss Francis, her toothpick suspended, stood in rapt contemplation. At the end of thirty minutes the spray was turned off and the containers rolled back into the car. Except for the artificial dew upon it, the moor looked exactly as it had before.

"Well, Weener, are you going to stand there and gawk for the next twentyfour hours or are you coming back with us?"

I could tell by their expressions how horrified her assistants were at the rudeness to which I'd become so accustomed I 'no longer noticed it. "It's not a success, then?" I asked.

"How the devil do I know? I have no crystal ball to show me tomorrow. Anyway, even if it works on the miscellaneous growth here I havent the remotest idea how the Grass will react to it. This is only a remote preliminary, as I told you before, and why you encumbered us with your inquisitiveness is more than I can see."

"Youre coming back tomorrow, then?"

"Naturally. Did you think I just put this on for fun—in order to go away and forget it? Weener, I always knew those who made money werent particularly brilliant, but arent you a little backward, even for a billionaire?"

There was no doubt she indulged in these boorish discourtesies simply to buoy up her own ego, which must have suffered greatly. She presumed on her sex and my tolerance, taking the same pleasure in baiting me, on whom she was utterly dependent, as a terrier does in annoying a Saint Bernard, knowing the big dog's chivalry will protect the pest.

When we returned the square was clean of all growth, as though scraped with a sharp knife. Only traces of powdery dust, not yet scattered by a breeze, lay here and there. I was jubilant, but Miss Francis affected an air of contempt. "Ive proved nothing I didnt know before, merely confirmed the powers of the deterrent— under optimum conditions. It has killed ordinary grass and some miscellaneous weeds—and that's all I can say so far. What it will do to inoculated *Cynodon dactylon* I have no more idea than you."

"But youre going to try it on the Grass immediately?"

"No, I'm not," she answered shortly.

"Why not?"

"Weener, either leave these things in my hands or else go do them yourself. You annoy me."

I was not to be put off in so cavalier a manner and after we parted I sent for one of her assistants and ordered him to load a plane with some of the cylinders and fly to the Continent for the purpose of using the stuff directly against the Grass. When he protested such a test would be quite useless and he could not bring himself to such disloyalty to his "chief," as he quaintly called Miss Francis, I had to threaten him with instant discharge and blacklist before he came to his senses. I'm sorry to say he turned out to be a completely unreliable young man, for the plane and its crew were never heard from again—a loss I felt deeply, for planes were becoming scarce in England.

94 As a matter of fact everything, except illegal entrants who continued to evade the authorities, was becoming scarce in England now. The stocks of petroleum, acquired from the last untouched wells and refineries and hoarded so zealously, had been limited by the storage space available. We had a tremendous amount of food on hand, yet with our abnormally swollen population and the constant knowledge that the British Isles were not agriculturally selfsufficient, wartime rationing of the utmost stringency was resorted to. The people accepted their hardships, lightened by the hope given by Miss Francis' work—in turn made possible only by me.

Though I chafed at her procrastination and forced myself to swallow her incivilities, I put my personal reactions aside and with hardly an exception turned over my entire scientific resources to Miss Francis, making all my research laboratories subordinate to her, subject only to a prudent check, exercised by a governing board of practical businessmen. The government cooperated wholeheartedly and thousands worked night and day devising possible variants of the basic compound and means of applying it under all conditions. It was a race between the Grass and the conquerors of the Grass; there was no doubt as to the outcome; the only question now was how far the Grass would get before it was finally stopped.

The second experiment was carried out on the South Downs. The containers were the same, the ceremonious interchange repeated, only the area staked out covered about four times as much ground as the first. We departed as before, leaving the meadow apparently unharmed, returning to find the square dead and wasted.

Once more I urged her to turn the compound directly upon the Grass. "What if it isnt perfected? What harm can it do? Maybe it's advanced enough to halt the Grass even if it doesnt kill it."

She stabbed at her chest with the toothpick. "Isnt it horrible to live in a world of intellectual sucklings? How can I explain what's going on? I have a basic compound in the same sense . . . in the same sense, let us say, that I know iodine to be a poison. Yes, that will do. If I wish to kill a man—some millionaire—and administer too little, far from acting as a poison it will be positively beneficial. This is a miserably oversimplified analogy—perhaps you will understand it."

I was extremely dissatisfied, knowing as I did the rapidly worsening situation. The Grass was in the Iberian Peninsula, in Provence, Burgundy, Lorraine, Champagne and Holland. The people were restive, no longer appeased by the tentative promise of redemption through Miss Francis' efforts. The BBC named a date for the first attack upon the Grass, contradicted itself, said sensible men would understand these matters couldnt be pinned down to hours and minutes. There were riots at Clydeside and in South Wales and I feared the looting of my warehouses in view of the terrible scarcity of food.

It wasnt only the immediate situation which was bad, but the longrange one. Oil reserves in the United Kingdom were practically exhausted. So were non-native metals. Vital machinery needed immediate replacement. As soon as Miss Francis was ready to go into action the strain upon our obsolescent technology and hungerweakened manpower would be crippling.

The general mood was not lightened by the clergy, professionally gloating over approaching doom, nor by the speculations of the scientists, who were now predicting an insect and aquatic world. Man, they said, could not adapt himself to the Grass—this was proved to the hilt by the tragedy of the Russian armies in the Last War—but insects had, fishes didnt need to, and birds, especially those who nested above the snowline, might possibly be able to. Undoubtedly these orders could in time produce a creature equal if not superior to *Homo sapiens* and the march of progress stood a chance to continue after an hiatus of a few million years or so.

The combination of these airy and abstract speculations with their slowness to produce something tangible to help us at this crisis first angered and then profoundly depressed me. I could only look upon the whole conglomeration—scientists, politicians, common man and all—as thoroughly irresponsible. I remembered how I had applied myself diligently, toiling, planning, imagining, to reach my present position and how a fraction of that effort, if it had been exerted by these people, could stop the Grass overnight.

In this frameofmind my thoughts occupied themselves more and more with the idea I had uttered during my illness. To write a history of the Grass would at least afford me an escape from the daily irritation of concerning myself exclusively with the incompetents and blunderers. Not being the type of person to undertake anything I was not prepared to finish, I thought it might be advisable to keep a journal, first to get myself in the mood for the larger work and later to have a daytoday account of momentous events as seen by someone uniquely connected with the Grass.

95 JULY 14: Lunch at Chequers with the PM. Very gloomy. Says Miss F may have to be nationalized. Feeble joke by undersecretary about nationalization of women proving unsuccessful during the Bolshevik revolution. Ignoring this assured the PM we would get a more definite date from her during the week. Privately agreed her dilatoriness unpardonable. I shall speak to F tomorrow.

Home by 5. Gardeners slovenly; signs of neglect everywhere. Called in S and gave him a good goingover; said he was doing the best he could. Sighed for the good old days—Tony Preblesham would never have shuffled like that. Shall I have to get a new steward—and would he be any improvement?

Very bored after dinner. Almost decided to start the book. Scribbled a few paragraphs—they didnt sound too bad. Sleep on it.

JULY 15: BBC this morning reported Grass in the Ardennes. This undoubtedly means a new influx from the Continent—the coastguard is practically powerless—and we will be picked clean. In spite of the news F absolutely refuses to set a definite date. Kept my temper with difficulty.

Came home to be annoyed by Mrs H telling me K, one of the housemaids, had been got into trouble by an undergardener. Asked Mrs H whether or not it wasnt her function as a housekeeper to take care of such details. Mrs H very tart, said in normal times she was perfectly capable of handling the situation, but with everything going to pieces she didnt know whether to turn off K or the undergardener, or both, or neither. I thought her attitude toward me symptomatic of the general slackness and demoralization setting in all over. Instructed her to discharge them both and not bother me again with such trivia. Tried to phone the PM, but the line was down. Another symptom.

As a sort of refuge, went to the library and wrote for four solid hours, relating the origin of the Grass. Feeling much better afterwards, rang for Mrs H and told her merely to give K a leave of absence and discharge only the guilty undergardener. I could see she didnt approve my leniency.

JULY 16: A maniac somehow got into The Ivies and forced his way into the library where I was writing. A horrible looking fellow, with a tortured face, he waved a pistol in front of me, ranting phrases reminiscent of oldfashioned soapbox oratory. I am not ashamed to admit nervousness, for this is not the first time my life has been threatened since attaining prominence. Happily, the madman's aim was as wild as his speech, and though he fired four shots, all lodged in the plaster. S, Mrs H and B, hearing the noise, rushed in and grabbed him.

JULY 17: A little upset by the episode of the wouldbe assassin, I decided to go up to London for the day. The library would be unusable anyway, while the walls and ceiling were being repaired.

JULY 18: Shaking experience. Can write no more at the moment.

LATER: I was walking in Regent Square when I saw her. As beautiful and mysterious as she was last time. But now my tongue was not tied; oblivious to restraint and ridicule, I shouted, rushed after her.

I—But, really, that is all. I rushed after her, but she disappeared in the idle crowd. People looked at me curiously as I pushed and shoved, peering, crying, "Wait, wait a minute!" But she was gone.

STILL LATER: I shall go back to the Ivies tonight. If I stay longer in London I fear I shall be subject to further hallucinations.

If it was an hallucination and not the Strange Lady herself.

JULY 19: Grass reported in Lyons. F has new experiment scheduled for tomorrow. Despite upset condition, I wrote six pages of my history. The work of concentrating, under the circumstances, was terrific but I feel repaid for my effort. I am the captain of my soul.

S says the cottagers no longer paying rent. Told him to evict them.

---

96 JULY 20: F's test today on some underbrush in a wood. Think in future I shall go only to inspect the results; the spraying is very dull. Wrote four pages and tore them up. S says it is impossible to evict tenants. Asked him if there were no law left in England and he answered. "Not very much." I shall begin looking about for a new steward. Hear the Tharios are in London. Grass reported beyond the Vosges.

JULY 21: Usual aftermath of F's experiment. Not a sign of vegetation left. In the face of this, simply maddening that she doesnt get into action directly against the Grass. Got no satisfaction from her by direct questioning. Can her whole attitude be motivated by some sort of diseased and magnified femininity?

JULY 22: Noticed Burlet at breakfast had left off his striped waistcoat. Such a thing has never happened before. Not surprised when he requested interview. He began by saying it had been quite some time since he put before me his plan for what he calls "vertical cities." Not caring for his attitude, pointed out that it was quite outside my province as an employer to wetnurse any schemes of his; nevertheless, out of kindness I had brought it to the attention of the proper people.

"But, Mr Weener, sir, people are losing their lives."

"So you said before, Burlet."

"And if nothing is done the time will come when you also will be killed by refugees or drowned by the Grass."

"That borders on impertinence, Burlet."

"I ope I ave never forgot my place. But umanity takes precedence over umility."

"That will be all, Burlet."

"Very good, sir. If convenient, I should like to give notice as of the first."

"All right, Burlet."

When he left, I was unreasonably disturbed. If I had pressed his scheme—but it was impracticable . . .

JULY 23: The Grass is in the neighborhood of Antwerp and questions are being asked in Parliament. Unless the government can offer satisfactory assurances of action by F they are expected to fall tomorrow. Assured the PM I would put the utmost pressure on F, but I know it will do no good. The woman is mad; I would have her certified and locked up in an asylum in a second if only some other scientist would show some signs of getting results. Did not write a word on my history today.

JULY 24: Debate in Parliament. Got nothing from F but rudeness. Wrote considerably on my book. I would like to invite Stuart Thario to The Ivies, if for no other reason than to show I bear no malice, but perhaps it would not be wise.

Riots in Sheffield.

JULY 25: Vote of confidence in Commons. The PM asked the indulgence of the House and played a record of Churchill's famous speech: ". . . Turning to the question of invasion . . . We shall not fail; we shall go on to the end . . . We shall defend our island whatever the cost. We shall fight on beaches, in cities and on the hills. We shall never surrender." Result, the government squeaked through; 209 for, 199 against, 176 abstaining. No one satisfied with the results.

Mrs H came to me in great distress. It seems the larder is empty of chutney, curry and worcestershire sauce and none of these items can be purchased at Fortnum & Mason's or anywhere else. I assured her it was a matter of indifference to me since I did not care particularly for any of these delicacies.

Mrs H swept this aside as entirely irrelevant. "No wellconducted establishment, Mr Weener, is without chutney, curry or worcestershire." The insularity of the English is incredible. I have not tasted cocacola, hotdogs, or had a bottle of ketchup for more than a year, but I don't complain.

The Grass is in the Schelde estuary, almost within sight of the English coast. I got nothing written on my history today.

JULY 26: Invited to see film of a flight made about six months ago over what was once the United States. Very moving. New York still recognizable from the awkward shapes assumed there by the Grass. In the harbor a strange mound of vegetation. Several of the ladies wept.

I went home and thought about George Thario and carried my history of the Grass up until the time it crossed Hollywood Boulevard.

JULY 27: The Grass is now in Ostend, definitely in sight from the coast.

JULY 28: Grass in Dunkirk.

JULY 29: F astounded me this morning by coming to The Ivies, an unprecedented thing. She is (finally!!!) about to undertake tests directly against the Grass and wants airplanes and gasoline. I impressed upon her how limited our facilities are and how they cannot be frittered away. She screamed at me insanely (the woman is positively dangerous in these frenzies) and I finally calmed her with the assurance—only superficially exact—that I was dependent on the authorities for these supplies. At length I persuaded her she could just as well use motor launches since the Grass had now reached the Channel. She reluctantly agreed and grumblingly departed. My joy and relief in her belated action was dampened by her arrogant intemperance. Can a woman so unbalanced really save humanity?

JULY 30: Wrote.

JULY 31: Wrote.

AUGUST 1: Attended at breakfast by footman. Extremely awkward and irritating. Inquired, what had happened to Burlet? Reminded he had left. Annoyed at this typical lack of consideration on the part of the employed classes. We give them work and they respond with a lack of gratitude which is amazing.

In spite of vexations, I brought my history up to the wiping out of Los Angeles. Leave with F and party at midnight for the tests.

AUGUST 4: It is impossible for me to set down the extent of the depression which besets me. F's assurance she has learned a great deal from the tests and didnt for a minute expect to drive the Grass back at this point doesnt counter the fact that her latest spray hadnt the slightest effect on the green mass which has now replaced the sandy beaches of the Pas de Calais. At great personal inconvenience I accompanied her on her fruitless mission and I didnt find her excuses, even when clothed in scientific verbiage, adequate compensation for the wasted time.

AUGUST 5: The government finally fell today and there is talk of a coalition of national unity, with the Queen herself assuming extraordinary powers. There was general agreement that this would be quite unconstitutional, but that won't prevent its being done anyway.

In spite of the stringent watch against refugees the population has so enlarged that rations have again been cut. Mrs H says she doesnt know where the next meal is coming from, but I feel she exaggerates. Farmers, I hear, absolutely refuse to deliver grain.

AUGUST 6: Interview with S C. Offered him all the facilities now at the disposal of F. I admitted I was not without influence and could almost promise him a knighthood or an earldom. He said, "Mr Weener, I don't need the offer of reward; I'm doing my best right now. But I'm proceeding along entirely different lines than Miss Francis. If I were to take her work over at this point I'd nullify whatever advance she's made and not help my own research by as much as an inch." If C cant replace F, I don't know who can. Very despondent, but wrote just the same. Can't give in to moods.

97 AUGUST 7: BBC announced this morning the Grass is in Bordeaux and under the Defense of the Realm Act every man and woman is automatically in service and will be solely responsible for a hundred square feet of the island's surface, their stations to be assigned by the chief county constable. Tried to get Sir H C—no phone service.

Wrote on my history till noon. What a lot of bluster professional authors make over the writing of a book—they should have had the neccessity every businessman knows for sticking eternally to it, and experience in a newpaper cityroom—as I had. Just before luncheon an overworked looking police constable bicycled over with designations of the areas each of us is responsible for. Sir H very thoughtfully allotted the patrolling of my library to me.

AUGUST 8: Grass in Troyes and Châlons. The assignment of everyone to a definite post has raised the general spirit. Ive always said discipline was what people needed in times of crisis—takes their minds off their troubles.

The prime minister spoke briefly over the wireless, announcing he was in constant touch with all the researchworkers, including Miss Francis. Annoyed at his going over my head this way—a quite unnecessary discourtesy.

Marked incivility and slipshodness among the staff. Spoke to Mrs H and to S; both agreed it was deplorable, saw no immediate help for it. So upset by petty annoyances I could not write on my history.

AUGUST 9: Glorious news. The BBC announced the antiGrass compound would be perfected before Christmas.

AUGUST 10: F denies validity of the wireless report. Said no one with the remotest trace of intelligence would make such a statement. "Is it impossible to have the compound by then?" I asked her.

"It's not impossible to have it by tomorrow morning. Good heavens, Weener, can't you understand? I'm not a soothsayer."

Can it be some scientist I know nothing of is getting ahead of her? Very dishonorable of the government if so.

Despite uncertainties wrote three more pages.

AUGUST 11: Riots in Manchester and Birmingham. Demagogues pointing out that even if the antiGrass compound is perfected by Christmas it will be too late to save Britian. They don't count apparently on the Channel holding the plague back for long. Possible the government may fall, which won't disturb me, as I prefer the other party anyway.

AUGUST 12: After a long period of silence from the Continent, Radio Mondiale went on the air from Cherbourg asking permission for the government to come to London.

AUGUST 13: The watch on the south and east coasts has been tripled, more as a precaution against the neverceasing wave of invasion than the Grass. It has been necessary to turn machineguns on the immigrant boats—purely in selfdefense.

The rioting in the Midlands has died down, possibly on the double assurance that permission for the removal of the French government had been refused (I cannot find out, to satisfy my idle curiosity, if it is still the Republic One and Indivisible which made the request or whether that creation was succeeded by a less eccentric one), and that Christmas was a conservative estimate for the perfection of the compound—a last possible date.

Brought my history up to the Last War.

AUGUST 14: Very disheartening talk with the PM today. It seems the whole business of setting a date was an error from beginning to end. No one gave any such promise. It dare not be denied now, however, for fear of the effect upon the public. I must begin to think seriously of moving to Ireland.

AUGUST 15: Grass reported in the Faeroes. French Channel coast covered to the mouth of the Seine. What is the matter with F? Is it possible the failure of the last experiment blasted all her hopes? If so, she should have told me, so I might urge on others working along different lines.

Motored to the laboratory and spoke about moving to Ireland. She agreed it might be a wise precaution. "You know, Weener, the jackass who said Christmas mightnt have been so far out afterall." She seemed very confident.

Came home relieved of all my recent pessimism and brought my book down to the overrunning of the United States. I am not a morbid man, but I pray I may live to set foot on my native soil once again.

AUGUST 16: No new reports from France. Can the Grass be slowing down? Wrote furiously.

AUGUST 17: Wrote for nearly ten hours. Definitely decided to discharge S; he is thoroughly incapable. No word from France, but there is a general feeling of great optimism.

AUGUST 18: Bad news, very bad news. The Grass has jumped two hundred miles, from the Faeroes to the Shetlands and we are menaced on three sides. Went up to London to arrange for a place in Ireland. I cannot say I was well received by the Irish agent, a discourteous and surly fellow. Left orders to contact Dublin direct as soon as phone service is resumed.

AUGUST 19: It seems Burlet has been interesting all sorts of radicals and crackpots in his scheme for glassenclosed cities. Local MP very reproachful; "You should have warned me, Mr Weener." I asked him if he honestly thought the idea practical. "That isnt the point. Not the point at all."

As far as can be learned France is completely gone now. It is supposed a fragment of Spain and Portugal are still free of the Grass and a little bit of Africa. It is almost unbelievable that all these millions have perished and that the only untouched land left is these islands.

Many irritations. The phone is in order for perhaps halfanhour a day. Only the wireless approximates a normal schedule. Wrote six pages.

AUGUST 20: Dublin apologized profusely for the stupidity of their agent and offered me a residence near Kilkenny and all the facilities of Trinity for F and her staff. Told F, who merely grunted. She then stated she wanted a completely equipped seagoing laboratory for work along the French coast. I said I'd see what could be done. Much encouraged by this request.

AUGUST 21: The arrogance and shortsightedness of the workingclass is beyond belief. They refuse absolutely to work for wages any longer. I now have to pay for all services in concentrates. Even the warehouse guards, previously so loyal, will accept nothing but food. I foresee a rapid dwindling of our precious supplies under this onslaught.

AUGUST 22: With all the shipping Consolidated Pemmican

owns I can find nothing suitable for F's work. Almost decided to outfit my personal yacht *Sisyphus* for that purpose. It would be convenient to use for the Irish removal if that becomes necessary.

Burlet's ideas have found their way into Parliament. The Independent Labour member from South Tooting asked the Home Minister why nothing had been done about vertical cities. The Home Minister replied that Britons never would permit a stolon of the Grass to grow on English soil and therefore such fantastic ideas were superfluous. ILP MP not satisfied.

AUGUST 23: Ordered the *Sisyphus* to Southampton for refitting. It will cost me thousands of tons of precious concentrates, besides lying for weeks in a dangerously exposed spot. But I can make a better deal in Southampton than elsewhere and I refuse to be infected by the general cowardice of the masses.

Speaking of the general temper, I must say there has been a stiffening of spirit in the last week or so; very laudable, and encouraging to one who believes in the essential dignity of human nature.

No new report on the Grass for four days.

AUGUST 24: The member from South Tooting has introduced a bill to start construction at once of one of Burlet's cities. The bill calls for the conscription of manpower for the work and whatever materials may be necessary, without compensation. The last clause is of course aimed directly at me. Naturally, the bill will not pass.

AUGUST 25: Flew to Kilkenny. I fear this will be one of the last plane trips I can make for a long time, since the store of aviation gasoline is just about exhausted. The place is much more beautiful than Hampshire, but deplorably inconvenient. However, since the Irish are still willing to work for money, I have ordered extensive alterations.

AUGUST 26: I have stopped all sale of concentrates. Since money will buy nothing, it would be foolish of me to give my most precious asset away. Of course we cut the deliveries down to a mere dribble some time ago, but even that dribble could bleed me to death in time. I have doubled the wages—in concentrates—of the warehouse guards in fear of possible looting.

98 AUGUST 29: The last three days have been filled with terror and suspense. It began when a patrolling shepherd on the Isle of Skye found a suspicious clump of grass. All conditions favored the invader: the spot was isolated, communications were difficult, local labor was inadequate. The exhaustion of the fuel supply made it impossible to fly grassfighters in and men had to be sent by sea with makeshift equipment. Happily there were two supercyclone fans at Lochinvar which had been shipped there by mistake and these were immediately dispatched to the threatened area.

The clump was fought with fire and dynamite, with the fans preventing the broken stolons from rooting themselves again. After a period of grave anxiety and doubt there seems to be no question this particular peril has been averted—not a trace of the threatening weed remains. The Queen went personally to Westminster Abbey to give thanks.

AUGUST 30: Work on the *Sisyphus* proceeding slowly. I have decided to keep my own cabin intact and have the adjoining one fitted for a writing room. Then I can accompany F on her experimental excursions and not lose any time on my book, which is progressing famously. What a satisfaction creative endeavor is!

AUGUST 31: The bill for the construction of Burlet's city was debated today. The PM stated flatly that the Grass would be overcome before the city could be built. (Cheers) The Hon. Member from South Tooting rose to inquire if the Right Hon. Member could offer something besides his bare word for this? (Groans, faint applause, cries of "Shame," "No gentleman," etcetera) The Home Minister begged to inform the Hon. Member from South Tooting that Her Majesty's government had gone deeply into the question of the socalled vertical cities long before the Hon. Member had ever heard of them. Did the Hon. Member ever consider, no matter how many precautions were taken in the building of conduits for a water supply, that seeds of the Grass would undoubtedly find their way in through that medium? Or through the air intakes, no matter how high? (Dead silence) The Hon. Member from Stoke Pogis asked if the opposition to his Hon. friend's bill wasnt the result of pressure by a certain capitalist, concerned principally with the manufacture of concentrated foods? (Groans and catcalls)

The Chancellor of the Exchequer inquired if the Hon. Member meant to impugn the integrity of the government? (Cries of "Shame," "No," "Unthinkable," etcetera) If not, what did the Hon. Member imply? (Obstinate silence) Since no answer was forthcoming he would move for a division. Result: the bill overwhelmingly voted down.

Since the Skye excitement everyone is inclined to be jittery and nerves are stretched tightly. When I told F she had missed a great opportunity to test her formula in Scotland she blew up and called me a meddling parasite. This is pretty good coming from a dependent. Only my forbearance and consideration for her sex kept me from turning her out on the spot.

SEPTEMBER 1: Encouraged by the Skye episode, a group of volunteers is being formed to attempt an attack on the Grass covering the Channel Islands. More than can possibly be used are offering their services. I subscribed £10,000 toward the venture.

Preparations for moving to Kilkenny almost complete. Even if F gets going by December and the Scottish repulse is permanent, I believe I shall be better off in Ireland until the first definite victory is won against the Grass.

SEPTEMBER 5: The Grass moved again and this time all attempts to repulse it failed. It is now firmly entrenched on both the Orkneys and the Hebrides. Terrible pessimism. Commons voted "No confidence" 422 to 117 and my old friend D N is back in office.

SEPTEMBER 6: *Sisyphus* almost ready. Find I can get a crew to work for wages when not in port. Luncheon at Chequers. PM urges me not to leave England as it might shake confidence. I told him I would consider the matter.

SEPTEMBER 7: F says she is ready to make new tests and what is holding up work on the *Sisyphus*? Replied it was complete except for my cabins. She had the effrontery to say these werent important and she was ready to go ahead without me. I pointed out that the *Sisyphus* was my property and it would not sail until I was properly accommodated.

99 SEPTEMBER 8: I shall not move to Ireland after all. The Grass has a foothold in Ulster.

SEPTEMBER 9: The Irish are swarming into Scotland and Wales. Impossible to keep them out.

SEPTEMBER 10: Donegal overrun.

SEPTEMBER 12: On board the *Sisyphus*. Wrote an incredible amount; still beyond me how anybody can call the fashioning of a book work. We left Southampton last night on a full tide and are now cruising the Channel about four miles from the French coast. It is quite unbelievable—under this tropical green blanket lies the continent of Europe, the home of civilization. And the bodies of millions, too. Except for a few gulls who shriek their way inland and return dejectedly, there is not a living thing in sight but the Grass.

I have reserved the afterdeck to myself and as I sit here now, scribbling these notes, I think what impresses me more than anything else is the feeling of vitality which radiates from the herbaceous coast. The dead continent is alive, alive as never before—wholly alive; moving with millions of sensitive feelers in every direction. For the first time I have a feeling of sympathy for Joe's constant talk of the beauty of the Grass, but in spite of this, the question which comes to my mind is, can you speak glibly about the beauty of something which has strangled nearly all the world?

LATER: Sitting on the gently swaying deck, I was moved to add several pages to my history. But now we are approaching the narrower part of the Channel and the sea is getting choppy. I shall have to give up my jottings for a while.

STILL LATER: F finally picked a spot she considered suitable—the remains of a small harbor—and we anchored. I must say she was overfussy—one cove is pretty much the same as another these days. Possibly she was so choosy in order to heighten her importance.

Repetition of the involved etiquette of inspecting the intended victim and turning on the sprays; only this time the suppressed excitement anticipating possible success made even the preliminaries interesting. Miss Francis and her assistants retired for a mysterious conference immediately after the application and I stayed up late talking with the captain till he was called away by some duty. It is now nearly two A M—in a few hours we shall know.

SEPTEMBER 13: Horribly shaken this morning to find the Grass unaffected. Even wondered for a moment if it were conceivable that F would never find the right compound—that nothing could hurt the Grass. Had I been illadvised in not going more seriously into Burlet's vertical cities?

F very phlegmatic about it. Says another twelve hours of observation may be of value. She and A rowed ashore over the runners trailing in the water and with great difficulty succeeded in hacking off a few runners of the sprayed Grass. I thought her undertaking this hazard an absurd piece of bravado—she might just as well have sent someone else.

Disregarding her rudeness in not inviting me, I accompanied her unasked to her laboratory-cabin. She laid the stolons on an enamelsurfaced table and busied herself with some apparatus. I could not take my eyes from these segments of the Grass. They lay on the table, not specimens of vegetation, but stunned creatures ready to spring to vigorous and vengeful life when they recovered. It was impossible not to pick one up and run it through my fingers, feeling again the soft, electric touch.

Miss Francis' preparations were interminable. If she follows such an elaborate ritual for the mere checking of an unsuccessful experiment no wonder she is taking years to get anywhere. My attention wandered and I started to leave the cabin when I noticed my hand still held one of the specimens.

It was withered and dry.

100 SEPTEMBER 17: The enthusiasm greeting the discovery that F's reagent mortally affected the Grass was only tempered by the dampening thought that its action had been incomplete. What good was the lethal compound if its work were final only when the sprayed parts were severed?

F seemed to think it was a great deal of good. Her manner toward me, boisterous and quite out of keeping with our respective positions and sexes, could almost be called friendly. During the return to Southampton she constantly clapped me on the back and shouted, "It's over, Weener; it's all over now."

"But it isnt over," I protested. "Your spray hadnt the slightest direct effect on the Grass."

"Oh, that. That's nothing. A mere impediment. A matter of time only."

"Time only! Good God, do you realize the Grass is halfway through Ireland? That we are surrounded now on four sides?"

"A lastminute rescue is quite in the best tradition. Don't disturb yourself; you will live to gloat over the deaths of better men."

I urged the PM to be cautious about overoptimism in giving out the news. He nodded his head solemnly in agreement, but he evidently couldnt communicate whatever wisdom he possessed to the BBC announcer, for he, in butter voice, spoke as though Miss Francis had actually destroyed a great section of the weed upon the French coast. There were celebrations in the streets of London and a vast crowd visited the cenotaph and sang *Rule Britannia*.

SEPTEMBER 18: Hoping to find F in a calmer mood, I asked her today just how long she meant by "a matter of time"? She shrugged it off. "Not more than four or five months," she said blithely.

"In a month at most the Grass will be in Britain."

"Let it come," she responded callously. "We shall take the *Sisyphus* and conclude our work there."

"But millions will die in the meantime," I protested.

She turned on me with what I can only describe as tigrish ferocity. "Did you think of the millions you condemned to death when you refused to sell concentrates to the Asiatic refugees?"

"How could I sell to people who couldnt buy?"

"And the millions who died because you refused them employment?"

"Am I responsible for those too shiftless to fend for themselves?"

"'Am I my brother's keeper?' If fifty million Englishmen die because I cannot hasten the process of trial and error, the guilt is mine and I admit it. I do not seek to exculpate myself by pointing a finger at you or by silly and pompous evasions of my responsibility. If the Grass comes before I am ready, the fault is mine. In the meantime, while one creature remains alive, even if his initials be

A W, I shall seek to preserve him. As long as there is a foothold on land I shall try on land; and when that fails we shall board the *Sisyphus* and finish our work there, somewhere in the Atlantic."

"You mean you definitely abandon hope of perfecting your compound before England goes?"

"I abandon nothing," she replied. "I think it's quite possible I'll finish in time to save England, but I can't afford to do anything but look forward to the worst. And that is that we'll be driven to the sea."

I was appalled by the picture her words elicited: a few ships containing the survivors; a world covered with the Grass.

"And when success is attained we shall fight our way back inch by inch."

But this piece of bombast didnt hearten me. I had no desire to fight our way back inch by inch; I wanted at least a fragment of civilization salvaged.

SEPTEMBER 19: F has not been the only one to think of the high seas as a final refuge. The London office has been literally besieged by men of wealth eager to pay any price to charter one of our ships. I have given orders to grant no more charters for the present.

SEPTEMBER 20: The enthusiasm is subsiding and people are beginning to ask how long it will be before thay can expect the reconquest of the Continent to begin. BBC spoke cautiously about "perfection" of the compound for the first time, opening the way to the implication that it doesnt work as yet. Added quite a bit to my manuscript.

SEPTEMBER 21: Mrs. H, in very dignified mood, approached me; said she heard I had made plans to leave England in case the Grass threatened. She asked nothing for herself, she said, being quite content to accept whatever fate Providence had in store for her, but, would I take her daughter and family along on the *Sisyphus*? They would be quite useful, she added lamely.

I said I would give the matter my attention, but assured her there was no immediate danger.

SEPTEMBER 22: Grass on the Isle of Man.

SEPTEMBER 23: Ordered stocking of the *Sisyphus* with as much concentrates as she can carry. The supply will be ample for a full crew, F's staff and myself for at least six months.

SEPTEMBER 24: Ive known for years that F is insane, but her latest phase is so fantastic and preposterous I can hardly credit it. She demands flatly the *Sisyphus* take along at least fifty "nubile females in order to restock the world after its reconquest." After catching my breath I argued with her. The prospect of England's loss was by no means certain yet.

"Good. We'll give the girls a seavoyage and land them back safe and sound."

"We have enough supplies for six months; if we take along these superfluous passengers our time will be cut to less than three."

Her answer was a brutal piece of blackmail. "No women, no go."

If F were a young man instead of an elderly woman I could understand this aberration better.

SEPTEMBER 25: It seems Mrs H's grandchildren are all girls between twelve and eighteen, which leaves the problem of fulfilling F's ultimatum to finding fortyseven others. I have delegated the selection to Mrs H.

SEPTEMBER 26: Grass on Skye for the second time. This invasion was not repulsed.

SEPTEMBER 27: The cyclone fans have been set up from Moray Firth to the Firth of Lorne. I am in two minds about asking the Tharios to join us.

The bill authorizing the construction of a vertical city at Stonehenge passed Commons.

SEPTEMBER 28: Grass reported near Aberdeen. Panic in Scotland. No more train service.

SEPTEMBER 29: Day of fasting, humiliation and prayer proclaimed by the Archbishop of Canterbury. Grass south of the Dee. All mines shut down.

SEPTEMBER 30: Every seaworthy vessel, and many not seaworthy, now under charter. I have ordered all remaining stores of concentrates loaded on our own hulls, to be manned by skeleton crews. They will stand by the *Sisyphus* on her voyage. Lack of railway transportation making things difficult.

OCTOBER 1: They have actually broken ground at Stonehenge for Burlet's fantastic city.

OCTOBER 2: Wrote on my book for nearly twelve solid hours. The postal service has been stopped.

OCTOBER 3: Hearing the royal family had made no plans for departure, the London office ventured to offer them accommodations on one of our ships. I had always heard the House of Windsor was meticulous in its politeness, but I cannot characterize their rejection of our wellmeant aid as anything but rude.

OCTOBER 4: Mrs H asks, Are we to live solely on concentrates now the shops are shut? My query as to whether this seemed objectionable to her was evaded.

OCTOBER 5: Grass in Inverness and Perthshire.

OCTOBER 6: F announces she is ready for another test. Under present conditions, the journey to Scotland being out of the question, we decided to use the *Sisyphus* again and the French coast. Leaving tomorrow.

OCTOBER 11: This constant series of frustrations is beyond endurance. In spite of F's noncommittal pessimism anticipating success only after the Grass has covered England, I feel she is merely making some sort of propitiary gesture when she looks on the darkest side of the picture that way. As for myself I'm convinced the Grass will be stopped in a week or so. But in the meantime F's work advances by the inch, only to be set back again and again.

We repeated the previous test with just enough added success to give our failure the quality of supreme exasperation. This time there was no question but what the growth sprayed actually withered within twentyfour hours. But it was not wiped out and not long afterward it was overrun and covered up by a new and vigorous mass. Such a victory early in the fight would have meant something; now it is too late for such piecemeal destruction. We must have a counteragent which communicates its lethal effect to a larger area of the Grass than is actually touched by it—or at very least makes the affected spot untenable for future growth.

What help is it for F to rub her hands smugly and say, "We're on the right track, all right?" Weve been on the right track for months, but the train doesnt get anywhere.

OCTOBER 12: Columbus Day.

OCTOBER 13: Grass in Fife and Stirling. BBC urges calm.

OCTOBER 14: Rumor has it work abandoned at Stonehenge. It

was a futile gesture anyway. I'm sure F will perfect the counteragent anyday.

OCTOBER 15: Mrs H announced she has completed her selection of fifty young women, adding, "I hope they will prove satisfactory, sir." For a horrible moment I wondered if she thought I was arranging for a harem.

OCTOBER 16: Decided, purely as a matter of convenience and not from panic, such as is beginning to affect even the traditionally stolid British, to move aboard the *Sisyphus*. Grass on the outskirts of Edinburgh.

OCTOBER 17: In a burst of energy last night I brought my history down to the Grass in Europe.

Disconcerting hitch. Most of the *Sisyphus*' crew, including the captain, want to take their wives along. I find it difficult to believe them all uxoriously wed—at any rate this is not a pleasure excursion. Agreed the captain should take his and told him to effect some compromise on the others. The capacity of the *Sisyphus* is not elastic.

OCTOBER 18: Grass almost to the Tweed. PM on the wireless with the assurance a counteragent will be perfected within the week. F furious; wanted to know if I couldnt control my politicians better. I answered meekly—really, her anger was ludicrous—that I was an American citizen, not part of the British electorate, and therefore had no influence over the prime minister of Great Britain. Seriously, however, perhaps the premature announcement will spur her on.

The erratic phone service finally stopped altogether.

OCTOBER 19: Riots and looting—unEnglish manifestations carried out in a very English way. Hysterical orators called for the destruction of all foreign refugees from the Grass, or at very least their exclusion from the benefits of the lootings. In every case the mob answered them in almost identical language: "Fair play," "Share and share alike," "Yer nyme Itler, maybe?" "Come orf it, sonny, oo er yew? Gord Orlmighty's furriner, aint E?" Having heckled the speakers, they proceeded cheerfully to clean out all stocks of available goods—the refugees getting their just shares. There must be a peculiar salubrity about the English air. Otherwise Britons could not act so differently at home and abroad.

Thankful indeed all Consolidated Pemmican stores safely loaded.

OCTOBER 20: As anticipated, the Grass crossed the Tweed into Northumberland, but quite unexpectedly England has also been invaded from another quarter. Norfolk has the Grass from Yarmouth to Cromer. F, the PM, and myself hanged in effigy. Shall not tarry much longer.

OCTOBER 21: Durham and Suffolk. Consulted the captain about a set of auxiliary sails for the *Sisyphus*. Moving aboard tonight.

OCTOBER 22: Heard indirectly that the Tharios had managed to charter a seagoing tug on shares with friends. This takes a great load off my mind.

Postponed moving to the ship in order to superintend packing of personal possessions including the manuscript of my history. F says it is still not mpossible to perfect compound before the Grass reaches London.

OCTOBER 23: On board the *Sisyphus*. What has become of the stolid heroism of the English people? On the way down to the ship, I ran into a crowd no better behaved than the adherents of the Republic One and Indivisible. I mention the episode lightly, but it was no laughing matter. I was lucky to escape with my life.

Nervous and upset with the strain. I shall not return to The Ivies till the Grass begins its retreat. Too restless to continue my book. Paced the deck a long time.

OCTOBER 24: The fifty girls arrived, and a more maddening cargo I can't imagine. I gave orders to keep them forward, but their shrill presence nevertheless penetrates aft.

I hear all electricity has been cut off. Grass in Yorkshire.

OCTOBER 25: F came aboard with the other scientists and immediately wanted to know why we didnt set sail. I asked her if her work could be carried on any more easily at sea. She shrugged her shoulders. I pointed out that only rats leave a sinking ship and England was far from overcome. She favored me with one of her fixed stares.

"You are dithery, Weener. Your epigrams have lost their jaunty air of discovery and your face is almost green."

"You would not expect me to remain unaffected by the events around us, Miss Francis."

"Wouldnt I?" she retorted incomprehensibly and went below to her cabin-laboratory.

The Grass is reported in Essex and Hertfordshire. I understand there are at least two other ships equipped for research and manned by English scientists. It would serve F right if they perfected a counteragent first.

OCTOBER 26: Have ordered our accompanying ships to lie offshore, lest they be boarded by fearcrazed refugees, for the Grass is now in the vicinity of London and England is in a horrible state.

OCTOBER 27: BBC transmitting from Penzance. Faint.

101 NOVEMBER 3: On board the *Sisyphus* off Scilly. The last days of England have passed. Heightening the horror, the BBC in its final moments forwent its policy of soothing its listeners and urging calmness upon them. Instead, it organized an amazing news service, using thousands of pigeons carrying messages from eyewitnesses to the station at Penzance to give a minutebyminute account of the end. Dispassionately and detachedly, as though this were some ordinary disaster, announcer after announcer went on the air and read reports; heartpiercing, anticlimactic, tragic, trivial, noble and thoroughly English reports . . .

The people vented their futile rage and terror in mass pyromania. Building after building, city after city was burned to the ground. But, according to the BBC, the murderous frenzy of the Continent was not duplicated. Inanimate things suffered; priceless art objects were kicked around in the streets, but houses were carefully emptied of inhabitants before being put to the torch.

These were the spectacular happenings; the emphatic events. Behind them, and in the majority, were quieter, duller transactions. Churches and chapels filled with people sitting quiet in pews, meditating; gatherings in the country, where the participants looked at the sun, earth and sky; vast meetings in Hyde Park proclaiming the indissoluble brotherhood of man, even in the face of extinction.

We heard the Queen and her consort remained in Buckingham Palace to the last, but this may be only romantic rumor. At all events, England is gone now, after weathering a millennium of unsuccessful invasions. From where I sit peacefully, bringing my history uptodate and jotting these notes in my diary, I can see, faintly with the naked eye or quite distinctly through a telescope, that emerald gem set in a silver sea. The great cities are covered; the barren moors, the lovely lakes, the gentle streams, the forbidding crags are all mantled in one grassy sward. England is gone, and with it the world. What few men of forethought who have taken to ships, what odd survivors there may be in arctic wastes or on lofty Andean or Himalayan peaks, together with the complement of the *Sisyphus* and its accompanying escort are all that survive of humanity. It is an awesome thought.

LATER: Reading this over it seems almost as though I had been untrue to my fundamental philosophy. The world has gone, vanished; but perhaps it is for the best, afterall. We shall start again in a few days with a clean slate, picking up from where we left off—for we have books and tools and men of learning and intelligence—to start a new and better world the moment the Grass retreats. I am heartened by the thought.

Below, Miss Francis and her coworkers are striving for the solution. After the last experiment there can be no question as to the outcome. An hour ago I would have written that it was deplorable this outcome couldnt be achieved before the latest victory of the Grass. Now I begin to believe it may be a lucky delay.

NOVEMBER 4: What meaning have dates now? We shall have to have a new calendar—Before the Grass and After the Grass.

NOVEMBER 5: Moved by some incomprehensible morbidity I had a stainless steel chest, complete with floats, made before embarkation in order to place the manuscript and diary in it should the impossible happen. I have it now on the deck beside me as a reminder never to give way to a weak despair. F promises me it is a matter of days if not hours till we can return to our native element.

NOVEMBER 8: Another test. Almost completely successful. F certain the next one will do it. My emotions are exhausted.

NOVEMBER 9: I have completed my history of the Grass down to the commencement of this diary. I shall take a wellearned rest from my literary labors for a few days. F announces a new test—"the final one, Weener, the final one"—for tomorrow.

NOVEMBER 10: Experiment with the now perfected compound has been put off one more day. F is completely calm and confident of the outcome. She is below now, making last-minute preparations. For the first time she has infected me with her certitude—although I never doubted ultimate success—and I feel tomorrow will actually see the beginning of the end for the Grass which started so long ago on Mrs Dinkman's lawn. How far I and the world have come since then!

Would I go back to that day if I had the power? It seems an absurd question, but there is no doubt we who have survived have gained spiritual stature. Of course I do not mean anything mystical or supernatural by this observation—we have acquired heightened sensitivity and new perceptions. Brother Paul, ridiculous mountebank, was yet correct in this—the Grass chastised us rightly. Whatever sins mankind committed have been wiped out and expiated.

LATER: We are out of sight of land; nothing but sea and sky, no green anywhere. On the eve of liberation all sorts of absurd and irrelevant thoughts jump about in my mind. The strange lady . . . Joe's symphony, burned by his mother. Whatever happened to William Rufus Le ffaçasé after he eschewed his profession for superstition? And Mrs Dinkman? For some annoying reason I am beset with the thought of Mrs Dinkman.

I can see her pincenez illadjusted on her nose. I can hear her highpitched complaining voice bargaining with me over the cost of inoculating her lawn. The ugly stuff of her tasteless dress is before my eyes. It is so real to me I swear I can see the poor, irregular lines of the weaving.

STILL LATER: I have sat here in a dull lethargy, undoubtedly induced by my overwrought state, quite understandable in the light of what is to happen in a few hours, my eyes on the seams of the deck, reviewing all the things I have written in my book, preparing myself, a way, for the glorious and triumphant finish. But I am beset by delusions. A moment ago it was the figure of Mrs Dinkman and now—

And now, by all the horror that has overcome mankind, it is a waving, creeping, insatiable runner of the Grass.

AGAIN: I have made no attempt to pinch off the green stolon. It must be three inches long by now and the slim end is waving in the wind, seeking for a suitable spot to assure its hold doubly. I touched it with my hand, but I could not bring myself to harm it.

I managed to drag my eyes away from the plant and go below to see Miss Francis. I stood outside the cabin for a long time, listening to the noise and laughter, coupled with a note of triumph I had never heard before and which I'm sure indicates indubitable success. There can be no question of that.

There can be no question of that.

The stolon has pressed itself into another seam.

The blades are very green. They have opened themselves to the sun and are sucking strength for the new shoots. I have put my manuscript into the casket which floats, leaving it open for this diary if it should be necessary. But of course such a contingency is absurd.

Absolutely absurd.

The Grass has found another seam in the deck.